Grosse Fugue

Grosse Fugue

A Novel
Ian Phillips

Alliance Publishing Press

Alliance Publishing Press

Published by Alliance Publishing Press Ltd
This paperback edition published 2012
Copyright © Ian Phillips 2012
The moral right of the author has been asserted
Alliance Publishing Press Ltd

ISBN-13: 978-0-9569992-0-7
Typeset in Times New Roman and Helvetica Neue
Book & Cover Design by Mark James James

Ian Phillips – A Biography

Ian Phillips is 58 and has been writing professionally for businesses and other organisations since 1993.

Graduating with a law degree in 1975 Ian worked in professional publishing before moving into the advertising and marketing industry. He then started his own consultancy offering communications and writing services.

At the same time, he began researching and writing "Grosse Fugue", using the spaces between projects to build the structure, characters and plot, as well as take the first tentative steps along the creative road.

When not helping clients or serving as a volunteer in education, Ian passes his time bolstering his passion for classical music and honing his bridge skills.

Married with two sons and living in North-West London, "Grosse Fugue" is his first novel.

For Elaine, Ben and Adam

Prelude

I saw the great man weep but once.

Never in all the time he'd poured out the billowing, black smoke of his momentous life had he truly cried. The odd moist eye and halting catch in the voice, maybe, but never streaming, silent tears. In the stillness of his private places Reuben could, I know, be overwhelmed, but in all the retelling the performer in him held his grief in check.

At least, until the full force of what was in the package hit him.

It had already been delivered to the Ambassador Hotel when the quartet arrived in Vienna to give a Schubert recital in the spring of 1968. The box was wrapped in nondescript brown paper and tied neurotically with far too much string. A note was taped to the top, his name inscribed on its envelope in a faux-Gothic script. Intrigued and impatient, he ripped it open and read the letter, scanning its formal German before translating aloud for my benefit.

> Dear Maestro Mendel,
> I cannot tell you my full name as the shame is a cancer
> eating me from within.
> Like my mother before me, I am a keen amateur musician
> and have followed your career with much admiration.
> My father died six months ago. While clearing his house,
> I came upon the enclosed hidden beneath some blankets
> in the attic. When I opened it and saw your name, I could
> scarcely believe what I saw.
> 'Vati' never spoke of the war, save to say he fought with the

Wehrmacht in various places too traumatic to recall. But I see now that this must have been a lie, for there is only one way in which he could have taken possession of your property.

I do not beg forgiveness on behalf of the German people, Honoured Sir, but do pray that my children may not be tainted by any guilt. Telling them what their grandfather did was the hardest thing I have ever done. But secrets are corrosive, particularly when it is wrong to keep them. We must face this poisonous inheritance as a family or be destroyed.

Not for one second does this parcel make reparation, but some part of me draws comfort that at last you will be reunited with what was taken from you.

I hope I have done the right thing.

Yours with the utmost respect and with apologies for writing in German rather than your mother tongue,

Gretchen S, Frau, Munich

Reuben's mood darkened. I sensed that in some deep, dank corner of his being lurked an inkling of what might possibly lie, still boxed, before him. He seemed reluctant, torn between the need to liberate whatever it was and fear of the memories it might ignite.

"Would you like me to do it?"

"No. Thank you, but this I should do myself. In the suite, I think, not the lobby."

As we walked to the lift he seemed distracted, and I knew better than to talk when he was in reflective mood.

Soon enough we reached his room, and immediately after the porter had been tipped and left, he set about the string. He rushed to remove the old newspaper and straw that filled half the box, not caring about the mess he was making. Parting the last of the packing materials, he saw at last what they swaddled. And froze.

"No, no, NO! Not now, not after all this time, it cannot be!"

Slowly he reached into the box and withdrew its prize, tentatively as though it were a Ming vase of the utmost fragility.

"My violin! My violin! My violin!" he repeated over and over, cradling the case in his arms like a baby. Beneath his closed lids, the eyeballs were flicking to and fro as the recollection of the last time he'd held it came roaring back.

"I never thought to see this again. Nearly twenty-five years ago! All that happened, all that time." His voice was firm, but bitter salt was now streaming down his cheeks.

He gently stroked the case before placing it on the floor and gingerly opening the clasps. There the violin lay, burnished golden-brown hue exactly as it had been the final time he'd played it, just before they had embarked on the train.

He didn't take it out, nor even draw his fingers across the slack strings.

"This was the fiddle I told you about. The one I stowed beneath my coat when we reached the camp."

The violin that kept him alive.

Now, when I think back over it all with a degree of distance, the abiding image is of his hands.

Veined and liver-spotted, joints enlarged and pads violin-hardened, those long fingers that would interlace in prayer-like contemplation resting invariably on the space between his nose and mouth as he bowed his head in thought.

But above all that, the inextinguishable remembrance of all they had done.

Fired rifles. Comforted babies. Shovelled shit. Defied death.

And made music.

I could not count the number of times I had seen them in action. The left hand would twist around the neck of his Guadagnini as its fingers danced along the ebony neck. The right stroked the horse-hair bow across the violin below the bridge, its rosin coating throwing soft sprays of sap into the air.

It never seemed to matter whether Reuben Mendel practised, rehearsed or performed. His entire being was focused on the action of his hands and the sound they coaxed from that golden, glowing wood. Sometimes it was as though the arm never moved, such was the silent ballet of the wrist and fingers. But often the music made such demands that joints and tendons strained as they sought the most taxing perfection.

And, at his end, when nothing but instinct remained, it would be that left hand which signalled his final parting with one last, defiant chord.

I was a shining child. By which I mean that from an early age I was seen as gifted, excelling (relatively, as it turned out) at the piano. When faced with the critical fork in the road, parents and teachers chose the one they thought was marked 'Genius'. Up until this point, my life mirrored Reuben Mendel's. But while his road was paved with triumph and tragedy, humility and resignation, mine was covered merely in false dawns and misplaced hopes, mediocrity and bitterness.

Until our paths crossed.

Only then did I realise that some bloom best in the shade. My life, so easy and self-indulgent compared with many others, was an uncomfortable existence, peppered by a nagging spiritual and intellectual hunger born of the dread of failing to fulfil my own-perceived potential. But meeting him for the first time in 1965 brought something approaching a personal epiphany, an instinctive knowing that this was someone who could blaze like the sun and provide the nourishment until then so clearly lacking.

My role was not to be that of a Boswell, chronicler of minutiae and selective commentator. It was more that, at the time of our initial meeting, this man who had seen and suffered so much was looking for someone to whom he could unburden himself of the broad sweep of his biography. By then a world figure, he knew that he would need to commit his life to writing but lacked the time and will to undertake it himself.

Already thirty-five, I was a failed pianist and dissolute freelance music critic, drifting between ad hoc assignments, be it recital (often in some depressing municipal building or private function), interview, review or article. Because of the huge amount of interest in Mendel and his colleagues, I had seized the opportunity to report on his string quartet's first complete performance of the entire Beethoven cycle in Israel, syndicating it around the world. He was kind enough to write to me with some gratifying comments. We met and almost immediately he shared his concerns about telling his story, waiting, I felt, for me to offer my help. Reader, I did.

Over the following years we talked at length. Or, to be accurate, more often than not he talked and I recorded. Anyone who has watched a recital by a soloist sans score knows the prodigious memory that great performers must cultivate. Reuben's recall of the details of his life was extraordinary. Once it was liberated, the flood could not be restrained, flushing out from the recesses of his mind conversations and incidents long-since hidden behind the opaque and protective curtain of time.

He shared his story in a sporadic fashion, as his busy diary necessarily dictated. When he was on the road we communicated by telephone or letter, and a couple of times, when we'd reached a particular juncture, I accompanied him on tour. But mostly we would sit on his veranda, overlooking the citrus groves of the kibbutz to which he would return when he sought either rest after performances or respite when the demons proved too much.

He would close his eyes and lean that noble head back so that the sun shone on his face, spotlighting the scar which ran from the bridge of his nose across the top of his left cheek and beyond his eye. The trademark mane of snow-white hair rested on his shoulders and I would see the feverish movement of his eyeballs beneath the lids as he reassembled the words and pictures of a specific incident, forming the narrative before he spoke. His silence was at first a little unnerving, but I soon came to realise that he would only ever speak when he knew what he wanted to say, and how he wanted to express it.

When he finally began, in English, he would do so softly and slowly, in that strange accent of his – London, but with traces of the German and French which life had required him to master. The occasional inflexion or mannerism would punctuate the flow, particularly when he appropriated the vernacular of the language in which the original scene was transacted.

I would transcribe my notes and recordings, and decide what fitted into the narrative scheme we had agreed. I then wrote from this source material, researching in and around the events he depicted to flesh out the story, creating what I hope is a vivid account of his life and the historical stage upon which he acted. Where his own words struck an especial chord, I have included them verbatim.

He never intended to publish in his lifetime, believing that to do so would suggest an end of attainment and ambition. So, from the moment we started, I would capture new phases in his life as well as his past history, ensuring that, when it finally saw the light of day, his tale would stand as a record of all that he had done.

I should say at the outset that I shared the vast majority of this book with its subject and he corrected some errors of fact and kindly refrained from commenting on the style, save to say that he felt that once or twice he thought he could hear me talking perhaps a trifle too loudly. I toyed with re-writing the sections to which he alluded (particularly the first three intermezzi), but in the end decided to leave it just as it was when he last looked at it. My only concession to change is the obvious one: to recount the events leading up to, and beyond, his final moments.

This then is the closest there will be to an official life of Reuben Mendel: musician, sage, survivor. It is, for me, a personal memoir of a man whose greatness was exemplified in the humility of his life and the gentleness with which he treated me, his inferior in every conceivable way. I hope it leads to an understanding not merely of the passage of his life but also to the way he sought a humanist path out of the destruction towards a new Jerusalem.

Perhaps I may conclude this prelude with the (treasured) note he sent me after reading the first draft. It contained simply the single verse appropriated by Primo Levi from 'The Rime of the Ancient Mariner' for the start of his own poem, 'The Survivor':

> Since then, at an uncertain hour,
> That agony returns:
> And till my ghastly tale is told,
> This heart within me burns.

I have no delusions that recording his tale extinguished the fire, but I draw some consolation from the thought that, just for a short interval, it did perhaps subdue the flames.

Chapter 1

For most of us it is enough to be born just once.

But for Reuben Mendel, life seemed a veritable fugue of births. Some painful, some joyous, yet all pulsed with the same themes: the throbbing rhythm of music, the *staccatissimo* of loss, the fortitude that comes from mastering fate; above all, the pregnant silence in the moment after the last note dies. And like the very etymology of 'fugue', each was not just a beginning but part of a continuing flight to what, seen in hindsight, seemed his inevitable conclusion, proof positive of Kierkegaard's truth that life must be lived forwards but can only be understood backwards.

He was a favoured son, not just of Gaia, although his prodigious talent would mark him out as different, but of more worldly gods.

The tortuous track that led Mendel's people to reside in the leafy suburbs of Victorian London was no different from that of his ancestors. A fear-fuelled flight from a hate-filled mob, forced expulsion, the hunger to do better than eke out a miserable living in some primitive village where only religion and superstition held sway – these were the main forces that impelled their millennial wanderings. Whatever the motive, the one common thread is that all of them, somewhere up the ancestral line, had been without means and shelter and friends. And all had built a life embedded in the soil of the lands they had washed up on, yet established with roots of such portability that, if need be, they could be withdrawn and replanted at short notice, a not infrequent occurrence.

Moses, Reuben's father, had fled penniless to London at the age of sixteen to escape an edict conscripting thousands of his fellow

Jews. He had lived the life of a devout student in the village of Skidel, one of the numerous *shtetls* that lay in the hinterland of Bialystok, cultural centre of a region beset by frequent changes of ownership and, at the time he fled, under the thrall of the Tsar. Skidel was like its cousin villages, tight-knit and primitive. Although his father Elias, the village rabbi, had sought to augment it with introductions to secular and political elements, Moses' education stood him in good stead only for life within the closed, devout community which was the intellectual heartland of his home.

In the never-changing landscape that encircled their never-changing lives, the climate shaped their year. Green during the short summers; dust whipped up from the street by wind and horses' hooves and wagons' wheels stung the eyes and choked the voice. White throughout long winters; Siberian winds hurled snow and ice at the exposed village and the residents' labours were ever harsher in the unyielding cold. The convulsions of industrialisation had passed the villagers by and the circle of life was still rooted in the land. Theirs was a hand-to-mouth existence that brooked no material advancement and rested on the maintenance of religious practices to secure a centre around which all could gather, hopes for eternal rest compensating for the misery of life.

There Moses and his father were, locked into a catastrophe that demanded the exile of the cream of male youth, for whom the Russian army meant almost certain death. When a red-eyed Elias led him to the little bridge over the river Niemen, Moses received instructions, a bag containing some clothes, religious accoutrements, a small knife, a few coins and an open letter. On the threshold of an unknowable future, the inadequacy of his upbringing stood stark against Skidel's dawn shadow. His grieving father took him in his arms and simply said the words that Moses remembered his whole life: "My beloved son, only now, when it is far too late, do I see how poorly I have equipped you for life. So locked was I in the immutable past of our forefathers, I never thought that things might change. Forgive me if I have failed you, and may the Lord bless you and keep you; may the Lord make his face to shine upon you and be gracious unto you; may the Lord turn his face towards you and give you peace."

The journey that took Reuben's father to London and his meeting with Leah Rodrigue became the stuff of family legend, a tale embellished with every retelling until it assumed Homeric dimensions. When Reuben recounted it, he did so within heavy quotation marks to emphasise that Moses was not exactly the most impartial or reliable source.

Moses embarked upon his escape as the sun began to rise over the Niemen valley, illuminating his way south-west towards Bialystok. Fording the river at Lunna, he travelled over the plain beyond and through the crop fields and animal pastures that chequered the countryside. But when he finally arrived, the Jewish community that was supposed to provide an initial sanctuary was in turmoil. The metropolis inevitably proved a magnet for the many villages in its long shadow, each racked by the trauma of the conscription order. Where Moses had been prominent in his own milieu but a day or two earlier, now he was but one of scores of boys and young men thrust from singular safety into a foreign world of anonymity, plural choices and numerous threats.

This new, alien environment was emphasised by the rush of adrenaline that Moses experienced when he came upon the main square on market day. It was overflowing with goods of every description: livestock, fruit, vegetables, herbs, spices; a seething cauldron of noise and fragrance that nearly overwhelmed him. As he pushed through the crowd he had no idea where he was going, only that Slavonic curses of the kind he was well used to from the locals in his home village rained about him, accompanied by kicks, slaps and punches. He did not know what the oaths meant, only that the vitriol which impelled the one common spit-drenched word, *yid*, was unmistakeable. He began to run, stooping and throwing his arms across the back of his head to protect himself, as the cacophony grew. Seizing the first avenue out of the square, he plunged blindly on, not looking behind.

Then, suddenly, he was free of the town and there he was, sixteen-year-old Moses Mendel, flying through a wheat field, the hurricane of fear at his back propelling him forward, away, anywhere but there. The hard ears whipped at his cheeks, chainlike stalks grappled at his ankles. Oblivious to the blood, he drove blindly on, bypassing every village, crossing unending fields and fording countless streams.

How long he ran Moses had no idea, but eventually he could run no further and he stopped suddenly, colliding with an unseen wall so high and wide it could only ever have been traversed by a giant.

At this point in his narration, Reuben paused and leaned forward, elbows on knees, chin cradled in his cupped hands. Then he spoke softly out into the far distance, as though to his long-dead father.

"I've thought a lot about this story over the years, you know. As you can probably tell, I never tired of hearing it. Papa loved recounting it to new people, invariably with novel twists and embellishment – but for a child it was just a thrilling adventure. As I got older, I began to wonder, what is it about an odyssey that seizes the imagination of Man? Do you think, perhaps, that it is a kind of wish-fulfilment, like dreaming of carrying out some death-defying act of bravery? When we immerse ourselves in such tales, we cast ourselves as the hero and imagine what we'd have done when faced with such odds. But very few are truly tested. By and large, life's not the stuff of Ulysses battling the gods to find his way home, or Buck heaving his laden sled and waging war against Arctic elements.

"But even so, deep within us all must lie the dormant seed of our primitive ancestors who overcame the frozen hazards of the Ice Age and harnessed the elements.

"We close our eyes and try to envisage what it must be like

– alone, stripped bare of all the trappings of normality, liberated from society's expectations. And so we turn vicariously to the lives of the celebrated, the solitary, the challenged, the heroes of fiction, so that we all might imagine what it is to be elevated to greatness, immortality even. Perhaps this in no small part informs the disproportionate clamour for this little book of ours.

"Father now saw himself in this heroic vein. He was, so to speak, cast adrift with the benefit of neither a useful education nor any practical experience. He had to rely only on those qualities which he'd been born with, and what little he had picked up in his sheltered sixteen years. How could he ever have known, ever even imagined, that what lay far ahead would put even his epic voyage into the shade?"

The flight from Bialystok was interrupted by the tearful removal of the long black curls of hair that dangled in front of his ears and marked him out to all the world as a Jew. This act freed him from his past, a violent but necessary severance without which he could never have survived. He emphasised the symbolism, with a sharp pang of conscience, by jettisoning the artefacts of religion his father had included in his luggage, both lightening the load and reducing the risk of discovery by the many anti-Semites who peppered his route whichever direction he took.

Moses soon realised the mordent truth of his father's parting words. Life in Skidel had not equipped him for a solitary battle against brutal elements, suspicious peasants, hunger and complete disorientation. Sixteen years of hearing Yiddish, a little Polish and very basic Russian, pouring over Hebrew script, learning by rote the Mosaic code and the Talmud, being weaned on the mystical tracts of the Kabbalah and the folk fables of Sholem Aleichem: this was an education that had only one purpose: to expunge any trace of the independence of spirit or physical and emotional self-reliance upon which mankind's progress had hitherto been based, and on which

Moses was now forced exclusively to depend.

It was with all this baggage that the only son of Rabbi Elias Mendel of Skidel cut a swathe across Poland, stealing food from farms, washing in streams, trudging on foot or wagon hopping – whether horse-drawn in the countryside or pulled by steam-powered train in the industrial north. During this voyage a physical transformation took place to complement the emotional. A thickening of sinew, the coming of colours to skin never before exposed to prolonged bouts of light, cold and wet, a broadening of the frame as though the very chemistry of the open air reacted with the latency of growth to speed the process of encroaching manhood.

Apprehension, the smell of freedom and the infinite variety of Nature combined to ignite in Moses the spark of humanity. His eyes glistened as the Arctic wind whipped his face, not just with tears from the smarting, but with the knowledge that here he was, alone, striding out as many had done before him to breach the barrier between the known and the unknown. When slumber was broken by nocturnal chorus or the beat of an owl's wings so close to his head he could smell the blood on its claws, he *knew* that here was where the ancients must have been. Huddled against a rock or lying upon the stony ground beneath the canopy of a tree, soaked to the numbed bones by the ice-cracked stream, they too had vainly sought recuperating sleep in the penetrating light of the winter moon.

While they were frightened by what had been lost and what the unknown future held, all this to Moses was the essence of life. Truth did not reside only in the arid words of generations of elders; he now realised that their, his, hermetic existence was but a cruel sham. Only through teeth sharpened on the crude stone of experience could the fundamental truths which the rabbis – yes, even his beloved father – had for centuries spoken be uttered. And what did they know of the bat's unerring flight path in the pitch black? Or of the orchid's quest for light? Or the salmon's epic voyage home to where it began? What, in short, did they know of Life? Moses knew. With all the hubris of youth, he grew tall in the sunlight of certainty, fed by the confidence of survival and the exuberant joy of liberty.

Following some obscure star that had guided untold explorers and wanderers before him, he finally arrived in Danzig, the main Polish outlet to the sea.

With wonder he stared about him. Reuben described his father's expression when recalling what he saw: eyes rolled up towards heaven, hand slapped on forehead, a breathily-phrased, 'Oy!' Beside Skidel, Bialystok had seemed another country. But this was a different universe. A skyline split by dockyard cranes, factories belching stinking smoke into the air, a teeming mass of people; all combined in Moses' mind to form a tableau of Gehenna, the often-mentioned but never described repository of lost souls.

In years to come old Moses would indulge in hindsight-honed analysis of what-might-have-been had he taken a different path. But he didn't. In the chilly autumn of 1889, on a date he never knew, he boarded a ship at Danzig as a cabin boy (no questions asked, no wages paid). He had no idea where it was bound, embarking in the knowledge only that wherever the ship went would be further from where he could no longer remain. And it was in this haphazard way that he arrived in the steaming cauldron of the lost, the lonely and the seekers-after-hope that was London's East End.

He never was able to say what drove him to slink from the silent coal carrier as she lurked at her mooring in the fog-laden early dawn. A sense of destiny perhaps, certainly a feeling of relief after the puke-wracked journey through the Baltic, round Heligoland and across the wild North Sea. More, it was the need to flee the slave-driver master who had sweated him like the bondsman he was: cleaning, fetching, carrying, slopping out, pouring copious quantities of liquor, so that Moses had been forced to learn the sailor's knack of sleeping on his feet. But later he would recall one motivation above others: the sound of Yiddish rising like a guttural siren call from the dockside

Babel, plucking the strings of nostalgia and loneliness that had so violently been tautened.

He found himself in a land he did not know, whose alphabet, let alone language, was indecipherable; penniless, and with no family, friends, familiar faces – his only asset the battered envelope still safely ensconced in the inside pocket of his filthy overcoat.

He wandered a while around the docks, trying to find the source of those few words whose unmistakeable inflection, rather than specific meaning, had summoned him to terra firma. But in the density of the clogged morning, he found nothing. Growing dizzy in his disorientation, Moses drifted away from the dock's warehouse areas, with their looming black spaces awaiting stock, back towards the mooring stations. He realised he had to wait for the fog to lift, so the morning light could give him an idea of where he was and where he might go.

He was by now an automaton, fatigued to the point where his bones ached and muscles throbbed, only propelled by the primordial urge for survival. He found himself drawn towards an open hut, its welcoming stove overpowering an instinct for danger. He slipped in and, magnetically drawn to the unmade bed under the window of the unkempt cabin, was asleep in seconds.

Moses would recall in graphic detail the moment of his greatest shock, a hand shaking him awake from the profoundest sleep he had ever known. He was completely disoriented, for the words that roused him were in his beloved Yiddish and fleetingly he thought himself back in Skidel.

When his eyes came into focus, he looked up to see two people gazing down at him: an elderly woman and a sombre man in a uniform. She had kindly eyes which more than made up for her appalling accent and grammar. She repeated the words again.

"How by this letter come did you?"

Moses instinctively felt for the inside pocket of his coat, only to find it empty. "My … my father, he wrote it for me."

The uniform spoke, and the woman translated: "And who your father is?"

"Rebbe Elias Mendel of Skidel."

"Is that what the letter says, madam?"

"Yes, Constable. It states that the bearer is Moses, only son of that honourable gentleman, and asks whoever finds him to treat him as befits a boy of such birth and to look well upon him.

"Now, Moses," she continued, reverting to her approximation of Yiddish, "you are the Anglo-Jewry Committee for the Resettlement of Russian Jews in the care of. Mrs Lily Jacobs my name is and for you taken I have responsibility. Do understand you?"

Moses nodded dumbly.

Years later, he would tell his son of the kind Lily Jacobs. "She was a second mother to me. My first, Miriam, may her dear soul rest in peace, died when I was but five years old. So for eleven or twelve years, I had no maternal affection at all, and although my father and sundry aunts tried to substitute, there is nothing to compare to a mother's love. I greatly regret that I can recall so little of her. Now, from nowhere, came this angel, to rescue me at my moment of greatest need. I have no idea of whether I was truly special to her, only that she made me feel so from that very first moment when she took my hand and told me that everything was going to be alright. And somehow I knew that it would be."

This was how Reuben's father was introduced to the foreign world of the anglicised Jew, integrated, safe – and far, far removed from the realities of life within the Pale of Settlement. Here he was free to roam as he wished, not afraid of assault, or worse. Here there was food aplenty, a more equable climate and freedom from the strictures of theocracy.

Lily was true to her word, and took him into her house. Why him, rather than the scores of others she had met through her work in the Docklands and among the burgeoning community of fellow exiles that filled the tenement buildings of London's East End?

Moses assumed that his position as the son of a rabbi from 'the mainland' was what clinched it, based on little more than the fact that for his first few months he was paraded among her milieu rather like a trophy.

This was fully in keeping with the reactions of the established Jews in England during this period of influx from the Russian communities. They felt their historic safety in some way jeopardised by these primitive arrivals, so different in language, dress, bearing and observance. They confronted these worries by embarking on a gentle process to acclimatise their brethren to the highways and byways of life in the British Empire. No greater success story could there be than to show that the son of a rabbi, reared exclusively within the closed community of study in the *shtetl*, could become a rounded Anglo-Jewish citizen who knew and appreciated his proper place under Victoria's benign gaze.

The re-education of Moses Mendel began with the language and it was not too long before he felt able, incorrectly as it happened, to hold his own at Lily Jacobs' cultural soirées of readings and light classical music, one of the monthly highlights of that peculiar class of aristocratic Jews, assimilated, yet apart. In truth, he was something of her pet project as his progress from darkness into light, as she romantically called it, was monitored on a regular basis by her peer group.

It was at one such gathering that Moses met his match, in every meaning of the word. Reuben recalled his mother's reply when he asked how she and his father had met.

"It was my first time at a Jacobs evening. My mother had discouraged me as she felt them a little frivolous, but my best friend Rachel had been to one and I nagged and nagged until Mother gave way. Well, I was seventeen, so it was high time! Naturally, Rachel and I had gossiped about what she'd seen, and my curiosity was aroused by her description of this Russian boy who had spoken a few words of English to her in an impenetrable accent not exactly enhanced by his mumbling shyness. But I'll have you know I wasn't looking for romance; it just happened, I'm happy to say.

"I'd thought long and hard about my dress and, though I say so myself, I looked rather fetching in a dark green satin gown with ostrich feathers and lime lace..."

"*Rather* fetching?" Moses had interjected. "Rather *fetching*? I swear the whole room stopped when she came in, just to look at her! I was at the other end listening to the poet who was talking about his imminent recital, I think. When the silence hit, I looked up and could not believe my eyes. Love at first sight, it was, I swear!"

"Moses, dear, don't be so silly. Look at me, I'm blushing, even after all these years! Anyway, I moved around the room, trying to avoid appearing gauche. I'm sure I failed to achieve that aim as I made small talk with various people Rachel introduced me to.

"Then, all of a sudden, I was there in front of your father, who was holding out his hand to me and saying something that sounded very much like, 'Ee am fair-r-ry plizzed to muyke yur akvayntince, Mizz Rodrigwey.' I can tell you precisely what it was that interested me – his eyes. They were so bright and alive!

"We started talking, and I suppose you could say we never stopped. It was rather like a cultural exchange at first. I was shocked by how little your father knew of the world, so I sought to give him an awareness that life was built on a vaster scale than his upbringing. I talked of Michelangelo and Mozart, Shakespeare and Goethe. And I helped improve his English by reading to him Browning and Keats, Austen and the Brontës. And all the while, I filled his head with the great symbols of Englishness – the monarchy and its history, the paintings of Constable, comedies by Sheridan and Congreve, the 'frozen music' of Westminster Abbey and Saint Paul's Cathedral.

"But it was not by any means all me. In turn, your father taught me the glories of Jewish intellectualism which Elias had clandestinely grafted on to his formal religious studies – Moses and Maimonides, even Spinoza and Marx. In my ignorance I struggled to reconcile this with the role of a rabbi, but Moses explained that it was the duty of all Jews to use their intellects to the uttermost, even at the cost of undermining religious teachings.

"He reciprocated my guided tour of literature with his own retelling of folk stories in their original Yiddish, tales and a language I never knew. He spoke too of Masada and Babylon, bondage in Egypt and pogroms in Russia. I knew much of this history, but he made it come alive for the first time. And in the twilight, when we sat in the gazebo at the bottom of the garden, my head on his shoulder, Moses would softly sing the songs of the *shtetl*, music that was somehow within me but which I had never heard.

"I can't pretend my parents were thrilled when it was clear that we were in love, but they welcomed him as the son they never had."

"That's true, they put me into the family business, taught me the ropes and that set us up. Then you came along, and we were the complete family."

His parents made an unlikely couple, by all accounts. And judging by the sole photograph that Reuben had from their wedding, Leah's dark complexion surrounding deep brown eyes and framed by waves of thick jet hair was certainly in sharp contrast to the pale, gaunt features of Moses who, despite his exposure to the rude autumnal elements of northern Poland and the even sharper winds and rain of the voyage, still retained the ghostly pallor of the perpetual student, deprived of sunlight and fresh air.

But more important than Reuben Mendel's physical inheritance was his genetic and cultural legacy: a paternal line that fetched its source in the great migratory sweep hewn out of hardship and prejudice which reached from the warm Mediterranean north to frozen Poland and Russia, and a maternal lineage that the name Rodrigue disclosed had somewhere in the dim and distant past originated in Spain. The two rivers of the great dispersal and the values that had preserved the flame converged in him, bringing a rich bequest: a commitment to justice, an unquenchable thirst for knowledge and an all-consuming desire for freedom.

But for that potential to be gloriously realised required a continual series of transmutation. This fugue of metamorphoses began with Reuben's 'second birth', its genesis an explosion of music that fired through the protective skin of his early years and detonated in his young soul.

Chapter 2

It wasn't that music was new to him, for he remembered from a very early age Leah playing the piano and softly singing of an evening. She had even tried teaching him the rudiments from the age of six but he showed no affinity and they soon stopped. So, until that momentous day, it was peripheral, never at the centre of his existence.

Some commentators have said of Reuben that whatever was played at the first concert he attended, the course of his life would have been the same. But he himself was never quite so certain. He probably would have been a violinist; and might even have made it to the stratosphere inhabited by the great interpretative instrumentalists – Heifetz and Kreisler on his own beloved violin, Schnabel and Horowitz the pianists, Casals, the greatest-ever cellist. But what if the concerto had not been Beethoven's sole sortie for the violin? What if the soloist had not been Fritz Kreisler himself? What if some other, lesser, mortal had been playing, say, the Mendelssohn or one of Mozart's? Or even the same piece but without Kreisler's own cadenzas? What, even, if his parents had not managed to get tickets for that much anticipated concert on the first of May 1907 when, as one critic would subsequently report, Kreisler played the Beethoven as if the great man had revealed it to him privately?

Sitting in the Victorian grandeur of London's Queen's Hall, eight-and-a-half-year-old Reuben Mendel, resplendent in a purple velvet suit with knickerbockers and white lace ruff, was blithely ignorant of the direction his young life was irrevocably about to take. He hungrily absorbed the sights and sounds. In the front row of the lower tier, stage right, Reuben felt as if he was suspended above the stalls, which were filled with the top-hatted and bustle-dressed, gossiping excitedly, possibly about the forthcoming music, more likely about the latest scandal concerning some hapless member of their social circle. His gaze rose to the chandelier-centred ceiling, its ornate surround rippling out across the entire surface before cascading down the wood-panelled walls that gave the hall its unique acoustic.

He shifted eagerly on his seat as the orchestra tuned up. Never had he heard such a sound! Every instrument a soloist, each with its own distinctive voice that could easily be distinguished by his perfect ear. And after Henry Wood arrived at the podium to conduct, Reuben basked in the frisson of expectant silence which emanated from the packed auditorium in that quiet place between the withering of applause and the beginning of music. This was Reuben's first experience of the hypnotic effect of absolute power – one man with several thousand souls absolutely fixed upon his every move and complete domination of his world. It would not be his last.

Reuben's memory was not yet developed but every detail of the concerto performance that followed was etched indelibly on his psyche, starting with the moment when the immortal Kreisler himself brought the hall to its feet, just by walking out with his violin tucked carelessly under his left arm, the bow held lightly, pointing groundward, between right thumb and forefinger. Not even a seven-year-old could mistake the tidal wave of love that seemed to cascade from some invisible source at the back of the hall. This was not the power of the conductor but something far more intoxicating: adulation. Whenever Kreisler slid his Guarneri under his chin, it was like Don Giovanni caressing a virgin's naked shoulder – an unmistakable statement of desire, soft as a rose petal, yet with a heart as hard as a diamond. He knew, *knew*, that his seduction would succeed, that his audience would fall just as surely as the one thousand and three did in Spain when Leporello's master roved the Iberian peninsula with irresistible priapic intent.

Five kettledrum beats fractured the anticipating silence. But the fifth was heard by very few – least of all Reuben – as the magical woodwinds entered, followed shortly by the strings. Bewitched, he sat through the ever-increasing tension as the orchestral *tutti* built to a climax, repeating through various combinations the soaring beauty of the main theme.

Moses and Leah, sitting to either side of their son, looked at him as the orchestra faded away to await the entry of the soloist. Later, they would be unable to agree on the expression transfiguring their young son – one thought it an angelic visitation, the other a Pauline revelation of the inevitable course of one's life.

As Kreisler's violin drifted upwards, Reuben was frozen, only his eyes moving imperceptibly as they followed the progress of the priceless instrument as it described an arc through the air. His gaze was fixed first on Kreisler's left hand as it positioned itself on the violin's graceful neck and then on his right as the locked wrist twisted the bow towards the four strings held taut over the deep-golden wood by the pegs in the scroll at one end and the ebony tailpiece at the other.

For Reuben, the sound seemed to take longer to arrive than a birthday. But when it came! Rising pairs of notes that seemed to go all the way to heaven; a sweet purity that brought tears to his eyes; an ebbing and flowing whose every shift of tempo and interplay of melody with the orchestra Reuben followed, glued to the music.

Not a muscle twitched during the entire first movement until the orchestra died away to leave the vacuum into which the soloist was allowed traditionally to display his prowess with a pyrotechnical solo that rarely gelled with its setting. Not so Kreisler. His own cadenza drew the boy to his feet, small body swaying with the rhythm as he imitated the rapid scaling and tumbling of the music. He became one with the short fireburst of notes and chords that reached the heights of the violin's range before waterfalling to its lowest reaches, all the time in keeping with the soul of the piece which framed it.

And when it was over, when the first movement had resolved itself, Reuben recovered himself in the sweet balm of the *larghetto*. The gentle melody stirred images of the rocking, lace-caped cradle in his nursery where Leah had softly hummed him to sleep, and he drifted along with its tranquil song.

All too soon the music had left that dreamland far behind as the slow theme dissolved into the finale whose joyous five-note motif danced headlong towards its inevitable end – the violin, like a benevolent Pied Piper, leading the orchestra towards a better place.

Reuben didn't applaud. Not for want of appreciation, neither to release the excitement that had built up during the forty or so minutes which had passed as the piece had progressed from its opening drum beats to the final ensemble. It was as if he was forcing every note, every nuance, all visual and aural recollection of the performance deep into his being, and that any motion, any sound emanating from within might infiltrate the process and become embedded in the music, rendering it impure.

And so he remained for the duration of the concert and for the entirety of the journey home.

When he had barely spoken for two days, Leah and Moses wondered whether they had done the right thing.

"Too rich for a young stomach – if you had to take him to anything, it should have been Strauss or Offenbach," opined the Rodrigue elders.

But the silence did not last much longer. Reuben himself recalled the period only very hazily, but did so in terms suggesting a plucking-up of courage for a life-critical moment.

"Mama, Papa," he eventually said, "I rather think I should like to learn the violin. May I? *Please?*"

The following day found the family trouping across Golden Square, London's elegant musical centre, and into the discrete charms of the showroom of Messrs J. P. Guivier, the city's oldest violin dealer. For a moment or two they drank in the atmosphere, a kind of hushed reverence with the instruments arrayed as though saints in a church. Reuben gazed around him, his eyes narrowing as he peered into the softly-lit corners of the store.

Hitherto, his life had been unremarkable, bright child though he was. But now, for the first time, his parents saw gentle stirrings of something great and serious. A kind of mist seemed to settle upon Reuben. It was as though he disappeared into a secret world where none may enter but him. In this place he could bring to bear the whole weight of what he knew, who he was – and what he might resolve with his own resources. It would prove to be as heavy as the yolks filled with water that his ancestors ported haltingly from the central well at Skidel. But for now, slender though they were, these faculties were brought exclusively to bear upon the selection of a violin.

No-one could pretend that the scene was entirely edifying. Reuben himself would recoil at the remembrance of him precociously rejecting a shopful of quarter-size violins as not being of the right colour. Leah soon enough realised that his quest was for a hue identical to that of Kreisler's Guarneri and suggested *sotto voce* that they might try to find one that matched its warm golden-brown luminescence. "But not its price tag, you understand."

Sure enough – and not before time as far as the young boy was concerned – buried in a remote alcove of the subterranean stockroom they found a battered, dusty violin case. When removed into the daylight and opened, the violin appeared to the boy like the genie in Aladdin, relishing the freedom of release and wallowing in the forgotten heat of a late spring morning. The wood, once it had been lovingly wiped with a yellow duster, fused with the colour of the sun and radiated an inner warmth as though its soul had been ignited by the rays and was now aglow.

The formidable Mrs Cohn, who owned the business, had quickly homed in on the family and taken control of the selling process. She tuned the long-slack strings and tightened the bow before rosining it. Reuben stretched out an impatient hand and took the tiny instrument to his chin. He grasped the bow and dragged it screaming over first the highest string and then, in turn, over the next three in descending order of pitch. His left hand began to feel its way around the neck, depressing one of the strings with the left forefinger as he pulled and pushed the bow across it, before forcing his middle finger to another string as he angled and re-angled the horsehairs whose sticky coating bit into the gut.

Moses' eyes began to fill with astonishment and he shivered as if suddenly chilled. He looked at Leah, whose expression was fixed with something far closer to fear, her stomach knotting with a nausea that made her head swim.

From somewhere deep within the cacophony, a ghostly form was slowly revealing itself, just as the sculpture hidden within a block of marble inexorably emerges from beneath the sculptor's apparently haphazard chipping. Reuben was playing the first theme of the Beethoven concerto he had heard a few days before. Rudimentary, of course. Recognisable nevertheless.

And Leah knew with an awful certainty that something inevitable had happened, one of those defining dawns whose light is both blinding and illuminating. Never would things be the same; never would the only grandchild of Rabbi Elias Mendel live a life that could in any way be termed normal. For just as she knew that Reuben was here displaying a facility that might indeed be genius, so Leah also realised that those who inhabit the outer margins of human endeavour often live there in crucifying loneliness.

She had only for a fleeting moment to reflect upon Beethoven's traumatic, unfulfilled search for a wife and then surrogate son, or bend her mind to his tempestuous, tortuous friendships. She saw in the vista of those turbulent auguries how reckless it is to expect those who are abnormal to lead lives that, in every way other than the quest for their own private unattainable Holy Grail, conform to the mores of society.

She thought she saw the future of her son. But she knew there was nothing to be done, save nurture the gift and lavish upon it all the nutrients necessary to make it grow, to stretch into the furthermost frontier of its scope and sweep out the last scintilla of raw plastic potential so that it might be gathered into his hand and shaped.

But she felt burdened, as though something had come between her and the sun. Sure enough, after Reuben had been cajoled into letting the violin have a nap in its case and the transaction was complete, they emerged into a sudden shower that stole the light which had warmed the wood. A changed day; for them, a changed world.

The whole house spoke eloquently of better days long since passed. Daguerreotypes of deservedly forgotten musicians, posing with their instruments or in studied postures at their composing desks, rose in careless parallel to the banister. Their faded gilt frames and murky glass weakly threw off stray rays of sun that had managed to penetrate both grimy window and yellowed net curtain which separated the hall from the outside world.

The stairs creaked as Moses, Leah and Reuben, their nostrils and throats thick with the musty aroma of perennially neglected furnishings, hacked their way through the shower of hovering dust and gingerly started their ascent to the studio. As they rose they navigated a meandering path that avoided the worst excesses of the loose rods and large threadbare patches which constituted the carpet.

A feeble, discordant tinkling trickled from a room on the first floor. It scarcely grew louder the nearer they approached; in fact, it stopped at an apparently unpropitious time in mid-tremulous bar. They barely had time to register their surprise before a torrent of guttural Germanic abuse and highly suspect syntax flowed under the door and cascaded down the decrepit staircase upon which they were perilously perched.

"Why do I with hopeless cases bother? Was this what I was meant to do? God help me! Did I spend by the side of Czerny's nephew's teacher seven years just so I should need listen to this rubbish! Why will you not practise like I tell you?"

At this, the door flew open and a tear-stained, ringletted figure in the most perfectly needle-pointed white lace dress with contrasted scarlet ribbons and black silver-buckled shoes bawled past them, hotly pursued by a nanny and the ruins of her future as a concert pianist.

"Why do they put their spoiled brats through this? All for appearances, not for love!" prefaced a further stream of threatening rhetoric from somewhere within the room that lay beyond the open door. "Do they think it's easy to become a genius? There are some things money can't buy. Talent, hunger, work and more work, wanting something so much you'd murder to get it. Ach, why can't I afford to teach the poor? They expect less – and give more!"

Too late did the Mendel Three seek to make their own escape. The stairs fulfilled their time-honoured role as an early warning system for intruders, and in a trice Madame Hartmann was at the door, her ample frame throwing a dark shadow that eclipsed what little light escaped her parlour.

"Ah ha, so this must be Master Reuben, yes? And Mister and Missus Mendel. Come, come in, come in. Mind me not. Since five years I've been teaching the Honourable Victoria St John-Maxwell, and, ach, it is hopeless! What is the point? Sometimes I am almost ashamed for taking their money but" – here a sigh to match her dimensions – "I have to eat."

Despite the inauspicious beginning, Moses took to her immediately. Perhaps he detected within her the spirit of someone who, too, had been forced to flee. Or did he see in her an inkling of his long-departed mother? Whatever, he led the charge up the hill and into her apartment.

After the formal introductions were made and Madame Hartmann had dispensed tea sweetened with rose petals for Leah and Moses, and some milk for Reuben, the boy's brief introduction to the world of music was rehearsed.

During the adult chatter, he wandered off to peruse the memorabilia of her life – a mantelpiece chaotically overcrowded with small, mostly damaged, off-white china busts of the pantheon of musical greats – here a Beethoven impersonating Samson after his fateful night with Delilah, there Mozart doing a passable impression of Van Gogh, next to him Bach modelling a Great Sphinx rhinoplasty. And interspersed with oval-framed silhouettes – mostly of the same composers when they were child prodigies – the walls, top of the piano and assorted small tables were covered with photographs of nameless musicians, some with faded inscriptions which may, indeed, have been made out to Fanny Hartmann herself.

Reuben brought the conversation to an abrupt end when he absent-mindedly brushed the keys of the battered baby grand while staring at the incomprehensible forest of notes on the score, held in place on the opened lid by two bent, burnished bronze prongs.

After a brief interrogation, during which she solicited his panoramic views on the world of music, Madame Hartmann, with one eye on her bank balance and the other on a final throw of the dice of (now vicarious) immortality, invited him to remove the violin from its case and show her how he held it.

Some hold a violin as if it were a Meissen figurine, only to be handled with the most delicate touch that lets it nestle on an upturned palm or be cradled protectively in the nook of the arm. Others treat it with a reverence approaching a breach of the Second Commandment, having to come into physical contact but that very fact being akin to sacrilege. Yet more are so dependent upon it for what they perceive themselves to be that they must dominate it, show how cavalier they are towards it by treating it with apparent indifference, swinging it in a reckless parabola towards the chin.

But Reuben belonged to none of these classes. For the boy did not so much recover the violin from its case as will its liberation, in much the same unconscious way as one requires the legs to walk or the hand to grasp a cup. It was a move as natural and instinctive as breathing, no need to take any deliberate action other than let the soul move the brain to impel the limbs. And when it left the case, the violin was no longer a static object but a very extension of the boy, a skein that cocooned him as a torch circled rapidly through the air haloes its holder in a frame of fire. His small body seemed to mould itself around the instrument, taking it unto himself so that where he ended and it began could barely be discerned.

He went to draw the bow across the strings but his teacher suddenly stopped him. For Madame Hartmann had already determined that here before her was the reason she had spent all those years teaching no-hopers like the one whose tearful flight had been the Mendels' overture. Now, she dictated terms with an assuredness that she had never known before, her coolness controlling the cascade of Germanic pronunciation that had constituted her welcome but thirty minutes earlier. After they were gone she was to think back upon her absolute certainty with a mixture of amazement and pride; in its confidence, logic and fundament of experience, her demands were imbued with an utter resistance to the possibility of rejection, as though she always had conducted business in an unequivocal manner that invited neither negotiation nor refusal.

"At half-past eight he will come every morning, bringing with him the fresh fruit to eat as a mid-morning snack. At midday you will collect him, and allow him a nap after his lunch, which should be something light; fish, I think, is best. From three to five in the afternoon, with tutelage in mathematics, science, philosophy and other such subjects you will provide him. I am sure that the need for this you see: his path of life is only just beginning, and we are seeing only so far as the first bend. We know not what might be hiding beyond. When older he gets he will wish the world to understand – he must have the, how do you say this, the tools? no, the weapons, yes, the weapons, necessary for this. In the evening he must practise the exercises which I shall require him to perform the next day.

"At the weekends, no music will he do, no study either. Instead, I am thinking that fun must be had, the zoo, theatre, anything he feels like doing and you are approving. In no time, there will be the day when he is no more the boy– but it is not yet here. If he has the talent, perhaps even genius. that we all hope he might, it shall come soon enough. Until then, our task, Mister and Missus Mendel, is to protect him against the worst effects of our false hopes. Too frequent is it that children's lives run aground on the rocks of adult expectations. So often I have been guilty of this, frightened to lose the pupil and encouraging the parents to believe that God Himself has kissed whichever part of the body their precious issue uses to produce some awful noise. You must decide whether Master Reuben is another of these or one of that rarest of children, the true wunderkind. I cannot yet say for sure, of course. I do promise you that I will do my best to find out, one way or another – and to tell you when I know.

"Even if he be so talented, you may feel that the life he will have is not what a parent would wish for their child. This I understand. So we will together spend some time also, so you can prepare yourselves for what lies ahead.

"I shall present my account at the end of each month, when I see how much time it has taken. It will not be very high but expect it to be paid immediately I shall. At the end of six months, we will see how things are."

Leah and Moses were won over, feeling that if she were a charlatan, her sheer *chutzpah* merited reward. Moses, in particular, had a peculiar perspective, believing that if people became so cynical that everyone was assumed to be prosecuting their own best interests to the exclusion of any other considerations, legal or moral, then life was just one massive Pandora's Box, devoid of even hope. Or, as Leah used to tease him, paraphrasing Tennyson, "'Tis better to be gulled and lose than never to be gulled at all."

The following day, Reuben took the first tentative steps towards his destiny. He recalled this time with affection tinged by more than a hint of regret. He put it rather beautifully to me: *"When my mind's eye wanders the passage of years, I think of my tutelage with Madame Hartmann and my parents as a golden time. For a boy of such tender years, to be the centre of attention without interruption was close to paradise. It was only later that I came to realise what I had missed. Close friends, the bustle of school, summer holidays at the beach. Idiotically idyllic, I suspect, but when you have never had something apparently desirable, that is often how it is."*

For the next seven or so years, his life was spent in a musical education of which Fanny Hartmann could scarcely believe herself capable, the perfect example of teacher made whole by the excellence of a pupil. And his parents performed their side of the bargain, replicating the mutual education that had been the basis of their romance, only broadening it with all the zeal of the self-taught to encompass the stuff of childhood that, for reasons rooted in their upbringings at opposite ends of the scale of wealth, they had both been deprived of. He was introduced to the world of nature; the botanical gardens at Kew, the zoological in Regent's Park. They brought him the Brothers Grimm and the fantasy of Hieronymus Bosch, the nonsense of Lear and the excitement of Stevenson and Scott. But more importantly, they exposed the rich pageant of his people's history. Moses and Leah programmed into him a fierce pride for an intellectual inheritance so often submerged in a mire of religious dogma, one that prized justice for all, morality that sits above law, the unending quest for knowledge and, most of all, personal independence.

On the blank page that was his technical knowledge, Madame Hartmann wrote the alphabet of music, the Rosetta Stone that would empower him to enter the world of the great composers and decipher their innermost musings. From the ubiquitous semibreve, crotchet and minim to the rarefied atmosphere of the semihemidemisemiquaver, he mastered the new vocabulary and how it should be articulated, learning where and when rests might be taken, where and when the pitch may shift, where and when the rhythm, momentum and sound may rise and fall, swell and fade.

And while he quickly became fluent in this strange new language, Reuben also learned to understand the physiology of playing the violin. Madame Hartmann showed him how to exercise the key muscles, ligaments, tendons and joints in order to provide the vital qualities of dexterity and stamina without which he would never play the concertos and sonatas she believed he was destined to perform. With the daily rubbing in of a liniment of uncertain properties intended to suffuse the flexors of the forearm, wrist and fingers with strength and elasticity, Madame Hartmann explained the pressure that holding the violin to his chin in any manner other than that which she taught would result in catastrophic wear and tear on his elbow; while even the slightest change of angle in his bow hand repercussed all the way to the shoulder, causing strain on the anterior annular ligament of the wrist and twisting the supinator longus which, in turn, placed wholly unreasonable demands on the biceps flexor cubiti.

He didn't pretend to understand – or even care about – the Latin terms with which she regaled him, but he got the message: it would ache in the short term and prevent him playing in the future. Although only a few steps into his journey, he was already painfully aware that the violin was more than merely prosthetic; it *was* him, and the thought of its amputation could no more be countenanced than decapitation.

As with all construction projects, he progressed from simple foundations to complex techniques. Scales upon scales were the layered brick of Reuben's musicality; *arpeggios* upon *portamenti*, *pizzicati* upon *archi*, the design and ornamentation to give the building its unique character.

Along a well-trodden path, she brought him to worship at

the altar of the greats – Bach, Mozart, Beethoven above all. And while Reuben even then cast a quizzical eye towards the unshorn undergrowth wherein lay, undiscovered, more pagan temples, he diligently followed her lead, launching himself into learning new works with the ferocious appetite of the long-starved.

And when she judged the time was right, she slowly introduced him to the distinctive challenges of performance. It was not enough to master music in the cloistered safety of a studio: Reuben had to play for audiences. At first, it was family and friends, and their extension in the sympathetic surroundings of Lily Jacobs' gatherings, a charming completion of one particular circle. Then, he ventured further afield and played in local halls which Moses rented for the occasion. Soon enough, word began to spread of a highly talented young violinist of enormous promise and engagements started to be offered by promoters always on the look-out for new talent. It took all of Fanny Hartmann's self-discipline to limit acceptances to a manageable number.

With the progression from tyro through note-player towards the rounded artist came the parallel development of boy to man – a thickening of sinew and muscle to mirror the blossoming of the sound that he started to produce with the violin; a broadening and lengthening that reflected his extraordinary ability to produce a seamless, seemingly infinite phrase; and, almost alarmingly, a vivid darkening of his eyes, a soul-revealing vista that encapsulated his questing for the inner meaning in the music that he played.

Therein lay his immediate disaster – and the seed of his later triumph. For no-one wanted thoughtfulness in their wunderkind – any maturity of purpose made the crowd feel uncomfortable, laying out before them something which they ought to have, but did not. A fiercesome display of note production, preferably louder and faster than the great names of the past, was the order of the day. As long as what was on show was that which could be marvelled at – caged like a newly discovered species, side-showed as some performing

Elephant Man, beyond the norm, freakish, perverse – then the honour of the audience was satisfied.

But woe betide he who brought fresh insight to the masters or, compounding the felony, sought to bring new music to its ears. Let him play Bach and Mozart, Beethoven and Mendelssohn, Tchaikowsky (not too often) and Brahms (not too slowly) – even the smaller-scale oeuvres of fiddle virtuosi like Paganini and Sarasate. Heaven forfend that a programme might introduce a strange cadenza to an old concerto or that a sonata be played at an unfamiliar tempo; heaven collapse if a piece was written in the last ten years.

Reuben was constant in his place. He would not pander to the common herd (as he saw it). His musical curiosity was ignited by a panoramic reading of philosophy, history, religion and politics that was a response to an insatiable hunger for knowledge and, at a deeper level, a personal credo. The profound questions that came to his mind provoked an equivalent challenging of received wisdom about the music he was learning, and of the repertoire itself. So he read around the notes, appreciating the composer's biography and thinking when he penned the piece being studied, extending the research to the era of creation so that he felt more in tune with its time. At the same time he would contact music publishers around Europe and even composers to ask whether any new pieces for violin were in circulation.

He outstripped Madame Hartmann in his breadth and depth of understanding, leaving him beyond her reach and protection. If he had a view as to a new way of playing a much loved classic, it would be aired. If he thought an innovative sonata had merit, it would be played.

By his own admission, realised through the dark veil of hindsight, this was not endearing. When his consciously intense programmes were interrupted by the scraping of the chairs, a chorus of huffing or a rising crescendo of ostentatious coughing, his nostrils flared and eyes flamed, revealing a haughty demeanour deemed unbecoming among the dominant classes in a Jew of any age, let alone one of his still tender years.

And like many demanding perfectionists, he refused to compromise, so just when others before him had been lauded at less than half his age – his beloved Kreisler, he who opened up this world to him, had started on his public travels when he was seven – Reuben's career stalled. Any bookings were in the sticks; joining an orchestra a humiliating acceptance of mediocrity and failure.

So he found himself staring at the future: at nearly sixteen, too old to be a prodigy, too young to be a doyen and with a growing reputation as a difficult artist. But the life-critical decisions that face all artists whose talents, ambition and fortunes are not always in harmony would be avoided.

Seismic shifts in the tectonic plates underpinning society would come between Reuben and his dilemmas, forcing him along a wholly unforeseeable path. Europe was unravelling, and the system of alliances which would drag the continent down into the slough was tightening its grip. By the end of it all, Reuben Mendel would be caught up in the tyrannical embrace of battle and marooned on a distant shore, changed forever by the profundity of his experience.

Chapter 3

When his neighbour's head exploded, Reuben was festooned in a shower of blood and bone and boiling flesh. A bright red cocktail – homogenised remnants of eyes, mouth, ears, nose, hair – dripped from his helmet and slid slowly down his face, its natural viscosity enhanced by the mud that caked him. He crouched below the parapet as yet another German shell flew overhead and with a lazy, practised gesture drew his saturated bow arm across his cheek and chin to detach the clinging vestiges of his erstwhile comrade.

For more than two years they had hoped it wouldn't happen. But eventually the wholesale slaughter bit so deep into Britain's resources that conscription for those over eighteen began and Reuben was swept up into the maelstrom.

While his father had fled a similar decree, he could not. So it was that Reuben, only grandson of Rabbi Elias Mendel of Skidel in the empire of Nicholas II, came to be enlisted to the service of the Tsar's cousin, George V, in his Sixth Platoon, 'B' Company, First King's Own Royal Lancaster Regiment, Fortieth Division, Third Army.

For Moses, the hardships that befell his son at training camp might have been softened with a tinge of nostalgia for his former life. But no amount of rehearsing the desperate existence by Niemen's banks could have prepared Reuben for the ordeal – the regime, living conditions, rations, people. Let alone the infamous trenches.

For as he readily acknowledged, Reuben had been reared as one of Nature's cosseted children, navigating the passage of his life through gentle brooks, not raging torrents. His hands were hardened only by the pressure of fingertip on gut string, the muscles strengthened by the hours of standing erect with violin under chin. His body had not developed in the sunlight of the farm, nor in the black of the mine, nor yet in the grease-soaked steam of the factory. His had grown tall in the dusty sunlight of Fanny Hartmann's studio. Neither had his head been required to concentrate on the racking grind of keeping the body united with the soul. He knew nothing of the twelve-hour shift two thousand feet below the light, and scarcely could imagine the sharp pain when molten metal attacked the naked torso, let alone countenance the prospect of a severed finger lying beneath the thresher. God forbid! In their stead the twelve-hour shift of endless repetition of Paganini's Caprices for solo violin, the white heat of Nietzsche, the raw satire of Swift.

But now he had to live with those who had not known one thousandth of what he had enjoyed. The origins his surname betrayed meant that officer status was closed off to Reuben. Not for him the gentle induction into army life; instead the cruel regime of sadistic sergeant-majors. Not for him the cuisine of the officers' mess; instead the canteen filth of mass-produced mush. Not for him the cosy comforts of the individual privy; instead the chorus of communal striving over rows of wooden holes.

For many of his colleagues, even these facilities represented something of an improvement. But for a member of the esteemed Rodrigue clan, they were Dante's Inferno made flesh, the only tempering of the heat coming through the occasional food packages which successfully ran the gauntlet of corrupt quartermasters and primitive refrigeration.

It was, however, the brain-numbing routine of the camp that was the source of greatest distress. The endless marching, trudging leaden-footed for long portions of the day, resulting in the need for liberal applications of castor oil to preserve several layers of foot skin and salve the gaping blisters. The interminable drilling, come driving rain, come snow and ice, rendered bearable solely by the mind-game of playing some piece of music that matched the rhythm of the left-right left-right about-turn shoulder-arms routine which the distorted logic of the British military machine determined vital to the success of a trench-bound war.

Reuben's keen sense of ulterior motive and subliminal messages – cultivated by long years of studying the coded concepts of genius – revealed the purpose behind these seemingly unnecessary activities. He saw clearly that men, whatever the altitude of their birth and culture of their upbringing, would not go willingly to the abattoir. Not, that is, without the dual action of unremittingly boring duties and the coercive threat of court martial. He realised soon enough that he best send that portion of his nature which marked him from the crowd into hibernation, and try to disappear into the crowded ranks.

Here were the first suggestions of qualities that marked him out as a survivor. The ability to merge into the background. An innate understanding of the melody and beat of power. A feline flexibility to bend with the fall, to bounce on impact. The dissimulation of his whole self. Battlefield cunning, knowing when to dive for cover, somehow sensing when it was right to plunge headlong into a water-filled mud-hole.

From where it came, none knew. Even Moses' random journey from Skidel did not explain it. And certainly none on the Rodrigue side could detect the slightest hint of the adventurer whose stock might have lodged in some remote branch of Reuben's vast genetic barn, waiting to be roused by the extravagant stimuli of chaos.

But one thing about him *was* new. The boy-man, who had for so long lived in a world peopled by adults, made his first friend.

Nowadays Isaac Rosenberg is rarely mentioned in the same breath as Brooke, Owen or Sassoon. But for a while among the cognoscenti he was thought to be greater than them all, if for no other reason than that the sheer quality of his verse transcended his modest origins and lowly rank, while his accomplishments travelled beyond poetry to prose and, extraordinarily, painting.

There, among the Anglo-Saxons, beneath the stultifying

inadequacies of an officer corps plucked fresh from those 'great' public schools in which the dying Empire's plenipotentiaries were perpetually bred, the two Jews were hurled together. Despite the difference in their own backgrounds, Reuben, faux-assimilated West End aristocrat and Isaac, East End ghetto-reared, recognised in each other not just the kindred spirit of the outsider, but also that they both lived the artist's life, a universe away from the experiences of their comrades-in-arms.

There in claustrophobic encampments – at the front and to the rear – they exchanged their worries and accomplishments, their ambitions and limitations. Under bombardments they cowered – Rosenberg composing verse, Mendel improvising on the harmonica, a mother's inspired gift that he'd rapidly mastered. In the quiet times they talked of Jewish history and German literature in hushed, conspiratorial tones – partly to avoid the accusations of espionage that could so easily spring from the paranoia of a ruling class in decline, even more to avoid being snubbed as intellectual snobs.

And yet, for all their obvious differences, the troop had a soft spot for its Jews. Isaac's verses spoke more for the ordinary soldier than those of more celebrated poets, while Reuben's improvisations came not from the classics but from the folk tunes of his youth, songs that were the very distillation of peasant culture and village life.

So, when that haunting, lonely sound floated out from the trenches or through the barracks, the music transported those who heard to reveries of better, safer times: hot bread fresh from the oven, stroking the loyal dog beside a welcoming hearth, thick soup slipping down to the stomach. And all the nuances of a life to which none would return, but which all could re-create, came flooding through. They may not know the origins of the tunes, could scarcely imagine the labyrinthine route of their arrival in a Flanders plain from a people dispersed along a languid arc from the eastern Mediterranean to the Russian heartlands. But they knew, *knew*, that they contained the common thread of shared hardships and mutual suffering and spoke of their fears and hopes, their yesterdays and their doomed tomorrow.

After a while, when he had finally exhausted his vast canon, Reuben found that his fellow foot-soldiers came to him with whistled snatches of their own past. A Norfolk yeoman dredged from somewhere way, way back a Fenland rhapsody which enshrined a rural idyll long since disappeared beneath the implacable teeth of a motorised plough. 'Jock', a Glaswegian docker, regurgitated in an impenetrable brogue the anger-pathos of the songs of Jacobite rebellion, at once mourning the absence of a king of their own and raging at enemy occupation. The reverberant bass of an American slave's son in a nearby trench assailed him with music that vented the poison of oppression, allowing the human spirit to find solace even in the deepest, most stagnant slough.

Like a prospector sifting the dredge of a rich river, Reuben's playing sometimes came upon a nugget of the purest ore. Such was the music and the setting that then – when the clear night sparkled cold and bright and quiet, when the rain for once withheld its incessant shafting into mud, when far-off shells paused their perpetual thud, and it seemed as though Nature itself was stooped to listen – then you could hear from somewhere down the long, silent line a single cry as gold dropped melting to the heart.

Under the crystal-speckled sky, the lost and broken could look up and know that loved ones too might share that canopy. And for a lonely soldier scared of dying distant from his mother, or a blood-soaked nurse so tired of dressing ragged stumps and sewing winding-sheets, anxiety and longing were cauterised, if only for those brief bars that drifted careless on the breeze, a rolling cloud of kindly gas to dull their pain.

There upon that blasted heath, Reuben learned the lesson Fanny Hartmann could never teach. Music is so much more than a series of notes, it is a living, breathing thing, demanding the oxygen of life, the wind of experience, if it is to take wing and fly to the heart and soul. It was a lesson that, once recalled beyond experiences yet to be told, would take his playing to regions and plateaux hitherto unknown.

The long winter that straddled 1917 and 1918 yielded to the blanket mud of spring – a cloying restraint that adhered to the legs, slowing progress to an agonising, freeze-frame suicide march.

But unlike so many of their confreres, Reuben and Isaac avoided calamity. It was, for a while, as though they were destined to survive with little more than the superficial wounds that are the stuff of life in the raw. And indeed there were compensations. The visits to the rear, where tobacco, alcohol and women (usually in that sequence) were all available in copious quantities, began to broaden Reuben's somewhat monastic upbringing so that he could, with detachment, look back on the horror of the war if certainly not with pleasure then with a sense that the experience was not without its positive facets.

Throughout the last weekend in March the regiment had been battling a German advance, soldiers decimated by vicious raking crossfire that took no prisoners, indiscriminate in its want of mercy. Still the bullets missed the two of them. Overrun, they retreated to reserve lines which all too soon became the new theatre. And still they resisted until, during a lull, they came to blissful, deserved rest.

But it did not last. As night began to fall and the few bedraggled survivors finally felt the pressure start to lift, the call went out for volunteers to renew the defence. If Reuben had had his way they would have stayed. But Isaac – for complex reasons rooted in a desire to stand tall in the teeth of a pitiless system – struggled up on feeble legs and began his weary way towards the burgeoning conflict around the village of Fampoux.

Reuben hesitated. But this new-found friendship exerted an even greater pull than the desire for rest, and his instincts won out. Hauling himself to his feet and leaning on his battered rifle, he hobbled down the darkening path in pursuit of the poet.

The clamour of battle grew ever louder. They were drawn to the noise as moths to a flame, hypnotically, magnetically, moving unthinkingly towards apotheosis. Vision diminished with each passing minute as night conspired with long-battered buildings giving up the ghost. Only the starburst of shells and half-hearted moonlight cast light in the smog of masonry dust that swirled epileptically, mingling with the smoke of war and the last flickering of twilight. Hearing could not compensate for the loss of sight as the cacophony of battle encircled them, assailing their ears with disorienting sound that buffeted them into a Bedlam choreography.

They stumbled through the rubble, back-to-back, crab-like, firing their carbines aimlessly towards what little remaining shelter was afforded by the dying village. No talk was possible, no words of comfort, no final farewells. Bullets flew, more houses fell, shells screamed overhead.

Blindly, deafly, they came upon a fragmented intersection where once the main street was crossed by alleys. Seeking respite, they turned up one. Clambering over the collapsed walls of the buildings on either side, they met blanket fire from a troop from Emperor Franz Joseph's elite guard. Instinctively Isaac dipped his right shoulder, tipping towards the enemy, shielding Reuben. He was shredded instantly, meeting the bullets almost willingly, while Reuben slid behind him into the black, welcoming embrace of a rain-filled crater.

Rosenberg died without a sound, and a light was extinguished much too soon to know how far its beam might shine. Mendel – wounded, captured, traumatised – lived, and the flame that would illuminate some of the darkest moments ever known spluttered and flickered, but remained alight.

Chapter 4

As he lay in limbo a horror-strewn zoetrope played an endless loop upon the screen beneath his restless eyelids.

Minotaurs roved a volcanic landscape. Stinking breath, poisoned clouds belching from monstrous nostrils. Suppurating yellow streams of acid pus. Putrid flesh, rotting in the dark. Screaming cadavers, their pitch ever shriller, rising from an icy stone floor slimy with gore, mangled haunches hanging from naked bone. Bellows of enraged beasts stalking the labyrinth, clawing, tearing hapless innocents lost in an inescapable serpentine infinity, forever, forev, for...

Fear ... a terror such as we, untouched, can never understand, spiking to agony, receding to dull, constant pain, plucking at the eyes whenever they at last can bear to open.

Who knows who has not been there what blackness lies within the shattered mind? Only those over whom the ebony cloak of despair has floated may know that entombed world wherein the damaged seek refuge from the demons they must confront when finally comes the time to wake.

Reuben never would be sure to what extent he elected to remain shut off from the world, choosing the safety of sleep over the danger of consciousness until catharsis purged his mind, alleviating the Sisyphean burden of unpardonable guilt. The recollection of those lost six months would remain a surreal montage of dislocated sound, vague smells and blurred light, recalled as an incomplete mosaic at uncertain moments throughout his life. But somewhere in the distance, the cacophony of hospital noise, a discordant concerto, could be heard: the thud and bang of slamming doors, the dull drumming of running rubber-shod feet, the cymbal clash of a hundred different metal instruments – and above all the hollow song of bereavement, an unceasing dirge of moaning.

There he lay, cheek by jowl with other casualties in the overcrowded ward of the Empress Marie Therese Hospital for Infantry, in Heiligenstadt, Vienna's leafy northern suburb where Beethoven once had roamed when summer's heat made the capital too oppressive. For all that Moses and Leah knew he was dead, his shattered remains lying in some forbidding pit, tangled inextricably with other unidentifiable portions of men, 'known', in the immortal simplicity of Kipling's universal epitaph, 'unto God'. And he might as well have been, for all the life he exhibited. Until that time when he was called back to take his place among the living by the vital force which had made him what he was – and would make him what he yet would be.

One late summer's day, when the hospital shutters were thrown open to admit the sultry air of rural Vienna, the village band came to play for those patients further advanced than Reuben along the road to recovery. This being Austria, the repertoire consisted exclusively of the genius of the country's favourite sons, born and adopted.

No single tune above all others could have roused him from the depths. It wasn't the melodies, although the outpourings of Haydn and Mozart, transfigured for wind and brass ensemble, might charm the birds from their perches. Nor yet the beauty of Schubert's songs, whose simple purity even this band could not obscure. Not even a minestrone made from tasty morsels of Beethoven.

No. It was the very sound itself. The harmonious noise of complementary instruments came together in numberless combinations, once soft, now loud, interplaying, weaving, dancing across the sky, skipping over the trim lawns that fell away from the bleak building down towards a trickling brook. Indeed it seemed as if the music was serenading the elements – the breeze susurrating through the trees, the bright, clean water sparkling and tinkling about the stones and rushes that stood in its path.

It was this symphony of life which summoned the broken soul of Reuben Mendel from its torturous netherland, calling him back to resume his journey.

Once roused, he began the creeping process of recovery, not of the body, which had in fact escaped relatively unscathed, but of the mind. Over the ensuing weeks he climbed stutteringly up, away from where he had been, a journey he would later come to see mirrored in Beethoven's favourite string quartet.

He recalled those last moments of Rosenberg with photographic immediacy and the images plagued every waking moment, and every sleeping one too. In his sweat-drenched bed he railed at all that had befallen him: the death of his friend, the separation from his mother and father, the overwhelming sense of loss that weighed so heavy it seemed as if sometimes he could barely breathe.

But slowly a kind of equilibrium came upon him, originating mostly in the unconscious awareness that he had descended as low as he would go and that he had, although still damaged, survived.

And it helped that signs of his past life began to reappear.

After months of refusing to believe he was gone, Leah and Moses had finally tracked him down. Using the Rodrigues' network of business contacts that included a medical supplies business, the simple question asked of all their customers – "Might you have an English soldier here, perhaps with amnesia or unable to talk?" – finally bore fruit. A personal visit by a distant cousin bearing a hastily despatched pre-war photograph confirmed identification, and now a letter arrived from London announcing their imminent arrival.

He shuddered at the prospect.

It wasn't that his love for them was diminished. On the contrary. It was the dread of seeing them after so long, knowing that what he had been, he was no longer; that he could not divine their expectations, and thus could not prepare for their hopes, their fears.

The apprehension that already pervaded his whole self ratcheted up as their appearance became ever more imminent. No firm date had been set, and each day that passed acted like a weight upon the next, piling on the pressure.

So that when at last he saw them from his brookside seat come nervously down the slope towards him, all pretence at stoicism failed, releasing a tidal wave of undiluted bile which grief, guilt and self-loathing had dammed in the reservoir of his soul.

A foam of spittle escaped his lips; tears streamed through the new beard which failed to mask the gaunt impress of life in the trenches and of living with the aftermath of loss. The storm grew in power, the stream of saliva ever more pronounced, the words increasingly incoherent as his tortured mind linked every injustice, real or perceived, to Leah and Moses and their parental failings.

His shoulders hunched, concaving his chest, from where whooping breaths announced the abatement of the tempest. His mother and father, having initially recoiled from the ferocity of the assault, quickly realised that this was why they had come. Their love was what was needed to ignite the pool of poisoned gas that had formed a malignant bubble at the centre of Reuben's being; their support was what was needed to help in the subsequent reconstruction. With their spark had come the explosion, an instant dissipation of the toxins which threatened his very existence.

When he recounted this episode, he flushed with embarrassment, even after more than half a century.

"The things I said to them, just to recall it makes my stomach turn. I vented a fury the like of which I have never known. The language I used was straight from the trenches, with no restraint. How could I have spoken to them like that? My only excuse is that I was not myself. And although I know that they forgave me, you know, I never forgave myself, and even now feel somewhat diminished whenever it comes to mind. Is it not strange how these threads, slight

but strong, run through our lives?"

Over the following days there were aftershocks, but they were decreasingly violent in their effect, increasingly apart, like thunder which rolls away leaving merely the rain as a reminder of its power. And as trees and animals regain scorched earth vacated by forest fire, so signs of Reuben re-exerting himself over life began to be seen as the glowing embers of his catharsis gave off their last light.

With the impeccable timing born of innate instinct, Leah came to the hospital one evening. Twilight had settled over the bank of the brook where Reuben had taken to spending his thoughtful times. She sat beside him without a word, allowing the soft music of the water to serenade their silent meditations. After a few minutes had passed and the mother sensed the son was ready, she placed upon his lap the violin case which she had so carefully nursed during the tortuous, impatient journey across war-ravaged Europe.

Reuben averted his gaze, staring with the vacant look of one whose eyes function yet who sees nothing, gazing long into the far distance to some lost world. But he could not ignore what he was. And even as he fixed on that lost horizon, his right hand drifted, seemingly of its own accord, towards the battered box, opening the lid and withdrawing what had been, until but a couple of years ago, his constant companion.

But what years those had been! Like all his comrades, Reuben was forever scarred and shaped by the carnage he had fortuitously escaped. The rest of his life would be spent in its long shadow, the transformation irreversible. If Leah had harboured any hope of getting the former Reuben back, she lost it the moment she saw him. It was her duty now to help him find his own way, burdened as he was by all that he had been through.

Having lain idle for so long, the violin was badly in need of tuning. He did it without hesitation, his perfect ear having survived perpetual bombardment.

His hands were not in such good shape, however. When they have practised for hours on end, daily, for weeks, months, years with no pause, the joints, muscles, tendons, tissues live in expectation of the discipline. They soon relax into the lassitude of freedom, and then the work needed to regain suppleness and stamina is awesome, an Eiger of effort.

But that was for the future. Perfection of technique never deserts the talented, even if physical powers wane. With a bow in his hand, the left jaw caressing the smooth ebony rest and his fingers pressing down the strings on the neck, Leah once again saw the little boy with the fruit of his precocious search in that instrument shop, aeons past.

As she remembered, so tears stung her eyes, and she wept for all that had been, for the years of sweated labour, for the lost childhood, for her broken boy.

And he too cried. Partly for the beauty of the sound he made, and partly for the lost safety of the time from which it came.

Mostly he mourned for Isaac, and poems that would never be written, pictures never painted. But also for himself, that he would not know the warmth of that sweet friendship, of the joy of insoluble, interminable argument through endless nights under endless skies. With whom now could he debate the questions to have corrugated minds since primeval flames flickered off the stony innards of a freezing African cave and all our ancestors gathered to share adventures and ponder the travails of life?

Chapter 5

With that first bowing, Reuben took the longest single stride on the road to recovery. Over the ensuing months, episodes of rage became shorter, the intervals between them longer, as he strove to regain his pre-war mastery.

Moses and Leah stayed in Vienna, finding an apartment where he might fully recover under their protective eye. In a tenuous yet palpable connection with Reuben's distant future, they settled upon rooms in Schwarzspanierstrasse, the very street that saw Beethoven's final days.

There, in the shadow of the place where that tempestuous genius composed his last two quartets, Reuben strove day and night to retrain his hands and ears, to dredge up from the deep places of his soul all that his first life, as he took to calling it, had meant. Why? He could hardly say himself. Everything that had happened led him to allocate music a lower status in the hierarchy of life than he had before. But something inside him could not be stilled, a restlessness to re-create the perfection in his mind's ear as actual sound … a perpetual pursuit that could never be fulfilled, but had always to be sought.

And in this way, the old Reuben began to exert itself over the new. Not to the exclusion of the ineffable sadness in which he lived both day and night, but to complement it and give it voice. A new humility pervaded his music so that, where once he was seduced by the superficial excitement of throwing off difficult works with the fewest mistakes and the maximum bravado, he now sought the inner tensions and emotions of more introspective pieces.

It was the humble beginning of a journey that would much later in his life place him at the pinnacle of music-making. For now, he knew only that he had discovered, there in the dozens of small music shops that dotted Vienna's back streets, a rich new seam to mine, of solo works, duets for violin and piano, trios and quartets, arrangements ad infinitum to express every mood from frivolity to dark despair.

He practised like a madman, sight-reading and relying on his memory to retain within him the notes as he drew them from the score before him. He played all day, windows flung open to the world, trying to mitigate the intense heat he generated, regardless of the temperature outside. Scales poured forth as before with Madame, and all the exercises she prescribed came flooding back along with the works she had demanded he master, only now they were augmented by the new pieces he had discovered. The focus was absolute, so that he looked only within himself, steeling his fingers, hands, arms, intellect and soul to the task in hand. Verging on monomania, he drilled as though back on the parade ground, and so was oblivious that there, in the most musical city in the world, he developed into something of a local celebrity, the Unknown Violinist. It became an unspoken understanding among those in the immediate vicinity of the apartment that, almost without fail, whenever you walked by there would be an outpouring of glorious sound, amplified echoingly by the large grey stones that made up the fabric of the building.

And word began to spread out, beyond Schwarzspanierstrasse and its claustrophobic parish, of the invisible fiddler who lurked within the shadows, playing with unsurpassed beauty.

One balmy autumn afternoon, Reuben was practising the fiendish second Partita for solo violin by Bach. The window was open in a forlorn attempt to entice some cooler air into the sultry room.

He reached the final movement, a looming landscape of crags and peaks, deep crevasses and hazardous ridges which only the most sure-footed dare traverse with any degree of certainty. For its full twelve minutes his right arm drew and drove the bow across the strings, twisting and tilting wrist and elbow as the fingers of his left hand danced a precise and assertive quadrille across the delicate neck of the violin.

Immersed as he was in Bach's profound sound-world, Reuben was oblivious to the small crowd that had gathered outside, rather than, as usual, just pausing or slowing their pace to drink in his serenade. It was only when the final long chord drifted off into the Viennese air that they were unable to refrain from appreciation and he rather sheepishly peeped out from behind a burgundy chenille drape to take a look.

Almost from the moment he had first picked up the violin beside the brook, something had been gnawing away inside him, the vague sense of change, of a dislocation between the now and the then. Until he looked through the window at his audience, he had been unsure of what it was. But as he gazed into the faces staring up at him with a curious mixture of admiration and envy, he realised that the pre-war Reuben would have looked down on them as something less than him. Yet now, he was different.

All that he had seen – his comrades' naked heroism and dignity in the teeth of appalling slaughter, the suffering they had shared as equals – transformed his self-perception, setting off in him a sense that he was wrong to distance himself from the rest of the world, that he lacked anything unique to say that merited special attention. He understood what it would mean for his music-making: he could never appear as a soloist again, and if he were to continue to perform, the anonymity of ensemble playing would be the only way forward.

He couldn't know that this process was, in fact, already in train. For the ripples of rumour about his impromptu recitals had reached the ears of the powers that ran Vienna's great Philharmonic. And among the audience for the Bach was Dr Franz Breuning, scion of the celebrated clan which had become Beethoven's surrogate family when he first settled in Vienna, way back in the 1790s. Wherever art and society intermingled, there for a century or more links to the Breunings would be found – whether it be amateur performance, the legal arrangements of aristocratic sponsorship, or simply innumerable acts of generosity and kindness upon which tempestuous creative souls frequently rely without actually being aware of their occurrence; not exactly taking them for granted, more assuming that things happen according to some mystical process whose causation need not bother them.

Several days later, Breuning rapped on the door with the silver top of his cane. Presenting his card to Leah, he entered the apartment, removed his top hat, and came quickly down to business.

"I heard your performance last week, sir. I know little of music, unlike some of my ancestors. But I do know one thing: our great orchestra has been badly affected by the war. Not only have some of our players been killed or injured, but our finances have been ravaged by the fiscal imperatives of our time. We are afflicted – and the only cure is fresh talent. Judging by the reaction of my fellow Viennese, you are obviously skilled. I understand that you were an English soldier. I have spoken with a few people at the Philharmonic – and they do not regard that as an insurmountable obstacle, provided you can play well enough. I have arranged for you to attend the Music Society tomorrow. There you will play for Herr Doctor Felix Weingartner, who will wish to hear two or three pieces of your own choosing."

Leah interrupted this stream, cup of tea and plate of cake in hand for the visitor. "Had you not thought to ask us first, sir?"

A slight chuckle. "Of course not, Madame. If you had said 'No', I should have been required to go and fetch Maestro Weingartner, who would then have convinced you that your son's talent is a public asset and you have no right to refuse its exploitation. Believe me, Ma'am, no-one, but no-one, refuses the Maestro. This way, I have saved everyone a great deal of time, no?"

So the following day Reuben walked into the neo-romantic jewel set in the heart of Imperial Austria that was the Golden Hall of the Musikverein.

In years to come, when the mood came for reminiscence and reflection, he would bend his mind to wonder what might have happened had he declined to go or if the audition had not pleased the great conductor. Perhaps he would have eventually returned with Leah and Moses to London, establishing a steady career as a jobbing musician. There, he may even have reverted to a career as a concert virtuoso. And in the doing, he would have been ensconced safely in the bosom of the British Empire when evil bestrode the vestibules of European culture, from Madrid through Paris and Rome to Berlin, Prague... and Vienna.

But that was for a different time. As it was, he waited for what seemed an age, pacing up and down, rehearsing in his mind the pieces he was to play. Over and over he went, picturing the notes on the page, the composers' instructions on rhythm, pace and style, hearing in his head exactly how it should sound.

At last, one of the many pairs of tall double doors leading off the corridor in which he'd been imprisoned finally opened. "Please to come in," invited a timid, pasty-faced woman of indeterminate age whose life had obviously been spent in perpetual panic. "The Maestro will see you now."

And there Weingartner sat, enveloped in that misty aura which attends those who know that they are recognised by those who know that they are not. It was different from conceit, more like being used to standing apart from the crowd, beyond the anonymity which is the habitual lot of the vast majority. Beside him sat another, physically even more distinguished figure.

"May I present Professor Arnold Rosé, our celebrated leader. So, you are the Englishman Breuning told me about. You wish to impoverish Viennese musicians with free, *al fresco* performances, I think. You have prepared some pieces for me to hear, no?"

Reuben nodded and bent towards his music case.

"A moment, please. My Philharmonic did not, I think, become great by having players who just know scores note by note. Here we breathe our collective soul into the music, even where they may be some risk of over-familiarity. So, you shall play a piece of my choosing – then I can see how well you love music, not whether you do it for the same reasons as lawyers transfer land, or cows chew cud."

Despite his nerves Reuben smiled, in part at the wit, but mainly for the instant feeling of having found a long-sought hearth, the inner glow that comes with coming home.

"You will not, Herr Mendel, know this piece, I think. It was written in 1910 by a Pole who was here in Vienna in 1914. It's the 'Romance' by Szymanowski. He will one day do something quite marvellous, I think."

He took the score that Weingartner offered. A brief glimpse told him all he needed to know. It was a lush, romantic piece with long, melodic lines demanding great technique and control. Sight-reading such works was always hazardous, and to make matters worse he realised that he would be accompanied by the old conductor himself.

He scanned the five-minute composition, logging time-signature, tempi and bowing instructions. Trying to buy some time, he flicked back over the pages but could put off the moment no longer. Like Horatio at the bridge, Reuben realised that the only way was to hurl himself into the foaming Tiber of notes, trusting to equal measures of blind faith, talent and luck to see him safely ashore.

So he jumped.

If Weingartner and Rosé had been expecting poor intonation then they weren't disappointed. Reuben's fingerwork all but deserted him. But the two maestri were not: they sought something else, that indefinable quality, the true musician's soul, an intuitive response to that mystical melange of rhythm, melody and harmony which has moved Man since that moment millennia back when, in some long-lost forest or frozen, flame-lit cave, a simian hand first swung a bleached bone hard down upon a hollow trunk or stone floor.

And they heard it.

"Why do you want to play in an orchestra?" Weingartner asked as Reuben allowed the final note to fade away to nothing. "You could almost certainly be a soloist."

The old Reuben would have shrugged his shoulders in a half-hearted attempt at modesty, his eyes betraying his true feelings of shock that anyone, even a world renowned conductor, could doubt his talent. But the new Reuben was of a different cloth, still ragged from the trenches, the vivid colours sprung from hubris now faded by brutal exposure to unforgiving elements, the pattern hidden beneath coats of dried mud and blood.

"Maestro, I'm honoured. Your opinion means much to me. I can't pretend I've long wanted to play in an orchestra. If I'm completely honest, before the war I'd have regarded it as something of a come-down. But I'm different now, the war's changed me. The idea of making music in the company of others feels exactly what I need. It hadn't consciously occurred to me until Dr Breuning's invitation to meet you. But from that moment it seemed to be right that, if I was good enough, I should do it. And to join an orchestra of such prestige and heritage, well I know it's more than most can ever hope for. I don't know what the future holds for me. I'm a foreigner here, a recent enemy even. So I can't promise to stay forever, even though I understand that *esprit de corps* is so important. But if you give me the opportunity, I will make this one pledge – to serve you and the Vienna Philharmonic with a full heart and with all my talents and skills, for as long as I am able."

With such new-found humility, Reuben joined the first violins of the greatest orchestra in the world. In one of the threads that made up the tapestry of his life, he found himself sitting directly behind Arnold Rosé. Player of a wonderful Guadagnini instrument, he also founded a celebrated quartet. His daughter Alma, with whom he performed, would rule the Woman's Orchestra at Auschwitz with the iron discipline without which no-one survived in that world *non pareil*.

For Reuben, this was now to be his tranquil time, that phase in a life when the foreseeable future is known, predictable, even secure, and the orchard that was planted during many years of study would bear its first fruit. Above all, it was a time to breathe deeply, stretch his limbs and see where they would take him.

Chapter 6

For those who knew Vienna in the immediate aftermath of the Great War, such a peaceful picture was mystifying, completely at odds with the actual state of the nation.

Decay was all around, the empire humbled, crumbling, its ruins trapped in a vortex of revolution. All of Europe lay as the dead of Pompeii, frozen under the dust of the huge eruption which had engulfed the cradle and heartland of western culture.

Austria suffered the most, all the tethering posts of its self-perception and identity savagely uprooted in the space of a mere four years. Its empire once had covered much of Europe's centre – now it was confined to a small, landlocked, mountain-ringed territory. The famed, near-octocentennial monarchy, the Fatherhead, the Voice, had been omnipresent in the halls of the great nations – now it was no more, its last embodiment, the anonymous Charles, slipping away to Switzerland in the dead of night at the deserted crossing-point of Feldkirch.

Worse than the perception was the reality. The fabric itself was in tatters, rent maliciously with shark-bite gashes and worn to translucence by the years of neglect. All the daily symbols of power – currency, infrastructure, economy – lay impotent in the gutter, limp and swollen for want of nourishment. Revolution hung heavy in the air, the spirit of change wafting on blood-red northerlies from St Petersburg via Moscow and Munich.

But they failed to breach Austria's mountain guard, and only the stale odour of violent rebellion wafted across Salzburg, its rotten corpse petrifying in the Bavarian heights. Insurrection failed to materialise, and instead Austria imploded, plunging into cathartic introspection fuelled by an unstable mixture of injustice, rage, rejection and relaxation – injustice of inflicted defeat; rage at the enforced truncation of its once-mighty body; the wholesale rejection of the previous ruling class; and the release of the coiled spring of pent-up anxiety which had been increasingly tensed during the long years of conflict, hardship and sacrifice.

The straight-lacedness of the Habsburgs unravelled with the velocity of a whip; morals were unshackled, hierarchies undermined and the frontiers that marked out the traditional strata of society obliterated. Everything was chaos, libertine; the untamed animal lurking within was let loose to run amok, sprung fresh from its prudish cage to scavenge among the virgin grasslands, fertile feeding grounds that could satisfy even the basest, most obtuse taste.

Every kind of perversion was on offer, the weirdest proclivity catered for. While for those whose mind craved escape into the singing labyrinth of hallucination, Vienna rained narcotics upon them.

The arts stalked the *zeitgeist*, plunging willingly, happily, into the morass. While Berlin carved its historic niche as the masterpiece of decadence, Austria, out of sight, matched – perhaps, even outstripped – it for cultural decay. Writers stopped writing, dramatists ceased dramatising, poets withdrew into themselves, their rhymes only for private musing. Music lost all its power, written for the time zone, locked on to a specific resonance whose power was dissipated almost upon its first utterance, such was its weakness.

Performance in opera, theatre and dance adopted faddish absurdities all designed, like every other artistic contrivance, to bring about the appearance of difference from what had gone before, to haul down a curtain of impenetrable opacity between now and the then which had inflicted death, defilement, humiliation and poverty on one of the great crucibles of civilisation.

Reuben relished, wallowed in, this corrupt atmosphere. He

started living the life that the combination of being a prodigy and a soldier had prevented. Rampant inflation made paupers of all; but even this did not matter. He dived into the black bread and coarse wine with the enthusiasm of the deprived. He enjoyed the camaraderie of playing with the orchestra, knowing the joy of being part of a community for the first time, a feeling enhanced by the new hardship of rehearsing and performing in freezing halls long since devoid of heating. And after the concerts, they would avail themselves of the many sources of pleasure the new Vienna offered, helping Reuben to improve the German he was striving to master.

"Yes, I must admit it," he recalled. *"I did make up for lost time. In the army I had, shall we say, some adventures of the extramilitary variety. But in hindsight I suspect these were far more a source of escape than a true rite of passage. Vienna was a different matter altogether. I suspect my parents worried about me, staying out all hours and coming home smelling of drink and smoke and perfume! But, you know, they never said a word."*

But it wasn't all play and music. What made him great never completely slumbered; and in Vienna Reuben found a spiritual home.

He drank in all that wonderful city had to offer, immersing himself completely in all its glories. There was no part with which he failed to be intimate, whether it was the gothic magnificence of St Stephen's or the simple pastoral pleasure of returning to Heiligenstadt, breathing the same rural air as Beethoven where, racked by his impending deafness and contemplating killing himself, he had written a moving adieu to his brothers.

Sometimes, he would go a little further and visit the small cemetery in Grinzing where Mahler – whose giant shadow still hovered over the Opera and the Philharmonic a decade after his passing – lay at peace beside his small daughter, Maria. On other days, he might just stroll around the Kunsthistorisches Museum and marvel not just at the splendour of the collections amassed by the Habsburgs during their eight-hundred-year reign but also at the building, with the exception of the Winter Palace in St Petersburg, perhaps the most stunning, most magnificent (certainly the most extravagant purpose-built) of all museum buildings.

His greatest pleasure was the Wurstelprater, Vienna's wonderful parkland with its fairground famed throughout Europe for the magnificent Ferris wheel bestriding its highest point. But in his foreshortened visitation to the joys of boyhood, Reuben headed for the Tunnel of Fun.

Even years after, despite everything, he could recount its every detail with child-like enthusiasm. The gothic entrance, a depiction of hell itself (so fitting during spasms of recall) with automaton devils bearing tridents, driving humans into the ever-opening mouth of perpetual retribution. The tunnel's bizarre passage brought other delights: tableaux of fairytales – Little Red Riding Hood, Puss in Boots, Snow White – which, despite the predictability of their static display, brought Reuben disproportionate pleasure as he drank in their every detail.

But it was the climax of the ride that stayed with him forever, a metaphor of his recent past and unknowable future. For the final stop was at Messina for a re-enactment of the earthquake in 1908 which had destroyed the Sicilian city founded by the Greeks some two and a half thousand years earlier and which, in retrospect, seemed an allegory for what befell mainland Europe six short years later.

The train with its worm of little open-topped carriages stopped in front of a stylised model of the historic port, Mediterranean houses with their typical white walls basking innocently in the warm sun. All too soon, the sky would darken, the earth tremble, emitting an awful groaning and hissing. Small children would cling to Nanny who, afraid to show her own discomfort, looked away and focused on some innocent diversion.

His pleasure was, of course, out of proportion; but it was for him a kind of release, as if the boils of his wunderkind and warfare years had to be lanced before he could even approach the steady world of adult order with which he identified service in the Philharmonic.

But while this touristica brought him superficial satisfaction, something deeper was afoot. For strangely, disconcertingly, Reuben found himself at home. During these early Viennese years he drenched himself not just in the city, not just in Austria, but in Middle Europe as a whole. Sometimes with the orchestra, more often on his own, he would take himself off to Prague, Berlin or Budapest (but not, to his regret, to St Petersburg or Moscow, where internal strife and xenophobia rendered visits impossible).

There he absorbed the passions of the past, the way in which cultural glaciers had moved through the land, depositing fertile residues and leaving in their wake irrevocable signs of their passage. Realisation began to dawn that this was his bedrock, not the bourgeois London upbringing which had so far served him well. Being sent to mainland Europe had not been the leaving he had assumed; it was an arrival.

He visited Jewish cemeteries, not for the religion but to absorb the names, the dates, the dust. And he envisioned the vast crescent sweeping down from the Baltic to the Balkans and bisecting the continent, seeing that the great rivers and trading routes traversing it were conduits for a mass cross-fertilisation of people, creeds, complex genetic cocktails, histories, folklore and music that came crashing together before splitting off into fresh avenues of thought and art, science and custom. He realised much of him lay along this arc, that numerous tributaries of his own river of genes had flowed along it on the way to Skidel and even, perhaps, from various Rodrigues who had journeyed east from Spain to traverse southern Europe to Greece or Romania.

With this gradual exposure to an expanse of his cultural history came the slow reconciliation of a disquiet that had increasingly nagged at him as war and recuperation receded into the background. It wasn't exactly the sound, nor was it precisely the air, nor yet the smells, the language, the way the people looked. It was all of these and more besides which made him aware that here he felt less of a stranger than in London.

He now began to understand why little of England's great artistic inheritance made any profound impact upon him. He had, under sufferance, tried the Brontës and Jane Austen, ploughed doggedly through two or three of Dickens' lauded novels, sniffed at the edges of Hardy, Eliot, Thackeray and Trollope, even sat through interminable evenings of restoration comedy and Victorian melodrama. None of it had moved him, even while he could appreciate the craft that lay at their base.

And he understood why English music had all but disappeared from sight after the great German and Austrian innovators – Bach, Haydn, Mozart and Beethoven – overwhelmed the modes and styles in which her greatest – Tallis, Purcell, Handel – had illuminated the world.

He now knew why he had remained unmoved, the experiences forgettable. England was hermetically sealed, its culture developed in a cul-de-sac, much like species of ape had ceased evolutionary growth while humans strode omnipotently on. Save for the Jewish immigrants en route to America from Russia (and many of those who stayed did so only because they had run out of money or were falsely led to believe that this was the 'golden land'), Britain was en route to nowhere, so could not be fertilised by the great migrations of traders, adventurers and the oppressed, all of whom stopped on their journeys long enough to leave something of themselves behind.

But here Reuben stood upon the moving, breathing earth of Europe; he felt its dynamism, and even as Austria froze in the winter after the Great Nullification, he sensed the ice cracking as the spark which had for so long fired the cauldron of European culture spluttered into life.

Yet, all the while he conducted his love affair with Vienna, the Viennese themselves grew madder. How they danced! Whirling, spinning, flinging, ever faster, afraid to stop, fearful of what ruination they may behold when the manic pirouette finally exhausted itself.

Like a delirious explorer in a distant uncharted village, surrounded yet totally alone, Austria wallowed as if under some spell, a mystical virus that infected all, regardless of age, class, education or trade. Fading, drawn seemingly unchallenged by an irresistible force down into the void – a descent marred increasingly by violence, factionalism and base immorality – she lurched drunkenly towards her doom.

But, somehow, she survived. The fever broke, leaving the patient limp, still drenched in the after-damp of sweat – but alive, and strangely stronger! Even Austrians were hard put to explain how they had avoided total breakdown. No satisfactory answers would be forthcoming, save that the expedience of politics, the need for our species to exert itself over events so that egos may survive, proved a potent brake on the decline, first slowing it, then halting it and, finally, with excruciating effort, reversing the momentum so that the country began to ascend.

When he wasn't working or exploring, Reuben would invariably be found book in hand. As his mastery of German improved, so he would devour the latest outpouring of literature in a time when the written word reigned supreme.

This was a period when fire dripped from the nib. Lightning rained from the heavens as prose and verse and drama thunderstruck the sky, illuminating the strife of life in all its teeming diversity: irony and tragedy, love and indifference, hatred and lust, farce and triumph.

Many of the names are now the stuff of obscure publishers or second-hand book stores. Who thinks of Hofmannsthal save, perhaps, as a librettist to Richard Strauss? Or speaks of Karl Kraus, critic and polemicist, the archetypal Viennese intellectual? How many read the embodiment of Freud in fiction and biographies by Stefan Zweig? What of Franz Werfel, whose plays and prose commanded huge popular acclaim, or the final flourishing of Schnitzler, fired by his imminent mortality? And where are those thousands of volumes of novels by Broch and Musil, poems by Rilke? Burned, all burned. Ashes, like so many of those who read them.

But for Reuben, they were ever-present friends, be it Werfel's novel on the massacre of the Armenians, a Zweig study of yet another literary great figure – or the latest copy of Kraus's periodical, *Die Fackel, The Torch*.

And it was this last who was the unwitting agent of the most sublime moments for the private Reuben.

Chapter 7

Karl Kraus. The name means almost nothing now, but there was a time when it embodied among creative Viennese loathing and opportunity, in equal measure. Approbation meant success, opprobrium ignominy.

Part of the spell he wove around the heads of the intelligentsia came with his magnetic one-man performances. On the seventeenth of April 1924, at the Great Concert House Hall, he was due to give his three hundredth reading, on this occasion from his gargantuan drama *The Last Days of Mankind*.

Anyone with even the wildest pretensions to intellectual importance simply *had* to be there. The clamour for tickets was unprecedented. Those who had by diverse means obtained one, donned the latest fashion, congregated at the vogue salons and talked up the expectation to fever pitch. And those who hadn't proclaimed a prior unbreakable engagement or the onset of some virulent disease to excuse their absence.

But the excitement was real for Reuben. (He, by the way, acquired his ticket from Arnold Rosé, whose wife's ex-sister-in-law, Alma Mahler-Gropius, was the nucleus of a large literary circle and a powerhouse of Vienna's cultural life.) Whilst the tingling anticipation was diluted by the need to rehearse a Wagner programme with the Philharmonic, even as he sawed away at the fiddle he was aware of a strange, ever-present excitement that he knew didn't come from the music.

In its time, 'Mankind' was the lightning conductor for bitter recriminations on the Great War. Its recreation of Viennese life during those four years when Austria plunged from absolute influence to complete insignificance resulted in a work of extraordinary complexity, intermingling satirical stereotypes with the unvarnished stuff of reality – military communiqués, civilian scenes, true events – to create a montage of those dreadful years, and their apocalyptic effect.

But the spellbinding performance lay not so much in the words, magnificent though they were, nor in the febrile, passionate intellect from where they sprang. No, what made the difference was the way in which Kraus *became* the characters who peopled the epic. Kings and beggars, generals and profiteers all came to life with a slight accentuated nuance here, the subtlest mannerism there; each faithfully recalled throughout the entire performance so that everyone present followed the ebb and flow of their respective fortunes.

Reuben's German was now good enough to follow much of the flood which swamped the audience, even if it was not yet sufficiently adept to contribute to the frenetic debates that filled the cafés after it was all over. He was, if truth be told, a little shell-shocked: Wagner by day and Kraus by night were enough to test even the sturdiest intellectual backbone. So he was in something of a daze as he wandered the streets in the sharp chill of the spring evening.

"Excuse me, but were you not at the Kraus performance tonight?"

Reuben started and spun round to be confronted with a sight for which he was utterly unprepared.

What it was about her he never could say for certain. Perhaps it was the light, a peculiarly clear night sky hung with sparkles of windblown frost which, leaping from streetlight to streetlight, haloed her black-velvet-hooded head. Or then again it might have been the chill-kissed rosiness that made her cheeks appear to glow, even through the breath which gathered about her as she spoke and awaited his reply. And Reuben would forever remember the stark contrast of the black and white of her eyes, moistened with cold, yet gleaming with a steely resilience.

But for now he tried to hide his surprise with a desperate attempt at the small talk of which he was so pathetic an exponent.

"Er ... I was ... Um ... were you? ... I mean, you must have been or else you couldn't have asked me if I was ... Would you, er, like, um, a coffee or, no I'm sure you wouldn't ... you must be somewhere, I'm sure ... But if not, um, that is, if you don't think me a little forward ..."

"I would love to. My name is Sarah Tenenbaum, Mr Mendel," she said in a refined yet soft voice while extending a slight, gloved hand.

He had by then known some women, but none, apart from Leah and Fanny Hartmann, had left their mark; all the others had given and taken but remained only faint impressions, if recalled at all.

But having battled their way to a small table at the back of the smoke-filled Café Central (shouting to conquer the noise from the furious debates that detonated at tables of Czech émigrés, German students and home-town intellectuals), Reuben felt a kind of unstopping, talking as he had not done since the trench days with Rosenberg.

The formalities were soon dispensed with. What she did (an editor at one of Vienna's premier music publishers, Schott), her father's job (doctor), her family's long-term presence in Austria (no Moses-style flights from Skidel coloured the myths of the family Tenenbaum; in fact the contrary was true as, in their quest for assimilation, a collective amnesia had set in). They compared the maternal contribution to their respective genetic confluences. Hers were Levys. (But what did that mean? That name was often given by confused immigrants who, when asked in an unknown tongue for their name by officials of whichever land they sought to enter, invariably replied not with the family name, but with the ancient Israeli tribe of which they claimed membership; thus so many Cohens and Cowans, Levys and Levis.)

How did she know his name? Simple really. "I often go to the

Philharmonic. In the Gods of course; it's far too expensive to sit in the stalls or the loggia. I didn't spot you at first; I've always had this thing for Arnold Rosé ..." (this last detail added with a becoming sheepishness that quite turned his head).

"I suppose it's the power ... but then again, if that's what you're after, why wouldn't you aim for the top and set your cap at Weingartner?" They laughed in unison at the mental image Reuben's remark brought forth.

Never had Reuben found conversation with anyone so easy, not even Isaac; so easy in fact that he forgot for a while how lovely she was. Only when something came along to interrupt the flow of their respective histories (her solid, assimilated Viennese life going back several generations, his one-step detachment from Skidel and the bizarre upbringing which is invariably the lot of wunderkind), what music they liked and books they'd read, places they'd seen (or, rather, would like to have seen) – only then, when the door flew open to admit another customer and a blast of cold night air, or a political debate at a neighbouring table erupted, did he pause to drink in her marvellous features.

In years to come, he'd find himself staring at her in his mind's eye, trying to analyse what it was about her face that kept him enthralled until their final separation. He would always recall that night, and when he did it was the eyes, a delta of smile lines fanning out from their corners, dark and glistening as they harvested their individual pasts to feed a collective future.

That's how it was. No compromise made to time or place. No acknowledgement of somewhere else to be. They became wrapped in a cocoon which only occasionally gave hint of the larger world which lay outside. The heat in the emptying café subsided and Reuben, never one of life's most robust physiques, put his coat back on. There they sat, the gauche and gaunt Reuben, drowning in an overlarge, dishevelled army greatcoat and Sarah, much shorter yet far stronger, dressed in the neat formal brown suit which she customarily wore to cultural events. Immersed only in each other, they were oblivious to their now sole tenancy of the café and the growing impatience of the proprietor, evinced by increasingly raucous coughing and the scraping of chairs as they were placed on tables before a sweeping exercise whose ostentation rendered it positively operatic.

Finally they left, walking out into an opaque Viennese night, the late sleet blurring its architecture, melting on landing and mixing with the dust of dry days and the detritus of city life into a muddy paste which globulated suckingly around overworked drains. But none of this registered at a conscious level, only embedding itself much deeper, to be recalled in later times, like childhood tastes or the scent of early loves which leap into the mind without obvious provocation. They were aware only of each other as – in silence for the first time since meeting – the two of them walked arm in arm across the sleeping city.

So began the years of serenity, a time of equilibrium and peace born of predictability that lent comfort and tranquillity to the soul. Never before had Reuben known such repose. And when it had ended, never again would stillness rest in any portion of his being.

Some have said that he, the eternal pessimist, was unwittingly laying down emotional and physical reservoirs, fuelling up a part so deeply submerged that it surfaced only in the extremities of human existence, when he would be picked up by the whirlwind, spun about in a firestorm of razored shards and abandoned alone outside those very margins that now ring-fenced his life, in the grey lands where no laughter rang.

But who could tell for sure? There were no outward signs of any such foresight.

"I did do a lot of reading of European Jewish history around this time; not a tale to inspire confidence in the longevity of our

security. Did I think it all might end? No, I can't say that I did. Could I feel the cold wind? Not precisely. But I never felt as rooted as the Tenenbaums; I was always aware of feeling different from the Viennese. I now realise that what I attributed to being English was, in truth, down to being a Jew – and that my in-laws should have felt the same. But if they did, they hid it all too well."

Life passed easily, even during the inevitable adversities, the rough and tumble of the daily life they shared with other middle-class families in Vienna during the Twenties and early Thirties.

The wedding was the first hurdle. If he had not yet reached the summit of affirmative atheism he was to attain later, Reuben was already far-distanced from the liturgy of Judaism. But this rational, conscious view ran full pelt into an equal, albeit instinctive, force rushing in the opposite direction: the marrow-resident sensation that there was a tie far deeper, far stronger than ancient words whose purpose and meaning was utterly alien to him. And, in any event, with Grandfather Elias lying mouldy in Skidel's clay mud, a mere two generations away, some continuity of observance appealed to Mendel's growing sense of history, an innate feeling of wanting to experience what countless kin in any number of locales – desert and ghetto, city and hamlet – had enjoyed down the generations: raising the wedding canopy and celebrating with the unfettered joy that only those who have known the deepest despair are able to express.

A small contingent of Rodrigues arrived by train, slightly unnerved at the prospect of meeting 'the *mensch* on the mainland' whom they felt they had somehow left behind. They were submerged by the deluge of Tenenbaums that had gathered at their local synagogue for a rare celebration.

Reuben had prepared the one line he had to recite, repeating each word as it was intoned by the rabbi. But he was not ready for what followed.

The cantor began to sing the Seven Blessings, a succession of ever longer verses providing both the musical opportunity and captive audience on which the natural showman thrives. He didn't disappoint.

As the long theme lines grew and the gently nasal voice rose and swooped, peaked and dived through a barely credible range, Reuben was strangely moved. It wasn't the words themselves; couldn't be as he barely recognised them, let alone grasped their meaning. No, it was the potency of their rhythm, a distillation of the tides of several millennia to which, whatever his personal credo, he was as much an heir as a rabbi's son.

He realised that, give or take the ad hoc accretions of a myriad renditions and the near exclusively oral record passed from successive masters to their acolytes, what now rained about his ears and assailed his innermost depths was a continuum stretching back to the olden days. These were the songs heard as the Moses-liberated slaves wed in the desert; these were the melodies that accompanied the first marriage after Jericho fell to a different Hebrew tune; these were the hymns that greeted every Jewish bride and groom whenever, wherever, the canopy was raised and their community invited to recognise their union.

Tears welled in his eyes, the misty sheen aiding the daydream. Musician that he was, he could not stop his mind from drifting to a magical passage from one of his favourite childhood books, *The Call of the Wild*. Only now did he truly understand Buck's visceral response to the wailing of the huskies. The songs that the dog first heard in the frozen Yukon and which Reuben was now so moved by were one and the same. Infused with the stories of all the ancestors, it was a bone-deep recital of all their travails, all their joys. And though for each the song was unfamiliar, they also knew that they had always known it.

It was in this reverie that Reuben plunged his shoe upon the glass, feeling it crumble underfoot, and heard the synchronous crunch simultaneously with the rising chorus of '*Maazel tov*'.

After the festivities were over, Sarah and Reuben settled down to a quiet life, never full of material riches but wealthy in other, more satisfying ways. Their small apartment radiated the warm glow that comes when life has attained a kind of balance. Once it had become clear that Reuben would settle in Vienna, Leah and Moses had moved there too. And although they were attentive to the newly-weds, they made sure that they did not impinge, so tranquillity reigned.

Work went well, and Reuben established for himself a comfortable routine of orchestral playing, supplemented by a little teaching income. Sarah continued at Schott until the time when she could no longer work.

When, in the spring of 1928, he learned he was to be a father, Reuben was beside himself with joy and anticipation, singing the hymn to fatherhood as heartily as the next man, lauding the expected event and serenading the baby Miriam when she was safely delivered. He wept that first time he held her in his arms, not just for the joy of continuity but, in some secret way, for himself.

Of course he was besotted, as he would be three years hence when the beautiful Elias came along. But something about those two small, dependent beings sometimes weighed so heavily that it seemed as if the burden might crush him.

In the dark of the night, when he walked up and down their nursery, singing over and over, *sotto voce*, a lullaby dredged from his own childhood, he wallowed in the perfect peace of a slumbering baby nuzzling his neck, breathing into it and exuding that special small, sweet odour. Even then, in that haven, he felt the tingle of distant apprehension, an indefinable pressure skulking out there in the night, silent as the Arctic wolf which prowls around the periphery of a camp, waiting the moment to strike. Could he care for them even now as they lived in peace, let alone the turbulent times which his inbred pessimism and understanding of history told him may not be too far away?

As they grew, so the duties expanded in tandem: instilling a sense of right and wrong, nailing down the fixing-posts for the fence which delineated their moral territory, balancing the desires of the parents with the needs of the children, laying out the ground on which they could grow, rooted in good earth yet free to reach for the sky.

He found it draining, the constant guard against deviation. It seemed as though the discipline essential for musical excellence deserted him when it came to fatherhood. And sometimes, awake at night, unease came upon him, a surge of adrenaline as he felt as though all he did was wrong, every choice mistaken.

And for a few years life continued in this staccato rhythm, the stop-go of parenthood, the striving for balance. Both Miriam and Elias flourished, precocious, sweet and bright. She had a gentle mien that haloed her, a skipping gait that sent the black cascade of hair she'd inherited from Leah rippling down her back. Her keen intelligence was allied to a benign and gentle character that instinctively made all who met her wish to be her friend. Elias was short, tending to chubbiness without ever being fat. He had a complete lack of *sitzfleisch*, that great Yiddish word, expressed always in terms of its absence, for the ability to sit still; and, in another sortie into that wonderful language, was a *labbes* – a kindly rogue, cheeky chap, one whose misbehaviour betokened a challenge to authority rather than a malign nihilism.

"It took me a while to become a father. At first I never really knew how to deal with them. But as they grew, and became, well, people in their own right, I suppose, then I think I did alright, even though I wasn't around as much as I would have liked or, perhaps, as I should have been. Miriam was always serious, wanting to discuss things beyond her years, reading a huge amount, popular with her school friends but never playing with them as often as I'd have liked. She showed early promise on the piano, and it was a joy to play together. Elias was another kettle of fish altogether, always up to mischief, testing how far he could go. Nothing malicious, mark you, just pushing the boundaries, seeing what he could get away with.

The challenge was how to protect his personality while setting out the necessary frontiers. I was always too soft, I suspect!"

And what of Sarah, Reuben's rock, the one who kept him sane? It was she who tended to Miriam and Elias, and upon whom the daily drudge fell. While he fiddled, she was burdened. And, strangely, more beautiful, even when she was pale through fatigue. For she found something resembling perfect peace, and an inner warmth glowed. With parents nearby to help out and her in-laws on hand to play their part and revel in the joy of giving their grandchildren pleasure, the circle was complete. She relished being a Viennese-assimilated bourgeois Jewish *hausfrau*, enjoying life on the fringes of its voluminous cultural life. And although she thickened with the legacy of childbirth and the impact of Viennese-Jewish cuisine, Sarah never lost that luminescence in the eye which first captivated Reuben.

Moses worked as an outpost of the Rodrigue empire, an ambassador, drumming up contacts and opportunities which could then be completed by others more schooled than he in the disciplines of commerce. It was perfect, as it enabled him time to educate himself as an amateur philosopher and student, filling the house with books, some of which he even opened occasionally.

In her turn, Leah revelled in being a grandmother, forging a fierce bond with her daughter-in-law and the two children. Through close ties with Samuel and Esther Tenenbaum, Sarah's parents, she plugged into a ready-made network that relished all the news she relayed from London, seen in jaundiced Vienna as a model of imperial governance.

During these times, when the good and easy life allowed the accumulation of physical and emotional fat, few doubted its perpetual sustainability, or considered that it could ever end. No-one bent their mind to gaze around and say, 'Nothing is forever'; so they couldn't ponder on what might take its place and, eyes down, rolled dumbly on.

But the storm clouds were gathering. The overture to the cataclysm was purely economic. As the 1920s began their death-throes, the world's markets crashed, driven onto the rocks by a lethal cocktail of greed and optimism. Across the entire spectrum of global capitalism came the deafening thud of plummeting – shares, fortunes, bodies of the ruined.

Faith in money was destroyed. And in its wake the anarchy which tracks the death of devotion began to flourish. Austria was not spared, and the mountains of near-worthless bank notes needed to purchase even the basics of life became commonplace.

There was a void left by waning belief, ebbing confidence and the vicious destruction of (illusory) security. Into the space oozed the divisive poison of scapegoating. The amorphous ocean of public opinion, formed by the precipitation of false expectations and fomented by an inescapable pessimism, began its mercury movement, slicking up on the beaches of all those deemed even remotely culpable for the destruction of wealth and comfort.

Under an unceasing bilious deluge, the patchwork cloth that had held Austria together through the aftermath of the war finally unravelled, as first the stitching began to show and stretch, tense and part, and then the very fabric wore and tore, small holes becoming huge, jagged gashes. Through the yawning wounds, the spirit of Austria, in all its livid ambivalence, came ever more starkly into focus. Who knows how it might have been had Hitler not risen to prominence and power across the border? Vacuous, idle thoughts! For there, under the pretence of beneficent nationalism a vast slavering monster was gestating and, like taurean Zeus seducing Europa, assuming a false form to squirm its way to German power.

As the political classes fell beneath the feet of an accusatory stampede, Austria shadowed its larger neighbour. Seipel, the brilliant, astute prelate, was purged, replaced as Chancellor by Dollfuss. But he, mimicking the Gadarene virus of oppression which spread from Berchtesgaden north to infect Germany, suppressed democracy and ruled by decree. Within two years – four before the formal Anschluss – Dollfuss would be dead, murdered as the Nazis attempted a *coup d'état*.

And while the public raged, in private every household was beset by degrees of agitation that ranged from the euphoric to the despairing.

For many in Austria, closer union with Germany couldn't come soon enough; the very thought sparked dizzy anticipation, filling sleepless nights and giddy days with that excitement unique to the expectation of a long-sought-after revelation. The debates among these good citizens revolved around what life might be in the Promised Land when all Germans were brought together as one under the saintly gaze of the Fürher. Like children looking forward to a boat trip, they saw only the pleasure of the cruise, the multicoloured flags fluttering in a benign breeze. Never for a moment did they envisage the malevolent undertow which, all too quickly, could sweep them to oblivion.

But there were others – intellectuals, Jews, artists, communists, even conservative democrats – who feared with an intensity equal to those whose passion for Hitler grew daily.

For those who live in safety, it is impossible to comprehend the debilitating effect of such unrelenting foreboding. Perpetual tension saps the soul. Nights are fractured by the gnawing unknown. And into dark voids leap suspicion, uncertainty and confusion, the worst imaginings, an avalanche of possibilities, each with its own family of ramifications that churn the brain, each with its own potential for utter catastrophe.

And the innate pessimism which lay at the heart of such thinking found near-infinite stocks of fuel with the grim news floating across the border. With Mussolini firmly ensconced to the south, contemplative Austrians felt themselves in an ever-tightening vice.

Utterly contradictory reports, often intentionally misleading, of what life could be like fed this frenetic atmosphere. From one source might come news of a healthy economy where public services functioned perfectly and none lacked jobs, a nirvana where all who worked hard benefited. From another came news of stone-faced hatred towards anyone not deemed to be of the new faith.

For those who now look back with incredulity that not everyone fled, think for a moment about Sarah. There she sat, surrounded by her beloved family, established in cosmopolitan Vienna where she could lay claim to a lineal presence (somewhat alchemised in the crucible of legend) stretching back to the sixteenth century. If truth be told, she probably would have said she was Viennese before Austrian, and Austrian before Jewish. But only slowly did it dawn on her that all the old tethering-posts securing these reference points were being violently uprooted. This State-driven vandalism of her loyalties was imperceptible, and irreversible. Like a sclerosis, the silent clogging of her capacity to make sound judgements was inexorable, postponing beyond the point of no return the time when therapy could improve her condition.

In that indefinable way by which the hypothetical 'if' crystallises into the concrete 'when', conversations in the Mendel household became more urgent, following the path of uncountable similar dialogues in an unknowable number of homes, some whispered as though to deny their necessity, others conducted tremulously, its participants scarcely able to contemplate the enormity of flight.

Like many others, when Moses, Leah, Sarah and Reuben talked, discussion evolved into increasingly fractious argument, veering from frustration at the historical inevitability of the encroaching nadir in Jewish fortunes to unbridled rage at its inherent iniquity. In particular, the ageing Moses reverted to his own history.

"My father, may his dear soul rest in peace, saw the writing on the wall, didn't he? He realised that there comes a time for action, and that, while there may well be better timing later, there also might be worse. I think the time has come to go."

But Sarah wouldn't, couldn't countenance it. "No. I can't. It's my home. I've lived here all my life. What about my parents? How can I leave them? Who'd look after them?"

"Bring them with."

"They'll never leave. Father was wounded in Bosnia in 1908; he's even got a medal from the old Emperor. This is *their* country. *You* may have no national allegiances and are able to live anywhere. They can't."

Moses tried to be emollient. "Let me speak to them, Sarah, tell them what it was like in Skidel, and how it compares with now."

"No. It would break their hearts. They are *Austrian*. Telling them their country no longer wants them wouldn't merely upset them, it would make them furious, and leave us estranged, forcing me to choose."

For the first time, Reuben saw the starkness of her choice. "Are you saying you might stay with them, rather than come with the children and me?"

"No! NO! But making the choice would change me – us – forever. I couldn't live with the not knowing, the guilt, if something happened to them. I'm all they have."

"I don't believe I'm hearing this."

Leah intervened. "Isn't this just what our enemies want? That we tear ourselves apart? To set children against parents, splitting happy families? We'll seek a way. But perhaps we should find it sooner rather than later."

And so it continued. After a while they became immune to the perpetual infections filtering in from Germany. Where once it had caused delirium in the streets, with groups of elderly Jews hunched together animatedly bemoaning the end of the hibernation of Jew-hatred and the younger generation stirring its blood with thoughts of vengeance, now the report of yet another humiliation, looting or killing sat fleetingly on the surface before vanishing like a soft flurry of snow at the onset of winter, an infinitesimal, neglected harbinger of the infinite bitterness to come.

What brought the Mendels' prevarication to a shuddering stop was not an act of physical cruelty or material misappropriation but the murder of the soul of society, culture. On the tenth of May 1933 across the border came news which froze the blood of all thinking people, nowhere more so than in Vienna, where the written word was prized above all other artistic attainments. The Nazis began their assault on the world of ideas, on the fruits of the free-spirited, those whose souls and brains combined to voice and shape our destiny through prose and verse.

After a slow crescendo of vilification and threat, the concerted campaign against books, innocent conduits of concepts now deemed evil either by virtue of their intrinsic qualities or merely because the pen with which they were written was wielded by a Jew, reached its climax. Brownshirts – precursor to the dreaded SS – acting as principals and *agents provocateur*, raided libraries, bookshops and private collections to abduct words. In an obscene *auto-da-fé* that made a reality of Heine's unforgettable prediction one hundred and more years before ("where they burn books, there eventually they burn men too"), words were martyred on pyres in town squares the length and breadth of the nation that gave the world Beethoven, Goethe and Kant.

Moses returned to the attack. "How long, how long must *we* wait to be attacked? This is a country which no longer has a heart or soul. Austria will follow, because Austrians are just Germans with a different currency. Even if it wanted to resist, how could it?"

Sarah remained adamant, her patriotism not yet completely defaced. "You go if you want. London awaits you, your family wants you home. I must stay. Austria will never allow such barbarity. Gluck, Haydn, Mozart – how could they have created all those glories surrounded by people capable of horror? No. It's inconceivable. It's …"

Her voice broke. Moses moved in for the kill.

"Look at Dollfuss. He's just a petty Hitler. What have your beloved Viennese bourgeoisie done to withstand him? Nothing. What did they do when offered that anti-Semitic bastard Lueger, may his name be blotted from history? Drive him from the city? I wish. No, elected him mayor. Mark my words. When faced with the hard choices, Vienna will do what it always has: succumb to the bullies and roll over in the face of intimidation – it's so much easier, after all."

Sarah was speechless, incandescent; Reuben hardly less so. In an atonal duet of violent proportions, they spat their protests with venom.

"How *dare* you? What do you know of Austria? Little more than you've picked up from the flyleaf of *Austrian History in Five Easy Lessons*!"

"Too far, Papa, too far. I'm beginning to worry about you. This is madness. If you and Mama wish to go then perhaps you ought. But we're staying, at least for now."

Before Leah could even voice a protest, Moses attacked again. "Are you blind? Or is it that you just won't look at what's staring you in the face? They despise us. Dollfuss has destroyed all trace of democracy here, and you mark my words, what Germany does today, Austria will do tomorrow. What this country was, it will not be again until the boil is lanced. You know that the Viennese are, at best, in two minds about us Jews. Half the time they hail our greatest sons, the Zweigs and Werfel, Schnitzler, Korngold and Mahler; half the time they spit on us. And now, without any constraints, they'll be free to do with us what they will!"

The exchanges became more acrimonious, increasingly personal. They spilled out of the confines of their own unit and began to infect relations with the Tenenbaums, similarly beset with uncertainty and fear.

There appeared no resolution, as if they were waiting for divine intervention to show them the way. But the source would be much closer to home. Sarah's mother, Esther, broke the impasse, having sensed the atmosphere and guessed the underlying reason. With the courage that only motherhood brings, one Friday night when they were all at the Sabbath table in the Tenenbaum apartment and the glow from the candles created a deceitful warmth, she spoke with a quiet resignation that quite broke the heart.

"Sarah, your father and I have been thinking," she began, turning slightly away from the others so that she faced her daughter directly. "When we brought you into the world, it wasn't so that you would be tied to us forever. We always knew the time would come when we must let go. If what is happening now had occurred when I was your age, and you Elias's, I would have left my mother, may she be at blessed rest, without a moment's hesitation. Of course, I would have been sad, heartbroken even. But I would have known it was the right thing to do. Perhaps it will be as bad as Moses thinks – it could hardly be worse. But your father and I are old, we've lived well – and long. We will miss you more than you can know. But at least we will know that you and our grandchildren are safe. Then, whatever God holds in store, we shall be content."

The air was heavy, full of a kind of prospective mourning, the anticipation of sadness. Leah looked at Esther, holding her gaze, pregnant with the deepest respect, understanding and gratitude. Moses looked down, his sense of shame mingling with relief that he would, after all, get his way. Reuben grasped Sarah's hand tightly beneath the table, trying to reassure her that it would be alright and that he was with her, come what may.

For Sarah, the tie that held her in Vienna was sundered. She was free to go, heavy of heart but lightened of burden. Reuben refusing to be dependent upon his parents once again, the only thing that now stood in the way of departure was his livelihood and, of course, their destination.

Salvation on both fronts came from an unexpected direction.

"Mr Mendel, a word in private after the rehearsal, if you please."

Weingartner had been replaced as *de facto* chief conductor by the gaunt Wilhelm Furtwängler in 1927 who remained a major presence in Viennese musical life, despite having left the post formally in 1930. The archetypal Germanic conductor: driven, tyrannical, uncompromising, distant, when he added 'if you please' the opposite was invariably the case, a wrong note or false entry having screamed at him out of the thunderstorm of perfect intonation and impeccable ensemble.

Packing up his violin, Reuben withstood the good-natured gibes of his colleagues in the immediate aftermath of the final rehearsal of Tchaikowsky's Sixth Symphony.

"Things'll be really *pathètique* for you, Ru."

"You look as sick as Tchaik was when he wrote that!"

"You want that I get you a ticket for the concert, Ben?"

"Can I have your rosin?"

Trying to appear unconcerned only served to encourage them further.

"Watch out for the trap-door in front of his desk; it's already swallowed two trombonists and a percussionist."

"Dive if his hand suddenly goes behind the desk – he's got a poisoned baton."

"Try busking on the Schubertstrasse."

The rain of remarks followed him out of the auditorium and faded away as he approached the holy of holies, Furtwängler's inner sanctum. He knocked.

"Enter."

"You asked to see me, Maestro."

"Close the door. Sit."

He placed his violin case beside the chair and sat down. For what seemed an age, but was in fact less than a minute, an oppressive silence hung over them. Furtwängler shuffled some papers, a clear distraction from what troubled him. Reuben was getting increasingly anxious, eager to ask him what he wanted but knowing he would speak when he was ready. The great conductor looked up and fixed him with a cold stare.

"I think that the time has come for you to move on."

Reuben opened his mouth to protest, but was silenced by an imperious hand.

"Be quiet and listen. It pains me to say it, but I don't know how much longer Jews will be safe in Austria. Already in Germany the Nazis begin to make your people bear the blame for all ills. Here, they will follow. I don't know when, but it will be quick and you may not have time to take everything with you.

"I have written to a couple of former students of mine. They run an orchestra and conservatoire in Paris and would appreciate the services of a leading desk from Vienna, both as player and teacher. They have arranged an apartment for you in Montmartre large enough for your entire family. I cannot say for certain that you will be safe in France – but I am sure you will be safer there for longer than if you remain here.

"No. Say nothing; I know what you're thinking. I would never say this in front of the others, but you have the stamp of greatness, Mendel. If, in years to come, you make of your life what I believe you can, then, just occasionally, think gently of me as one who saw you as you are and helped you on your way.

"Pax vobiscum.

"You will, of course," he added as an afterthought, "do me a service and refrain from mentioning my involvement to any but your most immediate family. Who knows ...?"

His voice tailed off, and the great man turned to gaze absently through the window, hunched in thought, his brow slashed by worry, the vast intellect locked in some inner battle trying to reconcile the conflict between the zenith of human achievement whose exposure was his life's mission and the slough of depravity already flooding his beloved Germany. No matter how Herculean the effort, it was futile.

Some things simply defy comprehension and must be quarantined in a grey zone beyond the reach of reason.

Chapter 8

This was how it began, their journey which would end in a place that, even now, defies belief.

Like ancestors arriving in Skidel pulling a handcart piled with possessions or fleeing, backs burdened, from Spain, Reuben assembled the belongings of his family and prepared for France. It was a hesitant, naïve departure, to be looked back at through the veil of tears as an innocent thing, touching in its attention to the unimportant minutiae of a comfortable, bourgeois life.

First there was the discussion of whether to liquidate the entire apartment or what to leave to await their return. They elected to take with them all their family photographs, a small selection of the vast number of books that filled every nook and cranny and Reuben's favourite gramophone records, no small undertaking when Schnabel's recording of Beethoven's last piano sonata alone took up no fewer than four seventy-eight-rpm discs.

Then the needs of the children had to be addressed. After much persuasion, ineffective incentives and no small amount of coercion, Miriam and Elias agreed that Pegasus, the vast rocking horse Leah had been unable to resist the previous Christmas, would be much happier staying where he was. The children were, however, unmoveable on more manageable artefacts. Protracted negotiations came to nought so brute force took over, and the neighbours were treated to the desperate spectacle of the youngest and last generation of Mendels being dragged screaming from their apartment, a trail of juvenile debris – dolls, tin soldiers, teddy – strewn forlornly in their wake.

So began their vocabulary of cold and endless words, hitherto unspoken.

Exile.

Impotence.

Distance.

Homeless.

Void.

Soon enough, others, even more lacerating, would be added, but for now it was the language of alienation that ravaged the Mendel household in Paris, shredding the reluctant unanimity in which they departed Vienna, dividing them as they retreated into shells where they were, for the first time in a long time, wholly alone.

For Sarah, thoughts were of what she had left behind: her country, friends and family; above all, her parents who when they hourly came to mind did so with grim foreboding.

Moses and Leah were stretched upon an ever-tautening rack. He wanted to continue their flight to London, and the perceived safety of an island. Leah felt unable to leave Reuben and the grandchildren, realising they would not be separated from Sarah, for whom abandoning the European landmass was simply too much, too soon. So Moses was forced back on his Viennese strategy: bide his time, using events as and when they arose to increase the pressure on the family to bend to his will.

In any previous moment in the last decade or so Reuben would have been delighted to renew the brief acquaintance he had made with Paris during a drunken furlough with Rosenberg. In normal times who could resist the urge to live there, drink in its spirit? Of all European cities, it is the one which draws artists, thinkers, lovers. But for Reuben it was now little more than a city living on past glories, a mummified reminder of a once wonderful past.

Musical life was stale, no innovation to speak of and even less tradition in the great masters for which his beloved Vienna Philharmonic was so rightly lauded. What recent native music there was seemed like gossamer; Debussy and Ravel, in particular, appeared to him no more than soulless form, while Les Six (although now split) was the archetypal example of a country devoid of its own genius revering domestic mediocrity in preference to foreigners (especially Germanic) of true and universal worth.

They suffered the dilemmas and friction with which a million families were riven. To stay? To go? If so, where – and when? For so many all that happened, in fact, was that one residence close to the outbreak of a plague was exchanged for another which, at that point, was perceived to be beyond the reach of an infection whose true virulence was presently unimaginable.

But such is the resilience of strong family ties that the Mendels settled down to a life in limbo. Did any of them think their journey had ended? Doubtful, though none dared speak of it. Had any of them thought where it might terminate? Moses excluded, probably not, although London, centre of a fast-diminishing empire yet to realise the growing distance between it and the nuclei of a new world order, seemed the obvious terminus.

Against this rumbling *leitmotif* of frozen uncertainty and fatal prevarication, Reuben set about establishing himself in the musical life of Paris. He worked with Furtwängler's contacts for a while before joining the newly formed Orchestra Nationale de la RTF in 1937.

They even tried to enjoy Paris, treating their stay like a holiday by cramming in as many of its wonders as possible. At first they were hesitant, setting out to explore the city as though it held hidden dangers. But slowly they succumbed to its many charms. The children embraced it more speedily than the adults, adoring climbs up the Eiffel Tower and Arc de Triomphe, requiring them to be repeated to the point of exasperation. The grown-ups absorbed the glories of the Louvre and revelled in the Bohemian passions which enveloped the café society, renting the evening with the heat of existential debate and a barren raging at the infection spreading through Germany which threatened this cosseted world.

So the Mendel tenure in Paris was typified by bouts of tourism and high-density lassitude, interspersed with shock waves of anger and apprehension as news filtered across the Maginot Line of the latest atrocities which went unchecked by the free world.

Then came the news that Sarah had feared.

On the twelfth of March 1938, the Anschluss with Germany meant that communications with her parents became increasingly fraught. Letters were turned back at the border, the telephone was never answered. Try as they might, they could get no direct word. Via diplomatic links between orchestra board members, Reuben managed to contact old colleagues in the Philharmonic. They visited her parents' apartment and, for a short time, relayed messages.

Then, nothing. No answer from the doorbell, no response from neighbours. It was as if they never were. A climate of suspicion had descended over Austria, a fog which shredded society and cut people off from one another. No-one was trusted; the only certainty was the perpetual uncertainty.

The days drifted into weeks. Silence. It was all Reuben could do to stop Sarah from jumping on the first train going vaguely in the direction of Vienna.

"If they're safe, we'll hear soon enough. If not ... well" – he shrugged – "what could you do?"

"I can't stand this not knowing. I have to find out what's going on. I *have* to."

Finally, one Saturday, after the weeks had melded into months, a crumpled packet bearing the name of her parents' synagogue arrived. The tortuous route of its arrival was betrayed by the bruised tattoos of Austrian, Swiss and French postmarks beaten out upon its surface.

Sarah opened it with shaking hands.

Dear Mrs Mendel

Rabbi Trachtenberg and the Committee of the Synagogue have asked me on their behalf to write to you with their sincere condolences on the passing of your parents, Samuel and Esther Tenenbaum, may they be forever counted among the blessed.

While the manner of their passing is not something which would in normal circumstances be condoned, we are not living in normal circumstances. Perhaps it may comfort you a little to know that your mother and father are not alone in choosing their own date and manner of departure, rather than living in constant fear.

Your parents were loved and respected in this community, but our loss pales into insignificance beside yours. All I can say is, in the time-honoured manner of our people: I wish you and your family a long life.

Sincerely yours,

Mr Avrom Kaplan

Beadle

P.S. The day before she passed away, your mother arranged to have lodged with us for safekeeping the enclosed, with its slightly cryptic covering note. If you are reading this then we have done as she asked.

Inside the package was an envelope with Sarah's address on it, bearing the handwritten legend: *Please arrange to deliver in whatever manner is most likely to ensure a chance of arrival.*

Sarah's strength failed her, the shock initially suppressing grief. She could hardly hold it, let alone bring herself to look at its contents. Reuben being out, she asked Leah to read it for her.

"Are you sure? Is this not something you should do yourself?" Leah asked when, finally, Sarah had broken free from her embrace.

"I can't. Please."

The pleading tone conquered Leah, and she tore at the top of the envelope with a sense of foreboding. Quickly, she scanned the contents. It was a single sheet, written in a frail, hesitant hand, punctuated with crossings-out and blots that betrayed the turmoil of its composition.

She paused at the end. "I don't think I can," she eventually said, feeling her heart might break were she to read it aloud. "It's something you must do yourself, privately, alone."

"No. You'd do it for Reuben. Now you're my mother too. You have to do it for me."

A quiet sigh of resignation overtured Leah's halting recital.

Our Beloved Sarah,
You are reading this. So you know by now that we are no more. Papa and I are old and tired. We miss you more than you can ever know. But we are content.
Our lives have been full, and you have been our greatest joy. To see you settled and happy with Reuben and our beautiful grandchildren is a blessing exceeded only by the knowledge that you, at least, are safe.
We are glad that you have been spared Vienna as she is. The ordinary Viennese hate us Jews as much as the Germans do – we are being treated like dirt already. You remember old man Goldfarb and his brother and sister-in-law? Why yesterday they were made to scrub the streets! On their knees! At over seventy! What next?
Your father and I cannot bear the prospect of that happening to us. We hardly ever leave the apartment, just in case something might happen. What if I go to get the bread – and never come back? What would happen to him then? No, we can't stand the thought. Better this way, that we take leave of this world as we have spent the major part of our lives – together, in peace.

Don't be shocked, my darling. God understands. We've lived honourable lives, done nothing of which we are ashamed, and can stand before Him and say: 'We are here, Lord, judge us. We are ready!' We go to meet Him happy and secure in knowing that you are beyond the reach of all this evil. He knows our sacrifice in letting you go. Our reward awaits.

Dearest Sarah. The tears fill my eyes as I write. Your father kisses you, as I do. I feel the softness of your cheek as if you were still a baby in my arms. Kiss Reuben, Miriam and little Elias for us.

Be brave.

Be strong.

Be happy.

Live.

Your ever-loving Mamma

From the envelope dropped a bank book, in Sarah's name. Its promise meant nothing, for what comfort was money in the teeth of brutal orphanhood, when the two strongest anchors of a life are simultaneously uprooted? The emptiness was all-consuming. She felt as though a hand had been plunged straight into her guts and wrenched them out, leaving a void where before had been fullness. And with that void came a kind of weightlessness, a sense of floating away from all she'd known , from a past well travelled, even if it had required a leave-taking of those two cold figures, now lying lonely across the border in a treacherous land.

From deep within her began the Wailing Song, a threnody that would become all too familiar but of which the family had as yet no real experience. No music sounds like this. Each rendition etched from the personal soul of the singer, every song immediately recognised even by those who have known no grief, as if, in the spherical cavern of time, a pre-echo of their own disaster ricocheted from the walls as a warning of what was to come.

It began as a soft moan, way back below her throat, a beating whimper whose hesitancy voiced her own unwillingness to accept the truth. As it journeyed through her it began to radiate out like an earthquake from its epicentre, a shockwave whose ferocity grew, convulsing her entire body. The hollow sound crescendoed as it sought release, fleeing simultaneously from mouth and nose, a fluid-drenched stream whose croaking rasp filled every room before escaping the apartment, so that those passing by stopped and gazed up at the shutters to wonder what calamity was being played out behind their blind gaze.

No sooner had she filled the house with her song than the catharsis began to subside. (Moses, returning with the children from the park, heard it and, forestalling questions, turned about, announcing his immediate need for ice-cream, before finally bringing them back and saying that their mama was ill and had gone to bed where Grandma was nursing her.) For hours, until twilight filled the room, Leah gently kept Sarah gathered in her arms, rocking her as though she were still a child, stroking her head while her own tears rode down her daughter-in-law's hair and mingled with the warm sweat which gathered at the nape of her neck. Leah's softly whispered 'Sssshhhh' had eventually brought some tranquillity and Sarah seemed to sleep a fitful sleep, broken only by sorrow-induced tremors deep within her dreamworld.

Reuben returned late, ignorant of what had occurred. With subtle eye movements Leah indicated the letter as her son came into his bedroom to be confronted by the Pieta-like scene of his wife limply at rest across his mother's lap. He took it into the light of the landing, an air of inevitability accompanying his reading. Although he had expected something like it, his reaction surprised him, a sudden ignition of burning resolution: no more of his family would die. This was not rage, neither was it revenge. More, it was a quiet determination that, whatever Destiny would throw, he would stand between it and his family so that none may be hurt without his prior destruction.

As for Sarah, what kept her from drifting away? The same emotions which prevented many in her position from giving up: love, duty, pride. What kept her grounded was that she too was an anchor; she could not afford, even in safe times, let alone hazardous, to relax her grip. So she tightened it, as if by holding hard to her remaining family, she could not be lost. She saturated them all with bottomless lakes of attention, damn-near drowned them, Reuben once reflected.

But she did survive, this crisis at least, finding in Leah a replacement confidante to whom she could turn when loneliness or fatigue threatened to overwhelm her.

("What of the contents of the account?" you might well ask. Gone, all gone, along with millions of forlorn others, snaffled, sidled, slipped, deep-pocketed by the faceless ones – bankers, accountants, lawyers; collective slime on the stagnant pool, choking what life there is in the trapped water below. Safe and secure, unlike the uncountable dispossessed.

"Once I tried to track down the money. Not from any need, but because my mother-in-law would have liked to know that it was used well. Never have I encountered such an unwillingness to help, such a blank-faced intransigence as I did from the several financiers I confronted. Asking them to return money was like inviting them to eat their own children. In the end I gave up. Life seemed too short to spend in such company. Despite the impeccable manners, I always left them feeling like I needed a bath, itching as though I'd been infected by lice. I suppose they're necessary, but ...")

After the grief came a settling-down, although, unbeknownst to any of them, it was on a level one stage lower than exile. This was the insidiousness of the destruction, astonishingly fast in retrospect, imperceptible at the time.

Moses still looked longingly north, but could do nothing to move

Leah. While he secretly hoped that the demise of Sarah's parents would undermine her links to the mainland, she would brook no discussion, hissing in their bedroom that it was far too soon to broach the subject ... not even on the eleventh of November 1938, the day after *Kristallnacht*, when images both awful in themselves and frightening in what they forebode spread across the world. It wasn't the dead, although they numbered in the mid-hundreds. Neither was it the shops, whose windows filled the streets with pools of glass. Nor even the tens of thousands rounded up and deposited without trial in concentration camps.

No, what serrated the psyche – even for non-believers – was two sights: flames escaping the ornate cupolae of synagogues across Germany and Austria, and the gravestones of their elders uprooted and fragmented.

The grand architecture of the great meeting-places of sophisticated Jews in Berlin and Vienna were the very symbols of their separate-togetherness. The solidity and ornamentation had seemed to enshrine the establishment of roots that were deeply embedded in the land on which they stood, the quintessential statement of acceptance. And they bore mute witness to a road long travelled; centuries of worship, growth, consolidation, safety, identity, parallel prosperity, learning, erudition, all bedrocks of a tradition that had spawned and withstood the prodigal sons – Spinoza, Marx, Einstein, Freud – the giants who quit the easy harbour of prescriptive religion for the uninviting, lonely voyage across the uncharted seas of our relationship with God, Society, Universe, Self. If all that could be reduced to ashes in a seeming instant, was there anything, anywhere, that could be taken to be safe, a haven, *home*?

And if even the dead were not immune to the virulent germ, then nothing was. The most radical rationalist, he who had purged the last traces of sentimentality from his soul, could perhaps stare unmoved at the vista of holy scrolls thrown out along the full length of their perfect calligraphy and trampled on by the pagan's unforgiving boot. He might even smile secretly at silverware being looted from a religion constructed on a decalogue which explicitly prohibits covetousness. And the smuggest assimilate, secure in arrogant apathy, may inwardly nod at an old man, lifetime spent in the devout service of God, as he is brutally shorn of beard or forced while wearing his prayer shawl to scrub the streets, as if such an archaic life lived outside the mores of progress somehow rendered such treatment self-inflicted.

But what could be done in the teeth of a systemic infection so remorseless that it needed to attack even the ground in which the ancestors of its victims lay quietly awaiting the day of judgement? The hatred of all things Jewish lay so thick upon these splinters of human timber that even the dead were fodder, the stones which marked where they lay not fit to stand erect but suited only to lie prone and crumbled beneath the oppressor's feet.

There is a bug called in Africa the Grazer. Its special way of killing, slowly, with inconceivable pain, is by the consumption of human tissue through an agonising process of gangrene and ulceration, from within. Its preference is for the soft, malleable flesh of a young face. Entering by stealth through infected water, it soon begins its irreversible progress up, through tongue and palate, lip and cheek, before feasting in the fertile lands within the eye socket. The unmistakable sign of its presence is massive deformity and gaping holes in mouth and cheek.

Kristallnacht was the infected water by which the Grazer entered the soul of Germany. Sipping at it, and finding that it quenched the thirst, Germans quaffed huge drafts of it, unaware of the menace within. The seductive thrill of having looted and murdered and humiliated God's chosen – all with no response save praise from their masters, indifference from the world and silence from Heaven – was the virgin meat on which it fed. The more it ate, the stronger it became, the greater the need for more. And so it grew, demanding more on which to feast, its very own *lebensraum*.

In Paris, turmoil beset the Mendel house. For Reuben, the passage was exact. He saw that the arrival of Hitler, Furtwängler's intercession, the Anschluss, the death of Sarah's parents and now *Kristallnacht* were all part of a continuum. His only problem: where was it leading? What if they left for Britain, only to find that Mosley took power or the Germans attacked? Despite its offence to his liberal pretensions, he could envisage a clear apathy were Germany to turn her face east and concentrate on Czechoslovakia, Poland, Hungary and the Soviet Union. Surely, if she were to do that, she could not, would not, look west at the same time. Even that Janus-faced Hitler couldn't, could he?

And there, in microcosm, was the dilemma which would trap them. They'd had it before, in Vienna. But then, once they had severed the cord between Sarah and her parents, there was a ready exit route. Now the questions returned, with renewed force and greater urgency.

The situation was deteriorating and even London seemed less of a haven. The failure of the Munich Agreement was a fatal blow to British prestige. Its chief minister was seen to have gone on bended knee to a man who had been perceived as something of a laughing stock, posturing with hectoring rhetoric, absurd salutes and a maniacal addiction to the trappings of power. Now Hitler was validated as a world player, outwitting the leader of the empire he aspired to surpass in both breadth and longevity. In a little more than five months after the deal securing Czechoslovakian independence at the price of the Sudetenland, German forces rolled through Prague, and it was clear that Britain was not what it was, its prior potency having succumbed to the flaccidity of old age.

And when Poland fell, the death knell tolled all over Europe, nowhere more dolefully than in France, where the deep, slow sound summoned from their tomb the ghosts of prior debacles at the hands of Prussians and Germans.

Music never lies. On the tenth of May 1940 the major German offensive against France began with a ruthless scythe through the Netherlands and Belgium.

Chapter 9

It was the speed of the advance that mesmerised France, standing helpless in the teeth of a devastating onslaught. Having breached the Maginot Line through the simple device of circumnavigation, the Germans sped from Abbeville on the twentieth of May and would take Paris a mere twenty-four days later.

Reuben moved decisively. He had already made some tentative arrangements. Unknown to any of his family, he had secured introductions to Sir Henry Wood, founder of the Promenade Concerts in London, in case they needed to flee to England, and Aymé Kunc, the director of the Société des Concerts du Conservatoire in Toulouse, should they need, instead, to go into hiding in France, or perhaps escape Europe via Spain and Portugal. As soon as the Germans had secured their bridgeheads in France and it was apparent that any Allied response would be woefully inadequate, the assertiveness of the survivor sprang once more to the fore.

He called the family together.

"We need to make a decision quickly. North or south? Britain is not the power she was, neither is she the haven we seek. Munich, Dunkirk, who knows where the next defeat will be for England? London is bound to be bombed. If he is to rule Europe, Hitler will have to destroy Britain, and dare not invade without first having broken their spirit. He'll never do that by sea. Ergo air. Ergo bombing, just like the Fascists did to the Republicans at Guernica."

"So, my son, the military strategist," snarled a bitter Moses, feeling the remnants of his paternal authority ebbing with every rational connection.

"No, of course not. One of the orchestra's directors happens to be an official in the Foreign Ministry. We got talking after a rehearsal a few weeks ago and it was he who made me realise. If you were to listen to him, you'd see – it's just logic, like chess really, a finite number of moves, each of which has its own ramifications. As you well know, I don't have that kind of brain, but I can understand when someone explains it. I never got chess, despite your best efforts to teach me, Papa. I appreciate there is a beauty in an elegant solution, but I can no more see myself envisioning it at the board than I could imagine creating the light in a Georges de la Tour painting. This is the same."

"So, our family in England is doomed ..." Moses sarcastically confirmed.

"Write to them if you're convinced, tell them to get to America – and soon. But for them and for us, similar logic applies to the crossing. To master Europe, Britain must be conquered too. You agree? America will support her, at least materially if not militarily, so it follows that the supply lines will have to be cut. Yes? Therefore, crossing the Atlantic will be very dangerous. I think we should take the risk, but we must aim to sail from Lisbon. Leaving from there will give us a less hazardous route, and Portugal is neutral, close enough to make it feasible – and less likely to attract the attentions of the Germans.

"I really don't know how things will work out, but I think we need to be ready. So, we're moving to Toulouse. I've thought about it – it's near the Spanish border but, should that be closed, we have other options – take to the countryside and hide or try to disappear by going to Marseille. It's not perfect – but I feel sure that our salvation lies in creating as many choices as we can.

"I've got a job. It won't pay well, but I can teach. We could possibly get hold of the Tenenbaum money in Switzerland, or maybe Mama's family could help if we need it. And here's some good news. A wealthy benefactor of the orchestra has granted us a long lease of an old house at a peppercorn rent, much run down apparently, where we might live secluded and safe."

It was clear that he was not to be controverted. A steely glint emanated from his eye as he looked at each of the family in turn. It was the moment that the son became the father, the father a son again, and Moses seemed physically to wilt in the white heat of the beam that radiated from Reuben.

The apartment was quickly liquidated; only the barest essentials were taken, sufficient for four suitcases plus the violin. No complaints or aggravation from the children this time, as if they sensed the urgency, picking up from the chaos of a rapidly emptying Paris that this was not like Vienna, when they had left on their own, leaving behind an anchorage, but more like departing what was merely a way-station on a journey whose end was not yet known.

They made their way through a teeming city beset by panic. Every transport terminus was a mass of people, shouting their way through the press of the crowd, dragging screaming children behind them, driving trolleys overladen with luggage at the legs in front of those who barred their way.

The early summer heat was exacerbated by the glass roof which arched over the splendid Gare Montparnasse, from which the train to Toulouse would depart. As the sun streamed through it reacted with the steam from the engines and the sweat of paranoia which permeated the atmosphere. Women fainted under the effect of the furs they wore, the price of overfilled valises. Men discarded top hats and top coats as their true priorities made themselves apparent.

The weight of absolute responsibility was growing ever heavier on Reuben's shoulders. He had assumed leadership, and now realised how onerous it was. The blood pounded in his temples, throbbing across the front of his brain, making him feel as though his eyes yearned for release from their sockets. His heart beat fast, almost audibly it seemed, and perspiration poured down his face. Over and over he rehearsed his plans, recalling the minutiae of his clandestine scheming. So many things could go wrong, each one likely to spark a chain reaction whose end was wholly uncertain. People bribed, tickets bought, timetables assumed, rooms and job waiting. What if all, if any, went wrong? Doubts assailed him, but there was no-one with whom he could share them, concerns about alarming the family overarching the need for a sounding board, reassurance, just for someone to listen! Questions avalanched. What if the choice of sanctuary was misjudged? Would the Germans outstrip their flight? How would they be received? Would this be their final sojourn before the torment was over?

The fact that so many others were similarly beset brought him no comfort. His was a peculiarly venomous form of loneliness, the solitude of being among people but apart, excluded by the immutable wall of his own responsibilities, his quasi-paranoid planning, scheming, counter-arguing. He became obsessed, near-deranged, as his mind spun through what seemed a million permutations with innumerable ramifications.

But, at least as far as the immediate travel arrangements were concerned, his unease was misplaced: he *had* thought of everything. Over the previous week or so the route had been meticulously prepared. Having paid a superintendent of the station, the family was spirited in through a staff entrance. Their passage to the train had been further lubricated by judicious back-handers to porters and conductors, so that they came upon their compartment in a first-class carriage with an air of relaxation quite distinct from their fellow passengers, several of whom could be heard to say, not too low under their breath, that once again the 'fucking Jews' had stolen a march and bought themselves an advantage.

But for now, safely ensconced, they could relax, certain that their escape from the epicentre of conflict would if nothing else buy them some time and distance in which to contemplate the next stage of their quest for freedom.

Of course, no-one knew how rapid and complete the French capitulation would be. No-one knew that France would be hacked in two, with the occupied portion stretching across its upper half and all the way down the Atlantic seaboard to the Pyrénées, and the remaining bleeding chunk run by fevered sympathisers and collaborators prepared to send to their death anyone condemned by Hitler. All that was known was that safety was no longer where they had been; that the distance between the German army and them could never be great enough.

A journey of inordinate length, fragmented and fractured as the infrastructure already began to sclerose under the turmoil of a nation on the move, ended as the train pulled into the station of the ancient city of Toulouse. Like every other main terminus, it exhibited the chaos of war; as many people were seeking to leave as there were trying to disembark. Although a house had been acquired on their behalf by Maestro Kunc, Reuben's scrupulous preparations had not extended to reaching it from the railway. But once more a stealthy transfer of francs made things easier, and a horse-drawn carriage that Reuben had managed to acquire on the cheap took them to their dilapidated accommodation in the south-west of the city.

As with the step down from Vienna to Paris, so it was with the descent from Paris to Toulouse. It was a fine place, steeped in a venerable history going back to the dawn of Christianity, including the touchingly germane, if somewhat distant, offer of rest to pilgrims on their way to Santiago de Compostela. And for someone coming from the surrounding villages, it was as Bialystok to the young Moses fleeing Skidel. But for the Mendels it was claustrophobic, made all the more so by the swelling population, drawn from all over France – and beyond.

If Marseille was the 'new Jerusalem of the Mediterranean' to the Nazis, then Toulouse vied with Lyon, Nimes and the other conglomerates of Vichy France to be its Haifa. It was less prominent, less exposed, but nonetheless a magnet for many Jews flooding west: Jews who, with an innate sense of rootlessness developed during their meandering diaspora, could rapidly settle anywhere, establishing demountable communities where religion, trade, education, disputation, literature and music each had their own tented pavilion, erected almost overnight, broken down even faster should the need arise.

So it was here. And although Reuben had never before felt a need to be with his clansmen, he now found pleasure in joining with the ad hoc chamber ensembles that sprouted in and around Toulouse. For the first time he came to enjoy the purity of amateur music-making, of duos, trios, quartets, wherein all composers seem to find greater expression and greater emotion. For the essence of ensemble is the suppression of the ego, the negation of the cult of the individual, be they conductor or soloist. He realised, musically at least, that he had come home and, although he needed the money that orchestral playing provided, some day, somewhere, this was how he would like to make music.

So they settled in Toulouse, but only in the sense that any want of flight now constituted racination. To live in Vichy France was to dwell in perpetual uncertainty. When, later, Reuben came to contemplate the two years they spent there, he did so with a sense of marvel bordering on the awe-struck. How was it that they could transplant themselves so completely? How had they duped themselves so absolutely that here, at last, was peace? After all, the rulers of Vichy hardly came to power with spotless hands, reaching rapid accommodation with Hitler and run by a military which, but a few decades before, had been willing to cleave their country by framing Dreyfus to protect one of their own. It was a regime which at the final reckoning deported – at best recklessly, at worst comprehendingly – more than seventy-five thousand Jews.

But they knew little of that. Whispers of atrocities within a grey universe that lay far beyond the imagination filtered from the east to places like Geneva – but they never penetrated the occupied zone. Reports of round-ups in Marseille were finessed by a self-deluding rumour machine in terms of *agents provocateur* or Allied spies, just as cousins in Poland and Austria, Czechoslovakia and Russia believed that a life of labour awaited them on resettlement.

They managed to put to the back of their minds the discomfort of the arrival in Paris, and to suppress, if not their demise then certainly the circumstances which led Sarah's parents to end it all. They even succeeded in sidelining the experience of the flight, focusing instead on the there and now, achieving a degree of equanimity by thinking of the present and immersing themselves in the detail of day-to-day life.

At first it was difficult, especially for Moses, who became increasingly fractious as he saw his life ebbing with little apparent purpose. Reuben's resourcefulness kicked into action.

"Look, Papa. You can either sit here moping or do something about it. The world's gone mad. The old rules do not apply. London's already being bombed, according to some reports. Maybe we would have been better off there. Maybe not. But here we are and we stay, at least until it's no longer safe. We're all refugees, we're all homeless. The city's teeming with Jews, so why not find out whether there are some Russians or Poles here? You may have left all that behind you, but then, so have they. You can brush up your language skills, relearn Yiddish. Who knows? You may even find some Skidelites!"

While the old man demurred, Leah and Sarah busied themselves in making their shabby accommodation at least serviceable and the children quickly made friends among the émigré community. And they began a project of gentle insanity that, when Reuben later contemplated it, broke him with its aching symbolism.

There, down among the damned, they started to develop a southern garden. It was driven by a mixture of needs at once both clearly pragmatic and absurdly idealised. The aim was to be self-reliant as the inevitable privations increasingly bit. Indeed, some element of the Rodrigue instinct for business now came to Leah as an opportunity for income presented itself. But more than that, it represented the dream of all who seek safety, and all who are deprived of the anchors of life – to be fed, clothed, sheltered. They dreamed of being dependent upon no-one but themselves, of needing nothing more than they alone could provide, of achieving the nirvana of knowing that, should all living beings but they be erased from the face of the earth, even then they would survive, harvesting what they had placed within the dry soil, watered, pruned and finally plucked, whether from tree, bush or direct from the ground in which it, like they, had rooted.

They hacked away at the undergrowth of the neglected earth, working as though they might not eat at all if they did not dig and hoe, sow and water. They planted for the present: staple green vegetables (peas, beans and lettuce), artichoke, tomato, aubergine and a rich variety of berries – and melon vines, peach and pear trees for the future.

Their striving bore fruit, both material and spiritual. They thrived on the pure foods that they grew, even as the shortages of wartime ravaged Vichy. The seclusion of their garden meant they could cultivate away from prying, jealous eyes, and they learned stealth in the ways they exited their house laden with produce for market.

But there was one aspect of their enterprise that defied concealment – and it was one which gave them enormous pleasure. Fragrance. For their garden was a profusion of scent, rising on the gentle breezes drifting inland from the seas and mountains that lay equidistant from Toulouse at all four compass points. When the aroma was at its most seductive, it seemed inevitable that, in addition to an abundance of birds and insects, other less welcome visitors would come knocking on the door demanding their portion. So the cellar became the Josephite storehouse where they lay down their harvest for the expected years of famine, while more overt supplies were kept in view to satisfy the curious and insistent.

There remained one section of the garden that, in the lonely years when it all was over, Reuben remembered with bitterness. Not for him the heady, nostalgic fragrance and taste of fruits, nor even the solid reassurance of vegetables. No, when he closed his eyes to revisit these last days of contentment, he saw only the small plot of sunflowers swaying at the top of their giant stalks, recognising in that crowd-like rhythm the congregation of another forest of yellow stars, moved as one by forces beyond resistance, requiring unswerving obedience to their implacable power.

While the garden grew, Reuben settled down to life in the modest musical world of Toulouse. His talent and experience illuminated the mediocre orchestra, and his tales of life under Weingartner and Furtwängler, the thrill of the Vienna Philharmonic, Rosé and the other great players, stretching back over half-a-century to the glory days of Brahms and Bruckner, Mahler and Wagner, brought pleasure and envy in equal measure. He enjoyed the celebrity and loved recounting the tales, seeing in the eyes of his audience the wonder of hearing about the world of their dreams, their imaginations becoming that mystical crucible where moderate talent is transmuted into brilliance and fame.

Moses, meanwhile, finally took his son's advice. He discovered a new old world of which he had scarcely dreamed, and recovered languages he thought he had forgotten. Sitting around in bars and cafés, drinking whatever ersatz liquor or coffee *le patron* had managed to acquire and inhaling dubious tobacco from a variety of exotic holders, he flew back through the years in the company of others who, by diverse routes of mind-boggling circuitry, had arrived in the ancient Gallic city.

In varying degrees determined by their ancient usage, the Yiddish, Polish and Russian of his childhood came tumbling out. As he sat with other refugees all their experiences merged into a coherent whole, the stuff of folklore, the collective conscience of a dispersed people.

But it was the songs which triggered the most emotional reminiscences. Music's power to evoke memory came rushing to the fore. Now the old men, their minds and voices liberated by drinks of doubtful provenance, were once again among their *landsmen*; in kindergarten, outside a synagogue, deep within the woods, beside a homely hearth, where all the growth of childhood and rites of passage had stutteringly, unstoppably, came to pass. In Yiddish and Hebrew, Polish and Russian, the lieder of life – religious, folk, marching, Zionist – from the cursed communities were once again aired, after who knows how long, as if newly minted.

Eyes moistened as each remembered parents, homes filled with laughter, harsh lives hacked out from unforgiving soil, even those tedious days spent in soporific study of the Torah. The enthusiasm of their invocation increased in direct proportion to the amount of alcohol consumed and the growing opacity of the smoke-filled room.

What linked all these men, there in the twilight of their lives, as the moon sparkled above the Massif Central and threw its cold gaze across the lazy waters of the Garonne, was the awareness that the songs were the same; familiar tunes, identical words, the shade of longing and regret shared as they looked back through frosted reminiscence. In the safety of remembrance lay all their hopes; in the uncertainty of the future, all their fears.

How long did any of them think it would last? There's none left now to ask. But they lived only for the moment, thinking more and more of the past, less and less of what might befall them.

Rumours continued to be finessed, whether it be of Nazi victory or defeat, firing squads patrolling the streets of Paris, bombs in London or an impending invasion of Vichy by any mixture of the Allies, Germans, Italians or Free French.

And in their very multiplicity lay the evasion, the wishfulness, the savage deceit that sat at the heart of these stories. This was the cruellest cut of all. For no matter how fanciful, how innately absurd the rumours, they could never encompass what was *actually* taking place. By a sadistic sleight of hand the Nazis devised that which could never be believed. So when at last the victims were confronted by it, they possessed no armoury with which to fight and – baby-defenceless – slipped to their destruction.

There was even a time when, if not exactly thinking that they might get through, people settled into the rhythm of attrition, not planning for unforeseeable eventualities and simply ignoring the inevitability of the future.

Until, that is, November 1942, when it arrived with an unforgiving vengeance.

Chapter 10

History is ambiguous about what finally broke Hitler's patience with Vichy. Perhaps it was the arrogance of certain victory, or the need for fresh conquests to satisfy the blood-lust. Maybe it was more than coincidence that Germany's move into unoccupied France took place in the same month of the Soviet counter-offensive at Stalingrad. It could have been exasperation at the enthusiasm of race law enforcement, or the desire to keep Italy, who looked after the south-eastern part of occupied France, on her toes.

Whatever drove the change in fortunes, for those thousands of Jews who had fled to that portion of France where they perceived there to be a less harsh regime, the realisation that they were wrong was swift and sure.

Round-ups began in the main conurbations – Lyons and Marseille especially. But the shouts of '*Raus, Raus!*', 'Out, Out!', with its raucous accompaniment of screeching tyres, running feet, boots thumping on splintering door, rifle butts shattering windows, sporadic gunfire, echoed also along the ancient cobbles of the historic *cités* of Avignon, Aix – and Toulouse.

The chemistry of collaboration is a complex compound. Where in one town the authorities would willingly throw all strangers to the sword, content only to protect the indigenous, in another all newcomers were granted sanctuary, the protector and the protégé links in the same chain, even if their positions were separated by sheer caprice.

The yield from the garden combined with its fortuitous rural setting to enable the Mendels to avoid the first wave of arrests. But despite its idyllic appearance, the old house with its pink slated roof and arbours began quickly to resemble the prison it had become. They dared not venture out, nor even open the white shutters that kept them from the daylight. The children could play only quietly in the basement, where the food store lay, its symphony of smells increasingly overpowering. Claustrophobia was the first enemy, for it was only at night, when the curfew was rigidly enforced, that they dared open the pair of small sloping doors that linked cellar to garden. Then they could finally breathe the fresh air coming off the Pyrénées, blowing the musty, dry air of the house from their nose, lungs, eyes and throat.

Now they all looked to Reuben for leadership, the mantle having drifted completely from the ever more bowed shoulders of the ageing Moses. In the half-light given off by the sun pouring through the slatted windows, he studied maps, making calculations of distance and velocity. He invented games for the children – who could walk fastest and quietest up the stairs, how far could they carry a suitcase while running, how many coats could they put on, how quickly could they fall asleep under the frosted sky, with its bright moon and crystal stars.

Miriam and Elias took only childish pleasure from the activities themselves; neither understood the significance. But the adults did. He was preparing to run.

At dusk, before curfew fell, Reuben would sneak out of the house dressed in peasant clothing and mingle with the inhabitants, armed with forged papers acquired at considerable cost via an underground source known to a fellow violinist in Kunc's ensemble. Listening to the frenzied conversations, he tried to form a mental picture of the lie of the land.

He even overhauled the rusty bicycle Leah had rescued from a garden shed and pedalled creakingly to the station. Merging with the crowd, melting into the turmoil, the enormity of the decision he faced stood before him stark and chilling.

The whole world seemed in transit. Swarming masses pressed around the railway, shuffling along, moving without individual will in directions determined by some unknown force. He saw the desperate, with fanned sheaves of impotent banknotes waved above their heads, besieging ticket offices, seeking a precious passport from the stricken city even while the *Fermé* signs were displayed. The sense of panic was all-pervading, magnified by the suffocating steam of the few trains that were preparing to move and the cacophony of pandemonium which filled the air. A discordant battle for supremacy was being fought. On one side, the normal sounds of the railroad – hissing steam, whistles, brakes, iron wheels on iron tracks, carriage doors slamming shut. On the other, the tears that accompany family bonds being sundered and a rising chorus of frantic *au revoirs* called after those departing, optimism doubled in the twin hopes of the messages being heard and the wish for speedy reunion fulfilled.

Twice, three times, he reconnoitred the town, moving carefully in shadows and doorways, or ensuring he rode within the pack of workers from the factories long since converted to the war effort. No-one took any notice; each was deep in his own world, calculating personal impacts and managing his own survival.

He quickly realised that he would need to go further afield. He knew that the chaos of landlocked Toulouse was bound to be replicated a hundredfold in ports and frontier posts which held out the prospect of escape from Nazi occupation, but he needed to check all the options.

He knew that when he broached the subject, he would face the combined wrath of wife and parents. So he waited until he was ready to go and, just before dawn, when the children were asleep, he told them of his imminent departure.

Moses was first to detonate. "You drag us all the way here, with no hope of getting safely home to London, and now you're going to disappear and leave us to fend for ourselves. What kind of son, husband, father, does that, eh?"

"One who's spent the last few years agonising about what's best, with no-one to confide in for fear of worrying them unduly."

"Well, all that succeeded in doing is making it worse now the time has come to tell us. We should have gone to Lon–"

"We didn't, we're here. When we're safe then torture me, Papa, with what might have been best. Now, all we can do is play the cards we've got. And I think I have to go and see what's happening along the coast. Options, that's what we need now, choices."

"So you find a boat, then what? The last Jew to thrive on water was Jesus. The only time you find us on a boat is when we're fleeing the land."

"Just so, Papa, like you from Poland, and all those who made it to America. It's an honourable tradition, and proven too."

"Oh, what's the point? Your mind's made up; why am I wasting my breath?"

"Are you sure this is best, dear?" Leah asked gently. Her voice faltered as she voiced their concerted dread. "What if you're cap … captured … or … or … worse?"

Sarah looked at him beseechingly, anxious for any sign of reassurance. None came.

"Mama, Papa, Sarah ..." His quaking voice betrayed the inner turbulence. "I can't give you the comfort you want. I've no idea what I'm going to find, nor what'll happen. But I have to go. And yes, I might not come back, so when I walk out the door, pretend I'm dead. Keep your heads down, carry on as we have, and if you have to leave without me then contact the orchestra and ask for Alain, the part-time librarian who looks after the scores. He'll maybe know how to help. Do not wait for me. Give Miriam and Elias a kiss and tell them I'll see them soon. When I come back, I'll leave a sign on one of the trees.

"No. No goodbyes. Don't look at me like that, Sarah. I have to do this, before we're trapped. You do understand, don't you?"

She broke. "No, NO! I *don't*. Papa's right. If you don't return, it's like we've been abandoned."

"Reuben would *never* abandon us," Leah insisted, maternal instinct reddening face and voice. "We've trusted him this far. We avoided what befell your dear parents, may they rest in peace. We got out of Paris, and if even half the rumours are true then we're well out. If he thinks this is what must be done, that's good enough for me."

"Look, we can debate this forever, but it won't make any difference. Don't let me go with angry words in my ears."

He didn't need to add "in case they're our last".

It was a trek reminiscent of that which his father had made so many years before, away from the near certainty of death in Russia and towards a hoped-for life in some uncertain place. On the trusty bike and dressed in the faded blue garb of the locals, Reuben had planned a rural route, travelling by day and sleeping in barns or under trees, traversing the small farms and orchards which dotted the landscape, taking a convoluted path through the villages and hamlets which were more likely to have so far escaped the invaders' scrutiny.

Cycling due east from Toulouse, his course took him past the distant, snow-capped Massif Central. He crossed rivers – Seillonne, Dagour, Vendrielle, Peyrencon – and their many anonymous tributaries before skirting Mazamet to the south, via the Forêt de Montaud.

There fatigue finally overcame Reuben. The emotional departure conspired with an unsustainable pace and the unfamiliarity of the terrain to deplete his stamina. It had taken him four days to reach the apparent safety of the dense woodland. Searching in the fading light for a secluded spot deep within its evergreen womb, he came upon a derelict gamekeeper's shed. No sooner had he entered than he lay down on the floor, wrapped his blanket around him and was gone.

He had no idea how long he had been sleeping when he awoke with a start, sensing that he was not alone. *Germans* was his initial thought, and his mind flew back to the family, waiting like so many others for news that would never come. He held his breath, recalling that the ramshackle room offered no hope of concealment. He heard the snapping of still dry twigs, protected by a deep carpet of dying and dead foliage but not so buried that the crack and splinter were inaudible. Surrounded by the sounds of encroaching danger, he sat bolt upright, stock still, each element of his being alert, listening for any sound to signify a change of direction that would take the enemy away from his sanctuary.

No such luck. The rotted door gave way with no sound of resistance, spun on its one remaining rusted hinge and swung there, creaking like a hemp noose swaying under the strain of the dead weight of a corpse. Reuben remained where he was, bracing his body for the impact of bullets. After an eternity two men appeared, then a third. But they were not dressed in Nazi uniforms. He had been found by partisans, who had tracked him since the moment he had entered the forest. They covered the ground between door and bed in an instant and forced him to the floor, boot on neck, driving his face into the cold, hard ground. He was briskly frisked and, comforted by the absence of weapons, the questions began.

He had already thought of what his story would be should he be arrested by the Germans or the Gendarmerie. But he had not prepared for this – being interrogated by those who might be sympathetic to his quest.

"Who are you?"

"What'ya doing here? Talk!"

Lack of preparedness initiated the dangerous truth. "I … I … I'm a Jew. I'm going to … er … Marseille to see whether I can find a way out for my family. I mean no harm to anyone."

"Where are they … your family?"

"I'm not going to tell you that! How can I trust you? What if you're captured, you may tell someone."

The knife came to his throat without so much as a whisper. He felt blood trickle down.

"Who are you to call us traitors?" snarled the unshaven, yellow-toothed warrior at the other end of the blade.

"I meant no insult, Monsieur," he rejoined. "Are you a family man?"

No reply.

"Precisely. You trust no-one with that information. In my haste, I said too much. That's all you'll get from me. Go on. Cut. Be done with it."

An uneasy silence filled the hut. Only the distant haunting of an owl broke the quiet. Reuben and The Knife held each other's gaze. In the Jew's eyes the Frenchman saw only the steeliest resolve. He weakened, and lowered the weapon. With the break in tension, nervous laughter ensued. Wine-soaked, stale breath heavy with garlic was exhaled in his face, and Reuben's back soon stung with the slaps of camaraderie.

"Come. Our camp is a little way off. We'll give you some provisions and help you on your way."

He was soon off again, with a full belly and a heart bursting with fresh determination to see his family. The dawn broke over Haut Languedoc, just before he crossed Mont Caroux. Beyond Bédarieux he forded the Hérault just south of the famous gorges.

Reuben's journey remained uneventful. He bisected the ancient towns of Nîmes and Montpellier at Vergèze before bridging the majestic Rhône at Arles.

He pedalled along the tracks which hatched the Camargue, pausing for several refreshing minutes to gaze at horses flying through the shallow water, spray all around their sweating fetlocks, and herds of black bulls grazing gently at the water's edge.

The final stage of his journey took him through Salon and Aix via the aptly named crest Chaine de L'Etoile, down to the Mediterranean and into the teeming cauldron that was France's greatest port.

Marseille was in total upheaval. Unholy teams of Vichy forces and the Wehrmacht patrolled the streets, occasionally swooping on an enclave of Jews or Resistance fighters who erroneously felt there to be safety in numbers. For the first, most shocking, time, Reuben witnessed a scene that was being played out across Europe: long lines of baggage-burdened Jewish families, some with overloaded handcarts, others with bursting suitcases or loosely tied sacks, were driven along to the rail head like cattle, cajoled and beaten in equal proportions, promised Eden in the east, threatened with death if they didn't hurry.

His days on the winter road had weathered and muddied him: with his mode of transport and faded blue drill peasant suit, he blended in with the hordes of French nationals who had descended on their second city. Discreetly he tracked the progress of the snaking, shuffling line, watching with disbelief the violence which drove it on. Those who stumbled and fell by the wayside were encouraged to continue by bullwhip, boot or rifle butt, only saved from immediate execution by the desire to avoid wholesale panic.

He sensed both his own impotence and that of the afflicted. Fleetingly, he wondered whether something could be done. No sooner had the thought been born than it was dead, killed both by pragmatism and the realisation that his priorities lay elsewhere. But Reuben registered something else: the apathy of the others who also watched the spectacle. He knew that he was on his own; that now all Jews were on their own.

When the line eventually arrived at its destination, it was not to that part of the station from which passengers departed, but to the ramped section for the loading of livestock. By the time they saw the nature of the transport, it was too late. The pressure of those being driven from behind proved irresistible – there could be no turning back, no rebellion, just the passive acceptance of entrapment.

Reuben filed it all away for later use. He realised that people treated this way in public view could expect no mercy when secreted from the risk of scrutiny. No-one who treated humans as cattle could subsequently look upon them as anything else. They were under sentence of death, as surely as animals at the auction are en route to the abattoir.

He had seen enough, and made his way towards the port.

"Stop! Papers!"

Reuben froze and, mimicking those he'd previously seen stopped, whipped off his cap in servility, slightly bowing his head to show inferiority and avoid defiant eye contact. He toyed with running, confidence in the quality of his fake identity card draining with the colour in his face. The baby-faced policeman studied it with all the intensity of an experienced counterfeit detective – but with none of the knowledge.

"Why are you in Marseille?"

"I look for work, Monsieur."

"What do you do?"

"Anything to put bread on the table, Monsieur. Labouring, farm work, clearing up. I'm heading for the docks to try my luck."

"When did you arrive? Do you know the curfew?"

"This morning. And yes, I know, thank you, Monsieur."

"On your way." He nodded perfunctorily and handed the card back without another word. Hopping on his bike, Reuben was off, down towards the port.

Unable to ask directly for passage, he changed tack and, taking his inspiration from the encounter with the policeman, he asked around for work, hoping to discover how the harbour worked. But it was to no avail. Thousands had had similar notions and his half-hearted efforts to insinuate himself into someone's employ met with immediate rebuff. With the curfew approaching, he sought lodgings among the hundreds of rooms which historically awaited inbound ships to disgorge their fully paid, thirsty, randy crews. Even these seemingly endless tenement rooms were full to overflowing, so he was forced to find a bench in a crowded, smoke-filled saloon.

After a glass or two of rough *vin de pays* and stale baguette filled with coarse pâté of uncertain vintage, the warmth of the fire, the bodies and the reduced oxygen conspired with the fatigue of his journey. Reuben was vanquished by sleep.

He awoke with the chill of dawn as the open door welcomed the cleansing salty air. The kindly patron had tolerated many others like him, so that when his brain kicked into gear and Reuben surveyed his sleeping companions, he realised that there was still no chance of work. He engaged a few of his fellow dormitory dwellers to see whether their longer duration could provide him with any shortcuts to understanding what the situation was. But the conversations carried out in a Babel of accents and aptitudes only added to his despondency.

"We're all trying to work our way out of here. But there's nothing, unless you want to enlist with Vichy."

"For my family I've tried a passage to get. But the black market, it is mean, afford it I cannot ..."

"And some of the boats – they look like they'll barely make it out of the harbour, let alone survive a rough voyage."

"I knew someone with a trawler who tried to make it to Corsica ... blown out the water by a U-boat less than two miles out. Hopeless, we're trapped."

Reuben knew it to be so. His mind bent towards his family and he left to cycle back, hugging the Gulf of Lion coast and checking the villages between Marseille and where the bay veers due south before stretching down to Perpignan and the Spanish border.

Back in Toulouse, agitation transfigured the Mendel home. The effects of daytime incarceration coupled with the uncertainty of Reuben's whereabouts were taking their toll. Claustrophobia had spread rapidly like a cancer, oozing into every last cranny of the old house so that escape from its pervasive oppression became impossible. The pressure of perpetual caution and the rising nag of anxiety were eroding self-belief, sowing poisoned seeds in the seat of reason and undermining future capacity to out-face the demons.

Among the adults, the ties that had thus far kept them together were fraying. Moses, increasingly cantankerous and with a barbed, guilt-sparking tongue which demanded respect as a right was, as ever, all for running. But the women were constant. Leah and Sarah spoke with one voice: "We stay until we can stay no longer. Then we talk to the librarian and go, even if Reuben has not returned ... and we never look back." Moses' angry reactions were emasculated echoes of bygone glories. Like nations no longer able to wage their own wars, or countries whose economies could be ravaged by distant speculators, his was the roar of the toothless tiger. He subsided, an ancient volcano that intermittently rumbled, threatening emptily. He seemed to age, a slight stoop more pronounced and the growing number of liver-spots on his hands and face more livid. And Leah, too, was much older than even when they left Paris; the last glimmers of black in her hair had ceded to the encroachment of grey and her gentle face now shone through a forest of wrinkles. But her eyes were still coal-black, even if the diet had left the whites a pinkish-yellowy tinge.

Sarah had grown into Reuben's regent and she ruled the house firmly. When Moses complained, she slapped him down, confident in herself and that Leah was by her side. She understood her role – to keep the family together, healthy and safe until her husband returned and reclaimed the throne. She was determined, and her face had hardened, with pinched creases at the corner of her mouth and a slight closure of the eyes. But at night, when the house was quiet and she lay in bed all alone, the crown at last set aside, she wept softly to herself, partly for what she had become and partly for the warmth and safety that she'd lost.

The children continued their playtime drills, unaware of anything but fun. To vary the games, new ideas were introduced. How to suppress a sneeze, going from dawn to dusk with nothing to eat, walking barefoot through the garden. During Reuben's absence, Miriam and Elias became leaner. By now fourteen, her body was changing, although the stress of their circumstances and restricted diet meant she looked young for her age. And despite the recent trials, Elias was also beginning to mature and tried to assume a manly bearing, particularly with his father away and Moses growing older before his eyes.

Exercises were designed to make them stronger, their feet used to punishing terrain and bodies more adept at processing optimum goodness from reduced quantities of food. This artificial process could never compensate for future trials, while the deprivation continued the erosion of their soft edges that had started when they fled Vienna. They were left more down-to-earth and ever less expectant of the comforts of life to which they had been accustomed.

Meanwhile, their father maintained his search along the north-western coast of the Mediterranean. From Marseille he rode west, cutting across the mouth of the Rhône as it flooded the Camargue, this time at its southernmost traversable points around huge pools, the Etangs of Berre and Vaccarès.

At every settlement, be it anonymous hamlet, little known village, town such as Martigues, Frontignan and Sète, or the southern reaches of larger conurbations like Montpellier, Béziers and Narbonne, he posed as a workman, looking for jobs. At each he was rebuffed, in terms varying from amicable sympathy to impatient indifference. But while his reception varied, one thing did not: the fog of palpable trepidation that hung over each community, rendering everyone he met suspicious of strangers even as their customary hospitality created a conflict, often resolved with a glass of wine or some bread to help him on his way. At each settlement not only was there no work but the ravages of war on the fishing industry that dominated the area were all too clear. It occurred to Reuben that while it might be possible to find an exit to freedom here, the chances were simply too remote to justify the risk. And while he might make it alone, the family would be too conspicuous, and too large a group, to transport.

As he pedalled, his mind wandered. From nowhere in particular a line from one of his childhood favourites, Sherlock Holmes, came back to him: "When you have eliminated the impossible, whatever remains, *however improbable*, must be the truth."

He had decided. The route to the south, and over to Spain, was the only hope. He feared it, recognised its innate dangers, but could see no other option. Before making off for home, he therefore headed down to the border and the Pyrénées, cycling along the coast all the way to the town of Cerbère.

His initial thinking was to take the family south-west from Toulouse via the Catholic shrine town of Lourdes and across the mountains where a score of assumed frontier crossing-points might afford ample choice. But his own pilgrimage in search of physical salvation had taught him one thing: information is true power, or rather the converse, lack of information is true impotence. His role as father, husband and son had impressed upon his entire being the irreducible burden of dependency. He interpreted it in many ways, not least that it imposed upon him the need to do his utmost to ensure their safety. So he set himself to explore the entire border from Cerbère at the Pyrénées-Or via Prades (where the great Casals would launch his music festival, as close as he could get to his beloved Catalonia without breaking his vow never to return while Franco remained in power) to the central region, ignoring the Pyrénées-Atlantiques for the simple expedient that it had been under Nazi occupation since the establishment of Vichy.

He hugged the frontier, scouting in twilight before night shrouded all and in the grey dawn before the sun burned off any early morning mist. He slept in shaded grottoes in woods and overgrown schisms in rock faces. Not daring to purchase a map in the abandoned tourist areas which scattered the region, he made his own, scratching with a battered pencil the line of the border and the distances between the many villages which dotted the landscape. Landmarks were noted as sighting-posts for when he returned with the family, preparing for a wide-ranging traverse of the mountain range before selecting the point of descent towards Spain.

He had long abandoned any semblance of hygiene. His cherished hands were ingrained with oil, while his one pair of trousers was stiff with the mud that squelched up from the tracks that he used. A rough beard gathered in the hollows of his face where the stress of his perpetual vigilance and the physical exertion of the odyssey had gouged shadowed corries down each cheek into the now scraggy neckline, winnowing what little fat had gathered at the jowls. He was aware of the stench that emanated from his unwashed body. The fastidiousness of his personal *toilette* had long been abandoned, his rank hair thick with grease and his rear caked with the evidence of constipation and diarrhoea brought on by his appalling diet of fruit and uncooked vegetables. Even the occasional stolen cheese or raw egg offered little respite.

But finally he had travelled as far west as he dared and turned for home, avoiding human contact in case his appearance would arouse suspicion, so skirting clockwise around Lourdes before heading north between Pau and Tarbes, then tracking east-north-east across country, approaching Toulouse from the south-west.

It was early morning when he reached the outskirts. The dank dawn mist accentuated the self-imposed curfew which had thrown a cloak of silence over the family; he could do nothing to jeopardise it, knowing that his arrival would spark excitement in the children. To avoid rousing the house, he rode past and beyond it, down and around the back streets, dipping into the city, shadowed doorway by narrow alley, trying to gauge its mood, feel the pulse. Far more military activity greeted him than had been the case before his departure, and even at that early hour the scenes at the railway station were reminiscent of Marseille. He needed less time to assess the situation, his innate cunning sharpened by the unstinting stress of his journey.

Turning towards home, he approached furtively through the

copse that abutted the bottom of their garden. Hiding the bike beneath a pyre of leaves which winds had harvested from the trees and deposited at the angle of wall and earth, he hauled his weary body, fast draining of energy with the onrushing prospect of true rest, up and over. Despite the cold, he settled down under his blanket and, beneath the large apple tree, fell fast asleep, relaxed for the first time since he had left over six weeks earlier.

By now the internal clock was a well-oiled mechanism. He instinctively realised that he had to wake early enough to warn Sarah of his return, but late enough that the excitement of his arrival could be controlled without arousing suspicion in any passers-by. He hoped that they had all stuck to the routine, so that he could prime himself to rise just as the waning sun was sinking towards the Atlantic, when Miriam and Elias would be tired from the combination of 'games' and the inevitable enervation of incarceration.

As the first shadows of twilight tinged the garden wall in pink he awoke, instantly watchful. He slunk towards the house, moving between the fruit trees and pausing behind one of the bushes and shrubs which dotted the plot. He progressed irregularly, relying on the increasing shadows to confuse the eye of anyone looking out from the house. He wanted Sarah to know he was back before anyone else. He used the agreed signal – the blanket thrown over an infant peach tree close to the kitchen window. This done, he crouched down beneath its young branches and waited.

He did not exactly fall back to sleep, but he was no longer in the garden. Rather, he inhabited that strange place between conscious and unconscious, allowing his mind to drift over the hardships ahead, not just for him but for Sarah, the children; even more so, his ageing parents. In that grey space between waking and slumber he drilled into his brain the route he proposed taking, harnessing the long-honed skill of remembering music to the detail of the journey he had just rehearsed, so that no time would be lost in the flight and each permutation of path over the mountains could be immediately recalled.

But throughout the entirety of this process a part of him remained fully vigilant, waiting for the house to stir. He was first alive to a sliver of light that oozed from beneath the kitchen shutter. Initially anxious about its visibility, he quickly realised that it was only so because he was beneath the sill, and the narrow gap at the bottom of the shade was all that the light had to escape through.

His heart leapt as Sarah carefully opened the back door, rapidly closing it behind her despite having shut off the light before drawing back the bolt. As he saw her stand there, waiting for a few moments to accustom her eyes to the dying embers of twilight, her husband, not so encumbered, drank in her features. He smiled the Gordian smile of one truly in love, that knot of desire, comfort, warmth, respect, faith and hope whose shape and complexity modulate as life exerts its capricious whims.

At first it seemed as if she wouldn't notice the signal, so intently did she drink in the magnificent sky, clustered with pinpoints of light and illuminated by the newly full moon. Afraid of alarming her, Reuben slunk silently back against the wall.

Suddenly she roused herself from the spell which the heavens had cast upon her and she turned, as she had every day for a month-and-a-half, to look forlornly on the peach tree. But this time its young branches were not naked. There, draped over a bough, hung her golden fleece.

Tentatively, quietly, she called his name, trying to control the excitement, her heartbeat rising vertically as with the imminence of harm or passion.

"I'm here, it's alright," he replied. "Don't come too close, I reek. No, please, I mean it, I'm disgusting. Bring out some water and soap, and I'll make a start here in the garden. Don't tell the others yet. I'd like to appear halfway like I looked before I left, even though on the inside I feel different."

She soon returned, by which time he had stripped off his putrid clothes and thrown them disgustedly to one side. She gazed at his naked body, its contours eroded to sharpness by the weeks of deprivation and highlighted by the moonlight.

Ignoring his warning, she moved towards him and enveloped him in her arms, pulling his head gently down into her neck. They stood like that, unmoving, until she backed away.

"What do you mean – different?"

"I don't really know," he said as the freezing water cascaded over his head, stinging his eyes and setting a chain of goose-bumps running down his arms and torso. "I've seen things, Sarah, terrible things. Lines of Jews, old, young, crippled, herded along the streets like animals, packed into freight trains. I won't say it in front of the others, but I was scared. I saw it first in Marseille, but all the signs are that Toulouse is next. Who knows what it all means? The only thing I know for certain is that we can't stay here. We've got to move – and soon. Let's get inside."

As he spoke, his mind's eye roved the landscape of his travails, excavating the newly laid layer of his memory and sifting the dross to extract what he now knew to be of value: experience, self-knowledge, a clear goal. He saw himself as the single beam passing through the prism, irreversibly transmuted into its real, undeniable components. He peered through the fog of the lonely nights in forest, mountain and lakeside, through the tangible insecurity which stalked the anonymous villages, through the thirst which had sandpapered his palate and throat, through the hunger which had driven him to speculative sampling of the unfamiliar fruits and fungi that proliferated in the countryside.

He saw himself as some mythic creature, half-man, half-beast. The former encircled his head in a halo of rational thought, determining his every step with a singular purpose which only now revealed itself. The latter was pure animal, driven with every instinct to ford the torrent regardless of its icy power, ignore the pain from the whiplash bramble in the blind rush through the wood, suppress any threat of failure. As the image formed in his mind he understood with a clarity so simple that its prior anonymity shocked him. He, Reuben Mendel, husband, son, grandson, musician, was, above everything else, a father. All that he had done, all that he was doing, all that he would ever do was for his children. For their survival, their thriving, their opportunity to do what he was doing in *their* turn, for *their* children. In this he was no different from the lioness dragging a dead zebra back to her cubs, or the eagle swooping endless skies to disgorge prey into the gaping crop of each demanding chick. He realised that the awareness of this near-holy burden would colour his every action until the haven which he sought was forever secured. He hit a groove whose sides reached up to infinity, so that whatever lay beyond was outside the ambit of his eye and his thought. It was a moment of nuclear purity, when everything in a life is gathered around an unarguable centre.

As soon as he entered the house Reuben was aware of the tangible difference in ambience that had set in during his absence. Their long imprisonment had taken its toll: his parents had aged and tension hung in the air like a malign cloud. He realised that they could not stay together in their current circumstances, even if his outlook on their prospects had been more optimistic.

The reunion was restrained, both by the continuing need for quiet and by the fact that it was clear that Reuben was troubled. Even Miriam and Elias sensed that they needed to temper their excitement, confining themselves to throwing their arms around their father and sobbing softly into his neck, relief at his return mingling with the apprehension that comes to children when confronted with radical changes in their view of the world.

He recounted his journey as if it were an adventure story, relying on adult intuition to read between the lines, to comprehend the silences and the small shrugs that punctuated the narration. Like Reuben so many years before with Moses, to Miriam and Elias this was every tale ever told, their father an ancient hero striding out to conquer evil, offsetting all that fate might throw at him with an exhilarating mixture of fox-like cunning and physical might. But for Sarah, Leah and Moses the truth was plain to see. They were being encircled – and the only escape route, to the south, was hazardous and would not remain open much longer. More than that, capture meant a voyage of unknown duration to an invisible destination in a manner fitting to livestock bound for the slaughterhouse.

"I know the route we must take. I've not yet sorted out how we go, but I have an idea. Now, I'm starving, so perhaps we can eat and then I'll explain."

He tucked greedily into the first hot food he had enjoyed since Marseille, letting the steaming vegetable broth scald his gullet as it made its way towards his ravenous stomach. After a couple of generous mouthfuls, he shared his thoughts with them.

"This is the way we will go," he announced, removing from a pocket the rough map he had made en route. He showed them, tracing the direction with a fingernail encased by the grime of the road. Leah only just managed to suppress her shock at the state of his hand, blistered, scored by foraging, roughened from the elements. Their eyes tracked his finger, showing how they would head south-west out of Toulouse, across the countryside to Tarbes, before dropping due south to Lourdes.

From there, he spoke of choices, continuing directly towards the border or heading due east to Bagnères-de-Bigorre and picking up the Adour river that rises in the central Pyrénées close by the Tourmalet Pass.

"After that decision," he went on, "we move by night or under cover of bad weather. Now, how to get out of Toulouse? I've been thinking about this. We can't just walk out, the trains are under constant surveillance and the chances of hiring a car are less than nil. So this is my idea …"

Chapter 11

The following Sunday, the last of October 1943, a caped and hooded Leah left through the gate at the bottom of the garden and circuitously made her way towards town. She joined the throng of worshippers heading for the gothic glory of the Eglise des Reubenins, mother church of the Dominican order and site of the tomb of the 'Angelic Doctor', St Thomas Aquinas.

Only so much preparation could be made for her mission. Some cursory research among second-hand bookshops provided the basis of the plan – but to call the detail sketchy would be generous. Reuben's plan was simple, yet profoundly hazardous. The family would pose as Catholic pilgrims, following a path beaten out by the feet of the innumerable devout and the desperate, travelling across the border to Santiago de Compostela by way of Lourdes.

As she shuffled into the church, Leah put behind her the fractious night just passed.

"I know I'm old and useless," Moses had spat, "but it is I who should go. It is one thing I can still do, walk and talk."

"No, Papa. Out of the question. You look and act too Jewish."

"So now you're ashamed of your roots! Anyway, why not send Sarah, why does your mother have to go?"

"Moses dear, think of the children. Listen to him."

Reuben spoke, his tone assuming a darkened hue as though he knew his words would hound him to the grave. "Papa, I honour all that you've done. When you were little older than Miriam you were forced to flee. Remember how you felt, the loneliness, the fear, the uncertainty. I don't want any of us to relive that. Trust me to do what is right for all of us, but most of all for the children – they have to be our priority. Were but one of us to escape, it must be Miriam or Elias. If it was an adult, that would be failure. You can't go, Sarah should stay with the children and someone must lead. Besides, Mama has always been a good actress. Remember the times we read Shakespeare together? She was always the star."

Chastened with velvet, Moses had bowed his head in acknowledgement of his son's irresistible logic – his beloved must don the mantle of those who still believed that Jews had personally killed Christ. The barbed irony tore at him. The direct descendants of Rebbe Elias would be assuming the guise of Catholicism to escape their enemies, adopting the posture and pathos of miracle-seekers in order to flee the latest fiend to drive them from their most recent rooting. He wondered what his father would say. He imagined himself in Skidel, back where warmth and aroma wove a sensual *pas-de-deux* through the small house, and even at his own advanced years thought he felt a paternal hand rest gently on his shoulder and whisper with a calm assurance, "Whatever it takes, my son, whatever it takes."

As she stepped across the threshold of the church, Leah was assailed with similar reservations. Within her, conflicting emotions formed and deformed like the sections of an orchestra, sometimes one section, others a single voice, then a conglomerate of several groups, worst, a nerve-jarring tutti – anxiety, suspicion, paranoia, the desire to flee, the need to remain.

Her sight became blurred and she came close to fainting as an eruption of superstition and deeply embedded monotheism exploded from within. But for the momentum of the crowd she might not have made it to the first tier of pews and steadied herself. She sought refuge behind one of the pillars, as though she would not be spotted by a disapproving Jehovah if she could not see the towering splendours of the cathedral, adornments glittering in the variegated colours of the sun passing through the stained-glass windows that encircled the altar.

Despite her years of abstinence from any religious practices, Leah had not completely shed the powerful and insidious early years of religious school, where the Ten Commandments and the *Shema*, Judaism's great protestation of the oneness of God, had been drilled into her, a long-submerged part of her very fabric. Now, through an adrenaline catalyst, they were released, all the more potent for their decades of suppression.

She was confronted with the discomfiture of idolatry and the deification of prophets, a frontal assault on the Mosaic Decalogue which she found incomprehensible whenever she set foot in a church, even as she marvelled at the creative genius which wrought the buildings and their ornamentation. When Leah was younger, hotter of blood, rage had been the common reaction, a welling of iniquity at superabundant displays of wealth, whether manifested in sculptures of the Madonna and Child, paintings of the Saints or the breathless beauty of a Mass set by the hand of a master.

But where once there had been a furious railing, now there sat a profound uneasiness. It was grounded in the cold awareness that a people who could be moved to brighten and smooth with kisses the toe of a bronze Saint Peter or, on their knees, erode to slippery concavity the stone *escalier* of a mountaintop pilgrimage, could also be moved to do absolutely anything. She saw that where the essential curiosity of humanity is exorcised by the copious stimulation of primitive doubts then no amount of rational pleading can withstand the forces unleashed.

With eyes opened as though for the first time, Leah saw the enormity of her mission. Crossing ostentatiously, kneeling, lighting candles, dropping coins noisily into any one of the many receptacles – anything to immerse herself in all this piety and to dissemble so completely that she vanquished the bilious distaste at the overt display of obeisance all around her. It all seemed an unbridgeable chasm between what she was and what she had to profess.

So when the air was suddenly rent with the sombre glories of Palestrina's *Stabat Mater*, Leah cast herself in the role of the mourning mother whose grief permeated every word, every note. She saw herself beside Reuben's open bier, placed her hands into his open wounds, touched the jellied blood that had congealed around them, aware at one level to the heresies that flooded her mind, oblivious at another to their inherent illogicality. She felt the sorrow choking her throat, rising up as she contemplated the vision of her only begotten bereft before her. It was not something Leah had in truth ever envisioned. Even when he went to the trenches or, worse, was lost when the war ended, she had never imagined him dead. The image filled her with a horror beyond comprehension.

She began to hate those who surrounded her, the intoxicating mixture of incense, candles, music and light blended with the constant hum of prayer and intruded upon her reveries, impinging just sufficiently to disturb them, intermingling so that her thoughts and qualms, the significance of her mission, splintered to the point of disorientation. The ensuing rush quite overcame her and she felt her knees buckle as she slid down the pillar, her flaccid, gentle face contorted as it rubbed against the cold, smooth stone.

"Are you feeling better, my child?"

Leah came round to find herself lying on a battered chaise-longue in a room lined with books and various accoutrements of worship. She slowly focused on the kindly face that hovered above her, and felt her hand being gently stroked. Uncomfortably aware that her blouse had been loosened, Leah raised her head to glance around her, absorbing in a single pan the alien surroundings. The nun who was holding her hand softly sought to assuage her:

"You are in the vestry, my dear. You were taken ill in the cathedral and we thought it best to bring you here, where it is quiet. Would you like us to send for the doctor?"

Blind panic gripped Leah, and she sought immediate escape. But while her mind was firm, her body was not, and she soon realised that she lacked the strength to move, even as her face betrayed her intentions.

"Be still, my fellow sister in Christ. Neither He nor His long-suffering Mother will mind if you miss Mass just once. Father, you'll pardon her missing confession, won't you?"

"Of course," came the beautifully modulated Parisian accent of the elegantly turned-out priest seated at the overflowing desk in his canonicals. "But I have no recollection of seeing you here before, Madame," he added with what Leah sensed was more than a hint of menace. "Perhaps you are from out of town?"

"If you please, Father, may I have a glass of water?" Leah sighed, ever so slightly overdoing a histrionic swoon as she sought to buy some time to gather her senses.

"Of course. Sister, would you be so kind?" The elderly nun left the room and Leah remained locked in an oppressive silence with the imposing, brooding presence on the other side of the room. As she collected her thoughts, she felt his eyes burning into her, and was driven to answer.

"You're right, Father, I have not worshipped here before. I recently arrived from Paris with my family. We hope to travel on a pilgrimage to Lourdes, and then to Santiago."

"Why? What miracles do you seek through the intercession of Our Lady?"

"None to rectify the tragedies of the past, of which we have been mercifully free. Rather to find holiness in these unholy times. We are not devout people, Father. We merely seek a place for quiet contemplation and feel drawn to the two shrines."

"'We'?"

"My husband, son, daughter-in-law and two grandchildren."

"I see. How do you plan to travel to Lourdes, may I enquire?"

"I hoped to receive the guidance of someone such as yourself."

"Uh-huh. And …"

At that moment the door opened and the nun returned with Leah's water.

"Sister, I will hear this lady's confession shortly, so I wonder whether you would mind leaving us for a while and, perhaps, prevent anyone from interrupting us."

"I'll be standing right outside, Father. Just call should you want me."

"Thank you, my child."

With that she placed the tray holding a carafe of water and a glass on the table and left the room.

"Now, where were we? Oh, yes. Lourdes. You were going to seek my advice on how to get there. Perhaps you can clear up something that is worrying me?"

"If I can."

"You said you came from Paris. That may be so, but not originally, I think. I am most interested in accents and yours is rather fascinating. You speak French well, Madame, but it is not your mother tongue. So, there is a lot of English but the way you pronounce certain letters, 'r' especially, suggests more than a hint of German."

"Well, I was born in England, but my father was a diplomat, so I spent quite a lot of my childhood in Berlin and Vienna."

Leah shocked herself both at the content and form of the lie, realising in the instant that she was locked into a battle of wits, a potentially deadly joust with an unknown protagonist who held the hill and could determine the pace and direction of the conflict. She was terrified and energised in equal measures, aware that she may give herself away at any moment, that he may follow the tradition of churches down the centuries and hand her over to the enemy, even while pretending to a holy neutrality.

"I see. And your father, what was his area of responsibility?"

"Commercial attaché."

"And your husband, what did he do? I presume, with respect, that he is retired?"

"Import and export. Father, is this really necessary? I don't mean to be brusque, but if you are able to help me then I would be grateful. If not then I should really be going."

"But did you not come for mass and communion, my dear?"

"No, Father. My family needs me so I must return as soon as possible. I was hoping for the assistance I seek and to make amends for missing mass when we arrive at Lourdes. I trust that would be acceptable."

"Well, it does seem rather irregular, Madame. You seek my help at an inopportune time. The service will shortly start."

"I do not mean to hurry you. I could come back later, if you prefer."

"No, that will not be necessary" he continued, a little curtly, like one doing his duty unwillingly, "I cannot help you cross the border. But what I can do is give you the name of an old and trusted colleague in Lourdes. He may be able to furnish a letter of introduction to his brother who, I believe, teaches at the Monastery of San Martin Pinario in Santiago. Now, if I am to write to my friend, I should be able to introduce you. Your name, please."

Leah froze, seeking refuge in drinking some water as she thought through a rapidly descending haze. She waffled. "My name, oh, how remiss of me not to give it you earlier, do forgive me, I'm not normally so discourteous. It must have been the turn I had. It's, er, Rodrigue, Maria Rodrigue."

"Aha, your husband has a little Spanish in him, I suspect."

"On his father's father's side, I think. All a bit distant."

"And his name, your husband's?"

"Mo ... Monty."

"Your son's, and his family?"

"R-R-Robert, Sarah and the children, M ... Michelle and E-Edward."

As she spoke, he wrote. He continued writing after she had finished and placed the note in an envelope, turned it over and scribbled a name and address on the front. He got up and walked over to a desk and pulled out some sealing wax. Lighting a candle, he continued: "This gives you no rights. I say merely that you requested an introduction, and I have done as asked. You understand?" he concluded, pressing the signet ring on the crooked little finger of his right hand firmly into the shiny red blob that straddled the edge of the flap and the back of the envelope.

"Of course."

"It is always a pleasure to help a pilgrim. Go in peace, my child." He blew on the still warm wax and handed her the letter.

"Thank you very much, Father."

As she walked towards the door, she turned, opening her purse as she did. "Would you accept a small donation? I'm sure you know many deserving causes."

"Thank you."

She handed over a few coins, and turned the handle to leave the room.

"Oh, one more thing, Madame Rodrigue."

"Yes?"

"Sholem aleichem."

The impact of the Yiddish 'Peace be with you' hit her like a blow to the solar plexus. She stopped dead in her tracks as though held by some unseen force. Her heart was exploding in her chest. She thought that she would die, reliving in a flash the skein of lies she had just woven, certain neither when he had realised that she was not what she claimed to be nor what precisely had given her away. Leah turned to face him, but he was already immersed in a book. She felt the colour rush to her face and all but ran from the room, nodded abruptly to the sentinel nun and followed the sounds of worship to guide her back towards the cathedral proper.

Leah struggled to regain her composure, aware that people were looking at her. She disguised her discomfiture as grief, drew her cape about her and lit a candle, which she placed on a spike beneath a painting of Mary holding the infant Christ.

As she walked down the southern of the two great naves, she glanced behind her and saw a familiar figure at the back of the church, beside the door to the sacristy. For a moment their eyes met, and she thought, even at a distance and in the shadowy light, that he bore a conspiratorial half-smile. Then she turned and, without a further glance back, fled, holding the precious paper to her breast lest it be damaged by the wind and rain which were now sweeping across the old town in vast sheets of impenetrable grey.

She headed south-west to mingle with the congregation spilling from the Cathédral St Etienne. As they poured away into the surrounding avenues and side alleys, Leah continued the walk home, relaxing as she realised that the combination of respect for the sabbath and the atrocious weather was keeping even the most assiduous policeman from the streets.

By the time she opened the gate at the bottom of the garden, Leah was completely exhausted, weighed down by the drenched cape and debilitated by the depletion of her emotional reserves. She fell into Reuben's arms and he carried her into the house.

After a hot bath, a couple of stiff brandies and some invigorating hugs from the grandchildren, she recounted the events of the day, waving the letter around her head like a trophy.

For the next two days they finalised their plans. More unavoidable selections of what they could take, with the single-minded objective of pruning their possessions down to two or three bags that could be easily carried. Not only to reduce the physical burden, but also to help maintain the deceit that they were pilgrims passing through.

Reuben had tackled the last problem – the best way to get to Lourdes. He'd looked at all the choices – train, pilgrims' bus, even stealing a car. In the end he opted for a taxi. He analysed it in this fashion: from his visits to Marseille and Toulouse, it was clear that trains were being inspected, if not systematically, then far too often for comfort. Travelling among pilgrims ran the severe risk of their near complete ignorance of all things Catholic being exposed. Despite help from the mysterious priest, he knew that, when weighed on the balance of history, the Jewish scales were tipped not by the righteous deeds of strangers but by their treachery. Stealing a car was the most attractive in that they could make their own pace and it gave them options, to hide, divert or make a run for it. What turned him against it was the risk of being caught in the act and his total inability with anything mechanical, so that a breakdown would render them stranded and hopelessly exposed. Thus it was a taxi, with all *its* attendant dangers of betrayal and abdicating mastery over destiny to an utter stranger.

During the last day, Reuben went into town and stood motionless in a doorway near the station. He was looking for one thing. For two hours he peered through the windscreen of every car that drove by. Finally, as the damp and cold had really begun to seep into his bones, he saw it. An old car pulled up with a small crucifix and rosary dangling from the rear-view mirror. A timid-looking young man let an elderly couple out of the back and recovered their suitcases from the boot. Reuben saw them pay the driver, and then he made his move.

"Monsieur, a moment, if you please."

A look of panic shot across the other's face, but Reuben was quick to put him at his ease.

"Have no fear. I only have a favour to ask of you. Would you drive me to my home and I'll explain?"

As he said it Reuben pressed a banknote into the man's hand and a look of understanding passed between them. During the journey the well-practised lie was advanced. Voicing it for the first time made him dizzy with guilt, but he had to gamble that the buttons he was pressing would work.

"My family is to make a pilgrimage to Lourdes. My children have both contracted some disease which has baffled the doctors. It means that they can barely walk – and they're getting worse. I was wondering whether you would be prepared to drive us there. We'd pay well for your trouble, but I dare not subject them to a long and tiring train journey. Well, what do you think? Can you help out?"

"It's a long way, Monsieur. My car is not too reliable."

"Monsieur, I am faced with risks at every side; each of our lives seems in daily jeopardy, don't you think? I am prepared to gamble on your abilities as both driver and mechanic. Are you prepared to help me gamble on a miracle for my children?"

The driver absorbed what was being said. His mind darted to his own young family, blessed with rude rustic good health, despite the poverty of a wartime diet.

"Oh, one more thing."

Reuben carried on with what he surmised was a trump card, judging from the impoverished state of the man's clothing.

"We may be gone for a little while, as we hope to pay homage to Saint James at Compostela. With so many desperate people around, do you know anyone who may be prepared to look after our house and tend our little orchard?"

"My name is Gaston Perrier. I would be delighted to help in both regards, Monsieur."

The final arrangements were made that night, with Perrier deciding it would be best to leave at first light. To maintain the fiction, Miriam and Elias were given a light dose of laudanum, sufficient to render them limp, as though their limbs were sapped of strength.

Three suitcases were packed; in one, Reuben's violin case was buried under his clothes. As the dawn broke to the east its weak rays were just strong enough to glow pink and orange over the distant hills. The taxi chugged softly up to the front door, a plume of exhaust trailing blue-grey behind the rusty back bumper.

At a given moment, first Moses and then Leah shuffled out as quickly as their ageing limbs would allow them, each with a valise. Gaston had got out to open the boot, and they put their luggage in before clambering into the back of the battered, dirty Citroën. As soon as they were in, Sarah and Reuben dashed from the house, she with Elias, he with Miriam, both slumbering, apparently nearly lifeless. They settled each child on a grandparent's lap before returning for the last case and locking up the house.

As they pulled away Sarah turned to throw a last look behind her, while Leah felt for the comfort of the precious paper that nestled in the inside pocket of her cape, crushed by the weight of the limp Elias. Moses was aeons away; his sad and baggy eyes rimmed red with the pain of flight and stinging from acid remembrance of an earlier uprooting, he distractedly stroked Miriam's hair as she dozed with her face turned towards his chest.

But Reuben did none of these. Gaston turned to look at him as he checked to his right that it was safe to pull out from the little road that led from the house. He was shocked by what he saw – a man transfigured, staring maniacally ahead, his eyes fixed on some distant point as through willing their rapid passing so that they could be far from where they were. Even at a cursory glance, he sensed the pressure electrifying his passenger. Reuben's jaw was locked tight so that the muscles of his neck stood red and proud, and the veins at his temples throbbed blue with the furious blood that was pumping through them.

The Frenchman started, frightened by the passion he saw before him, confidence draining as he suddenly realised that he had wedded his fortunes – *Diable*, his very *life* – to these complete strangers. As he studied them in his mirror, his vision, now made more acute by the adrenaline surge, piercing the grey half-light of the car cabin, he realised that, come to think of it, they did look rather Jewish. How could he have been so blind? What was he doing here, saving Christ-killers? And at such risk, not just to himself but to his whole family.

As he drove along Perrier shot glances at Reuben. Before too long the sight became too much and, suddenly, without warning, he slammed on the brakes and brought the car skidding to a halt beside the verge. Plucking his rosary from the rear-view mirror, the driver got out and walked to the verge, kneeling down on the wet grass. Reuben spun around, imploring Sarah with a glance for some kind of guidance, all his doubts returning with renewed vigour. What to do if he refuses to go further? Return to the house they had now exposed to one at best unsympathetic, at worst treacherous? Should they run? Not with the children immobile. Nothing to do but sit and hope no-one came along. At least the hour was in their favour.

Perrier prayed, prayed harder than he'd ever done, not even when labour threatened both wife and first-born. His mind was a mosaic of images. The most recurring were of children, his and the ones lying limp in his car. He realised that this was a test of faith, that the temptation to do the wrong thing had to be resisted, the Devil's work. But what was the wrong thing? He closed his eyes, seeking a vision. But nothing came, save the formulation of a question in his mind: *What am I doing here?* The answer emerged, albeit with what seemed to his passengers excruciating slowness. Surely the only Son had arranged for this to come to pass and it was not for Gaston Perrier to question the ineffable workings of the Holy Trinity. No turning back then, and anyway, he couldn't dump the family on the road and abandon them to God-knows-what. That *had* to be wrong, whatever else may come to pass.

Thus rationalised, his mind became certain, and the little man returned wordlessly to the car, turned the ignition key, nodded imperceptibly at Reuben and pressed his foot to the floor, grating through the gears. The old car picked up speed and headed south-west towards Tarbes.

Not a word was spoken but, with the open road stretching out in front and no sign yet of troop movements or major migration traffic,

Reuben tried to relax, despite the oppression caused by Perrier's actions and his failure to explain himself. Yet the vigilance that lurked at the centre of his survival instincts now lay on the surface of Reuben's skin like a soft cloak, light beads of sweat covering his brow and cheeks despite the chill wind that blew through the cracks of the ill-fitting windows and rotten door seals.

"Turn right after the bridge," he ordered Perrier as they crossed over the infant Garonne at the tiny village of Boussens.

"Why, Monsieur? It is so much quicker by this road."

"I do not want to be stopped, so I figure that we would do best to travel by the backwaters, cross-country."

"You know this part of the world well, then?"

"Quite so. I have walked and ridden here a lot. Will you trust me?"

"If you are honest with me."

"It would be better for you if some things remain unsaid between us. You understand?"

"I believe so. You have a route?"

"Yes. We will avoid Tarbes completely, and go by way of Lannemezan, Capvern and Bagnères-de-Bigorre. We then cross the Adour and head due west to Lourdes. First, though, I think we should take a small break. There is a small roadside café about ten kilometres from here."

"A good idea, if I may say so, Monsieur. I need some coffee."

They set off again after a half-hour break. Miriam and Elias were both still dopey, but the adults were fully awake, even if they were not at the same heightened level of consciousness attained by Reuben, rejuvenated and stimulated by the hot caffeine that was now flying round his bloodstream.

They sensed the onrushing Rubicon, the moment of no return when Leah's letter would determine their collective destiny. In the flights from Vienna and Paris all three had felt that Reuben was master of their future, and had planned as carefully as the circumstances would allow. But now things were different. They were hurtling towards the unknown. What if Abbé Lafayette, whose name in copperplate script adorned the front of the envelope, was indifferent to their plight? Or, worse still, was as alive to their race as the priest in Toulouse? What if he didn't exist, and the letter was merely a ruse to get rid of a troublesome visitor?

The temperature in the cabin of the old Citroën rose as the tension mounted. Perrier was aware of it, and he accelerated as the hormonal rush provoked by his own situation began to assume control.

"Slow down," chided Reuben. "These roads can be tricky. They're not well made, and farm vehicles can come at you with little warning. Besides, we could be in for some nasty weather. Looking at the mountains, there's a storm brewing."

Sure enough, large black clouds were gathering about the distant peaks, great rolling banks of menace which, even as they all hunched their shoulders to look up through the low windows of the car, began to empty their load, refracting the rays of sun behind into a curtain of prisms. The winds which accompanied the downpour buffeted the car, hammering it with weighty pulses of water that seemed to demand that the Citroën halt its progress and bow down to the voice of Nature.

But almost as soon as it had reached its full force, it was over, fading into distant rumbles that reminded Sarah of the Vienna Philharmonic under Furtwängler playing Beethoven's Pastoral Symphony in the glorious Musikverein. It all felt so long ago. The rush of nostalgia fused with a sudden remembrance of all that was lost. It brought her to tears of anguish which she swallowed hard to suppress, leaving her closed eyes full but her cheeks dry.

Silence resumed when the thunder subsided, broken only by squelches, rattles and knocking as the old car bucked and bounced through puddles and turned the earth to a light brown mud that splattered up, restricting the view. Primitive wipers battled valiantly, the one in front of Perrier performing just sufficiently to permit him an adequate view of the rustic road.

Each remained locked into their own private world, and it was in a mood of rising apprehension that the filthy car bumped along the waterlogged route that ran due west in the long shadow of the Pyrénées. They traversed the beginning of its foothills before descending into the pilgrimage town that stood as a beacon of hope to all those prepared to suspend rationality and succumb to the belief in its power to alleviate suffering – Lourdes.

The small town was already awake, the day-long services at the grotto of the miraculous apparition having started shortly after dawn.

Reuben had long realised that much would have to be left to chance. Despite the recent break, everyone in the cab was becoming irritable, the expressed need for fresh air and a leg stretch disguising the desire for some sort of conclusion to their journey, as if the very fact of its closure was more important than the manner or the outcome. So he took another gamble.

"Mother, may I have the letter, please?"

He looked once again at the address – *Abbé Lafayette, Basilique de l'Immaculée Conception, Lourdes* – and then turned the envelope around to study the impression made into the wax. He spoke, but it was more like thinking out loud, underscoring the unspoken conspiracy into which Gaston was now being drawn.

"Well, it's decision time. We cannot be certain precisely what the note says; neither do we know what reception we shall receive. We could ignore it and go our own way. Or take the plunge."

The family knew that he was not inviting comment; the driver didn't. Without understanding a word of English, he could tell by the way Rueben toyed with the envelope that he was weighing up the pros and cons of a critical decision. Any residual feelings of subservience finally disappeared beneath the mantle of co-conspirator that had settled over him.

"Look, Monsieur, I haven't risked everything for your courage to fail now. Your only chance to flee is to take every tiny piece of good fortune God and the Holy Mother, begging your pardon, throws your way." Leaning over and peering at the name on the front of the letter, he continued: "He's a priest; he won't betray you. Have faith. You've got this far. Go further."

Reuben was relieved to have the burden of responsibility removed just once from his shoulders. The irony of its coming to pass – a devout Catholic whose entire church was wreathed in the suspicion of Nazi sympathy and collaboration – was not lost on him, and for the first time in a long, long while Mendel was light of heart and spirit.

He laughingly threw an arm around his new friend's slight, bent shoulders: "You're right, *mon vieux*. We'll go straight there. *En avant!*"

The mood in the car relaxed as Gaston pulled away from the increasingly busy Place Peyramale where they had stopped to study the town plan. The family picked up on Reuben's euphoria, sharing in the sudden release that accompanied the decision. Even the children began to rally, shaking off the worst of the effects from the tranquilliser and even urging a family singsong. That, however, was further than the adults were able to go, and Miriam and Elias were mollified by Sarah's concern that 'kind Monsieur Gaston' was tired and needed to think very hard about his driving.

It was not that easy to find their way around. Although police were thin on the ground, apprehension hung in the air like an invisible veil and the town was peppered with those busying themselves only with their own interests. With no map of Lourdes, they sought to recall the plan they'd seen in the square, but it lacked the necessary precision to find exactly where the Basilica was, and it was clear that the number of natives among the various groups of people was in direct inverse proportion to the number of languages they could discern.

But this apparent confusion was balanced by a critical

counterweight – the local population's habituation to strangers. They were well used to explaining directions by sign and the minimum of verbal guidance. So, steeling themselves against the alarm being immediately raised, Perrier pulled up beside an old man sitting on a bench at the roadside and Reuben, accentuating the German in his French, approached him and said in a quizzical tone enhanced by shrugged shoulders and a rapid move of the head from left to right, *"Basilique de l'Immaculée Conception, s'il vous plaît?"*

The veteran Lourdois turned his sun-beaten, wizened, toothless face towards them. Taciturnly, in an inimitably impenetrable accent, part Catalan, part French, he gestured them a few turnings back off the road they'd just travelled, his expression betraying his astonishment that more stupid pilgrims had missed the spiritual heart of the town.

Finally, after what already seemed like a full day's travel but which, in fact, had taken them only until mid-morning, the tired Citroën came to a rest outside the Basilica.

Reuben had already decided what to do. Without prevarication, he would go straight to the Abbé and present the letter. But first, another severing.

"Gaston, this is where we must part. We will need to cross the border as pilgrims among a host of other pilgrims, and besides, you must get back to Toulouse before curfew. I have no words to express our gratitude but here, this is the fare we agreed, plus a little on top, and the key to our house. The rent is paid for five years. I hope that someday we may meet in happier times. Go in health, my friend."

"Thank you, Monsieur. I, too, hope that a better world may see our rendezvous."

Sarah came up to the little, dishevelled chauffeur and threw her arms around him, burying her face in his neck. "Thank you," she whispered in his ear, her voice breaking with emotion. "Take care of our little home. We look forward to seeing you there when this is all over. And if … if we don't return then perhaps you'll plant a peach tree, and when you taste its fruit for one small moment you will maybe remember us, no?"

He could say nothing, but with eyes rimmed with red he went over to Leah and Moses, shaking their hands while gently rustling the children's hair. He turned and, with no glance over his shoulder, slid into the driver's seat, revved the engine … and was gone. They all watched the car until it disappeared from view, obscured by an evergreen cluster that hung over the road at a gentle right-hand bend.

Leah placed a restraining hand on Reuben's arm. "Reuben, I'm going to go in, not you. After all, I got the letter and it may mention me. Besides, I feel, well, you know, parental, as if this is my baby, my contribution – so I'd like to see it through."

Even Moses couldn't argue, his instantaneous change of hue owing more to dread than rage, draining blood from his face and temples.

Reuben saw the strength of her position and handed back the precious envelope. As one, the family watched her as she pulled the hood of her brown cape up over her head and strode purposefully off towards the door, visibly shuddering as she mingled with other pilgrims, on crutches, deformed, rotten with disease, entering to say the rosary in the hope of intercession.

With the experience of Toulouse behind her, she was now steeled against the expectation of being overwhelmed. So she was taken aback when the atmosphere was completely the opposite: an air of quiet contemplation filled the domed building, the silence broken only by the insistent, dull muttering of the devout throng that knelt at timeworn pews or waited for a confessional booth to be vacated. Leah quickly sized up the building, her only interest being where the Abbé might be found. Feigning prayer, her hands open-webbed over her eyes, she watched to see from where sacristan or curate emerged or which transept they used when leaving the Basilica. Making her decision quickly, she moved up the nave and took a left at the chancel before walking boldly towards a large door, knocking and entering without being invited.

"Can we help you, Madame?" enquired the less surprised of the two young curates who were busy preparing for the next Mass.

"Forgive the intrusion, Father," she began, instinctively looking towards the meeker of the two. "I am looking for Abbé Lafayette."

"He, he's not here, I'm afraid," the one she looked at replied haltingly.

"Who wants to know?" the other demanded brusquely in a tone that distinguished him immediately as assertive, if not precisely rude.

"Whom do I have the privilege of addressing, Sir?"

"Father Patrice Duplessis, at your service. And you, Madame?"

"Marie Rodrigue."

"And what is it you require of the Abbé?"

"I have a letter of introduction from the Cathedral at Toulouse. My family and I wish to make a pilgrimage to Santiago and are given to understand that he has a brother who could give us sanctuary."

"I see. Another one, eh?" continued a sceptical Duplessis. "Well, we are not expecting him back for a while, he's a little, er, frail these days. Why don't you leave your letter with me and I'll make sure he sees it when he returns? Come back after lunch, at about two o'clock."

"No disrespect, Sir, but I would prefer to keep the letter with me, if you don't mind. Thank you for your time and advice. I shall return later."

"As you wish. Until then, Madame."

He bowed a cursory, almost Teutonic bow and returned to his work. His colleague, who had during this brief exchange been fixing Duplessis with an icy stare, darted forwards to open the door for Leah.

"I shall walk you to the side door, Madame Rodrigue, and you can avoid the other worshippers." He took her rather too familiarly by the elbow and ushered her away. "This way, if you please. If I may make a suggestion, you are clearly tired from a long journey, so I think you will find the air of our peaceful graveyard rather restful. Try that seat over there, I beg you, just for a few moments, by that fresh grave. *Adieu.*"

He was pointing to a bench that sat in the shadow of the dome. Leah didn't understand his insistence but decided to humour him. "Will I not see you later, Father?"

"I do hope not."

She was completely nonplussed, aware that there was clearly some subtext being spoken but in a foreign tongue of which she was entirely ignorant. When the curate had gone back inside she went round to the front to meet up with the others, quickly appraising them of the situation.

Reuben was perplexed, unable to understand Leah's report. But his instincts were sharp, and he decided to investigate the graveyard. "Which bench, Mama?" he asked.

Leah led him towards the seat and the two of them sat down. He urged her to repeat the conversation once again, trying to find the Rosetta Stone that would reveal the true meaning of the several elliptical comments. Leah had recounted accurately, but he didn't get it; not, that is, until after a good five minutes in quiet contemplation he got up and paced back and forth along the path. As he walked he looked down to the freshly turned earth where a very recent interment had taken place. He froze as he saw one word, the surname of the deceased.

Lafayette.

"Mama, we're going. Now!"

She followed his gaze, stifling an involuntary scream as she instantly understood the significance of what he had concluded: the treacherous Duplessis – his instant lie about the Abbé – the planned arrest – the gentle, anonymous second curate – his cryptic attempt to expiate the sin of his colleague.

Hand-in-hand, they walked briskly from the graveyard and hurried to meet the others. Reuben called on them all to follow him. He sought out a crowd, instinctively following a large group headed towards the dark Grotto at Massabielle where Bernadette met with her visions, the emotional epicentre of the town.

Passion filled the air, as supplications mingled with the grief that negates faith. The atmosphere was thick with suffering as the lame and the diseased threw themselves on divine mercy, drinking deeply at the last watering hole before the endless desert of their own mortality.

So no-one would notice them as they sat to take stock. But in truth there were no longer any options.

"Our only hope is Lafayette's brother in Santiago. We're going to have to make our own way there, trusting to the training we all underwent in Toulouse. This will not be easy. But we've got this far, so one more heave and we should make it. We'll stay until dusk and follow the faithful out of town, then head south towards the mountains."

All his careful planning now came to the fore; the battered paper on which he'd sketched the rough map of the Pyrénées south of Lourdes was all that lay between them and capture, a passport not to any country, but to life itself.

For Moses especially, this was a return to an earlier time, one he had thought had passed him by forever. His bald head was now balanced with a full silver beard. Taken with the watery eyes, the image that would later come to Reuben was of the old man in de la Tour's *Saint Joseph Charpentier*, a kind of infinite sadness permeating his whole being, as though he knew the future. For now, the remembrance of a previous flight energised Moses, the power of recall fuelling a resurgence of prior authority.

"We can't just go. We need some basic supplies. It will be cold on the mountains, Mother and I are not young, neither are the children strong enough to maintain a rapid pace. We should buy some blankets and a tent, if we can find them, plus matches. If we could lay hands on a proper map and compass, all the better. You and Sarah will have to carry a rucksack as well as your cases. That means the violin will have to go, although it might make good firewood."

"Papa, you're right in every respect but one. I can't let go the violin; I'd rather chuck my suitcase. Don't ask me why, but I feel that the Germans, for all Hitler's philistinism, have produced some of the greatest musicians the world has seen. Perhaps if they see the fiddle, they may look on us a little kindlier than might otherwise be the case. I'll manage, somehow.

"Will you go and buy the provisions? As your French is not so good, they're more likely to take you for a foreign pilgrim and ask fewer questions. Pretend that you're going to the mountains to commune with God! You know, hands clasped in prayer, and a wet-eyed, beatific look of holiness and awe."

Moses feigned the prescribed expression. Despite their dire circumstances, the family had to suppress the hilarity that often accompanies stress. The old man was not convinced. "What on earth would my father, may his dear soul rest in peace, think of all this?"

"Take Elias with you. A grandfather and grandson on a pilgrimage could help, and in any event, you'll need him to carry stuff. We will mingle with the crowds here. Be quick!"

So off they went, hand-in-hand, the newly invigorated ancient and his excited young assistant. Meanwhile, Leah, Sarah, Miriam and Reuben returned to the permanent crowd around the Grotto, sitting quietly, slightly to one side so that they might feign devotion while watching for the return of the other two.

By now, the afternoon was wearing on, the winter sun sinking into the Atlantic, and the danger was growing that they would draw attention to themselves, the only ones not praying among the mass of supplicants for mercy. Reuben's mind was furiously active, trying to calculate how far out of town they might get on foot before curfew.

He decided to gamble.

"I'm going to get a taxi to take us to the town of Cauterets. We'll say we have lodgings there. If we can't find anywhere, we will sleep in the open. There are some caves not too far from there and we might be able to find one if it's not too late."

That this was not rejected out of hand, that the notion of this noble, cultured family skulking in the caves of an unknown wilderness was not utterly absurd, served only to prove how far they had fallen.

Before any discussion could be joined, he walked off in search of a cab. Lourdes was full to overflowing, a mixture of refugees, devotees and military on the move, and those inhabitants with cars and the good fortune of a source for petrol could make some much needed cash, as any pretence at regulation had long since broken down.

And still the auguries were deceptively good, teasing them along the road to salvation. For just as Moses and Elias were returning with some provisions, he found someone prepared to take them the thirty or so kilometres.

A rapid passage of francs accompanied the bundling of people and baggage into another ancient Citroën. The driver (an educated man embittered by his need to be a servant to the debris which regularly washed up on the shores of his holy town) started the car and they lurched away from the roadside. Moving with sufficient speed to leave town, but without so much fuss as to attract attention, they journeyed in oppressive silence through the dank afternoon clouds that rolled from the mountains in front of them, mountains that were at once the hope of freedom and a barrier to it. Oblivious to the raw beauty of the torrential Gave de Cauterets, through whose gorge the rough minor road they travelled cut, they only had private thoughts of the next rung on their ladder of descent.

"Your hotel, Monsieur?" their surly chauffeur asked finally as the journey came towards its close.

"Just drop us in the town square and we'll walk from there, if you please."

"As you wish. But hurry up, the curfew will be shortly upon us and I must get back to Lourdes."

They screeched to a halt near the old spa. "*Voilà!* We are here. Out you get, quick as you can." They had barely closed the boot before the car revved up and tore away from them, leaving them standing beside the road surrounded by their luggage and the bag containing a small tent, blankets and the other supplies Moses had just bought.

"Papa and I will wait here with the children. Sarah and Leah, you try to find a room or two for us to sleep in. I reckon we have about an hour. If you don't have any luck, we will head out of town tonight. Here, take some money in case you need to tip someone. Quick! Go! Hurry!"

Fortunately, a small auberge down an unlit alley had one twin room available. Despite her exposure to the holiest of pilgrims, *la patronne* was no stranger to sharp-edged negotiation, especially in a seller's market. The cost was disproportionate to the facility provided – but not to the brief respite it afforded the Mendels who, as soon as they were safely ensconced behind the door, collapsed into that peculiar realm of fatigue familiar only to those exhausted by prolonged pressure.

Knowing that this could be their last shelter for some nights, they settled quickly, allowing no time to unwind. Explaining their need for an early night in terms of the exciting trip to the mountains the following day, the two single beds were pushed together to accommodate Leah, Moses and the two children, while Sarah took the battered old armchair and Reuben the floor.

Sleep was slight, the accumulation of strange noises disturbing to all but Miriam and Elias, who were gone just as soon as their head hit the bolster. But even in that half-life between waking and sleep, the adults allowed themselves to reflect on how they had come to be here, on those they had lost or from whom they were parted, on the unknowable adversity that lay just beyond the sunrise on those slopes in whose towering shade they slumbered.

Dawn broke through the snow-laden clouds that shrouded the peaks, and the family rose with it. They hastily worked out the minimum that could be carried and decided on the two largest cases, the new bag and the violin. An impromptu rota would emerge as they walked.

The traditional breakfast was downed rapidly; the boiling coffee scalded the adults awake while sweet hot chocolate kick-started the children. Fresh baguettes and croissants were heaped with butter and strawberry jam to pile on the necessary calories (and those that weren't were pocketed for later consumption). A perfunctory *"Au revoir"* – and they were gone.

Reuben reckoned that the walk was about seventy kilometres and would climb about fifteen hundred metres to where they would first try to cross the border, around Port de Boucharo, close to the vast limestone amphitheatre Cirque de Gavarnie and, unbeknownst to him, a centuries-old route between France and Spain, much favoured by smugglers and other assorted villains. He had designated a route that would keep them to the graduated lower lands of the range, so they headed due south from the village, following his rough sketch that signified where the Lutour waterfall left the Gave de Cauterets and plunged to its eponymous valley. From there they would walk through the shadowed valleys of Ossue and Espécières, circumnavigating the Lac d'Estom, rising all the while towards the Pic de Tantes, the frontier – and freedom.

On his recce, he had dared not go too close to the border post, so he would be guessing precisely what to do. But his faith in the twin expediencies of luck and money was resolute, and he believed that the creativity which had imbued his leadership of the family would be robust enough to react to whatever challenges lay ahead.

The greatest imperative was the decision of how far and how fast to push the others. Of Sarah, he was confident; but the others? His parents were old; the children weaker than they should be at their age. The climb was slow and steady, but it was a climb nonetheless, and in mountain air more rarefied than they were used to. So, seventy kilometres in how long?

In the end, Reuben settled for the pragmatic solution: wait and see, push – but not too hard – then take a view and judge when refreshment and rest should be earned, when it should be offered as a reward. He hated thinking like this, but it was the only way he could see to manage the fleeing pack. He couldn't be certain about trusting *la patronne*; she could easily have raised the alarm if she was at all suspicious. But he rationalised that worry away on the basis that, were it so, there could be no flight, and they would be trapped soon. Ergo, it was not so. Nevertheless, the sooner they were off the ill-kempt road out of Cauterets, the better, so he hurried them along.

Since their arrival in Paris, when his responsibility for the family finally became absolute and the deterioration in the political and diplomatic climate demanded forward planning, he had been given to reflecting on the importance of options, of having a choice at any given moment. During the long nights, the silence of the sleeping house had oppressed him, knowing that their security was in his hands. He vowed that whenever and wherever it was within his power he would bring about a plurality of directions, a kind of self-proliferating insurance which would always create its own set of actions, any one of which they could elect to pursue. So it was with the route to salvation.

Although he had not shared it with them, his cold calculation went along these lines: *If the border is unprotected, we cross, heading overland for Santiago, Lafayette's brother – and sanctuary. If it is protected, I will send Father ahead with money. He's the oldest, therefore more likely to earn respect and sympathy. Also, his language skills are the least reliable, therefore easier to bore an apathetic guard. Last, he is the least indispensable so that if he is arrested, the rest are relatively unscathed.* His guilty heart missed a beat as the vicious truth of his analysis cut a swathe through his soul, but the intellect was dominant and he knew it to be right.

Finally, what if the border were unpassable at any point within reach? The choice was clear: stay, thanking Nature that when ancient Iberian island collided with mainland Europe and forged the Pyrénées, it determined that the new range would be composed in part from porous limestone, empowering millennia of wind and water to burrow deep towards the earth's mantle, creating cavernous havens for the cold and wet, the lost and the hunted.

They would revert to an ancestry far more distant than Skidel, more in keeping with the romantic harking back of Jack London's Buck that had come to him under the wedding canopy in that former life, long since dead, when the feast that preceded their present famine was upon them. Nothing had readied them for a troglodyte existence – and he knew how hard it would be. But he reasoned that if ancient ancestors, far less sophisticated and wise than he, had managed to build viable domestic units over thousands of years, then should not the Mendels (at least for the few short months that he hoped were all that was necessary) be able to survive secluded in the dark beneath the tumultuous surface?

Was this madness? Of course it was. But then the world in which they had been swept up was insane. Whatever similarities it once had shared with perceived normality were now gone. New paradigms demand new values, new thinking, new directions. The old is poisonous, hobbling and dangerously beguiling.

Looking back from days of comfort, peace and plenty, who can say how fanciful was the notion that these six, six of millions plucked from the safety of the known and planted in a wilderness where nothing was familiar, could prepare to survive savage days exposed to Nature's forces? But then what know we of such times, of what *we* would do if hurled back to rely upon long suppressed instincts of survival, conjured from the furthest reaches of the spirit by the desperate summons of necessity?

In more peaceful times the thought of a simpler life had appeared seductive. To live away from the bustle of Vienna, to breathe clean and tranquil air had appealed, especially to Sarah. She romanced the prospect: to walk on hills, to spot the buzzard, kite and eagle wheel wing-stretched on high thermals, to know the call of a host of animals, the scent and taste of a thousand flowers and fruits.

But now, as they trudged their way through torrent-forged valleys and churned up muddied banks and across soggy foothills, there was no time to relish their surroundings – for this was no voluntary ascent to a higher, more cherishable life but a forced climb away from death. Progress was slow, so that the first half-day took them little further than the beginning of the Vallée du Lutour. Reuben was relieved in one way – he now knew what their pace would be, reckoning that two more nights would get them to the border. Now he calculated how they would need to eke out their food, water being no problem with the many streams that peppered their path.

Reuben had originally made some key milestones by which to mark their route, keeping the massive sentinel of the towering snow-clad Vignemale like a lowering Pole Star diagonally to their right at south-south-west as they bore due south. With only the rough sketch and its broad-brush features and inaccurate scale to guide him, he would have doubted his ability to get to Boucharo. But Moses had acquired a second-hand map, albeit of uncertain vintage and, marking on it the twin peaks of Vignemale and Monte Perdido in whose bisection the intended crossing point approximately stood, Reuben now felt a little more confident about their goal.

So on they ploughed, increasingly caked in mud as the slush and rain cohered beneath their feet, sucking at their ankles to restrain them, rendering Reuben's initial estimates of journey length absurd. Soon enough the diversions planned to keep them all from thinking of how tired they were began to pall, an entire repertoire of songs exhausted within a couple of hours, and the concentration required to keep a foothold precluding the enjoyment of their surroundings or the attention necessary to spot a spectacular act of nature.

They rested frequently, often beside a stream to drink. At around four in the afternoon he called a halt. The light was already failing and he had spotted an inviting cave opening and went to explore. It seemed clear, no debris to suggest recent occupants, so he lit a fire about two metres inside its mouth and went to collect the others. The sight of the warm fire had precisely the effect he had intended, the others rushing towards its welcoming flicker, a beacon that signified some kind of arrival and putting all their travails behind them for that moment.

Food was still not a problem, their supplies both bought and snaffled sufficient to satisfy a hunger in any event diminished by the fatigue of the climb. They ate little, and in silence, each one relishing the soothing crackle of the dry sticks that they had all gathered to stoke the fire, gazing distractedly into the flames and dreaming of – who knows what? – but better, warmer, safer times, long gone, all lost.

In no time they were asleep.

"Raus! Raus! Juden, raus!"

Reuben was first to his feet, crouching like the caged animal he was, shoulders hunched up behind his ears. Despite the now cold cave, sweat came immediately to his brow, beading at his temples. He motioned silence to his family.

But it was too late.

"We know you are in there. Come out – no harm will come to you. You have the word of honour of a soldier of the Reich. If you do not come out by the time I have counted to five, we shall come in and get you. *Ein!*"

They looked at one another, Sarah gathering Miriam and Elias to her, Leah holding Moses.

"Zwei!"

All of them turned to Reuben, who was glancing around and behind him, cursing silently that he had led them into a trap, or at least had not checked to see where the cave led.

"Drei!"

"There's no choice. We have to go with them. Gather our belongings; at least if we're carrying them, they'll know we're not armed. Children, this is the next stage of our great adventure. Try not to be afraid; they may be loud and rough but they will not harm us. Alright?"

"Yes, Daddy," they chorused.

"Vier!"

"We are coming out. We have children with us."

"Schnell! We don't have all day. You've wasted enough of our time already."

The six emerged from the cave to be confronted by three Wehrmacht soldiers from one of the snatch squads patrolling the border region. Rifles pointed straight at their heads.

"Stupid Jews! Shouldn't have built a fire so close to the mouth of the cave. March down the hill, and make sure you don't fall over."

Standing on the unmade path they had travelled along the previous day was an army truck, wheels caked with mud where it had traversed many fields and plunged through puddles and fords, engine running and a cloud of blue smoke visible as the fumes hit the cold Pyrénean air.

Barely able to keep their footing under the pressure of the required speed, they all slipped and slid, coerced by a repetitive *"Schnell!"* shrieked at them by the corporal. The children were lagging; one of the patrol pushed his gun up to the shoulder and scooped one under each arm and ran in front of the others to make sure they won the race.

Giggling half through fear and half through exhilaration from the rush down the hill, the sound of childish laughter jangling across the valley jarred with their circumstances, a cracked bell tolling flat but loud and long.

The gentleness of the Nazi conduct only served to beguile them for what would soon happen. But for now they accepted it as the norm, no more than should be expected from the people who gave the world Goethe and Schiller, Bach and Beethoven.

Their belongings were thrown in the back of the truck and they were pushed up into it, to sit on the narrow benches that ran up either side. Two soldiers sat at the end by the open door, the other got in the front to drive.

The lorry roared off, hurtling down towards Cauterets, hurling them about so that they cowered in the corner and tried to get some purchase by huddling together in a complex knot. Moses had his arm thrown tightly around Leah, their eyes closed to stave off the sight of their grandchildren locked terrified between Sarah and Reuben, small dark faces splattered with mud and terrorised eyes ringed black with fatigue.

"Where are you taking us, please?" Sarah finally asked.

"You speak good German."

"We're from Vienna."

"Ach, Jews from Austria, might have guessed. Thought you could escape the Führer, eh? Huh!"

"So, where are we going … Sir?" Reuben pushed, remembering just in time the subservience he learned in Marseille.

Steadying himself by holding the metal supports for the canvas roof, the younger of the two soldiers went straight up to him and leaned forward. He stared straight into his eyes, their noses almost touching as he spat with a venom beyond contempt: "You will learn one thing quickly: in the Reich, Jews have no rights to anything, especially answers. Understand?"

The initial belief that it may not be too bad withered before such unbridled hatred. With no way to see where they were going, they could only try to image the journey in reverse. Clearly they were headed back to the place of their last shelter. But then?

The family fell into an oppressive silence, absolute but for the insistent gunning of the engine as it was driven at breakneck pace on roads not built for speed. Moses had begun to think about bribing their way out of it. He tried to plant the thought in Reuben with an extraordinary smattering of French and his own brand of Yiddish, accompanied by none-too-subtle facial and hand gestures. A barked "No talking!" put a stop to it. Uneasy quiet dominated once again.

Reuben's mind was working overtime, attempting to trace their journey against his earlier voyage around the area. But it was impossible, and after an hour of trying and focusing on keeping the children from falling, he lapsed into a kind of trance, allowing events to unfold in their own time and their own way. Occasionally he and Sarah exchanged glances, their fingers entwined behind as they encircled Miriam and Elias. But the looks were devoid of meaning, the perfect manifestation of impotence which, for the first time in their flight, had now utterly overtaken them.

Suddenly the truck screamed to a halt. Nervous, they awaited developments, relieved at least that the tossing and pitching had ceased and they could gather their breath. One guard remained while the other could be overheard in conversation with the driver. They could work out neither where they were, nor precisely what was happening as voices were muffled and the view out the back still obscured by a dark green tarpaulin. After a few moments it was thrown open and another family – a mother, father and two infants – similarly beset with the haunted look of all the hunted, were driven into the truck, their cases chucked in after them.

The missing soldier returned to his station, the engine was restarted, gears engaged, and they were off again. Reuben guessed that they had indeed been in Cauterets, confident that, in the glance available as the new prisoners entered, he had recognised the old spa. Assuming he was right, he tried to imagine the journey. They were heading north, back along the road that led to Lourdes via Argelès.

But then they veered left and, judging by the undulating ground that exaggerated the absence of suspension, were headed if not precisely cross-country then certainly along ill-kempt roads, unmade and traversed by iron-wheeled agricultural vehicles that churned to mud their customary paths.

They were now travelling west-north-west, away from the route with which Reuben was familiar. No more words were exchanged. The absence of conversation was tyrannical, bearing down on them. For another hour it prevailed, as the noise of the engine receded into the background, leaving a space that was filled with a claustrophobic pressure. Their individual reflections were fractured only by futile attempts at eye contact and at keeping some semblance of balance as the army truck was thrown about by the furious velocity and appalling terrain.

Eventually Sarah broke the untranquil quiet, addressing the guard sitting nearest her, the one who had not yet had the opportunity to display his hatred. "Sir, the children need a drink of water and to go to the toilet. Would it be possible to stop for a moment, please?"

His look made her blood freeze, for it bore the impress of uttermost contempt as though she barely existed, a disdain reared on the drip-feed exposure first to ridicule, then to fury, last to unconfined hatred, its expression coming in the guttural accents of the southern German peasantry. "Let 'em drink their own piss, we're not stopping."

"But, Sir…"

Sarah never saw the punch coming, failed to appreciate either the risk or the significance of his having laid his gun to one side. He brought his right hand from behind his left shoulder, catching her with tensed knuckles full on the right side of her face, spinning her round, felling her instantly. Reuben instinctively sprang to her defence, but his leap was taken as an attack by the other guard who, rising quickly, swung his rifle at him, catching him on the left temple and stunning him.

"For God's sake," wailed the woman from the new family,

clutching her children to her breast. "Sit down and shut up or we're all dead!"

Once more silence settled on the prisoners, four children looking blankly for succour from six adults who, for the first time in their young lives, were unable to provide it. Sarah and Reuben recovered themselves soon enough, albeit nursing cuts and bruises. But what actually hurt was the atomic shock of this first exposure to the unrestrained hatred they had as yet avoided. Even though Nazism had marched triumphantly across Europe, only now were they swept into its blood-soaked hand, ready to be crushed by its unforgiving grip.

And still the lorry rocked and bucked over the Pyrénean landscape, throwing its cargo across a filthy mud-caked floor, its driver insensible to the discomfort and fear that each successive pitching exacerbated.

Another hour and more passed. They settled into a kind of ennui, a lassitude that numbed their thought processes, infecting them as if it were a virus, stilling the body, sapping the will, so that when the truck finally ground to a halt it took them a while to recognise that fact, and to prepare for disembarking.

Once more they heard the words that spelled extinction for millions:

"Raus! Raus! Juden, raus!"

Intermezzo #1

Dieser Weg für die traurige Stadt,
Dieser Weg für ewiges Erleiden,
Dieser Weg, die vergessenen Leute zu verbinden ...
Verlassen Sie alle Hoffnung, Sie wer betreten!

This is a world where nothing
that ever went before means *anything.*

Forget comfort and safety.

And the power of money.

Disabuse yourself of the notion that you might be master of your
own destiny.

All
that
was
order
is
now
chaos.

All
that
was
predictable
is
reduced
to
mere
caprice.

All that was known must be forgotten.

To believe in justice is weakness.

Yearning

for

freedom

is

delusion.

Remembering sufficient food brings madness.

Hoping for life is fruitless …

and for release, futile.

In this world, time is measured on scales unknown.
Three hours at attention in the snow is without end.

Each day

lasts

                                                              a

life-

                        time,

                                          fading

            into

                                          the

next,

their only separation
a terror-soaked night with fractured dreams of better times,
            drenched in the enervating certainty
                  of tomorrow's violence,
                              and probable death.

                              The agonies of hunger,
                  sickness,
exhaustion
            lacerate the soul with serrated barbs,
tearing at the essence,
                              ribboning identity.

Sometimes, the 'lucky' times, it merely throbs, nagging away in
                  deep, bleak background.

More often,
it shrieks between the ears,
driving scalding stakes through the eyes
to burn the brain.

Pass through this frontier post,
enter a land
whose only escape is death.

Even for those whose life
is not extinguished there.

Read not only the lines, but what lurks between,

beyond the compass of vocabulary,

in that place where words lose all their value,

a currency devalued to dross,

castrated by stunning inadequacy in the face

of that which demands description,

yet whose very nature defies it.

And if you chance upon a remote oasis
during this benighted journey,

pause

and

reflect

for a while

on
a
world
beyond
words.

Chapter 12

They had arrived at Gurs. Built for refugees from the Spanish Civil War, it was now 'home' to several thousand other Mendels, those who had sought freedom and safety, only to be trapped at the last.

The camp, whose vista of hundreds of low huts greeted them as they were turfed mercilessly from the truck, nestled in the shade of the Pyrénées on a low plateau, north of Oloron-Sainte-Marie. It was their first sight of barbed wire enclosures, of the disconnected walking aimlessly, of unvarnished squalor, of those with too little food and too few clothes, of the ravages of disease. It was a first sight of what the rest of their lives would be.

But it was also a deception. For here, in the brooding shadow of the mountains, a chaotic surface belied the malign, organised schizophrenia that lurked beneath. It was the duality in the dark heart of the camps, whether transit, concentration, labour or death, which would confuse, shock and ultimately shatter the vast preponderance of their inhabitants.

They were herded into one of the huts, already full to overflowing. Their first exposure to the filth, the smell, the hollow look of the camp dweller was a hammer-blow, defying comprehension, a script written in a language whose alphabet, let alone vocabulary, was unknown.

It was all part of the diabolic plan, seducing them into an inferior normality with the beguiling promise of safety, even while acknowledging the poverty of their surroundings. The German strategy was simple: design a project so beyond the boundaries of belief that it would fail to occur to even the most unreconstructed pessimist, the severest, most vitriolic critic of Aryanism. Complement it with a smooth reassurance whose deceit would become apparent only when absolute defencelessness had set in and flight was impossible, partly because of geography, mostly because of the negation of individual will, the complete devastation of self and soul.

So the process began its work upon the Mendels. They queued to eat. They queued to wash. They queued to defecate. But even at this shuffling-off of the last trappings of decent, comfortable bourgeois lives, so the double blind kicked in. For within Gurs, culture did not merely bloom, it burgeoned, exploded, like flowers exuding scent when the season is ripe and their time has come.

Here, in the antechamber of hell, where overcrowded barrack huts slept sixty, on thin, rank mattresses, where one thousand shared eight taps of burning ice-cold water and eight stinking latrines, here the arts flourished, allowing the spirit to escape, if not the body. Productions of Ibsen and Shakespeare, Schubert song cycles, cabaret revues, magic shows, piano recitals and chamber music. So beguiling, so enriching that even the camp officials and local population came in order that they, too, might for a few moments commune with the best of what we are and forget the bestiality that roundly beset their lives.

The sight of Reuben's violin case was a passport to the centre of this perversity. His musical pedigree took him into the inner circle of artists who re-created themselves, throwing off the luxurious apparel of ego and a dependency upon idolisation to become intimate performers, to play just for the purity of the quest for perfection, isolated from the need to earn, the plaudits of the press, the baying of the crowd; to play just for the joy that can come when, *in extremis*, a glimpse is won of better times and softer climes.

To Reuben, it was like spinning back through the last twenty-five years to a time when his music brought some solace to his comrades in the trenches. And he repeated much of that repertoire. Folk tunes, praise songs and lamentations recalled ancestral hearths, whether primitive *shtetl* or middleclass townhouse, keeping at bay for a short time the icy blast through broken window, the nagging hunger, the perpetual fear, and delivering a kind of consolation, though fragmented through the prism of their shared suffering.

So for a while, even here, they were able to settle down, accustoming themselves to their new way of life, shorn of all comfort, security, certainty for the future. Instead they learned swiftly that to live for the day was to *live*. With the sight of the camp being steadily emptied by trains taking inmates 'to the east for resettlement in labour camps', they knew that each single day, each single *hour*, that they remained there they were not en route to some nameless unknown destination. This was their only comfort.

Reuben had seen in Marseille and Toulouse lines of broken Jews queuing for trains just like these, had heard rumours of identical exercises across France, and even of the wholesale destruction of the ancient Jewish communities of eastern Europe. All this told him one thing: they were inextricably part of some massive design, a schematic ensnaring the whole continent.

And there was no escaping its all-seeing eye, its all-grasping hand. As he watched the population of Gurs drift silently away, no word of protest, no howl of rage at the encroaching dark, borne into the night on trains whose rattle knelled like old bones in a wooden coffin, Reuben knew, *knew* with a certainty which brooked no denial, that they too would leave the camp, luggage in tow and heads bowed, their bruises fresh and the past closed down behind them with the finality of a funeral.

Flight was not an option.

"Of course I thought about it. But a moment's consideration revealed its impossibility. To get myself, even Sarah, out was extremely hazardous, but not utter fantasy. But the children? Mama? Papa? No chance. And to leave them ... Well, who could even contemplate such a thing? It was a feeling of total entrapment, along with an inkling of foolish hope that the most pessimistic outcome

might yet prove untrue."

When he calculated their time was close, he took up his violin as the autumnal afternoon wore on. Impromptu, he started to play Bach, the giant Partita with which he had serenaded Vienna to announce his recovery and arrival. But now, in these surroundings, it took on new meanings of rage and grief, desperation and loss, dispossession and, above all, panic for the imperilled future of the children. There in the midst of a condemned crowd that emerged wraith-like from the gathering gloom and encircled him, crouching, sitting, lying on the freezing ground, he launched into the Chaconne. The vast movement assumed the appearance of a ghost parade, of ancients long gone, and those still fresh and raw in the mind; an endless catalogue, ragged with the sobbing of the heart-sore, a wake-dirge for the past and what was yet to come. Edges were sharp, and where *portamento* might once have glided notes together to soften the rises and falls, now they leapt *staccato*, barbed and brutal. The sound was amplified by the still air, seeming to echo off the mountains and hang in the cold like frost-sparkle so that, at the end, when the bow had reached the bottom of the down stroke and the last tremolo had been wrung from the music by the vibrato pressure of an iron-tough finger, the silence was absolute, and the living dead dissolved back into the twilight, as though the music had wept valediction for them.

Before they settled to yet another restless sleep, he told them, "We will soon be moved on, a long train ride, very uncomfortable. We must try to stick together, or at least in pairs, so that none of us is alone. If one gets separated, they must try to find the others, not the other way round, as we dare not split up. Children, one of you will go with Mother, the other with Grandma; you can decide between you."

His daughter looked up at him with black eyes, her face gaunt with hunger, cheeks sunken. Such was the insidious nature of their decline that they were generally oblivious to each other's foetid state, but Reuben couldn't help but notice the filth that matted her hair and was ingrained in the once-soft skin.

"Daddy, Elias should go with Mummy. He *is* younger, and anyway, I can look after Grandpa."

"At that moment, it was all I could do to stop myself crying. It seemed an angelic thing for her to say, especially in such a state. I hugged her hard then, and sometimes it's as if I still feel her in my arms."

The end of October 1943 dawned grey with impending snow. Laden clouds obliterated the mountains, ready to weep their load upon the next train that had drawn up to the sidings to await its cargo of human livestock.

The mixed force of Vichy militiamen and Nazi troops came early for them, before the troubled sleep had left their eyes. They moved through the huts, an unspoken understanding loitered among the final remnants of the thousands that had passed through Gurs in the last three years that now was *their* time to depart.

The practice was well-established, a potent mixture of cajoling, coercion – and undiluted cruelty.

"Only one bag, Jews, only one bag!"

"That includes the fucking fiddle. Choose. NOW!"

Quickly, Reuben emptied half the contents of his battered valise indiscriminately on to the floor of the hut and pushed the violin case into it, forcing it closed and trusting to the fealty of the old locks.

They joined a long queue of the forsaken, standing beside the railway spur that led from the camp far into the distance. The goods train was familiar, a regular visitor since long before the Mendels had taken up their forced tenancy. In truth they had remained indifferent to the actuality of boarding and travelling, not allowing themselves to dwell on something that may not come to pass, what with the rumours of German defeat in North Africa and Russia circulating, accompanied as ever by the ubiquitous dream of an imminent invasion by the Allies.

But now there was no avoidance, either emotional or physical;

and Reuben was only dimly conscious that he, like the lines he'd espied on his search for escape, was now shuffling, worldly goods in one bag, towards a cattle wagon.

The entry was unforgiving.

"Schnell, Juden, schnell!"

Even though they might be incapacitated, old or feeble, blows rained down on the shoulders of those who hesitated.

Reuben lifted Sarah up so that he could pass the children to her. Then he pushed Leah into the train, and lastly his elderly father. Finally he yanked himself up and in. He had barely pulled himself clear of the sliding door when it began to scream in its rusted groove as it was forced rapidly shut. And then, in the immediate silence that followed the deadening thud of bolts being thrown, the unmistakable rattle of chains and padlocks.

The lash of dark caused a moment of recoil. When their eyes became accustomed, they looked around and realised the new depths to which they had sunk.

There must have been thirty, maybe forty, others with them. Little room to lie down properly, some token straw to soften the wooden floor. No light, save that from a small grilled window at the top of one side of the wagon and whatever could seep in where the timbers of the wagon had warped through years of exposure to wind and rain. At one end, an empty bucket whose purpose was clear; beside it a barrel of water, bound to spill the moment motion began.

Reuben gathered his wits. Last in, there was precious little wall space, but he got the family to sit down quickly, backs against the door, trying to claim a piece of territory.

The clanking of captivity receded up the line. Sarah settled Miriam and Elias as best she could, exchanging dimly realisable glances with Leah and Reuben. Terror was now etched visibly on their faces, an acid gnawing eating at their insides as the wretchedness of the imminent journey became apparent.

The wailing started almost in unison with the first pull of the engine, jolting those who still stood, causing them to grab their neighbour to avoid falling. Despite the outside temperature, the heat began to rise as the crying started, sweat and tears mingling.

"I can't breathe! For God's sake, give me some air!"

"My baby, my baby, she needs to be changed; please, some room, I beg you!"

Reuben tried to instil some order. "We're going to be together for a long time. It's going to get worse, so we must try to work together. First of all, let's rig some kind of curtain around the bucket. And why doesn't someone try to ration the water? It won't last long."

Individual survival instincts were not yet sharpened; they did not know what awaited them. So they grudgingly agreed to some semblance of order, of co-operation. But any arrangement was doomed to be overtaken by rapidly degenerating conditions and, sure enough, debate subsided, defeated by the rocking motion of the train, the stifling heat, and lack of food. Soon, the sound of retching drowned out the subsiding sobs and the pervasive odour of vomit added its own notes to the swelling miasma of sweat and waste which suffused the carriage.

Their fellow passengers came from the widest disparity of European Jewry, an ultra-orthodox rabbi who had ministered to the émigré community that had gathered in Marseille breathed the same foul air as the atheist Mendels, and in between them lay every shade of opinion and belief.

But *this* gathering of the universal clan did not, *could* not, would never fulfil the traditional feature of voluble discourse that habitually accompanied a Jewish congregation. Morale had long been drained by the increasing imminence of capture. Now that it had, at last, happened, there had been a palpable venting of tension which, taken with their surroundings, drove them into a collective torpor, a kind of coma. And in its wake came a plunge in the temperature, as heat and horror subsided into catalepsy, shifting the ambience from oven to freezer.

Now, where bodies once had sought some cooling space, they oozed together, not in any sense of sharing but with the unconscious intention of theft, trying to absorb without compensation a few precious degrees of warmth. Individuality leaked from them, pooling itself in an amorphous farrago of limbs and twisted bodies where the beginning of one was the middle of another, the end of a third. Like a manic tide ripped from its immemorial rhythm by a freak wave, the faceless morass ebbed and flowed, as first one segment was disturbed by the undertow of an element that had pins and needles or cramp, then at the opposite end another maze shifted and unravelled as someone needed to use the bucket.

For countless hours they remained like this. It was neither sleep nor sleeplessness, rather a numbing apprehension combined with growing hunger, thirst and cold. They inhabited a stasis, strung between life and death, powerless.

But for all its thousand cuts, its choking purgatory, in one respect Reuben found the journey therapeutic. For the first time in as long as he could comfortably recall responsibility drained from his shoulders, a black burden lifted from his back by the violent destruction of their self-determination. As he rocked through the long, slow ride, half-standing, half-slumped upon neighbours similarly dominoed, he found a perverse mental equilibrium in which he was able to close down his mind to all around him and drift away on song-borne wings to somewhere safer, warmer. His sense of smell and hearing shut down, freeing him so that the mental exercise of fingering the notes while a sound picture played in his brain was unencumbered by the sorrow and filth that infected those around him. For an uncertain time he was elsewhere, liberated both from the freight train itself and the burden of perpetual concern for the family.

In this trance-like state he was initially oblivious to his father tugging at his sleeve.

"Reuben, Reuben!" came the urgent whisper. "I need to go."

He recovered himself to readjust to the surroundings, registering the deterioration in both physical and mental conditions within the carriage. The passengers were splintering, both as family units and within themselves, their disintegration palpable.

The bucket was full to overflowing, liquefied shit, the putrefying mixture invading nose, stinging eyes, clogging throat. To use it was an abandonment of decency, as the modest curtain no longer served. Evacuation in public – the sign of profound weakness, of pending mortality – previously performed in private, now exposed to all. But by the time desperation had vanquished Moses, so that he would have gone in his trousers, anyone looking would not have seen, their gaze glassy with indifference and distance.

"No-one's interested, Papa, so just go. I'll hold my coat open."

But the footing was treacherous as they stepped on prone and half-erect figures, pursued by curses muttered with no threat behind them, sliding over the spreading filth that slicked out from the brimming bucket.

Squatting slightly to maintain a semblance of balance, Reuben averted his eyes as he held his coat. But his ears could not be closed to the vile noise as Moses added to the floating morass of those who had been before. He felt his stomach start to churn and pulse, an acid rising in his throat and it was all he could do to stop himself vomitting.

Moses looked around for something with which to wipe himself, but could find nothing, so he used his handkerchief, folding it carefully in ever smaller squares in a fruitless attempt to make a half-decent job of it.

Suddenly, as they were returning to the others, the train stopped and both men were pitched headlong against the door. Almost immediately a dissonant tattoo began to reverberate through the train, a primitive code which at once signalled to each wagon that it was not alone and called for succour to anyone outside who had the means and courage to help.

People started to stir. Sharp elbows jabbed scrawny sides,

seeking the glimmer between the wooden boards, a promise of light, of clean air.

Weakened arms impotently shoving cold meat, exhausted neighbour sagging under little pressure. The downtrodden now literally so. Brittle bones cracking under pressing feet, seeking fresh oxygen as the distant sliding of opening doors grew ever closer.

Now their turn, and the press of those keen for their ration pushed the Mendels hard against the door. They shoved back, just in time to gain some space between their faces and the hard, pitted surface as the door was brusquely slid open.

"Bucket!" was the harsh greeting, and in harmony with a collective in-breathing the foul container was passed gingerly from hand to hand until it fell to Reuben to empty it. He placed it carefully in the opening, and jumped down.

"Move yourself, Jew! Get going! We haven't got all day."

Reuben was forced to pick up the bucket quickly. Allowed no leeway for its noxious contents, he had to walk rapidly towards the dilapidated building that the other members of this first of many *scheissekommandos* were bearing down on, similarly burdened.

"If you spill any, you pick it up with your hands," spat a sallow soldier. Reuben concentrated as though he were back, far back, in the days of calm, embroiled in the fiendish fingerwork of a Paganini Caprice, and managed to reach his goal with the contents more or less intact.

They each emptied the bucket, holding their breath deep within as a sentinel against an incursion by nausea, certain in the feeling that were they to cede ground to their revulsion they would be overwhelmed by it. They closed down their senses of sight and smell, tipped, and fled. But the velocity of their return to the train could never be fast enough – and they were accompanied by short, sharp prods and impatient thumps about their heads and shoulders from the small truncheons that each guard carried at his side.

They could not know, but they had stopped at Drancy, the

infamous way-station through which most of France's Jews and other undesirables had passed on their way to the east – and almost certain death.

More carriages were added – and many more people, 'pieces' in Nazi vernacular, crammed into the existing wagons, notwithstanding the chorus of complaints and curses that greeted them.

Now, where there had been discomfort that none had previously been able to imagine, there stood a new horror. To the filth, the hunger, the unquenchable thirst, to the heat and the cold, came swiftly the purulent face of the death-plague.

Not the galloping taking of the innocent. No, this was a spreading of a different contagion, in its own way even more lethal. What took hold was a virulent infection that sapped the will to live, as if those who succumbed had been drained of their last antibodies. And indeed it was so. Those who boarded the train, whether at Gurs or Drancy, did so physically weakened but with a paradoxical optimism, seduced by the lie that the final destination in the east promised safe, albeit hard, resettlement. But with the journey itself the cruel deception was finally exposed to all but the most hardened optimist. No-one with the slightest scintilla of objectivity could believe that even the lowliest servant of the Reich would be treated in this fashion. Thus they were lower than the lowest of the low, and had lost any hope of influencing their destiny.

The mood shifted, a joint realisation that the reaper whose scythe had been sharpened so audibly during the preceding months and years was now harvesting their part of the field. Children set up a waif-like lament, adults a slow ground-bass of dull sobbing. Parents began to wilt under the persistent pressure of seeming strong. Many of the elderly in the carriage – especially those who had languished longer than the Mendels in the camps dotted around France – were already drifting, no longer anchored by the need for willpower, accepting the inevitable.

"Move, Madame, you're lying on my leg! Move, I said!"

The man gave up any pretence to manners and rudely pushed the elderly woman slumped across his feet. She rolled off, and he saw with horror her fixed, immutable stare, the mask of death. He failed to suppress a cry of revulsion and, in the way unique to crowds, an immediate comprehension rippled through the wagon. A low threnody, a prospective requiem of self-mourning, spread out from their carriage and joined in an inaudible chorale with the similar songs that were emanating from every other wagon.

The train continued its sporadic passage eastwards, via Nancy and Breda before approaching the ghost town of Lodz, second largest city in Poland, emptied of its half million Jews in the previous two years.

The death toll rose, as did the pitch of ever-more desperate voices. At frequent halts and numberless stations pleas for water, even if only dripped through cracks, went unanswered.

By now the meagre rations were long exhausted. The stop-start progress whereby the train remained in sidings or in spurs from the main track to allow troops and supplies to go by had sapped their food supply, and what remained of their water was stale and tainted by the all-pervading stench.

And then when time, in that mystifying quirk of travel, seemed to have lost all meaning and been traversed in a kind of semi-conscious torpor, a sudden stop in an anonymous spot within a forest, hidden from gaze. Somewhere between Lodz and their unknown destination, the train came to a halt in a snow-heavy copse. The silence was deafening as it ever is when a perpetual sound no longer heard but always there, in background, ends. Then the rattle of padlocks and the sliding of doors announced the opening of the wagons. Simultaneously the low chorus began. The parched choir, one in every wagon that had rolled remorselessly through the nights and days, chimed in feeble, cracked voices:

"Fresh air."

"Plenty of food."

"Hard work but fair conditions."

Night had grouted the spaces in the wagon's deformed shell. Blinded by the cloak of invisibility thrown over them, they mistakenly assumed that their destination had been reached. Every one of them instinctively drew to themselves that which they loved the most.

Reuben flung open his valise and tucked the violin case, imminent, unknown lifeline, under his right arm. He threw the other around Sarah and pulled her close to him. She, in her turn, clutched the children to her breast. Moses and Leah, now empty vessels, bereft of spirit, grasped straws and each other, adding their own fragile extemporisation to the theme that was wafting the entire length of the pernicious train.

"They said a labour camp."

"Working in the east."

"Hard but fair."

"Enough food and water."

Moving closer and closer, muffled voices became more distinct. Fear. No. Panic.

A different noise, previously unheard, not quite deadened by the laden trees and thick white carpet. Gun shots, but not machine-rapid; pistol-pointed. Raucous shouts now decipherable.

"Throw out your dead, Jews," spat with venom. Whip crack. "Just your dead, *Scheiss-Jude*. Look at your filth. Have you no shame? Fucking vermin."

Now the Mendels' turn. Deceptive, star-encrusted winter sky revealed as rusted door shrieks open. Sudden rush of air. Breathe it in quickly. Store it. Turf out the stiffs.

"You!" screeched at Reuben. "Get the dead out. Anyone more dead than alive?" accompanied by the menacing waving of a Luger. "Hey, old man, talk to me, you still breathing?"

A fatal silence from the ancient slumped against the wall opposite the open door. As his mouth moved to speak, a single report and blood spewed from a clean hole in his forehead.

"Him too, *schnell, Jude*!"

How many? Five, ten, now twenty-two. Nearly half of all who had left France. And of those, who had passed mourned, or even acknowledged? Just the first two or three. Thereafter, none, save perhaps those whose family noticed and who wept silently and rocked the corpse to salvage heat and memories.

The blast of air and sound had snapped Reuben into action, and he stuck the violin behind Sarah. Jumping down from the wagon, he took the lifeless, limp forms from those who had manhandled them, like baggage, to the open door. The luxury of respect was long gone, and he flung each corpse, even the fresh old man, blood oozing, over his shoulder and staggered the fifty metres or so into dense woodland. As he dumped them, one at a time, he knelt and scooped up handfuls of precious snow and ran back to the train. He caught Sarah's eye and dropped the priceless clumps of frozen water onto her lap. She quickly dispensed the elixir to her children and parents-in-law, before suggesting to the remaining passengers that they find some receptacles to store what they could, uncertain as to how much longer the journey would last.

Despite the horror of the undertaking, it represented a brief respite, the chance to try to evaluate what was happening to them. The ice-cold sting of the snow on their lips, palate and throat rekindled a spark, but the heightened awareness brought no relief, only fuel for their anxiety.

Soon enough, the train restarted, turning south some miles beyond Lodz, and headed for its final destination.

It was not long reached.

After three more hours of sporadic progress, they slowed to a near crawl. Those with a view through some of the rotted slats reported some distant mountains, dimly visible through the grey dawn now breaking over the transport. The rest was bleak, a marshy valley hewn from the earth by the constant pressure of the Sola flowing into Poland's main artery, the Vistula.

Then, with a familiar jolt, the engine started up again and rolled slowly up to a long, remote platform. Instinctively they knew that this was the end of their journey. Even so, they stood at the small station until dusk had long fallen. Tension swelled, exacerbated by the assault on their senses of an alien force. Discordant sounds mingled with the waft and wave of strange odours and flavours to assail them, all blind in their wagon: barking (slavering German shepherd dogs awaiting impatiently their next taste of flesh and bone), thuds and cries (the swipe of whips and their contact on emaciated shoulders), revving (motorbikes, lorries and jeeps), smell (burning flesh and fat-saturated smoke), cloying taste (ash-laden air). At one moment someone shouted: "Music. I'm sure I just heard music," but he was hushed quickly by a thousand imputations of insanity. Above all, the screams of furious Nazis, demanding action and immediate responses to their orders. The now-familiar, ominous *"Raus, raus"* rent the air with venom. The temperature in the Mendel wagon rose as their turn inexorably approached, a sweaty tension mixing with the omnivorous odour to accentuate the ragged edge along on which they were tottering.

And then it was their time. The door shrieked open for the last time to reveal a scene of incomprehensible madness, for they were at the infamous ramp of Auschwitz. A cacophony of noise, baggage strewn everywhere, people wandering, kicked, beaten into line, forced to drop what little luggage they had salvaged and protected on the journey. Dogs strained at leashes, desperate to sink their fangs into the weakened carcasses that limped from the train. In amongst the milling crowd appeared spectral shaven-headed figures in faded, filth-encrusted blue-and-white stripes, sifting and collecting the discarded dross of their fellow travellers' lives. In the distance the lowering sky glowed vermilion with fire from five tall chimneys.

Reuben dropped down and helped the others from the carriage.

It was dusk and the searchlights that had stolen their sight as they emerged from the wagon began to lose their effect. The Polish winter hit them hard, but still they drank in the frozen air in a futile attempt to cleanse their throat and lungs of the putrefaction that clung to them, matted in hair, absorbed into the warp and weft of their clothes, lodged in nostrils and under fingernails so that they seemed as if enclosed within it.

Whips hit them as they tried to recover their luggage. But they lacked the strength to duck, the will to fight, sapped as they were by the totality of their decline. They had vomited, pissed and shat in shameless exposure; they had become indifferent to everything. They were nothing, disinhibited, deprived of the tethering-posts of their life.

Intuitively, surreptitiously (or so he thought), Reuben made the move that would forestall his death. In an instant he had seized the violin and, turning a rapid circle, stowed it beneath his coat.

"In line, in line, *schnell, Jude!*" snapped a guard, poking Reuben in the back with a sharp thrust of his baton, pushing him into a line distinguished only by the fact that they were only young and middle-aged men. All the rest stood in another line, the women, the old, the young.

On a gravel path beside the track, the two queues shuffled in approximate parallel towards two desks, the Mendels several hundred places from the front. They stood for a moment, then began to move forwards as those next in line moved in their turn. Reuben watched as Sarah gathered the children to her, each protected by a single arm. Fatigue had rendered Miriam and Elias to vacancy, all questions stilled, fear so great it backed them deep into the embrace of their mother, small eyes wide, black voids, the lifelight extinguished. Their grandparents were ageing before them, stooped with the agony of exhaustion, all skin colour drained with fright and hunger and the pain from the loss of their dignity. Sarah tightened her grip around Elias and pulled him even closer to her. Although she couldn't see his face, she knew the tears were silently rolling down his face, even while he pretended to bravery. Tiny movements in his shoulders and neck betrayed him. Miriam, her fourteen-year-old virgin lustre that might otherwise have bought dubious respite, even survival, in the camp brothel now lost to the ravages of flight and fatigue, made to break away as she momentarily remembered her promise to look after Moses. But the thought died as it was born and she subsided back against her mother. Reuben and Sarah exchanged the occasional glance across the narrow divide, but they knew that they were now enslaved to a different power, one over which there could be no influence, and after a while they withdrew further into themselves and the thoughts that none may know.

"I can't recall the time between lining up and the intervention that saved me. Most of what we went through is carved into my soul but that precise period is gone, I think because those last moments together are too precious to expose to the vagaries of recollection, as though to dredge them up might start their decay."

Suddenly, a harsh, wet whisper in Reuben's ear, first in Yiddish and, when that elicited no response, in German, both with a heavy hint of Polish:

"Don't turn round. Just listen. I saw you."

"What?"

"I saw you take your violin."

"So?"

"Quiet" hissed the mysterious voice. "I'm trying to help you."

"What do you mean?"

"See those flames? Know that smell? It's Jews being burned. Is that your family over there?"

No answer came as Reuben, head spinning with shredded credulity, desperately sought to gather his thoughts.

"The Germans are selecting who will live and who will die. Sent to the right, and you live, at least for a while. To the left, gassed in large chambers and then burnt. Only those who are useful go to the right. None of your family will be chosen to live. Your wife won't leave the children, and the old folks will have no choice."

"So?"

"*You* have a choice."

Reuben felt flaming bile rise in his throat, ejected by a stomach churning with revulsion and panic.

"No. I don't believe you. You're lying."

"Turn round quickly and look at me."

Reuben turned to view his Jeremiah, sunken cheeks, bottomless hollows at the back of which sat empty eyes ravaged with disease. He was swaying with a limp, to and fro, trying to simulate activity and disguise their conversation.

"I am one of the fitter people here, if you can still call us 'people'. This place is called Auschwitz, the arsehole of the world. It's a death camp, where you either work and then die, or die immediately."

"No!"

"Yes!"

Now they were all nearer the desks, and Reuben noticed that for every one person standing to the right, all of them younger men, eight or more hovered to the left. And they were all old, female or children.

"You must decide!"

"No!"

"Decide."

Sarah noticed his agitation and had seen his mouth moving, even though she had been unable to make out the words.

"Reuben, who are you talking to?" she whispered across the space between them.

He did not, could not, respond to Sarah's question, indicating weakly towards the man who had melted back into the throng to continue the scavenging process.

"This man, he was saying …" He was unable to continue.

"Saying what?"

"That … that …" All his words had failed him and he could no longer talk. For what would he say? "*You* must die, while *I* might live"? Or, "I could choose life over death, when you cannot"?

"I know what you're thinking," came the man again after a few moments, busying himself by stooping to pick over a battered suitcase that lay open on the ground. "Can't imagine life without them, eh? Think again. Here, the only life is to breathe for another hour without the gas in your lungs. Survival is everything, food the only currency. Here, just *you* matter; all else is nothing. You can save no-one but yourself. And there is no point dying just for a few extra minutes of togetherness. Try to live so that we might see the fuckers hang, to tell what happened here. Your choice."

The family shuffled along, each lost in bewilderment at the devastation that surrounded them, already inured to the foul air, not wondering – save Reuben, plagued by knowledge he dared not share – about its cause, nor about the tall chimneys belching blood-red flames into the sky.

Sarah and the others reached their desk before Reuben.

"Over there, with the other families!"

They meekly complied.

Reuben arrived.

The SS officer looked up at him with no sign of acknowledgement. A moment's assessment, and then he nodded in the opposite direction where a group of men stood.

"I wish to remain with my family."

The soldier's eyes opened wide and he made to rise. But before he could get to his feet, The Whisperer intervened.

"Wait, Hauptmann, if you please!"

He came hobbling up at a trot, whipping off his cap as he spoke and averting his eyes from the *Übermensch*. "I saw him arrive with a violin. Commandant Schwarzhuber wants more musicians for the orchestra. We need him badly, Sir."

A moment's thought, weighing up the dilemma: fulfil the Holy

Writ of the Führer and speed the destruction of the sub-race or suck up to his boss. He chose the latter, with barely concealed contempt. "Take him."

"No, as I said, I wish to stay with my family," declaimed Reuben, recovering his haughty spirit for one last show of defiance.

The whip came from nowhere, slicing open his face from the bridge of his nose right across his cheek. "Here, there is no 'No', Jew. Go with him. Now!"

Reuben stretched out a desperate arm as his nameless saviour pulled him away from the ramp: "Sarah, Mama, Papa!" They could still hear him calling – "Sarah, Mama, Papa!", "Sarah, Mama, Papa!", "Sarah, Mama, Papa!" – receding, ever more receding, until finally he was gone.

The family disintegrated, unable to comprehend this latest catastrophe and, in their blind ignorance, convinced of his inevitable, immediate death.

Moses slumped to the floor; Leah was no longer by his side, but somewhere else, shoulders folded, her only words a whispered, "My son, my son."

Sarah was aghast. In an instant, and before she could register what was happening, he was gone. His cries were echoing in her ears. Instinctively she reached for the children.

Other prisoners were driven to raise Moses up. Sarah encircled the children to her, their tear-soaked faces buried in her belly. Prodded by batons, they were driven deeper among the condemned, Reuben's final words reverberating along the empty corridors of their soul. The selection rolled remorselessly on.

Near catatonic, Reuben was swept up in a maelstrom of activity to whose direction, rhythm and tempo he was utterly enslaved. Processed by unseen hands, ordered by unheard mouths, kicked by unfelt feet, he was stripped, shaved, showered, given an ill-fitting striped uniform with wooden clogs, tattooed – and finally taken off to Barracks 15, the hut where the orchestra was based.

As he nursed the stinging pain from the crudely stitched gash across his face, Reuben was approached by Szymon Laks, conductor and arranger of music for the capricious assemblage of instruments that passed for the Auschwitz Men's Orchestra. His rank was signified by a silver lyre that sat on an armband at the top of his left arm, in stark contrast to the faded yellow star and number sown on his old striped uniform.

In French tinged with a Polish accent, he spoke, holding Reuben's eye even when he tried to avert his gaze from the unavoidable truth. His tone was urgent, delivered with a clipped authority that invited no debate.

"You are new here. There is much you do not yet understand. So let me tell you what is going on. Your family is dead or, if not yet, soon will be. There is, and was, nothing you can do to save them. If you can play, you have a chance of lasting a while. I forbid any greater ambition. You will still need to work. The food is filth, but as long as you're part of the orchestra there should be a ready supply. No matter how disgusting, you must eat everything you can get hold of. If you can't play, I will throw you out and you'll be on your own. A word of advice. We are in hell. Don't try to understand anything. All is madness. But you have been handed an opportunity that one day you may come to see as a blessing. We are all in the same boat. We never know when our time will come. This is a world where we are at the whim of anyone with power – guards, doctors, other prisoners, dogs even. We are nothing. Sometimes we're in favour, other times one of the *kapos* who hates music will make us do hard labour. Or threaten us with escape up the chimney. Concentrate only on the now, even when you're abused by jealous prisoners for your apparent privileges. You owe nothing to anyone – except your orchestra colleagues whose own life may depend on your performance. So far, although you don't yet believe it, you've been lucky. Wásko spotted you, not a Nazi, or else you'd be dead by now. Now, tell me about yourself and then you must play something for me."

But Reuben wasn't yet ready for this rational discourse. He was adrift, all alone on a leaky raft, with inundation inevitable. He refused to believe in the reality of the island being laid out before him as his salvation; too much had happened too quickly for him to trust his senses, his intellect. He was assailed on all sides by shame, fear, loss. It was as if the beneficial force that was guiding him to potential safety was not to be trusted, an illusion, a malign joke that existed only for as long as he believed in it. Thus he was already trapped in the surreal inconstancy of the camps, where all preconceptions were turned on their head and all prior experience counted for nought.

He sensed a reply was awaited, so he broke the first rule of Auschwitz: when someone in authority tells you to do something, you do it without question.

"I would prefer to play first, then talk."

With Laks he was lucky.

"In future, when told to jump, you must jump, without question. But I, we all, know what you are going through, so play. Next time, though?"

Reuben looked at him with a mixture of resignation and dull acknowledgement of his power, succumbing to the realities of the situation, picking up on the fact that all those in the orchestra maintained a slight but discernible distance from their leader.

As with all things of value in this place, his own violin had disappeared when he showered. He would never know how it ended up in that Munich attic but the most likely path was via 'Kanada', the storehouse so named after a land of fabled wealth which was crammed with all manner of artefacts taken from the trains and their passengers.

He was handed a violin by one of the other players. With an instinct established over many years, he wrapped the fingers of his left hand around the neck of the violin and instantly plucked the strings to see if it was in tune. A couple of slight tweaks on the pegs at the scroll-end, a minor twist of the small metal pin at the bridge and he was ready. As ever with Reuben Mendel, when the violin rose to his chin, he was transformed. Even here, surrounded as he was by a world beyond understanding, beyond the ability of those who were never there to know what it was like, he dredged up the strength to find music. Strange to relate, he didn't play from his huge repertoire of classics, but instead found himself back at an earlier time of horror, when he had improvised on Jewish tunes in the trenches. As he drew the bow across the strings, the adrenaline that was pouring through his body empowered the most extraordinary control of line and tone. There, in that hut, surrounded by a degradation only the surface of which he had yet been exposed to, he pulled from the fiddle one of the songs of the *shtetl* that all around instinctively knew, whether from recent forced departure or by deeper feelings lodged within from more ancient exile.

By now it was night and the camp was settling. In the silent moments, when exhausted workers and broken captives unfit for labour stole precious minutes between ravenous eating and merciful sleep to ponder the course of their lives, those close enough caught snatches of the subversive melody. With the power of music to transport heightened by their condition, they took flight and were, for the briefest of time, free.

Laks interrupted the all-too-brief reverie. "No! Stop! You mustn't play Jewish music, only German or approved classics."

Reuben thought again and started to play Wagner, back from the days under Furtwängler, the main theme of the *'Liebestod'* from *Tristan und Isolde*, the cathartic moment of realisation that the perfect love is dead. He drew the long, languid melody from deep in the lower register of the instrument, thrumming the slow bass rhythm with his thumb while double- and treble-stopping to create the impression of ensemble. All in the room knew why he played it, and each saw a montage of the loved and lost drifting out of reach before them. In a matter of moments the door opened softly and an SS officer came in to sit quietly on an empty chair. He was joined by a second, then a third and, finally, a fourth. For that short time they were equals, conjoined in communion, taken by the music to places they would all prefer to be, murderer and pending victim both, linked across the heinous dogmatic void that divided them by the purest of common ground: the desire for peace and the longing for love.

Reuben could not know that, as the violin ascended to his chin, his family descended the steps to the sham shower; as his fingers phrased chords, other fingers unfastened clothing; as bow bit into gut, fingernails scraped at unforgiving walls, clawing impotently for escape, while those familiar beloved voices which had once sung Schubert and nursery rhymes, often scolded, frequently seduced, demanded attention and comfort, those unmistakable voices now screamed for air.

"In my very worst moments I can see them, gasping for breath, holding each other as the awful realisation hits, that this, this ... was ... their ... end.

"I know what it was like in there. I've read the reports of what the Sonderkommando found when the chamber was unlocked. But I can't let myself believe that their last moments were of blind panic and the futile crush to find air.

So I like to think that I can hear them, I distinctly hear them, whispering names for the final time. I wonder whether Mama thought first of me, and then held Papa tight to her, and if they subsided together, so that one wasn't left alone, even for an instant.

"And my beautiful Sarah. She, I know, would have understood and calmed the children. I can see her mouthing the words 'Schlafet, Schlafet, meine kinder', kissing their heads and holding them close, 'and when we wake, we will be safe ... and all will be well, all will be well'."

When he had finished his audition, the SS men slinked silently away, afraid to reveal the weakness betrayed by the moisture in their eyes. Laks spoke. "Enough. I've heard more than enough. You sleep in my block tonight; tomorrow we'll wake you early and explain the ropes."

Compared to most, Reuben's baptism was gentle. He didn't go through a heartless induction of rigorous medical, physical exercise and back-breaking labour. Whisked as he was from the ramp, he was ripped straight through the ice without an agonising, slow immersion.

Yet still he slept head-to-toe with another, on the middle rank of the three-tier bunk, with only dank, soiled straw for a mattress. Still he had to piss in a bucket which, if your timing was wrong and it overflowed, you had to carry outside and empty into the latrine, even in the treacherous frozen Polish winter. Still he had to watch over the precious bowl, without which he would not receive the disgusting ration of black bread, frequently made of sawdust, and thin soup made of all-too-obvious ingredients, such as mouldy potatoes (a good day), hair, dead mice or even buttons. Still he had to undergo the early morning roll call, starting at half-past four in the open air regardless of the harshness of the weather, be it freezing winter or the perpetual rain and mud in the spring. Still he had to go through the debilitating expectation of the next selection when, for no reason, sheer caprice could determine whether you were next to feed the insatiable monster in his lair.

Still he had to get to grips with a world for which no prior experience was preparation. Still he had to remain constantly alive to the camp's byzantine jurisprudence, be it the rules governing 'organisation' (where the universal marketplace of trade and barter enabled the acquisition of priceless calories to augment the starvation diet), or the specific violent proclivity of each Nazi or *kapo* (pistol whip, dog attack, boot in bollocks) so that at least it might be prepared for, though never avoided.

And still, when the orchestra had finished its morning duties outside the kitchen as the prisoners were marched off, he had to join a labour group which, as with everything, was unpredictable in its harshness, duration, location and the degree of malice shown by the leader. Being in the orchestra afforded at least some relief, in that work could start only after the other groups had tramped off, and had to end before them so that they could be serenaded while they dragged their exhausted, broken bodies back through the gates with those lying words *ARBEIT MACHT FREI*, and somehow held themselves up during the interminable roll-call that each day balanced the books, even by counting corpses.

To those who would know no such privileges, what he had was paradise. But for Reuben, it was searing purgatory, the totality of descent thrown into high relief by the acuity of his senses, fired as they were by a ferocious *mélange* of apprehension and grief, vigilance and deprivation.

They never worked singly, so the members of the orchestra laboured in ad hoc pairings and small groups, according to the task. Despite their mutual dependency, this was not the place for friendship. Far too much was at stake for the shackles on trust to be entirely unfastened. The atmosphere was not suspicion, as such; rather, awareness that one false step might condemn them all. But a degree of intimacy was inevitable with the claustrophobic existence, hedged by never-ending anxiety and mutual dependency.

During the work, or the small snatched moments of precious rest, they exchanged short biography ... but only of their musical histories, never of family.

Most of the time, the labour broke backs and sapped energy. Hauling coal, logs or stones by neck-crushing yoke or hand-ripping rope from one part of the camp to the next, frequently for no apparent reason, promised only exhaustion exacerbated by futility. At times like this the fatigue weighed upon them more heavily than the loads they were required to haul. Such muscle-fraying weariness reduced them to silent agony, when the eyes close and the mind withdraws into itself, as though to escape the nerve-jangling pain.

But at other times, joy upon joy!, came the welcoming lighter and potentially enriching duties of working in Kanada, sorting through an abundance of treasures whose owners no longer existed. Alternatively, it might involve bringing the cleansed apparel of the deceased from the storage camp to be readied for transport to Germany. And if there were items of no apparent value – spectacles, prayer books, photographs – they would simply be left to rot in chaotic disregard.

Occasionally Reuben might be required to participate in the unpredictable one-off, like moving over to the women's camp the full canteen of cutlery that had been harvested during their time in the camps by the gypsies prior to their wholesale liquidation.

But far too frequently he had to plunge deep into the blackest filth in the camp, the physical manifestation of Auschwitz as *anus mundi*.

Which is how it was that Reuben Mendel, formerly of the first violins of the Vienna Philharmonic and only grandson of Elias Mendel, rabbi to the now-defunct Jewish community of Skidel, came to clean that incarnation of festering putrefaction – the mass latrines which received the slimy, cankerous waste of a polluted diet. Such was the effect of what they ate and the pressure to perform that often the need of the body to expel it was irresistible, so that when its time came, its time came, and no amount of willpower dredging the long-expended dregs of self-respect could forestall banishment of the poison. So all around the rancid facility lay shit of every consistency, colour and odour, a seamless vista of filth that assaulted eyes, nose, mouth, throat, permeating everything and everyone.

Danisch, the head prisoner at the main extermination centre in Birkenau, loathed music, conducting a one-man war against the orchestra behind the back of the commandant. He took the greatest delight in nominating musicians for the filthiest tasks in the camp: cleaning the latrines and clearing the trains.

It often fell to Reuben to apply quicklime with spade, shovelling into the ditch behind the latrines as much excrement as possible, churning over the earth when rain had turned it to mud. For only then, when the soil was neither baked dry nor frozen hard, could any effective progress be made without recourse to a rusty pick. And even when he was forced, bone-tired, to swing the ancient tool over his shoulder and fragment the tortured ground, the mere covering of the noxious material was insufficient to prevent its odour from pervading not just the air that they all breathed but their very being. For hours on end they did this, under the watchful eye of the *kapo* and his cudgel, always ready to whip the *scheissekommando* into ever-more feverish activity.

Not that all of them were bad; most were so close to evil it made no difference, any semblance of humanity lost to the twin forces of disproportionate power and death-fear. But once or twice the Hungarian was assigned and he, at least, would turn a myopic eye towards reduced activity, and only spur himself when his own survivor's antennae warned of approaching danger, a rare event, given that the SS avoided the latrines. But these small salvations were no comfort, for even the very thought of them might kindle hope, the deadliest of all emotions.

But regardless of how repugnant the duty, no matter how sickening its prospect, even this assignment under the most hate-filled guard was preferable to the trains.

For it was there, in among discarded suitcases, soiled clothing, caked waste, that frequently were found the rotting remains of the elderly who died en route, or the emaciated, swollen corpses of babies, interred under rotten straw by grieving parents seeking a charade of funeral rites. When Reuben had emptied his own carriage of stiffs, it had been in ignorance of what awaited at journey's end. Now, mostly inured to horror, the only time he recoiled was at the ramp, the last reminder of his vanished bloodline. It was then, when the prospect of finding tiny cadavers quite overwhelmed him, that

Reuben, feigning illness, sought asylum with a doctor in the hospital who found his own relief in listening to the orchestra.

The cunning that had saved him before came once again to his rescue. He realised, as had every other musician, that the solace they could bring held huge material value.

Their 'work' had two sides: the public and the private. For the mass of the camp, they had to play martial tunes of crass Teutonic origin – 'Berlin Air', 'German Oaks' and the like – to accompany columns of labour groups on their dreaded trek to factory, mine, quarry and, at a slower tempo, on their exhausted, racked return. This was supplemented by regular concerts for staff, with the occasional attendance by prisoners.

But it was their private assignments that proved lucrative. Often the complete ensemble that delivered the *oom-pa-pah* rhythm so beloved of the authorities – brass, percussion and some woodwind – was put to one side and the more melancholy, sentimental strings were preferred. For after a hard day's slaughter, many of the SS liked to sit in the privacy of their apartment or at a table in the camp brothel and be soothed with music. Reuben quickly learned the tariff. Not hard currency, of course, for it had no intrinsic worth, but precious tradable goods – chocolate, alcohol and, above all, tobacco.

What's more, in that Babel he grasped that his English, German and French were in huge demand, as lovers sought to cross linguistic barriers, traders traverse commercial frontiers – and guards lay the ground to flee inevitable defeat by being able to converse with their future captors, whom they hoped would come from the west, rather than the dreaded Russians.

There was an unspoken third aspect to their music making – the rare, secret, stolen moments when they played for themselves in duets, trios and quartets. In these clandestine sessions, passed off as practice, fellow inmates walking by, or lying on the ground, reconciled to their destiny, or standing in line for a selection, or awaiting transport to a certain grave heard some theme that wafted on a burnt breeze and fell gently in their ears, an ephemeral notion that there was another world, one where kindness and culture still held sway.

This was his life, if it can be called living. His entire body was coiled with the tension of perpetual vigilance, making sure that his cap was removed and head bowed whenever authority came into view, steeling himself against the next arbitrary blow, an unknowable number of illogical rules that demanded nothing but blind obedience. Only the fleeting hermitage of sleep and the snatched bars of introspection brought some respite.

His existence was pure bedlam. It veered insanely from the frenetic and frantic, particularly the tension-soaked moments when selection seemed inevitable or the sudden malign intervention of chance appeared unavoidable, to the static and somnolent, characterised by numbing tedium when the grinding routine of unending roll calls, assembly at a staged execution or dire marches dulled the brain and drained the spirit beyond ennui to a kind of waking coma.

The days dragged by. One blended seamlessly into the next. The only distractions were the endless quests for food, the manifold devices to boost the calorie intake. The focus was absolute, a drilling down of consciousness on to one precise point – the need to survive. A perpetual mantra filled his playing, whether at the gate or moonlighting for the SS: "Don't stop playing: play to live, to remember, to tell of what you have seen; don't falter, play the notes as if they're your last."

"This time in my life, well, of course, it never leaves me. But the strange thing is that the images are not clear. They're like a sepia photo which simulates the lack of detail in a Monet. You know what the picture is, but the lines are blurred, as though I am peering through a dust storm. There's a limitless sea of people; a handful I recognise but most have no faces, all of them mingle aimlessly, a

teeming crowd that spreads over the horizon and out beyond my vision, top and bottom, left and right. They neither walk nor run, but shuffle, face towards the ground. It is like I am hovering above these minuscule, anonymous people, lost, wandering alone in a featureless landscape. There are no buildings, and although I can't identify the smells and sounds, I'm aware that my senses are assailed by a foul stink and my ears are assaulted by a cacophonous din that tears at my head. Every time it takes me a while to realise that the opacity is caused not by dust but by smoke. Despite this lack of precision, the overwhelming impression is of a vast population, indeterminate in every detail save those I can specifically recall: Laks, of course, my saviour; and Wásko, who rescued me. Others from the orchestra – Heinz, the Greek doctor, his friend Michael, some others whose names, to my shame, escape me. But I have come to think of my memory as a fiercely protective friend, and I trust it to remind me of what I need to know. Nevertheless, I am permanently torn: to live with these ghosts is unbearable; to live without them, now that is unimaginable ... unimaginable."

Did he think of his family? Apart from the days when ramp duty might be in the offing, never. He drew down an impenetrable curtain between the present and the past, harnessing every precious ounce of physical and emotional energy to the now, the recurring moment, the immediate and imperative need for vigilance, his waking mind a three-hundred-and-sixty-degree radar scanning for danger.

And when sleep came, what dreams then? Like most, of groaning tables, laden with food so rich that if they could eat it now it would surely finish them off. Or of happy childhood times in London, filled with sunlight. And of music, played for pleasure, no duress – of chamber pieces with joyous tunes thrown carelessly from instrument to instrument. But they were dreams that never finished, aborted always by a harsh reveille.

All the while he played the appetite of an insatiable malignancy continued to demand ever more sustenance; and not just where

Reuben was.

In other camps built exclusively for industrialised genocide – Belzec, Chelmno, Majdanek, Sobibor, Treblinka – and those where it was an acceptable by-product of hard labour, cruelty and calculated indifference – Bergen-Belsen, Buchenwald, Dachau, Flossenbürg, Ravensbrück, Sachsenhausen – unknowable numbers, ravaged by disease and heart-sickness, waned and died, or hurled themselves on electric fences, or just awaited death, by gas or gun, boot or fist.

Untold incomprehensible tragedies played out against an ever blanker expression of apathy. For it was only through indifference that survival was possible, only through switching off the instinct to care, to even *notice*.

In that world was where Liebeskind died. Forced to witness his wife and child murdered, hair white overnight as he watched over his son in Treblinka's crematorium, his 'Lullaby for my Little Son in the Crematorium' was saved for posterity when he was not, a threnody for all the children still sung by those with no wish to forget:

> Crematorium black and silent
> Gates of hell, corpses piled
> I drag stiff, slippery corpses
> While the sun miles in the sky
> Here he lies, my only little boy
> How can I cast you into the flames?
> With your shining golden hair
>
> Lulay, lulay – little one
> Lulay, lulay – only son
> Lulay, lulay – my own boy
> Oy ... oy ... oy.
>
> Oh you sun, you watched in silence
> While you smiled and shined above

Saw them smash my baby's skull
On the cold stone wall
Now little eyes look calmly at the sky
Cold tears, I hear them crying
Oh my boy, your blood is everywhere
Three years old – your golden hair.

Lulay, lulay – little one
Lulay, lulay – only son
Lulay, lulay – my own boy
Oy ... oy ... oy.

And beyond that, all those others, choking, overwhelming quantities that cleave to the soul; all those for whom no songs were written, for whom none remained to sing the mourning, to place the stone of memorial visit on the grave; all those whose only grave, to steal Celan, is in the breezes, in the clouds.

For a year or so this was Reuben's existence, the endless repetition of performance and labour, interspersed with shards of fear and the perpetual quest for food. Time lost all meaning, measured only in the elapsed moments between food, or when respite might come from work, or the imminence of night, and sleep, the welcome shut-down of consciousness if not recuperation. How was it they could stand, eviscerated by hunger and riven by fatigue, for freezing hours in winter dawns and dusks? The will to live, or rather not yet to die, shored up the wasted muscle as though the whole skeleton was splinted. The brain, the soul closed down so that treacherous thoughts could never weaken resolve. He grew ever more accustomed to the suffering around him, and finally even the ubiquitous reeking receded into deep background. Like a heavy man on thin ice, the absolute centre of concentration was avoiding a mistake, whether of intonation as he was playing or of camp 'etiquette' when he was not. His entire being came down to that one function: no flirtation with providence. If he failed to survive, it must not be through any fault of his own.

Yet even as the transports began to decline, and the regime assumed a fractionally less harsh mien, so the dangers of liquidation grew as the authorities moved to hide their deeds and eliminate witnesses. He was saved by the rapidity of the decay, so that individual self-preservation – whether by flight or the pretence of belated kindness – became the Nazis' paramount driver.

Escape attempts, the revolt by the *Sonderkommando* in the very crematoria they had been forced to empty and in which they were due to be dispatched, the sound of gunfire from the rapidly encroaching Red Army – all these combined with the increasing frenzy of the remaining Nazis to create an ever more surreal atmosphere as order broke down.

Reuben had only one idea: keep with *Kapellmeister* Laks, knowing that his salvation thus far was due to him. So when in late October 1944 the wildfire rumours spread that half the camp, including the orchestra, was to be evacuated, he made sure he stuck with him and helped close up the music room.

They were taken for delousing, shuffling along in a single file until (dreadful moment) the shower room came into view. Even though they had been reassured, no-one believed anything they were told. As they stripped they had no way of knowing whether they would emerge. Some retreated into prayer as the doors slammed shut, breath held as they waited, expecting the oxygen to run out and the suffocating gas to fill their nostrils at any moment. Reuben was now deep within himself, in lands he'd never travelled, and he allowed himself for the first time since arrival to think on those he had loved, and for happy times to be relived, even as he awaited his death. A small smile turned the corners of his mouth, and his eyes slowly closed as the images came and went. He was, in the moment of death, at peace.

Then, after what seemed an eternity, rattling pipes and a low gurgling announced the advent of water, a momentary release from the rising fear despite its acid cold.

Driven from the sopping chamber by whips and darker threats, they were given old striped uniforms and led towards the gates. But this would not be one of the infamous death marches when all but the living dead were forced at gun point to walk at speed due west towards the shrinking interior of Greater Germany, their route bespeckled with the corpses of the shot and the exhausted. Herded back onto the very trains that had brought them to that hell, they were taken, without food or water and with the minimum of blankets, to Sachsenhausen, and from there, scattered among the one hundred or so satellite work camps that littered the area.

Winter had set in early that year, so that by November the weather was bitter. Reuben found himself working underground in an arms factory. For six long months (though he knew little of time) he and the other slaves harvested from death camps laboured, dawn to dusk, loading and unloading heavy materials and carrying them up steep slopes in blizzards and ice, rain and mud.

With no music to provide release, Reuben finally closed down, losing even the long-held power to play in his mind, his already thin body wasting down to skeletal, the intellect dulled to void. Now they were all alone, marooned on their own private islands, oblivious to everyone and everything, automata who worked without speaking and dragged themselves stooped and laden-legged to and from the places they were directed, adrift in a waking half-sleep; when sleeping, tortured, half-awake. All time was lost, all functions unconscious, unplanned, eyes empty of awareness, ignorant of who was the latest to drop.

Beyond fatigue.

Beyond thought.

Beyond hope.

And then finally the decay that, unknown to them, had eaten full into the soul of the Reich finally brought down that portion of the rotting edifice where they were ensnared.

On an unknown date in April 1945, they were dragooned one last time, corralled in the forecourt on a dank spring dawn. The commandant summoned up one last show of bravado:

"Prisoners! Today the victorious German army is on the march and we must leave this camp to move closer to Berlin. Remember to say wherever you go that you have been treated according to universally recognised rules. On behalf of your Fürher and the people of Germany I thank you for your service to the Reich and wish you Godspeed on your journey."

Unable to comprehend either the meaning or attitude behind his words, the prisoners dragged their broken bodies and what remained of their frayed muscles out of the compound under an armed guard; a ragbag of troops not fit by dint of age or infirmity to merit even the rapidly approaching front line.

For three days they limped westward, towards some unknown destination, shuffling along, sleeping rough, scavenging food, partners in adversity with the decrepit soldiers who accompanied them.

When the fourth day broke, they awoke with the dawn, alone, unguarded, *free*.

And, in every way, lost.

Without the sentries, the band disintegrated, suddenly shorn of control. But at the same time they were energised, as though their souls had been dormant, awaiting the lifting of the burden before exerting themselves over their shattered bodies. It was a kind of delirium, a huge explosion of chemicals that had until now lain frozen beneath the permafrost craving for survival.

Some sought weapons for protection or vengeance; others, shelter and the welcome embrace of rest; more still, food. Finally deprived of the violent, coercive parentheses that had enclosed them for so long, they unwound, though each kept within himself the necessary barriers to ward off the demons.

For Reuben, it was music. All the tunes he had ever known were liberated, as if a long-hidden library had been discovered and unlocked. He wandered down the road they had been travelling, alone, hungry, cold, shuddering as the defences began to unravel with the first symptoms of trauma. He sang, his weakened voice seeking forever louder solace in the songs of his youth, classical lieder he had learned with Leah at the piano, hits from the operettas and shows his father had loved so much, hymns from the life of poverty enjoyed by the eradicated Jewry of East Europe, international anthems to hardship and injustice that had filled the trenches. As he filled his lungs with free, clear air, anything that forced him to mine his past for tune and lyric sufficed and was shrilled noisily into the air.

For Corporal Nathaniel Scott, American GI from Mississippi and the advanced guard for his troop, it was not a vista for which he was at all prepared. As he and two comrades rounded a bend in the road that led east out of Buchberg he heard the sounds of the pseudo spiritual 'Ol' Man River' renting the silent, cold spring morning in a cracked, high-pitched whine. As the unknown singer reached the unforgettable couplet "But I gets weary and sick of trying/I'm tired of living, but scared of dying" Scott came face-to-face with Reuben, wrapped in a tattered greatcoat liberated from a roadside corpse, filthy, faded striped suit and cap, ill-fitting clogs padded out with rags, shaven head betraying the scabs of malnutrition, face hollowed and grey, hobbling down the road in a trance, devoid of awareness, walking like a blind man, staring, unseeing, oblivious to his surroundings.

The soldiers paused, taking in the shocking, surreal vision.

Scott spoke first.

"Hey, man, how you doin'?"

Reuben stopped dead in his tracks, song dying in his throat, dark-ringed, sunken eyes agape in astonishment at the battle-worn, mountainous man standing huge before him in the middle of the road, machine gun at the ready.

"A – A – American?"

"Yes, sirrh."

"Then I will live?"

"You bet, sirrh."

"Why?"

With that one word, the one word that would haunt him, haunt them all, forever, he imploded, the last vestiges of inner strength evaporating in the moment, so that, to Scott, it was as if he collapsed slowly from within, and the big GI had to move with unlikely speed to catch the limp, empty body before it hit the ground.

And what of the man that the corporal caught in his strong arms? The Reuben Mendel who had alighted at the ramp in Auschwitz had been willowy, the strengthening of frame by his long voyage in search of escape beginning to wane as the deprivations of Gurs and the train journey took their toll, the full head of hair just tinged with the suggestion of silver at the temples, entirely in keeping with his near forty-five years. Despite the rigour of that first camp and the appalling rail trek across Europe, he was unbowed – exhausted, but still alert enough to retrieve the violin and to show defiance, even at the imminence of his own death.

But the man who slumped into Scott's embrace was not the same. Although closer to forty-seven than six, he looked a dying seventy or more. The flesh of the face was gone and dark ravines lay where once his cheeks had been. The depravity of his features, with eyes cowering in the recesses of their blackened sockets, accentuated the bone-proud skull, now betraying the hint of pure white where the most recent shaving had just begun to grow. Skeletal wrists and ankles that hung shockingly below too short rags were translucent, finger bones clearly visible, muscle consumed by over-activity and under-feeding.

"Why?"

The soldier scooped him up and carried him gently back towards his colleagues. Tears filled his eyes as the delirious Reuben, light as a child, heavy with burden, repeated the same word over and over and over again:

"Why?"

He laid him softly in a lorry, swaddling him in thick blankets as he would a baby, and they drove carefully back to the nearest field hospital.

"Why?"

Intermezzo #2

It is time to pause and play the numbers game, if you have the stomach for it. Now it's all over, and Reuben has survived, the moment is here for a stock-taking.

We're going back to the moment when the Mendels fled Vienna. Multiply that scene a million times, the detritus of a million families bestrewn in street, along corridor, on cattle wagon floor, or abandoned to some unknown future in wardrobe, drawer or cupboard. All those dolls never again dressed, regiments of tin soldiers never again arranged in serried rank, forests of books whose leaves would never again be turned, pages folded, spines broken by a reader impatient for progress. Who can envision a single million, let alone the estimated *six* million annihilated Jews? How can mere words elucidate inconceivable numeration? Truly what we seek to understand embraces not only the attributes of the avalanche but also the sheer quantities that were swept away.

But dare we contemplate the head-spinning numbers, we who, untouched by its malignant power, sit secure in our comfort zone, wallowing in full stomachs, warm hearths, solid roofs, effective clothing, private sanitation?

For just like its perverse beauty lay in its very inconceivability, rendering readiness impossible, so the numbers destroyed lie beyond the ability of the human mind to fathom.

And so we fall back on analogy, illustration, desperate to configure a way of bringing it within our conceptual capabilities:

$$6,000,000 = [1 \text{ per day x } 16,000 \text{ years}]$$

The death-chain shackles us back through all we have ever known to a time when next to nothing was known. Sure, some cave art and primitive sculpture (for the instinct to shape our environment is primeval) but no pottery or metal work. Perhaps the rudiments of agriculture, but no domestication of animals. No houses, villages or towns, cities or countries, but troglodyte packs whose territory was no more secure than any other primate's. Just ice and rawness, bleakness bedecked with volcanic landscapes and vast territories where not even one of what we are now stirred. From the nothing of then to the everything of now, each and every one of the connecting days would bear one hollow-eyed, shaven, skeletal corpse.

If that is a journey too far then bring it closer to home.

Between the birth of Jesus of Nazareth and the celebration of its second millennium, a mere three-quarters of *one* million days would have passed. To get to six million, place a family consisting of four grandparents, two parents and two children on each single day since 0 AD, close your eyes, and imagine that tortuous passage of time from then until now. Each and every day carpeted with three generations, that family of eight hollow-eyed, shaven, skeletal corpses.

From the heyday of Rome to its decline, through the uncharted first thousand years with Christianity's triumphant march, the birth of Islam, the advance of native Americans, the dominance of the Khans, the hidden development of innumerable tribes across the globe whose gentle ebb and flow have avoided the scrutiny of all but their own oral historians.

And that first millennium is but one half of the journey. Never forget. Each and every day carpeted with three generations, that family of eight hollow-eyed, shaven, skeletal corpses.

Reflect, if you will, on the second half of the journey, the second thousand years, on the multifarious travels that take us from the dark and wild days of those one hundred decades to the lives we have today.

Driven by burgeoning populations and the ever-growing needs of an increasingly sophisticated populace, just watch the development of nations and super-nations, from what were once small towns to powerful city states and cantons, uniting by (frequently coercive) coalescence to become regions, then countries, all with their own emerging governance: monarchies, democracies, theocracies, autocracies. The wars, the struggles, the injustices, the politicking, the manoeuvring as peoples jockeyed for power, for position, for posterity in the continuously shifting sands of history. All those micro-events and macro-movements. Each and every day carpeted with three generations, that family of eight hollow-eyed, shaven, skeletal corpses.

At the outset, communication was rudimentary, hand-written and constrained by distance and time. And now? The path has taken us from illuminated manuscripts through printing and the telephone to satellites. A world that was limited to a tiny circle radiating from a parochial base has now expanded by road and rail and air to reach around the globe, and beyond. Each and every day carpeted with three generations, that family of eight hollow-eyed, shaven, skeletal corpses.

Envision how knowledge and understanding have flourished with the founding of the sciences that led from Copernicus through Galileo and Newton to Einstein and humans walking upon the Moon. And the voyage within Man himself – from trepanning for headache relief to heart transplants, from da Vinci's elementary anatomy through an unending war with disease, from Freud's journey into the soul to the unravelling of DNA, our biological essence. Each and every day carpeted with three generations, that family of eight hollow-eyed, shaven, skeletal corpses.

Or imagine instead how our species has, over these last one thousand years, expressed its dreams and fears, hopes and frustrations, loves and hates. Close your eyes once more and imagine candlelit Tuscan rooms in which Giotto fathered painting and Dante narrative verse, or the vaulted cathedrals of Rome for which Palestrina formulated the foundations of music. And see all those darkened, musty ateliers where their progeny – Michelangelo and da Vinci through Caravaggio and Rembrandt to Monet and Picasso; Shakespeare and Cervantes through Goethe and Racine to Whitman and Tolstoy; Bach and Mozart through Beethoven and Schubert to Mahler and Shostakovich – gave voice to all our striving. Each and every day carpeted with three generations, that family of eight hollow-eyed, shaven, skeletal corpses.

So whenever we hear the dread phrase 'six million', let us not shrug it away as a number too vast to encompass, but rather we should meditate on its immensity and imagine the line of dead that leads way back to the times when all that we now know was nothing.

But before we consign it to the feedstock of imagination, perhaps let us think on one more aspect of these multitudes: the heart-breaking lost potential of the destroyed and the life-denied. For who knows what glories were thwarted by direct destruction and the indirect abruption of those uncountable genetic and cultural rivers?

What scientific breakthroughs were left undiscovered by dead and unborn Einsteins? What suffering remained unalleviated by dead and unborn doctors? And injustices left unredressed by dead and unborn lawyers? How many Stradivari remained un-bowed by dead and unborn Heifetzs? Or Steinways unplayed by dead and unborn Schnabels?

All those lives, wasted, precluded. What might have been? What might have been!

Chapter 13

This was the dead spot in Mendel's life, for he could recall little of what occurred. Piecing it together years later, he came to know that he was taken from the hospital to Bergen-Belsen, now liberated by the British and where special units had been trained to nurse back from the brink those who teetered on its edge.

Slowly he recovered, even though this time there was no mother to place a violin in his lap, no one on whom his fury could be vented. Apart from more sophisticated care and better medicine, what accelerated healing was the repository of experience that he now possessed, a greater maturity than when first he faced a long and hazardous road back. But something else was driving him, the ambition voiced by Wásko at the ramp: "Try to live to tell what happened here."

He was alive. The time had come not for retribution but to make sure that the world knew how his family had come to ash. As his strength began to return it rushed to fuel his tongue, and the words came in a deluge not of grief, as all the pain lay yet too deep, but of history, events, a seamless narrative, sea-bed trawl of every minutiae, until his mind begged for respite. It was as if the very act of articulation gave all that had happened a life of its own, independent of Reuben.

He explained his background and all that had come to pass, everything, from the trenches on. The telling and retelling of his story – shocking, but no more so than any other survivor's, and a lot less fortuitous, miraculous, than many – eased his recovery and repatriation.

Europe was drowning in the stinking pus of war. At every roadside lay the discarded remains of lives in flight. In every city centre thronged thousands of the lost, dislocated from family, homeland, their very selves. Societies no longer existed, and people wandered, dazed and broken, from the ruins of one anchorage to the shattered remnants of another.

Often they were gathered in displaced persons' camps, sometimes the very same sites in which their recent horrors had been played out. Not for Reuben. His explanatory exuberance secured a berth home, as those for whom a home still stood were shipped out as soon as possible.

It took six more months, a full year from when he, Laks and the rest had left Auschwitz, before the train that brought him from the coast pulled into Waterloo. But the London to which he returned just before Christmas 1945 was so different from the one he had last seen, on a family visit, in 1932. It had been ravaged, much of it reduced by bomb and firestorm to rubble, leaving mounds of fragmented masonry and the charred skeletons of buildings. The atmosphere was austere, burdened by the realities of 'victory at all costs'.

And he too was altered. But whereas he had changed irrevocably way down to his very core, so that all remained of the old Reuben was some physical similarity, the Rodrigues had not. They had suffered deprivation, but not of the kind that impels reconsideration of the very stuff of life.

They took him in, smothering him in a love borne partly from grief at the loss to their own lineage and partly from some deeply inset sense of guilt that they, Jews too, had been spared the destruction.

Yet when Reuben spoke of all that had come to pass, they knew they ought to listen, but couldn't bear to hear. They joined the eternal debate of what it meant, and how Yahweh could have stopped his ears to suffering and to the slaughter of the innocents, for whom Miriam and Elias loomed large as lost totems. And when there could be no answer, they resiled into their pre-war superstitions and habits, as if nothing could be allowed to change, as if the story that Reuben had recounted was like that of Abraham and Isaac, a parable of the test of faith, and were they to allow even the suspicion of doubt to come to mind then they would have failed.

He felt the distances between them growing; they were of a different time and, not having endured what he had, could never understand. He began to withdraw into himself, sitting in a chair, staring blankly into the far distance.

The nights were worst, when the silence of the house allowed him to hear the din of the camps playing in his head, the endless hum of whimpers, screams, whip cracks, the fizzle of electric wire welcoming another to its embrace, the hoot of a train. And when sleep finally came it was accompanied by nightmares, horror-filled mosaics that woke the house with their screams and curses.

Finally the fractured nights brought the whole family to distraction, and after a discussion they invited the rabbi in to talk to Reuben. This was not the wisest idea.

"Reuben, you have a visitor."

"I don't really wish to see anyone."

"But he's come especially to see you."

"I don't think so, if it's all the same to you."

Rabbi Baum forced his way into the room and announced himself with an unconvincing informality.

"Reuben, my boy, thank you for seeing me."

"What do you want?"

"Your family is rather worried about you, and thought that you might appreciate the chance to talk."

"With you?"

"Well, yes. I have spoken with one or two who were also spare –"

"Spared? You weren't going to say 'spared' were you, Rabbi? This isn't going to be a trotting out of some formula about deliverance, is it? I don't know how the others reacted, but let me make this easy for you. I wasn't plucked out of the valley of death by some unseen hand.

Luck, pure luck ... oh, and don't forget the ability, the *willingness*, to throw off all pretence of civilisation, forego any interest in decency. Animal instinct, no shame, pure fortune to find people to warn me, teach me the ropes in a place for which no preparation was possible. That's all it was. Shameless cheating, lying, thinking only of me, not giving a damn about anyone else. But above all, just luck."

"And do you not consider that this luck may have had some providential origin, some larger purpose?" Baum countered, feigning gentleness but inwardly uncomfortable about where the conversation was going, unaccustomed as he was to having his authority challenged and being engaged as an equal in philosophical debate.

"You really don't want to have this discussion," Reuben went on, as though reading his mind. "I don't know how long you've pondered these things, but I've thought of little else since I began to get better. Don't try to argue about divine intervention. I see from your eyes that you can envisage the repercussions. If I was saved, why not the others? And why all those children? This is not a road you want to go down, is it?"

A prickly pause.

"I thought not.

"I don't know what experiences you have heard about. I haven't a clue what other survivors are going through. But I know what *I'm* going through – it's mine, and mine alone. It's not just all that happened, the things I keep seeing, the sounds that won't go away. It's ... it's ... look ... I ... I ... k – k – KILLED them, don't you, can't they *see* that! They're all dead because of *me* ... Mama, Papa, Sarah, Mi ... El ... the children ... it's *my* fault. They trusted me to keep them safe – and I failed them, completely failed them! I said to them, back in Toulouse, if only one of us makes it, it should be one of the children. But *I'm* here, not them. So what's the point, what's the fucking point? What does your precious Talmud make of that, eh?"

Reuben lapsed into silence, hunched over, and Baum regarded

224

the broken man before him, slumped in the armchair. He wanted to reach out to him, to place a hand on his arm and squeeze just to let him know that he was not alone. But a force prevented the intimacy, as though Reuben embodied a new power in the heavens that countermanded everything the rabbi had been taught and represented some malign threat to all the points of reference that had constituted his life. He was unable to touch him, for he was, in a truth that must never be uttered, profoundly scared of Mendel and his kind.

He knew, deep within a dark, secret place where none had strayed, that there was no way to reconcile what Reuben had experienced with the existence of a god to whom he, Rabbi Baum, had utterly dedicated himself and upon whose worship the entire edifice of his existence was constructed.

But he couldn't just leave either, so they sat there in a heavy silence until dusk began to fall, the room now cast in shadows.

Eventually Reuben stirred.

"Look, I appreciate your concern. I know they're worried about me. I also know that my presence discomforts them, as well as reminding them of their loss. While I'm here, they can't move on. And perhaps I can't either."

After Baum had gone, Reuben began to think that maybe the rabbi's visit had not been without value. During the next few days his mind began to turn away from the past with which it had been obsessed and to try and envisage what the future might hold. His grief and guilt lay heavy, and he thought he heard Miriam saying: *"If you think of the future, you will leave us behind."* And he himself called out, as though shouting might carry his voice to them all, wherever they were: "NO! NEVER! While *I* live, you do, in here and here," knuckling heart and head. He slumped low in the armchair as he fell to thinking.

An idea once born can never be unborn, and Reuben started to stir. One evening, when the Rodrigues were gathered for the main meal of the day, he joined them as they repaired to the drawing room for coffee.

"I just wanted to thank you for looking after me and to apologise for being such a burden. I've decided to find a flat somewhere; it's time that I moved on and tried to make something of my life before it is too late. It means, I think, that you shall not see much more of me. To make the step, I have to strike out on my own. You know, I've never really been alone and healthy. I wonder what it will be like. I'm scared but it feels like something that I have to do."

"Reuben, my boy." Leah's brother, Joseph, the elder of the family, pushed back his chair and stood up. "We have little idea of what you have been through and I know I speak for us all when I say that we are proud of what you are, and honour all that you did to save your – and our – family. If we have appeared insensitive to your suffering or intolerant of your recovery, we hope you find it in your heart to forgive us ..."

"Uncle ..."

"Ssshhh. Remember this – wherever you are, whatever you do, this is your home and the door is always open."

"Uncle Joe, please ..."

"Hush. Now, have you thought of the practical matters, like money?"

A sheepish, embarrassed lull.

"Typical of you artists. Well, you know you're quite wealthy, don't you?"

Bemused look.

"Of course not, how could you? Well, when your Grandmother Hannah, may her dear soul rest in peace, passed away in 1935, your mother and I inherited a large sum of money. As she died when you were all in Vienna and things were a little uncertain already, we decided to leave all the capital here. As you are her only heir, that money is now yours. You remember you had to sign some papers while you were recovering before they would let you come home?"

"Yes."

"Well, they were sufficient to obtain probate, and the money is now lodged in the bank in your name. Here, take the cheque book. Be free, and go in health."

Reuben fell into the old man's warm embrace.

At the turn of 1947, having found lodgings in Hampstead, he began to immerse himself in London's cultural life, visiting galleries, going to concerts and the opera, watering the roots of his life that had lain unnourished for so long.

Hermit-like, he took up the violin again. In a repeat of his initiation, he sought out once again the showroom of J. P. Guivier, now located in Mortimer Street and, explaining his history and circumstances, threw himself on the owner's mercy. He knew the sound he wanted – a resonant, mellow tone with the capacity to sound sharp-edged when needed. Reuben spent days playing on a variety of instruments as much as his unconditioned hands and arms would permit, waiting to hear that mystical quality.

The finding of it was wreathed in coincidence. The owner, in fact the son of Mrs Cohn who'd sold Leah and Moses that quarter-size fiddle aeons ago, took him to one side.

"Mr Mendel, would you kindly step this way into my office? I heard that a truly special instrument might be coming to the market and took the liberty of asking whether it would be in order for you to try it out. The executors of the estate concerned consented, once I had told them your tale and promised them the utmost discretion. I hope you do not regard that as in any way impertinent."

"Not if it is as good as you imply."

"It has some history. Would you like to know it first?"

"No. Thank you. I would prefer to judge it on its merits."

Mr Cohn turned to the open violin case on his desk and removed the instrument with due reverence.

"I have tuned it but ..."

Reuben had already started to pluck the strings, tweaking the bridge, twisting the pegs and turning the fine-tuners before reaching for the bow.

A couple of scales, runs and *arpeggios* and he was ready to put it through its paces. Under his fingers, the violin seemed to glow in the heat which he generated from the Bach Partita that contained the Chaconne. The fiddle felt somehow at home, nestled safely between his jaw and shoulder.

He stopped, brow furrowed.

"This is it, this is definitely it! Utterly beautiful tone, so dark and rich, yet with plenty of bite."

"I hoped you would think it so."

"It's strange, but it seems a familiar sound. You had better tell me the story."

"You know or, rather, knew, this instrument and its previous owner."

"Really? How come? I don't recognise it."

"That is because you usually saw it at a different angle."

"Please stop being cryptic and put me out of my misery."

"Arnold Rosé was exiled in London. He passed away recently, on the twenty-fifth of August last year to be exact, while you were recuperating. This is his 1773 Guadagnini."

"He was here, in London? And I never knew! Oh, if only I'd known, I should have visited him. Now I shall play his violin. I must visit his grave."

"You will have to go to Austria. He was buried in Grinzing, with his wife, in the same cemetery as Mahler."

"That is a good thing. I shall pay my respects whenever I go to Austria. Perhaps he'd like to hear a few notes played on his own fiddle.

"Now, to business."

Having finally found it, Reuben was aghast at the price tag, but a conversation with Uncle Joe reassured him that, first, he wouldn't starve and, second, there was nothing his mother would have wanted more than that her grandson own such a wonderful instrument. With the astute businessman leading the negotiation, the deal was done.

His precious violin safely secured, Reuben practised for hours and hours, solitarily, retraining body and mind through rigorous, punishing exercises, rehearsing all that he had learned with Fanny Hartmann so many years ago, and everything he had picked up since. When he ate it was simple fare, bread and cheese, a little sausage, anything that didn't require cooking.

He rarely slept, finding in one of those bitter-black ironies which would baffle and shock him for the rest of his life that *arbeit* actually could *macht frei*. For when he was deep within the music he was, for that moment, nowhere else, not even in perpetual hell; there, immersed, drowning in the notes, unable to consider anything but engraving them onto his mind and perfecting their intonation, he was liberated from the sights and sounds that assailed him.

Even when sleep became necessary, it was unwelcome, to be discouraged and put off as long as possible, for fear of the dreams that came when his guard was down, in the uninhibited terrain of his unconscious. So, when he became too tired to play, Reuben took to roaming the ancient Heath, often in the dead of night, enjoying the sounds of nocturnal urban wildlife, relishing the wet grip of dew-heavy grass and enjoying the air, even when it was clogged with smog.

He found again his memory, filling it with music that he studied in libraries. It was all chamber music, whose sound world reminded him of the precious moments of release provided in hell: Haydn's pioneering work in the string quartet, Mozart's perfection of the genre, Beethoven string trios and his sixteen quartets (especially the 'late' final five), Schubert's glorious contributions to set beside his piano trios and, above all, the two quintets for piano and quartet (universally loved as the 'Trout') and the towering piece for quartet plus an extra cello.

He sought to fill every last fragment of his mind, as though trying to replace what lurked there. But he failed, as fail he must, the elasticity of his intellect expanding to accommodate it all.

For another year he saw no-one, met with no-one. He remained in his apartment, building muscle, reading text books on technique, listening to the gramophone and wireless for performances by famous quartets like the Busch.

Then he emerged. As 1948 faded into 1949 his cocoon could no longer contain him. He sought a quartet that he might join, and when he couldn't find one, formed his own, placing an advertisement in the musical press to find a second violinist, violist and cellist. Hundreds replied, and he bent intuitively towards the émigré community, those who had fled Europe before the war and been interned as aliens.

But first he wrote to Furtwängler, care of the Musikverein:

Dear Maestro,

I hope that, despite the dozen or so years and the tumultuous events that separate us, you may remember me, and that this letter finds you well. Thanks in no small part to your pre-emptive action, I survived the worst ravages of Hitler, although my beloved family did not. If we have the opportunity to meet again, perhaps I shall tell you more.

Maestro, my reason for writing is simple. I am forming a string quartet and would be honoured if you would allow me to show my gratitude and admiration by granting permission for it to bear your name. Without wishing to appear in any way obsequious, I think the 'The Furtwängler Quartet' has a resonance that speaks to the interpretative tradition which will lie at its heart. I hope, too, that it expresses the ambition to endow our music-making with a level of authority to match that which, perhaps through a romantic prism I do confess, I recall our Philharmonic used to exert under your baton.

I would like to say that I read with shame of what happened in Chicago and of the criticism of your conduct during the war. If explaining what you did for me could help redress the balance then I hope very much that you would feel able to call upon me.

Respectfully yours,

Reuben Mendel

Vienna Philharmonic, First Violins, 1920–1936

The reply came as fast as the postal system would allow:

My dear Mendel,

How pleased I was to see your name at the bottom of your letter, and how sad I was to read of your loss. I was, as you well know, never one for words, so I thought I might share with you what Beethoven wrote to his friend Wegeler when devastated by the knowledge that he would soon be deaf:

> *I will seize fate by the throat; it shall*
> *certainly not bend and crush me – Oh, it*
> *would be so lovely to live a thousand lives!*

I am not impertinent enough to even attempt to understand how your tragedies compare; only to hope that you too might master your grief and triumph, as he did. I am flattered indeed that your chosen vehicle will bear my name, and I thank you from the bottom of my heart for your generous thought and kindly remembrance. I sense, however, that not even a Musikverein full of those I might have helped a little would suffice to mollify the mob.

I pray that, this time, my earlier wish will indeed come true for you:

Pax vobiscum.
Furtwängler.

While waiting for the reply and with the money liberated from Leah's estate, Reuben hired a hall and prepared the auditions. In parallel, he made some discreet enquiries, anonymously acquired that last haven, the house in Toulouse, and arranged for a local lawyer to inform the residents that they could stay there indefinitely.

As he sat in the venue waiting for the first of the players to arrive, he began to doubt what he was doing. He had thoroughly studied the audition pieces for each instrument, but confidence in his ability to recognise kindred and complementary spirits started to leach slowly from him as water from an imperceptibility cracked vessel. He thought he had in his mind's ear a clear impression of the sound he sought, one that sacrificed nothing to ensemble and pure harmony but had at its heart a grittiness, an edginess made of pure steel. Could he recognise it in the artificial environment of an empty, cavernous room?

These qualms stayed with him through the first two sessions of violin, viola and cello. Soon enough, however, he tuned in to the noise they each made and how their personalities shone through, and he slowly came to realise what he did like by hearing and seeing what he didn't.

In addition to playing, some whose quality and bearing appealed to him were invited to talk for a few minutes, impromptu, about their favourite pieces and what made them special.

Finally he chose three men, not for the perfection of their playing, for he knew well the pressure of the audition, remembering both Weingartner and Laks. He was looking for that extra something: passion, intellect, the desire to penetrate the finest music that many composers ever produced.

Two were German, one Austrian – each having made the trip to London before the war, when the Mendels had not. They had all lost relatives in the camps; and philosophically saw music as the bridge to cross cultural, racial and generational divides and unite people in neutral territory free from politics and dogma.

Erich Weintraub, the second violinist, was willowy; his long, thin legs were disproportionate to his trunk and seemed to have a life of their own on stage, at one moment tucked right under his seat and the next flailing in front of him as he rocked backwards. A shiny pate surrounded by wild, wispy, brown hair made him look like a professor and indeed he talked like one, fast, clipped but with the soft centre of one who was confident in what he spoke.

Felix Löwy was the group's violist. The spitting image of Trotsky, with round, black-framed glasses, a thick moustache and goatee beard, he was permanently hyperactive, with a feverish intellect that fuelled a voracious appetite for reading. He would never be seen without a dog-eared book protruding from the pocket of his overcoat or jacket. When he performed he exhibited a rabbit-like energy where he would burst into motion and slide across his chair.

The cellist was Leon Friedländer. Father figure to the quartet, he was approaching sixty, grey haired and with the air of wise resignation worn by those who have seen much and lost a great deal. He never spoke of his past, nor mentioned any family. And, in the unwritten rule of quartets, the others never asked. But the three younger men turned to him for advice, and it was he who arbitrated the inevitable disputes of repertoire, interpretation and schedule which would pepper their working lives. In performance, he exhibited an aristocratic bearing, back ramrod straight and very little lateral movement of his body, save when the music drove him to it by its demands of speed and sound level.

The Furtwängler Quartet was launched in the summer of 1949. They rehearsed well for four months solid and had retained a concert agent who realised that London thirsted for great chamber music. A booking was secured for the Wigmore Hall and they made their debut in a classic programme of Haydn, Mozart and Schubert.

Critics immediately noted the perfection of ensemble, their ability to understand instinctively how each partner would play. They suppressed the tendency to overdrive, tending to hold back rather than press forward, a typical Viennese approach.

And it was so therapeutic. Reuben was the dominant personality, his unruly mane of snow-white hair (maintained as perpetual defiance and a symbol of individuality and survival) tossed to and fro with the rhythm of the music. The medium afforded him the perfect fusion of orchestral anonymity and the oratorical opportunity for a soloist. They were an instant success, filling a void that had been left by the passing of the great inter-war groups like the Busch and the Rosé. They enjoyed a friendly rivalry with the Amadeus, but always seemed prepared to take more risks, even if doing so jeopardised elegance and smoothness of ensemble.

For Reuben, fame brought a surprise benefit over and above its material advantages and the partial escape that accompanied his total immersion in preparation and performance. A letter arrived from Paris shortly before they were due to perform there for the first time.

Dear Mendel,

I cannot tell you with what joy and no small degree of
pride I read of your survival and success!
I am established here in Paris and read of your imminent
arrival here. I would so welcome the opportunity to
renew our acquaintance, this time in comfort and safety.
If you feel able (and willing!) to spare some time, it would
give me enormous pleasure to meet again.
I await your reply with anticipation.
Respectfully yours,
Szymon Laks

Reuben wired him immediately.

Maestro,

Shocked & delighted to hear from you.

In Paris from 16th – Georges V – 5 days.

Arranging 2 tickets at box office Salle Pleyel for 1st concert + invite to green room & dinner.

Hope you can make it – wire back if need to change.

Can't wait to catch up and hear your story.

Thank you for getting touch.

In haste,

Mendel

"Meeting up with him after such an interval, both of time and emotional distance, was more difficult than I could ever have imagined. Of course, the balance of the relationship was skewed by the fact that he had dominated it, and I was permanently indebted to him. But it was something else. He is a marvellous person, whose heroics in saving the likes of me are largely unsung. However, the bond was too tenuous and traumatic, a bit like meeting an old colleague only to discover that the only thing you had in common was the workplace. He was, I guess, too close to my loss, unlike other survivors with whom I have congregated. We still correspond regularly, but I have felt the need, selfishly I should add, to steer clear of too much intimacy, so that our main topic of conversation is music, on which he is endlessly stimulating."

For the next five years their celebrity grew alongside their repertoire. The Furtwängler Quartet's performances of the Schubert String Quintet, with the second cello performed by the golden players – Casals, Piatigorsky, Tortelier – were famous, as were their renditions of the Beethoven middle quartets, the three Razumovsky, the 'Harp' and the 'Serioso'. But they never performed his late quartets.

Wherever they went, they were asked the same questions: "When will you play late Beethoven?" Every time they answered the same:

"When all of us are ready." And when pressed, whoever was the spokesman replied: "We study them, we rehearse them, but we are not yet ready to perform them."

They knew the time would come when Reuben felt that he was ready. And all the while he stalled the mystery grew of what it would be like when the most enigmatic of quartets took on the most enigmatic works in the repertoire.

For Weintraub, Löwy and Friedländer knew that the works were not just the greatest musical challenge Reuben faced but, far more significantly, that they constituted, *en bloq*, the severest, most daunting emotional peak he would have attempted to scale since his liberation.

Intermezzo #3

Sometimes, when the music has finally faded and the mind reverberates only to its memory, the temptation to wonder whether Beethoven knew what he was achieving can be irresistible. Did the colossus truly realise as his quill etched notes and chords in the flickering candlelight of shadowy rooms that a journey like no other was in train? Dishevelled, indifferent to the mounting squalor invading his modest lodgings, as he sat at the battered Broadwood hammering out those massive creations on the worn keys and scratching them with multiple blotted corrections onto staved paper, was he even aware of what immortal, inexhaustible riches were pouring from his turbulent soul? When he wandered the fields of his brother's estate at Gneixendorf, the peasants who encountered his manic waving and shouting had no inkling that he was working through music that would astound, move, inspire for as long as the art itself is practised. But did *he*?

Or was it of an entirely different nature, an involuntary outpouring of something pure and essential that could no longer be contained? A stream from the unconscious wrought in beauty and miraculously sculpted by immaculate technique; a reflex response to a life shaped by torment whose end could now be perceived if not predicted and which demanded a closure fitting to its epic, earth-altering proportions?

By what magical process could he revisit his whole being and call forth all its travails and mould them with his will, expressing them with the sole intention of their destruction so that he may, at the very last, find long-sought tranquillity? There he sat, drowning in the glacial gathering of his own fluids, driven to cleanse, to sweep out all the sadness, frailty and frustrations that he had suffered.

It is comforting to think that he knew all this, that this most testamentary of geniuses was etching out of his own soul an emotional codicil to the political and spiritual will he so generously bequeathed to mankind in the Ninth Symphony and *Missa Solemnis*. There he sat, marooned on an island of deafness and loneliness, gazing out across the limitless ocean of his life to the teeming masses which he loved and yet from which he stood so far apart. His final gift would be the greatest – the unvarnished revelation of the self, the quartering of the intellect and the soul so that all may gaze upon it and understand the very essence of what it is to be human.

For such music there can be no programme, no literal explanation of each phrase, every movement. But what may be laid out is something akin to a map. Not an X-marks-the-spot route to treasure (though treasure it undoubtedly is), but more like one of those ancient representations of the celestial skies, an interpretation of what can only be perceived imperfectly and incompletely but which nevertheless presents a key to understanding, one of a number of paths to appreciation.

In the history of the theatre there have been so many great plays that it is impossible to say which is the greatest. *Hamlet? Hedda Gabler? Phèdre?* Who could possibly decide? But for sheer drama, for the naked exposure of existential angst and the courageous confrontation – with eventual triumph – over the most deeply embedded antagonist, then Beethoven's final set of string quartets stand without equal. Liberated from the limitations of language, the works are the five acts, in twenty-six scenes, of a heroic epic wherein our Odysseus undertakes the most arduous voyage of all – deep into his own being.

The pinnacle of western music, Beethoven's late quartets were the great man's last thoughts before he embarked upon his eternal journey. Profoundly personal, difficult, yet when penetrated an inexhaustible exchequer, they are the quintessence of music, the Everest for any ensemble, every listener. And like their Himalayan counterpart, the view commanded from those great heights hits the soul with a luminosity almost painful in its intensity. Standing on that proud promontory, the gaze encompasses all the music ever written, and everything heard subsequently is forever in its shadow.

But for Reuben Mendel, Beethoven's late quartets were much more than even this. His fear of performing them was absolute because he saw mirrored in them the catastrophic passage of his own life, the profoundest exposition of the tragedy whose shadow enveloped him. And though the voyage on which they took their composer would eventually reach harbour, the passage was fraught with danger, full of terror.

He understood what they meant to Beethoven, that they presaged Freud's self-analysis or, more pointedly, Primo Levi's Auschwitz writings: a journey to be undertaken only by the very bravest, those for whom eternity would be preferable, whose liberation can come only when the demons which hover are turned upon, chased, hunter turned hunted, haunter turned haunted, tracked deep down to the bleakest reminiscence of the past where the poison seeps from the walls, floor, ceiling, where no light shines, where the howling of the painful years bounces off the walls in a ceaseless cacophony of screams ... and where the only interruption comes with the fragmented echo of the voices of all the lost ones. Only when the monster has been pursued to its lair at the barbaric heart of the maze is the torch brought into the dark corners and the skulking minotaur, that malign Gordian knot of the profoundest wounds that life has inflicted, burnt beyond recall.

Thus Beethoven seized and sealed his fate in his five late string quartets. Embarking upon a journey without parallel in the world of art, he announced his odyssey at the start of the first with momentous chords, firm in their resolve to rush headlong to the fray.

And through that first and its successor, the music ebbs and flows, descending all the while towards the beckoning crucible where all time is sublimated into the purest essence. Occasionally the hero drives on towards the final battle, knowing that the serenity of triumph can only be enjoyed after the battle has been fought. Sometimes he hesitates before the enormity of the task, lacking the belief in his ability to annihilate the fearsome enemy. Every now and then he lingers as though in some gallery to gaze at vignettes from his history, cast upon the dripping walls by a mystical projector.

The slideshow deepens, the impression moving from superficially bright colour through aged black and white to immortal sepia. He sees his mother, shallow-breathing on her Bonn deathbed while, forever in the distance, he, her young son, flies frantically back from Vienna ... scared he would be too late to cradle her head, to kiss that still warm brow, to whisper the last and longest goodbye.

The picture flits back and forth in a random review of his life. Flashes appear of his hopeless father – of paternal torture at the keyboard, of embarrassing, drink-sodden rescues from the police, of lies about his age so that Mozart's precocious virtuosity might not overshadow Ludwig's slower development. Friends, patrons and lovers materialise to speed him on his way, summoned from his memory in apparently haphazard fashion, some encouraging, others not, but all threads in the tapestry that made him what he was.

The descent continues. Darker images come into focus. Physical frailty pervades his thoughts. The sweaty nights when fever seemed to invade his whole being, numbing the brain as well as the limbs. The relief in recovery tempered by the certainty that illness would come again, afflicting some as yet untouched part of his strong, racked body.

Until, at last, the destination hoves into view. The third, the middle, the emotional centre of the quartets. The theatre for the final battle, where the hero will come face to face with the Hydra, and fight it to the death, head-by-head.

At first they circle each other, eyeing their adversary, seeking out points of weakness, assessing points of strength. The tension builds, the first locking of horns comes ever closer, the space between the two ever smaller.

Beethoven braces himself. The penultimate movement is the springboard. Looking back, he would say that none of his works had ever moved him quite as much, and that merely to recall it would take him to tears. The regret at what he had lost – hearing, his Only Beloved, the chance of offspring, music never written – and the reminiscence of pain were synthesised into a single whole. During these several minutes, the entirety of existence is condensed into a timelessness where numerous mistakes, so many missed opportunities, all the bitter twists of fortune hang suspended, crudely exposed like one quartered in an ancient judicial ritual. And in his languid, anguished meandering around the central pillars of his life, Beethoven saw that they were finite, that he could encompass them with his massive will, that – for all the pain they had brought him – he was huge, powerful, dominant, a giant whose shadow fell upon them and cast them into darkness. With that realisation came fury, undammed after so many pent-up years, the river arriving in full spate, torrents, frothing, tidal waves of rage ripping a narrow gorge through sharp mountains bedecked with snow. The *Grosse Fugue*, the final movement, high plateau of the five quartets. Three towering peaks of splenetic release, separated by uneasy, too-rarely sunlit valleys in whose benign shade the soul could regather itself for the next assault. Catharsis, a cleansing abrasion so absolute that it reaches down into the pitchiest bottom of the darkest crevice, that lost place where all fearfulnesss, all hatred, all injustice, all desire for vengeance are annihilated, crushed by the mighty fist of core humanity and hurled far out of sight into the nethermost outpost of the universe. And, at the last, emerging from the heroic battle in which he confronted all those demons and slew them one by one, Beethoven stood haloed in the shimmering light of his looming sunset.

The next, penultimate, quartet, a staccato climb away from the theatre of his triumph ever higher to safety, the bloodied stage receding into shadow, was Beethoven's own favourite. Well might it be so. He knew that what he had done would stand forever among the bravest of voyages. It was almost as if the hero he buried in the Eroica had risen again to complete a journey prematurely abbreviated. And in the end he could begin to contemplate all that he had done with the gentle smile of one who knows his work is finished.

So, at last, he emerged into the light. His final complete work, the fifth quartet, apart from the rest – an exclamation mark crafted in the beauty of tranquillity to end a life. No wonder he could go laughingly into eternity. Valediction made in other late, great works for piano, orchestra and voice, all his affairs in order, the sense that the circle was finally complete, he was ready to embark on Hobbes' great leap in the dark, at peace with himself.

All this Reuben saw as clearly as Belshazzar saw the inauspicious writing on the wall. And with an equal clarity he knew that, for him, there was no hope of redemption, no chance of serenity, if the gauntlet was not picked up, if Beethoven's ultimate challenge was not confronted. He might fail; the obstacles the cycle presented might just be too onerous to navigate. But to fail would be better than to avoid the conflict, to live forever with the never knowing and with the permanent shame of capitulation without endeavour.

And what, finally, of the ultimate shock of genius, the last music to flow from that worn, wonderful quill, the movement he wrote after everything else to replace the *Grosse Fugue*?

Rueben explained the Furtwängler Quartet's position with great clarity.

"You know, of course, that Beethoven succumbed to suggestions that he write a new finale to the quartet numbered thirteen. No-one understood the Grosse Fugue; *they were completely baffled by it. To this day people are still amazed that he agreed. But it seems obvious to me. He did it because the movement had fulfilled its purpose; it had purged and liberated him. He could afford to discard it for he no longer needed it, so to speak.*

"In performances of this quartet, we have never played his substitute movement. We rehearse it, of course, but for us, it has never really worked. We played all the preceding movements knowing that we would not face the ultimate challenge, the music that made sense of the rest. If I may extend your theatrical imagery, my colleagues and I felt as if it would be like staging Hamlet *and substituting 'To be or not to be' with a greetings card. We only ever performed it as an encore to the last quartet, its rightful chronological, stylistic and psychological place."*

Chapter 14

In musical circles, rumour had been rife for some time. At the United Nations Concert of Reconciliation, being held to commemorate the tenth anniversary of the liberation of Auschwitz, Mendel would return to the camp and for the first time the Furtwängler Quartet would play one of the Beethoven late quartets in public.

For Reuben, the decision to play was driven by the location as much as the occasion. He had this anxiety that rippled through his entire being, a harbinger of horror; inevitable, if not yet imminent. With no warning, shivers would wash over him and icy tingling cascade from scalp to sole. He had been unable to identify it, attributing it vaguely to his perpetual sense of apprehension. But when the quartet's agent was approached about the concert, there had been an instant crystallisation. He realised that the conjunction of camp and concert represented what had been nagging at him. It was as if an unknown Rubicon lay just around a slow, meandering bend and after so long the curve had just straightened to reveal it.

Weintraub, Löwy and Friedländer were surprised when he suggested they do it. They too had ghosts to exorcise but theirs were neither so massive nor legion as his. When they sat down to discuss what they would play, Reuben's logic was irresistible.

"I only want to do it if it's late Beethoven, the Thirteenth with the *Grosse Fugue*."

"Why?" asked the paternal Friedländer, first to react after a few moments of stunned silence.

"Look. I realise I've been putting it off too long. We have to play these pieces. If not now, when? Honestly? I shake every time I think of playing them, but that's exactly why I should do it. Look, I'm already trembling. Do you remember what Furtwängler wrote to me when I asked his permission to use his name? It was about Beethoven seizing fate by the throat. I've been pussy-footing around this. I see now that I have to go back, that's what's been gnawing away; and I have to play late Beethoven in public. Thirteen will be the most difficult for me, so I'm thinking, what the hell, why not kill the two birds? Do you think I'm wrong?"

"Only you can say, Reuben," said Weintraub, having reflected for a while. "If you think you're up to the strain, I hope I can speak for all of us when I say that we're with you."

Löwy had a different angle. "About time. I've kept *schtum* for a while now but enough's enough. We've waited way too long. People expect it; we expect it – so let's get on with it. The sooner we start, the better. I reckon we're the best in the business, maybe the best there's ever been. But we'll never prove it without playing the Five. I'd prefer to do it as a complete cycle. However, once we've done one, we'll be away. Let's do it – and do it with Thirteen."

Friedländer closed his eyes, a quiet smile upon his lips, a contented father whose children were making him proud in their maturity, as though it was his gentle guidance that had brought them to this state of grace.

After their schedule was adjusted, they had a clear month in which to prepare. Having studied it both as individuals and ensemble, the process of embedding the notes and structure was already well in hand. They stepped up their rehearsal time, knowing that the expectations upon them were increasing with every article that rehearsed their joint and several histories.

Reuben became quieter and quieter as the date of departure loomed, withdrawing deep into his own thoughts. They all recognised the signs and left him alone. No longer needing to practise, all they discussed now were the subtleties of intonation, the synchronicity of ensemble, the minutiae of entries, for the score was imprinted on their collective conscience and the tempi ingrained in their souls.

The time came, and Reuben was alone, adrift. The weight of anticipation was heavy upon him and his shoulders hunched with the burden. Three days before the concert they travelled by ferry and train, arriving in Kraków, where they were due to stay. Last time Reuben had arrived in Poland it too was by train. But now it was different, being met at the station by a group of dignitaries and a brass band.

The four Jews had talked of this moment, when they would set foot in a nation whose hatred of their people was so strong that thirty-nine camp survivors, having somehow passed by the yawning abyss, were massacred in Kielce just one year after the war. They listened to an interminable speech from a short, rotund man with a tarnished gold chain around his neck whom they took to be the mayor, welcoming them in effusive terms that were almost believable.

As leader, Reuben replied, short both in duration and tone, the heat of his words vaporising the winter air around him.

"We thank you for your greeting. For us, of course, this is nothing to celebrate. We are here to pay homage and to play music that will make people think about what happened on this soil. We shall use our time here to reflect on what occurred a handful of miles from here, and to share with Poles the solidarity that comes with common suffering. As fellow victims of Nazi atrocity, we hope that relationships between our two peoples need never hark back to darker times when we were neither welcomed here as we have been today nor safe while we stayed."

With that they purposefully picked up their suitcases and instruments and went to the official car that was waiting for them.

As they drove, Reuben was far away, completely silent, gazing from the window but not seeing. The others were similarly lost, conjuring into their minds images of what the land must have been like but one decade earlier.

They were settled into the ancient Hotel Pod Róża, in the city's historic heart, and tried to rest. When he couldn't sleep, Reuben walked around the town and then wandered down to the old Jewish Quarter. Although now *Judenfrei*, nothing could eradicate the signs of two hundred years and more of a bustling, burgeoning community. Reuben drank in the spirit of the place: old, dead synagogues, ancient cemeteries, on doorposts the ghosts of *mezuzot*, the time-honoured symbol of a Jewish home. The very pavement seemed impregnated with the phantoms of the thousands who a mere fourteen years earlier had been hounded across the Vistula and into the ghetto.

He was much as he had been in London in the immediate aftermath of his departure from the haven with the Rodrigues. For, like then, he knew that a vast black obstacle stood between him and his future, and that it had to be surmounted or circumnavigated if he was to survive.

Before visiting the Philharmonic Hall they went to the main camp at Auschwitz and then travelled the handful of kilometres to Birkenau, killing centre of the complex. While Löwy had discovered that some of his family had perished in Dachau, Friedländer and Weintraub had lacked the will to find out what happened to so many of their relatives. So each took the visit as totemic, a symbol of what had come to pass for their own bloodlines.

Reuben, of course, knew. His silent vigil in the Orchestra's barracks and outside the kitchen where they had played twice daily was for lost and sundered lives.

But Birkenau was something altogether different.

As he walked the snowy, stony path that led through the decrepit camp, Reuben was aware of the crunching underfoot and wondered whether Mama and Papa had heard similar noises as they were driven by screaming guards and raging dogs towards annihilation. He thought of Miriam and Elias, afraid beyond comfort. And he imagined Sarah, shuffling with dull resignation, broken like the rest of them. All he was certain about was this – that never for one moment would she have lost contact with the children, and that the greater the fear, the louder the cries, the tighter her grip would have been.

The others kept their distance, each locked into his own reminiscences. Reuben wandered distractedly, roaming through the rotting barracks. The sounds and smells had never left him, just as he had never left the camp. But now, for the first time in nearly ten years, they rushed from the nagging background to the forefront of his mind.

He grew dizzy as an insane mosaic crowded in upon him, the pieces jostling for prominence. Marching music battled with the thuds and screams of beatings. Machine-gun rattles vied with the dull threnody of resigned mutterings. Insistent groaning clashed with the screech of cattle-truck doors.

When he came upon the remains of Crematorium III and its gas chamber, he tentatively descended the icy steps with the reluctant gait of all those who had preceded him. Although the rubble prevented him for entering, he squatted down to peer through the chaotic masonry.

Even with distorted perspective and fragmented sightlines, he could imagine the blackness there must have been when the iron doors were slammed tight on the packed room. He stretched an arm as far into the ruins as he could, striving to run a hand along a frozen wall and trace the invisible lines made by desperate nails clawing for release. His mind's eye fixed on their ending, seeing the piles of naked corpses heaped semi-standing in the centre of the chamber or crushed against the door. Recognising his loved ones frozen in death and covered in the filth of hundreds of final moments, Reuben was overwhelmed.

The enormity of it all engulfed him like a tidal wave and he dashed back up the steps just in time to retch into the stiff white grass. Blanched with revulsion, he stood up and turned circles, the landscape of wooden barracks, trees and wire fences merging the faster he spun, his chest heaving as he gulped huge draughts of cold air through nose and mouth into his lungs. Giddily he stuttered around the random pile of bricks, tottering in a daze, aimlessly, wanting to be anywhere as long as it was far from where he was but finding it impossible to wrench himself away.

And, as he slowed, Reuben found himself at the edge of the pool.

The virgin snow gave way beneath him and he heard the crack of ice as he broke through the thin crust of frozen water. He looked down, into the depths, and saw that it was neither blue nor brown, but grey. Hypnotically drawn to its depths, he knelt, ignorant of the cold and wet that soaked through his trousers. His bow arm swept through the coagulated film that covered the surface and the cupped hand swooped back up. The consistency of the liquid reminded him of the viscous tissue that had covered him in the trenches two lifetimes ago. He peered at the contents and the truth concussed him.

Ashes, saturated globules of ashes, filled the pool, discarded atoms of, who knows, his own family?

Like a primitive undergoing some rite of passage, he buried his face in the glutinous mixture, smearing it across his brow and cheeks, in his hair, eyes, nose and mouth. And from deep within him came the howling, tearing at the mournful quiet of Birkenau. Huge waves of sound rang from him, low like a tolling bell, ringing out the dirge of disaster. The unstopping was absolute; doubled over, kneeling in the water, muddied, haggard face rising from his knees to way back, pointing at the baleful winter sky, torso rocking to and fro, side to side.

His three comrades came when the noise reached them, as did others, running to view the commotion. And Friedländer and Weintraub raised him up, for he was lost to the world and beyond resistance, even as the reverberations rippling through his being began to subside. They moved swiftly from the camp and got him back to the hotel. A doctor was called and a sedative administered.

"He is close to a breakdown; you must cancel the concert."

"No!" came the croaked voice of Reuben, muffled by pillows and dulled by the narcotic that had already started to shred his senses. "No." But nothing more came as he drifted deeper and deeper into the welcome tranquillity of induced sleep.

He was now beyond disturbance but Löwy nevertheless lowered his voice:

"Let's see how he is tomorrow. We can do nothing until then."

The wintery dawn hung forebodingly over the ancient Polish town, heavy with threat of yet more snow to land on the fresh fall that greeted the quartet when they rose the following morning.

Reuben had always woken early, one of the less malign legacies of the camps. So when he had still not come down for breakfast by seven o'clock, Löwy went to check on him.

Knocking gently and getting no answer, he softly tried the handle and gently pushed against the unlocked door. Lit from the corridor, the curtained room was in complete disarray.

The bed was a wreck, sheets and blankets on the floor suggesting a deeply troubled night. Clothes were strewn all around. The violist tiptoed in, lest Reuben was in the bathroom or asleep in a chair.

He switched on the light when he was sure the room was empty, and rapidly scanned it before checking the open wardrobe. When he couldn't find what he was looking for, Löwy dashed from the room.

He ran up to Weintraub and Friedländer in the dining room.

"He's gone!"

"What do you mean, 'gone'?"

"The room's a complete mess and there's no trace of his fiddle."

"The camp! He's back at the camp."

"Oh my God! What's he going to do?"

"How the hell do I know? But given how he was yesterday ... "

"This is bad! Let's go; we may not be too late!"

They flew from the hotel, just as the mayor was arriving to see how preparations were going.

"Car, driver, *now!*" commanded Friedländer.

Picking up on their panic, the official rose to the occasion, turfing his chauffeur out of the driving seat.

The three musicians hurled themselves into the car as it moved off, skidding on the slushy surface, the gears grating reluctantly at a velocity for which they were never designed. Somehow, it stayed on the road. But the passengers were oblivious, gripped with fear for what they might find. When they arrived at Birkenau it was not yet light. After the engine was killed, there was silence, apart from the low hum of a battered old taxi whose engine was running to keep the sleeping driver warm.

No sound came from the moribund camp. The dead quiet was deeply ominous. While the mayor sought out a gatekeeper, Weintraub, Löwy and Friedländer separated, certain that Reuben was somewhere near.

After a few minutes, Weintraub called out.

"Here! Over here! There's a gap in the fence and there are footprints in the snow."

Löwy took charge. "No time to wait. Let's get in."

He wrenched up the wire and they scrambled under.

"We'll separate. Call if you find anything."

They fanned out, one to the left and the Women's Camp, another to the Men's on the right, the third straight down the rail track that bisected them.

Nothing. No sound, save that of their own breathing, their own feet crushing the long grass standing stiff and proud of the white that blanketed the camp.

Suddenly, although at different parts of the vast enclosure, they heard it. From deep within the silence it came, the tumbling baroque of Bach, cleaving the uneasy tranquillity with a clean, sharp blade of sound. Their eyes followed the source of the music to the black heart of Birkenau, the burnt-out gas chambers.

And then they saw him.

Violin case in hand, he had somehow clambered up the snow-covered rubble heaped above the ruined crematorium which had just the day before so overwhelmed him.

Now, Reuben stood tall and wild-haired, silhouetted against the milky inkling of dawn. Dressed in an open greatcoat that flapped around his knees, he swayed in harmony with the music on feet planted like anchors on the upturned edges of two sloping slabs.

Transfixed, his three colleagues slowly, quietly, approached where he was perched, arriving almost at the same time as he bit deeper into the Chaconne. But where in Gurs it had been a lament and protest for former lives and present travails, here it was a song of loss, a parting serenade for the ghosts that filled the death camp, waiting to say "Adieu" before they could at last leave and seek some rest.

And in his playing were distilled the stages of his life, first as son, then husband and finally, father. In the Pyrénean transit camp a bitter edge had foamed across the peaks and troughs of the music, a sense of injustice permeating every note. Here there was no room for rage. This was the time to remember in full, perhaps for the first time, all that had been lost: the laughter, the moments when the children came for comfort, or just a cuddle, the joy of fatherhood; the nights of tenderness with Sarah in his arms, the first time they had known each other, their initial meeting; back, beyond the trenches to the peaceful life in London they destroyed forever; and finally to recovered fragments of his childhood, beside his father at the zoo, or on Leah's lap.

He was transfigured. Eyes gently closed, a slight smile played across his face. He was reprogramming his memory, dragging from behind the tungsten curtain of his trauma the benevolent remembrances whose associations his psyche had thought it best to bury. He played with a softness they had never heard before, as though he was lulling his family to perpetual sleep, trying to hold them in his hand and cushion their passing, as if to say, "I've come to say goodbye. No need to wait any longer. It's time to sleep now."

Smoothing the edges, rounding off the sharp ascents and descents, he gave the eulogy he could not give before in the only way he knew. And when the ending came, he elongated the phrases until near their breaking point, desperate to postpone the parting for as long as possible. And at the long last downstroke his whole body folded and he hung there, bent in half, teetering with the heart-pain of his loss.

His friends climbed to his side and held him up before they gingerly descended the heap of stones.

"It's okay. It's okay. I'm alright."

And then, as they left the camp:

"I had no idea, no idea at all, that that was what I needed to do. I've felt them at my shoulder all the time, *there*, like they wanted something but couldn't tell me what. I know it's irrational, but I realise that, while they all had each other, I had no-one to bid farewell to. Now at last I feel as if it's done. And in good time for tonight.

"Sorry, if I scared you. I've been rather selfish."

"It's alright, Ru," said Friedländer. "We're just pleased we won't have to play string trios tonight."

They returned to town, courtesy of the much relieved mayor. After freshening up at the hotel, they made their way to the auditorium to test the acoustic with a few small pieces.

After lunch, the four musicians went off to rest in their rooms. But Reuben couldn't sleep. His mind was on fire, and until he liberated his thoughts onto paper, repose was impossible. When all that possessed him was finally free, a kind of torpor settled upon him and he managed to relax.

After a short while he came round, unpacked a small brown-paper parcel he had brought with him and went in search of a barber.

The first half of the concert had been Beethoven's last piano sonata, whose end is of infinity, fading away like some ghost reluctant to leave, as though wanting to be around the living forever even while knowing it can never be.

There was no interval, just a few minutes of introspection as the piano was moved and four seats brought out, along with music stands and scores. Weintraub, Löwy and Friedländer came out and sat down. There was no sign of Reuben, save his empty chair on which the Guadagnini had been placed.

Without warning, the Philharmonic Hall was plunged into the black of lightlessness, the night of a gas chamber where nothing thrives but death. The audience grew still, cohered by expectation, disconcerted by the unknown.

The awareness among those closest to the stage of movement from the wings rippled instantaneously through the audience. As it reached the back, a single white spotlight suddenly and starkly illuminated Reuben.

Feet wrapped in rags and clogs, shaven-headed, he wore once more the striped uniform.

Silence. Shock. Not even a gasp to split the tyrannical quiet.

At length, he raised his head. The notes he had written earlier rustled in his hand redundantly as he spoke into the darkness, directly to the unseen throng. "When I walked out, under that mendacious sign, I never once looked back, and never intended to return. The rags I wore soon rotted, but these were the clothes I was wearing when an American GI found me walking blindly along the road. Some deep-seated urge drove me to keep them, because, quite frankly, my mind was not functioning at all. I never thought that I would ever wear them again. But it felt right to put them on one last time, as I seek to confront the horrors that visit me every day … and every night.

"The music we are about to play is a battleground where genius, the greatest and best of what we can be, wrestles with the monsters that surround it … and triumphs.

"Although I worship Beethoven, I do not seek to deify him. I merely wish to say that his courage in facing the worst of his turbulent life lends courage to us all, and tells us that to live in fear is not to live at all. Spinoza said that peace is not the absence of war. So living is not the absence of death, but a positive affirmation of what we can achieve.

"Coming to this place, standing in front of you, clad like this, playing this music is the beginning of my renaissance, I hope. I do not know how this performance will go. I ask you to indulge me, as my colleagues have.

"But before we start there are things that must be said. Remember what happened to we Jews, gypsies, homosexuals, dissidents. The terror we felt when cattle trucks carried us, thirsty, hungry, filthy, into an endless night. Imagine what it was to be blinded by light and deafened by noise as we were pulled from our trains, punched, kicked, beaten, barked at by man and dog. As you listen to this music, think of the queues for tattoos, the mountains of hair shaved from heads of those who no longer knew themselves, the teeth, the glasses, the false limbs. Parts of what we were pillaged, recycled, so that nothing of us would remain.

"And put yourself in line as you go to the right, and life, or left, to die. And what it felt to see ... parents ... grandparents ... wife ... children take the other route, not knowing truly what this separation signified.

"No words can do this justice. Only if you were there could you know the sounds, a cacophony of screams and sobs and sighs, the sporadic rattle of gunfire, the whips, the thuds, the gallows' creak, the short, sharp sizzle when the desperate found perpetual relief on the electric fence. Only if you were there could you know the smell that even now pervades my dreams – and those of thousands who, like me, survived. Only if you were there could you know the cold, even in summer, that lodged in the marrow, radiating through our bodies so that no part knew warmth. Only if you were there could you know the ever-present fatigue which numbed your being, even to the point where thinking, remembering, wishing, *hoping* pained beyond hurt. And only if you were there could you know the hunger, gnawing at your guts, demanding to be satisfied, while knowing all the time that it never would be.

"When you listen to this music, try to remember this ...

"That these hands went behind latrines and shovelled stinking shit. These hands emptied the poisoned, rancid filth of thousands, all forced to perform to order, without paper, without privacy, without time. These hands scooped it into buckets, and carted it away.

"Finally remember this. These hands played marches, waltzes, serenades while work gangs went to laboured death.

"And ...

"These hands played the *'Liebestod'* as my parents, wife and children descended to their death, as they choked ... maybe even while they burned."

He sat down. They all took up their instruments as one, looked at each other, and intoned the opening chords.

In the life of every great artist there is a sublime moment, the quintessence of cohesion when technical perfection fuses with an inner drive, conspiring to serve the higher purpose. Where what is seen in the mind's eye or heard in its ear as the sketches are etched with obdurate pen in some forlorn atelier leaps irresistibly to life.

That moment, when a work appears in all its glory, when the paint is vivid or the marble smooth, when the notes fly from the page, merging into a crystal constellation whose image all can witness and understand, that is when artist and observer are joined in a revelation and know that they have seen the perpetual mysteries, the eternal truths, the questions answered.

So it was on that pivotal day for the Furtwängler Quartet, when the four players fused into a single organism. Until that moment their ensemble had been praised for its beauty of intonation, for the seeming perfection of their unity. But this was overwhelmingly different.

Where the music demanded introspection, they penetrated deeper than seemed imaginable, revealing as yet unplumbed regions of human experience. When it took wing, they catapulted the audience through the stratosphere from where they could, Icarus-like, look down upon the world and see it for what it was.

And all the time Reuben's words burned in the mind, spooling images of what had come to pass close to where they now were seated. So when the Cavatina started, its tear-soaked regret, its bitter-sweet reminiscences brought the audience to the threshold of the gas chamber door.

All eyes watched Reuben as he appeared to hesitate over every note as though each was one more step further from life, closer to death. Each man attained timelessness, a mastery of control, bows hovering over the strings, fingers assured on the neck, embodied in the music, a trance state as surreal as Auschwitz is to those who cannot imagine how it was, or even *that* it was.

Those close enough to the stage could see the tears which streamed down Reuben's face, knew that he was once again playing the *'Liebestod'*, once again imagining Moses, Leah, Sarah, Miriam and Elias shuffling down the steps to their oblivion.

The music dissolved into silence, the interval between the notes became unbearable, the waiting for the next just long enough for suspense, just short enough for momentum. There is a nausea which comes with great emotional music, a dizziness which traps you in its maw and allows liberation only when it is ready. So it was here. The audience was now as one, bound together by an electricity which shocked through them; breathless, they were at the mercy of the quartet. Some shifted, others sat bolt upright scarcely moving, more still bent over in their seats, not wishing to hear, unable not to. Many openly wept, imagining what visions were playing in his mind, all too aware of what played on theirs.

The sudden violence of the assault was brutal. The transition to the *Grosse Fugue* vicious, unforgiving, a *kapo*'s whip attack, without pity. Someone cried out in the dark. Reuben grunted.

Nothing could stop them now. For a full quarter of an hour the music was flung between the instruments, the tranquillity of several respites only serving to stem their rapidly diminishing reserves of nervous and physical energy. Sometimes their playing tottered on the abyss of chaos, but never once did they falter. It was as if the souls of all the murdered millions had taken hold of their fingers and, puppet-like, manoeuvred them with an unlearnable speed and dexterity.

Reuben was transformed. Where but a few moments before his face had been etched in grief, rage now contorted him, and his countenance was of madness. Eyes fixed wide open, not seeing. The veins of his temples prominent, blue. Chin locked, mouth slightly agape.

Despite the chill that blew from the wings of the stage, sweat poured from him, turning the collar and back of his jacket black. The faded blue-and-grey striped sleeve became a hypnotic blur as his right arm drove the bow up and dragged it back with even greater force, while his left flew along the neck and thumped his fingers onto the strings. He rocked in his chair, moving to the edge and leaning forward, then sliding back. His colleagues mirrored him; they bucked and moved, bobbed and wove, a spiky impromptu ballet which served only to enhance the drama.

As each peak came in view, so their ascent became more aggressive. Reuben stormed at all he had seen, all he had been forced to do. He hounded out the music, dragging it screaming from the page; his eyes, even when open, were somewhere else, no need for a score as each note and chord, every pause and pluck, was seared onto his soul like a tattoo.

Even the less turbulent intervals in the relentless assault brought little relief; all knew that until the final release there could be no respite in the quest for catharsis. Tension built upon tension and, just when it seemed no greater intensity could be achieved, the quartet miraculously found a further dimension where the sound they made reached deeper sonorities and struck faster, surer tempi.

As they hunched their shoulders and dug deeper, heaven itself seemed stooped to weep, at first lightly and then with lancing currents, puddling the streets around the hall, washing to the surface of the entire camp hinterland the long-nestled ashes of the dead as if they, too, were drawn to hear. Stretching as though choreographed, the quartet bent their backs, the scrolls of the three shoulder-borne instruments pointing towards the sky as they embarked upon the final charge. The rain beating on the old roof drummed a reverberant rhythm, underscoring the ferocious music as it reached for its irresistible climax.

Four bows bombarded the strings, four left hands flew up and down the necks, fingers still firm, the harmony still absolute, even as the pressure became unbearable. The final bars:

bahh ba bahhh – ba.ba.ba.ba : bahh ba bahhh – ba.ba.ba.ba : ba.ba.ba. – bahhhhhhhhhhhhhhhhhhhhhhhhhhhhhh

Sound draining into silence. Where but a moment before the air had rung with fury, now only the shockwave lingered. Reuben remained unmoving on his seat, bent double, every last fibre and cell strained to breaking point, wrung out. The other players were equally drained, even if they had not been to where their leader had.

"I've never talked about what I – we – felt when those last notes finally faded. Obviously, the four of us discussed later, knowing it was a one-off, of course, if for no other reason than we couldn't recall exactly what went on. As you know, I completely reject all notions of a life beyond. Yet while I played it was as if I could hear voices whispering, telling me: 'Sing our song, for we no longer can.' And after, well, I can't speak for the others but the feeling was one of total emptiness. If this doesn't sound too strange, I was how I imagine a volcano to feel after an eruption, completely void after an almost interminable build-up of boiling, turbulent pressure. Sometimes I wonder what might have happened to me were it not for that concert."

The audience stayed, no words, not even hushed whispers, as though awaiting permission to leave. For what seemed an eternity, no-one moved.

Finally, Reuben stood up and as he did his colleagues – and everyone in the hall – rose with him, almost as one. No-one clapped. The camps were never the place for applause, never one where joy could reign. Even when liberation occurred, it was greeted with the dull resignation that survival was not life, that to have lived through the inconceivable would be to cohabit with it for as long as breath remained. And from the moment that Reuben had walked out in his stripes, the auditorium had been elevated into an annexe of Auschwitz. For that hour it was home to regrets and suffering, loss and grief.

After the quartet had departed the stage, the audience shuffled silently away, knowing that upon them now lay the impress of a greater moral authority. By being present during Reuben's transformation, they became witnesses to his rebirth, and whatever lay in store for him they could testify that he had earned the right to be heard.

Chapter 15

The quartet didn't perform again for almost a year; not just because of their total fatigue and the need to replenish their physical resources, but more due to the vacuum which opened up in that part of the combined make-up which made them musicians.

They had teetered along the brink of the abyss, staring down into the bottomless gorge which can devour an artist as completely as the bear consumes a salmon; a massive, implacable embrace of jaws and teeth which takes in head, bones, everything.

The fact that they had survived with their psyche and technique intact was a measure both of their aesthetic judgement and technical skill. But they needed some time away from the constant routine of preparation, rehearsal and performance. So they each went off: Weintraub to Paris, Löwy to the USA and Friedländer back to Vienna.

For Reuben, the draw was different. He felt the need to be among those who had known the night that he had known, shared the cold which had numbed his bones; who could still smell the stench of invisible filth and ubiquitous burning flesh which lurked forever under the fingernails, insensible to cleansing; who felt the ceaseless gnawing, whether born of loss, hunger, fear … or guilt.

This feeling for the kinship which remains unspoken reacted with an ancient determination to go back to the land, to avoid the strain of performance and to rest his strained tendons and aching joints.

No-one could have predicted the impact of the concert, the way it propelled Reuben, the quartet, Beethoven and the Holocaust into the consciousness of the world. It thrust them all into the limelight so that when he arrived in Israel Reuben was welcomed as an honoured son. But he eschewed all celebrity and settled quietly on a small *kibbutz* in the fertile lands east of Haifa, away from the dangerous borders with Lebanon, Syria, Jordan and Egypt.

As he planted and harvested, hoed and watered, he relished the feeling of sweat pouring from him, the sun hardening his skin and the dry earth sifting through his fingers. And although the faecal odour never completely left him, the pleasing aroma of freshly picked oranges on his palms began to take the edge from it.

But best of all was the community, the evening concerts around the fire or in the canteen when Reuben played the songs of their shared heritage: Sephardic medleys which enshrined the essence of the cultural marriage between Jew, Moor and Spaniard; and Ashkenazi airs which encapsulated the very different struggle through the hard lands of Eastern Europe. His repertoire grew as he learned, trenches-like, new tunes – partisan defiances from the forests of the east, old Biblical songs rescued for the new Israel, ancient arias of lamentation and mourning.

But in his quest for recovery, what helped the most were the long conversations as he and those other survivors capable of release spoke, some haltingly, others torrentially, of guilt and pain and the agony of remembering, of the narrowness of escape and the breadth of experience, of the endless nights fractured by vivid dreams of foul corruption, raucous sounds and fetid smells. The irresistible urge to tell and re-tell expressed a pathetic futility: pursue the chimera of dilution lying somewhere far distant, each recounting an illusory step towards an unattainable goal which sat beyond the ever-lengthening horizon.

Yet no matter how often the survivors and those who cared for them reached some level of understanding that no blame attached to the living for not having died, the nagging agony persisted. For some, the guilt, the loss was still too much to bear, and by their own hand they put an end to it.

Reuben ran it through his mind hundreds, no, thousands of times. The guilt of having survived, of not having saved the family. Questions assailed his nights, and sometimes, apropos of nothing, when he went about his daily chores, he would be assaulted by the sheer enormity of it all, stopping as though coming up against some unavoidable wall whose span and height precluded circumnavigation.

But gradually he reached a plateau of equanimity. He didn't precisely quell the turbulence; that was always prone to erupt at unpredictable times when some external stimulus or just the chemistry of his brain sparked fresh turmoil. It was more that he learned to live inside it, almost welcome it as a sign of sanity, of *life* itself.

In those endless debates around the fire, with the clear Mediterranean sky sparkling above, he began to put aside the unanswerable, destructive 'what ifs?'.

Far more complex were the moral issues. Had he compromised music itself by playing in the orchestra? When he ate, and so deprived another of food, did he commit some crime of self-preservation? When he serenaded SS officers in the brothel, was he bringing them comfort and so restoring their enthusiasm for the next day's work? By the very fact of survival in that place, had he shuffled off civilisation, rather than affirm life by dying without accommodating evil?

For all these dilemmas there could be no resolution. Survivors and counsellors worked slowly to rake over the evidence of each story and so reveal the truth behind each tale. They never stopped the dreams, the shredded nights, but slowly they reached that place where shame began to recede and actuality took its place.

Reuben, too. He came to realise that he was not to blame, could not be blamed, either for living when Sarah, Elias, Miriam, Moses and Leah had not, or for their deaths. It was, he finally reconciled, the Nazis, and all their apologists. It was they who dehumanised humans. Who designed the Final Solution. Who implemented it. Who created a world where innocents were coerced or tricked into submitting to their own destruction, incapable of conceiving of a pre-existing scheme to expunge from the face of the earth them and those who shared their blood.

But something was still missing. A void was opening up within him, caused by that growing unease which accompanies the feeling of a task unfinished. It was not sufficient for him to come to terms with his own part in everything that had happened; his intellect quested after a notion around which to make some sense of it all. He was hopeful it would come to him, but it was elusive, niggling away, demanding a resolution and increasing the irritation as it grew, slowly and inexorably, like a growth threatening to consume him.

For the time being, Weintraub, Löwy and Friedländer came to Israel and the quartet prepared to return to the concert hall. The Suez crisis and subsequent long-planned engagements postponed it until 1959, but that allowed the publicists at Carnegie Hall to build subscriptions for their first complete Beethoven cycle. It was a triumph. The Auschwitz performance had reinforced their own individual self-confidence, both in their technique and, more importantly, in their ability to communicate the essence of, especially, the Five. And their audiences projected their own expectations, so that the frisson during each of the six concerts made for legendary reviews and fond recall.

After the performances, which had been made more strenuous by the surrounding excitement, they remained in New York for two months, giving master classes to students from the Juilliard and relaxing before embarking upon a coast-to-coast tour. During their stay Reuben continued to sense the exhilaration of the undiscovered road that buzzed around inside his head, the edge on the hunger ever sharper, the frustration at its elusiveness dispiriting.

One afternoon, he wandered into the Metropolitan Museum of Modern Art and came across *I and the Village*, a classic Chagall painting depicting the artist's childhood in a Russian *shtetl*. It struck a chord, and he went in search of more works by the same artist.

When he found them, in gallery and book, he was consumed, devouring them and their symbolism with the enthusiasm of a child. The lives depicted could, of course, have been the inhabitants of Skidel, but that was not precisely it. He felt an instant relation, and finally what had been tormenting him began to take shape, emerging from the indistinct backwoods of his mind into bright, sharp focus.

The world exposed in a raft of oils, lithographs and gouaches that brimmed with colour, character, fable and folk-life was *his* world, even though the vanished life and religious superstitions which permeated it were utterly alien to him. He realised that there was a seamlessness to being of his people that made them all, regardless of observance, one. That unity was manifested in the six million, his own parents, wife and children included, selected for death for no reason other than their birth.

Epiphany. And in the blinding moment of crystal insight, he saw not only the destination but the route.

Chapter 16

He moved with astonishing speed. While neither preparation nor playing betrayed the turmoil within, the urge to progress filled all his other waking hours, as though the vision might dematerialise if not soon made flesh.

When they weren't rehearsing or performing, he read copiously, foisted himself on people he imagined would be helpful to his quest, thought, planned, schemed. The quartet was due to play the series of quartets over six months in Boston, Cleveland, San Francisco and, finally, Los Angeles. He decided that the end of their journey would be the most auspicious place for the launch of his plan. The community spawned from the large number of Jewish artists who settled there after fleeing Hitler boded well for a sympathetic audience.

During the train journeys and the downtime between recitals, he worked on what he would later refer to, in tongue-in-cheek homage to Jonathan Swift (though without his satirical edge), as *A Modest Proposal for the Liberation of the Jews*. In it he sketched out the rationale for a new movement which had as its objective nothing less than an alternative community for all those Jews who yearned for their heritage but could not cross the threshold of a synagogue. He called it The Fellowship of the Yellow Badge.

He peppered the media and wrote to every influential and potentially supportive Jew he could think of, scouring telephone directories for relevant organisations. He sweated his new-won reputation and the charisma that surrounded his story to stimulate interest. It was a single-handed odyssey of self-exploitation, confidence in the strength of his idea unshakeable.

He discussed his thinking with Weintraub, Löwy and Friedländer. When he told them about it, his mood darkened, even as his eyes flashed with a martyr's passion. They sympathised, both with the idea and his need to do it, while expressing concern for the future of the quartet. But he reassured them: "Six months on, six months off; careful scheduling. If the idea gathers the kind of momentum I hope for then I'll establish a small full-time staff, manage commitments and be a figurehead. Trust me. You know I sleep little, think much. We'll give it a go, no? And if you think it's not working, all I'll ask is that you give me the chance to choose. If it's the Fellowship, you keep the Furtwängler name and its legacy and find another fiddle."

It was agreed. When they arrived in Los Angeles, the concert promoter had reserved the hall they were to play for an extra night, after the cycle was complete. Private invitations were sent out, media presence was assured by the magnificence of the series, played with a blistering intensity as though the inferno that burned within its leader had ignited spontaneous fires in them all and the heat fused them into a composite whole. All that those who were invited knew was that Reuben Mendel would make an important personal announcement, followed by a brief solo recital.

After they had played Beethoven's substitute movement for the *Grosse Fugue* as an encore, anticipation was high. Following a short break to allow Reuben to relax and gather himself, he walked out onto the stage, now empty save for a simple wooden lectern. He drew from his pocket a sheaf of notes.

"Thank you all for coming, and for indulging me. I have only one purpose this evening: to share with you a vision I have of a new Jerusalem, an intellectual 'city of peace' that reconciles our blood-soaked past with a future full of hope, empty of fear. I hope that under its blazing banner all Jews, be they observant or assimilated, leftist or rightist, of Israel or the Diaspora, old or young, male or female, can march beneath it on a new road, paved with the suffering and death of our kinfolk.

"I would like to start by reciting a short poem, written by one of the men who saved my life, Isaac Rosenberg. It was written at the height of the First World War in 1916, and is entitled "The Jew":

> Moses, from whose loins I sprung,
> Lit by a lamp in his blood
> Ten immutable rules, a moon
> For mutable lampless men,
>
> The blonde, the bronze, the ruddy,
> With the same heaving blood,
> Keep tide to the moon of Moses,
> Then why do they sneer at me?

"My friends, for every people there are defining events that resonate down the ages, mutating through multiple retelling, assuming new significance as their relevance and implications wax and wane with the spirit of the times.

"We Jews have known more than most, for our history is long and we have excited the sneering admiration, envy and hatred of those people whose lands we have settled during our endless wandering or who claimed the region we have coveted as our own.

"As you bend your mind towards the watershed events of our history, whether the epic scale of the Exodus, Sinai, destruction of temples, Roman occupation, exile, the meandering Diaspora or the less epoch-making acts of heroes like Bar Kochba, Esther, Judith or David, you realise one thing above all others. Each has been subsequently annexed by the rabbinical authorities to bolster their political power. They have patiently awaited the passage of time and the passing of survivors, all the time deflecting challenging questions and finessing inconvenient logic. Then, the legend is woven from this skein, the involvement of God entwined in the pattern to suggest divine intervention or retribution. In this way, the self-styled 'learned' rabbis become the unique arbiters of our history, sole repositories of understanding and interpretation, the only route to our traditions, the guardians of what we know and how we should know – and thus of what we think and how we should think.

"I know that I shall be accused of bitterness, of impertinence, of heresy even. So be it. But I believe that in some quarters of religious governance can be seen the quintessentially evil. I see it in the abuse of education, that great bastion of Jewish tradition, so that it intends to narrow the mind, not broaden it. I see it also in the subversion of beautiful (perhaps even God-given) intellects for the purpose of puerile sophistry, narrow political advantage and self-aggrandisement, rather than for the benefit of the greater good, the whole of humanity. And above all I see it in the futile attempts of religious authorities to approach the greatest catastrophe to befall our people, principally because they know, I sense, its utter irreconcilability with the continuance of worship.

"We Jews are at a crossroads. The Holocaust is still so very fresh, the wounds raw and gaping. Yet we must make sense of it. To do otherwise, to pretend it makes no difference save as a shield behind which we may shelter to stave off the spears of criticism and thwart the arrows of disapproval, is to render the suffering and death of so many little more than a convenience.

"I cannot permit that. At least not without trying, without putting forward an alternative path.

"For me, the Holocaust is *the* watershed event in Jewish history. What went before is obscured by its mass; and what comes after may only be guessed at. I believe it to be nothing less than the death of Judaism, the birth of Jewishness, in the sense of the whole Jew emerging from centuries of ambivalence and moral compromise. In his recipe for our destruction the Nazi created a mechanism not just for our survival but for our fulfilment of a world role. Through what we have borne we must become torches for justice, flames against oppression, lights of tolerance, warriors for the needy. Where the weak are crushed beneath the heel of the strong, there we Jews must be, exploiting our intellectual and material resources for their benefit.

"We can only do this if we are liberated from the suffocating bondage of religion, if all Jews are suffused with the glory and the tragedy of our past. The rabbinical annexation of the Holocaust has begun. I look at those grotesque memorial stones which are beginning to appear in every synagogue, every cemetery, and I feel the rage rise. I owe it to the memory of my children and all those slaughtered without the capacity to form judgements on their sacrifice to stand here now and say: They did not die as martyrs, 'sanctifying the Name'. Many of the millions, given the option (which they were not), would never have endured the humiliation, the agony – and the death by labour, by injection, by beating, by bullet, by gas."

His voice began to rise, the colour coming to his cheeks, each phrase emphasised with a stony, forceful resolve and the slamming of fist into palm.

"They were not martyrs, for they had no choice. The essence of martyrdom is the preference for a pure death over an impure life. But they died because of what they were, because at least one grandparent was Jewish. Nothing else need be said. From that simple fact cascades a morality to which each of us is heir, a history of which each of us is part, a responsibility for which each of us is liable, without limitation, without debate. Apply a religious precondition, believe it avoidable by assimilation or apathy, and those imperatives erode to nothingness just as surely as rock fragments and turns to dust beneath the insistent attentions of wind and rain."

He paused. The level dropped to little more than a whisper, the tempo even more deliberate.

"I am often asked: 'Was God at Auschwitz?' I reply: 'If you need to reconcile that place with the existence of a deity worthy or demanding of devotion then do what you must. Pray for intercession to a supposed being who failed to intercede if you have to, if you are even able to.

"But whichever side of this line you stand, it no longer matters. What *does* matter is making sense of that which lies beyond comprehension. He may exist. He may work in mysterious ways. But for me that is an intellectual desert, an abdication of responsibility so absolute as to defy rational argument and exist in a barren land, far beyond reason.

"I was an atheist before I entered hell. I remained one there, never exhorting the omni-absent deity to intervene on my behalf during those many times when it might have been easy to succumb to that temptation. I am still here, able to speak for those who are not. I do not argue against religion. For those who need its emotional, spiritual and psychological comforts, I wish them well and envy them the certainty it must bring. But that has never been enough for me. And it is not an adequate commemoration of the millions. When the rabbis are through with it, the Holocaust will become a shining example of God's love of the Jews, evidence of the unique covenant between us. And then those like me who revel in the greatness of our contribution to the advance of humankind will be lost forever, our right of congregation rescinded by dint of non-adherence."

Once again, his voice started to rise.

"For we who saw rampant evil, and those who reading of it know which path their life must take, cannot pay the huge price of assuming a cloak of belief, of bending the knee to a non-existent authority, of cauterising the bleeding wounds of our conscience for a semblance of security. And for what? For the seductive refuge of never thinking for ourselves and allowing our individuality to become subsumed into an amorphous, impotent whole.

"I am a Jew. There was a time when such a statement, while never denied, meant little or nothing. But slowly, as I married and fathered, so its meaning came to resonate. And since my family was obliterated because of it – and I so nearly followed them – I have come to see that it was everything I am, and all I shall ever be.

"In 1951, I went to Princeton University and met Einstein. He shared with me something he had written in 1934, as the Nazi stranglehold began to exert itself on Germany: 'The pursuit of knowledge for its own sake, an almost fanatical love of justice, and the desire for personal independence – these are the features of Jewish tradition which make me thank my stars that I belong to it.' How beautiful! And so say I – and I now proclaim it so that all might hear. I revel in my history, my heritage, my culture. I think on all our great forebears, even back to Moses, and I am giddy with pride. I wallow in their works, the chemistry of challenge, of curiosity, the endless quest for truth. I roll up my sleeve and reveal my clanhood; I know that its stamp impresses on me – and all my clansmen vicariously – obligations we are bound not to shirk.

"I am a Jew: yet I reject Judaism. To say I am Jew*ish* is wrong, as it suggests a choice which can never be made, a gradation remote from the absolute. Not possible, certainly not now when all that condemned us to die was that absence of choice, stripped of all appeal, without any qualification.

"It is hard to know how to advertise this position. All our outward displays of kinship are religious. So what is one like me to do? My solution may well infuriate and offend. But after due consideration, I shall forever display this on my lapel."

He drew from his trouser pocket and held up what appeared at first to be a simple brooch. Enamelled in a shade of deep yellow, its six points were edged in black. Written in a gothic script across the body was the one German word: *Jude*.

The audience collectively gasped.

"In doing so, I follow the great Yiddish clarion call of Robert Weltsch in 1933: '*Tragt ihn mit Stolz, den Gelben Fleck.*' From now until my final breath, I shall obey him and 'wear it with pride, the yellow badge'!"

His tone moderated from the high colour of passionate crescendo, descending to a more reflective hue.

"Those who have followed my life may recall a time during my 'great flight', *ma grosse fugue* as the French would almost say, when my family and I sought refuge across the Pyrénean border in Spain, having fled Toulouse by taxi. Our driver was a wonderful man, Gaston Perrier, with whom we became fast friends during our short trip to Lourdes. As we took our leave (and even now I see her tear-streaked face facing me as I stood behind him) my darling Sarah hugged Gaston tightly and made him promise to look after our lovely house in Toulouse and plant a fruit tree in remembrance of us.

"A couple of summers ago, I finally found the courage and went back to that last seat of tranquillity, just to recharge my memory, although I was more than a little curious to discover what had become of it, and him. I had bought the house outright in the late Forties but kept my ownership secret, only permitting the lawyer to inform the Perriers that they could stay there indefinitely. It took me a little time to find the old place; my recollection of the area was somewhat imperfect. But finally I came across it.

"Gaston was not the kind of man to encounter the Furtwängler Quartet and therefore knew nothing of my tale. So when he answered the door, older of course, as are we all, the light of recognition ignited only after a few seconds of puzzlement. The tragic emptiness in his look as he realised I was alone even now makes my stomach churn and eyes prickle. His silent embrace said everything, but he took me by the arm and, without a single word, guided me straight to the garden whose beauty they had, if anything, enhanced. The heavy fragrance, the sultry heat, the noise of sundry insects as it basked in the baking sun was nearly overwhelming. He looked back at me and I saw the profoundest grief in his eyes. It was not the sense of loss, more the sorrow of knowing finally what had befallen all but me, the desolation of knowing that words could not bring comfort. Instead, he guided me to a peach tree, hung heavy with round, pink, plump fruit, exuding that alluring odour. He plucked from one sagging branch a particularly inviting piece, handing it to me as he said: 'Never for one moment forgotten, Monsieur, be the tree bare in winter, blossomed in spring, full-fruited in summer or dropping in autumn. Madame's tree and I have waited so long. Thank you for coming; it cannot have been easy. Please, eat.'

"My friends, as I sank my teeth into that succulent flesh and felt the juice dribble down my chin, I suddenly saw that peach tree as a metaphor of our people. Wherever we go, we must enrich the places we pass through, leaving a little of ourselves behind, so that all the peoples of the world can stand as one and say: 'The Jews are our friends, for they give of themselves and their history so that we all may learn from their bloody past.'

"We Jews cannot be divided, we *must* find a way to rejoice in our shared past, to live out what Romain Rolland said so wonderfully in his great opus, *Jean-Christophe*:

> The Jews have been true to their sacred mission, which
> is, in the midst of other races, to be a foreign race, the
> race which, from end to end of the world, is to link
> up the network of human unity. They break down the
> intellectual barriers between the nations, to give Divine
> Reason an open field.

"We cannot do that if we impale ourselves on a stake of division, torn between observance and assimilation. I think of all that unites we Jews, no matter what the religious differences, and I am energised. The history and the legends, the literature and art, language and humour, similar expressions and inflexions, whether rooted in Yiddish or Ladino. The mouth-watering cuisine, the yearning and joyous music. All these draw us together. But now, one thing above all others makes us one. That all of us were condemned to die, not for beliefs or crimes or by tragic accident, not even through personal flaws, but because of one fact: the blood – undeniable, undisguisable, unavoidable. Ignore it or forget it and we shall, once more, be doomed.

"As I have said, I cannot allow that sacrifice to be made without a fight. And even though I might fail in this, as I failed when I sought in vain to save my family, I know that I must strive to make these beliefs a living, daily reality.

"So I am launching a new movement, The Fellowship of the Yellow Badge. Tomorrow, in major newspapers in this country and Europe, a manifesto will be published that calls on all Jews to forget our differences and unite in a great and noble cause: to bring peace, justice, freedom and fairness to all parts of the world and bridge the many divides that separate the peoples of this great and bountiful planet.

"For my part, I am pledging six months of every year that remains to me to play for charity, to participate in debate, and to urge on my fellow Jews a new fellowship, a new sense of tribe, born not in divisive religion or partisan politics but in Rolland's 'sacred mission'. It will, I hope, enable anyone with Jewish blood in their veins, whatever their beliefs, to re-connect with those magnificent strands that bind us.

"I dedicate this service with the Fellowship to the eternal memory of my marvellous parents Moses and Leah, beloved wife Sarah and beautiful, innocent children Miriam and Elias, who died because of their blood. Under its flowing yellow banner may all Jews be united with their heritage in an atmosphere magnified by the beauty of selfless service and untainted by politics and religion.

"And now is the right time for this, while we witnesses still live and suffer, breathe and agonise, endure and mourn – and seek a meaning for all that befell us. Shakespeare said it perfectly:

> There is a tide in the affairs of men
> Which, taken at the flood, leads on to fortune;

Omitted, all the voyage of their life,
Is bound in shallows and in miseries.
On such a full sea are we now afloat,
And we must take the current when it serves,
Or lose our ventures.

"Are we to be bound in the shallows of intellectual abdication and the miseries of spiritual compromise? Or shall we float, heads held high, on the sea of moral confidence, marrying the obligations of our legacy with a world view consistent with all that we have known and endured?

"The time has come to decide."

Silence fell as the audience pondered the power and import of his words. For this was little more than a declaration of war against a religious hegemony that had enjoyed millennial power, no matter that he would say later that he never sought to convert those who worshipped, only to offer shelter to those who, like him, were homeless.

He took up his violin and started to play. The hushed hall was filled with music of impossible melancholy. The base tune was a traditional setting of *'El Molei Rachamim'*, the lamentation sung over a Jewish grave when the stone is consecrated a year after death, denoting the end of mourning, a new spring after a winter of sorrow. But the yearning melody, evolved over centuries of cantorial improvisation, became something quite different under Reuben's hands. Where barely understood words intoned into a rain-drenched wind as it whipped across a desolate burial ground lose their meaning and thus all reason to be, their abstraction into pure tones elevates them into the consciousness of everyone, equally.

The power of music to move is an awesome force. How they were stirred, flying back through time, across the years and miles, knowing that wherever their ancestors had laid their head, there too they had laid their dead. Whatever labyrinthine passage had brought them here, the connection was absolute. The commonality of the shared blood-flood, compressed through the gorge of history and suffused with common experience and the promiscuity of survival, was made flesh in the *portamento*, swooping down to the lowest register of the violin, before ascending, sliding, skidding, to the top.

And each successive peak, mirroring its preceding trough, appeared to those who cared to think that this was Reuben's life and it was *their* collective past. So that when the music did at last fade away all that remained to do was sit and wonder, stand and leave, each in his own world, heir to the past, trustee of the future.

Who of them could say which was strong enough to bear the burden?

Intermezzo #4

This is an advertisement.

<u>A call to Jews throughout the world:</u>
Unite and Fight for a Brave New Future!

My fellow Jews,
I call upon you in the name of my murdered family and our six million brothers and sisters who have no voice.

Fifteen years have now passed since the full immensity of what befell us dawned upon the conscience of the world. We are, understandably, still in collective denial. And not just us. The whole world seems intent on putting the incomprehensible behind it and moving on with all its many problems, tensions and uncertainties. But *we* cannot move on. Not until we have made some compact with our tragic past.

There are some who deny the very fact of our catastrophe. They we spurn with contempt and pity. Others deny its uniqueness, and with them we can engage, but only in a sterile debate of comparative suffering. And then there are those, the vast majority of whom are Jews, who deny its significance. Until we resolve *that*, we will never find the tranquillity we so richly deserve. Having our own land will not bring peace. Pretending that the Holocaust was an aberration will afford us no comfort.

Trying to continue as though nothing has changed offers only angst and emptiness.

So I humbly offer a new path to this great family of ours, a kinship that girdles the world and which, in its finest, has illuminated and shaped the human condition.

Whether we seek the elusive definition of 'Jew' in the religious, racial or cultural, our tribe is divided along many fault lines. Between the secular and religious (and within the latter along the widest spectrum of observance and opinion from ultra-orthodox to progressive). Between the Diaspora and Israel. Between pro-Zionist, anti-Zionist and agnostics. Between Ashkenazim and Sephardim. Across traditional political lines. Finally between those who contemplate the stuff of being a Jew and those for whom it has no significance and who are, intellectually and culturally, totally estranged.

If you are a believer, I invite you to reflect upon what the Almighty intended when He permitted our terrible suffering and failed to intercede. Remember that He visited this catastrophe not with the surgical precision used on the Egyptian first-born but with an apparently indiscriminate sweep of His hand that caught up grandfathers and mothers, parents and children. Above all, the children.

If you are secular then remember this: It would have made no difference. You could no more deny your destiny than you could your need to breathe. There was no hiding. Escape was fortuitous. Pleading conversion, indifference, even contempt held no hope for survival.

The undersigned Jewish artists, writers, composers, performers, doctors, scientists and lawyers have pledged to provide 10 per cent of their earnings and one month a year to The Fellowship of the Yellow Badge.

We undertake to work for the needy and advocate on behalf of those with no voice. Through our resources, contacts and abilities we shall fight injustice, challenge power and expose hypocrisy.

We do this to honour our six million brethren who died because of their kinship.

We do this in the name of the uncountable children denied the opportunity to serve their fellow man.

And we do this to build a new fellowship of Jews, forged in the flame of oppression and toughened in the searing heat of genocide. In a spirit of camaraderie and joint enterprise, we will operate outside politics and religion to attain independence and freedom of belief, thought and action.

Join us, and turn the shame that once our enemies sought to impose upon us into a powerful engine of purpose, belonging and humility and so live out the true meaning of our founding principle:

Tragt ihn mit Stolz, den Gelben Fleck!
Wear it with pride, the yellow badge!

Chapter 17

After the launch, Reuben's life took on a new momentum, interspersing concerts with a global voyage to spread the word, put his violin to work and grow the membership. Despite approaching an age when people begin to reap the harvest of their life, he found himself new-planting. Taking cuttings from the tree he had nurtured, he traversed the world, invited to Jewish communities to explain the Fellowship, play for funds, support campaigns – or just simply talk: of loss and loneliness, of the guilt of surviving and the pain of separation, and of the unslakeable thirst for redemption.

This great unstopping rejuvenated him. The sense he had begun to make of his loss rendered him more able than he could ever have imagined to reflect on his family's descent. He gained a vital element of distance, so that he now could look over his shoulder at the years behind, years that somehow he had negotiated. He contemplated the endless nights, the barbaric dreams, the waking moments when the cruellest terrors transfixed him.

And he saw that he had survived.

How he did not precede Celan into the Seine or Levi down the stairwell? Who knows? Perhaps the visions became too bright to behold, the soundtrack too loud to avoid. It was a question he pondered often – and not just when yet another child of the Holocaust was unable to live any longer with the horror of remembrance, the shame of survival.

But he always believed that music was his salvation. Where others dealt in words, the currency of reality, he worked with notes, whose abstraction permitted release and then, from somewhere above the fray, reconciliation.

He knew without thinking that whenever the haunting was upon him some theme or phrase would return from the long-lost time when he was safe, calling him back from the black lands. It was not the sound itself; it was the feelings and associations it engendered: security rather than danger, warmth instead of cold, a full stomach replete not with gnawing guilt but with the weight of wholesome food, a fear-free zone in whose space he might roam unhindered.

With this realisation Reuben came finally to embrace the essential difference between originator and interpreter. Creative spirits are driven to pull screaming from the soul the images that lurk within, while the interpreter is born to give their works the wings which took them to the hearts and minds of others, there to nourish those whose senses they assailed. And while he knew that his important job was entrusted only to the few, nothing he did, not even when navigating the treacherous vortices of Bach or Beethoven, came close to the birth-pain agonies that accompany the process of bringing into being a work of art.

It was around this time, in his early sixties, that an annoying snippet of memory first began to worm its way into his mind. He found that more and more he was drawn to minute fragments of one particular melody, a wistful, simple air whose origin escaped him as he tried to piece together the haphazard notes that came to him. And the more he strove to remember what it was and where he had heard it, the more recalcitrant the theme became, obstinately refusing to reveal itself as though the very act of seeking drove it further from him.

As is often the way with desperately sought recall, remembrance came when it was least expected. He was in London for a Rodrigue wedding and a notice in the morning paper for a lunchtime lieder recital at the Wigmore Hall caught his eye. He hadn't been to a concert for a while and could not even begin to recall the last time he had exposed himself to the beguiling beauty and ineffable simplicity of Schubert's songs.

He settled into his seat once the small frisson caused by his arrival had subsided. The magic of Schubert is just this: with the barest of resources, single voice and piano, whole worlds are conjured in miniature – from the opening bars to the conclusion often but a few minutes. So Reuben was quickly taken from the charming auditorium on a boat trip across a lake, then to sit beneath an apple tree and listen to a nightingale. From there he paused beside a brook to watch a trout weave its innocent way to an angler's hook, before Shakespeare's hymn to Sylvia and Gretchen's poignant paean to love transported him to that far-off place where only the greatest of art can take you.

Then, out of the silence that followed *'Meine Ruh' ist hin'*, a ghost began to emerge. From the piano, slow, gently rocking chords formed a melody at once new and familiar. Reuben's closed eyes flashed open, blazing with amazement and relief. The dislocated notes that had been meandering through his mind were suddenly ordered before him in all their deceptively simple beauty.

Accompanying the recognition came an image long lost to time. He was at the top of the stairs in the family home in London. He could only have been two or three, yet there, pyjamed, he knelt in the warm dead of a late summer evening, still soaked in slumber, peering secretly through the banisters to the drawing room where Leah sat at the piano, softly singing.

The miracle of memory threw out not just the scene nor only the tune, now fully-formed, but the very words that had lodged inviolate in some dark, deep cul-de-sac within his brain.

Unlike the original moment lifetimes ago, he now understood precisely what had moved Schubert to compose 'To Music'.

It was a simple and touching hymn of thanksgiving, an explicit appreciation of music as the bringer of love and hope, consolation and escape.

The words arrowed their way to his very centre, fired from a bow cast in the purest gold by Schubert. They epitomised him, and he came to understand that his life, for all its pain, was blessed, not by some dead deity but by the very fact of being. His inbred talent had fused with all the receipts of his life to create an indivisible whole, a conglomeration of the physical and moral which imposed on him an absolute duty to talk and play, to state his views and muse on what it meant to be alive.

Such was the liberation that music delivered. For he had the consolation of knowing he would never be alone, that whenever loneliness and despair became too much to bear he need but pick up his violin and close his eyes. From somewhere instinctive would emerge a piece to serve as a hermitage when what was needed was a quiet place; or as a quarry when he sought to vent the boiling rage which poisoned his entire existence and screamed for release through gaping fault lines.

He was Ahasuerus reborn – but with a profound difference. This Jew would not wander aimlessly, cursed to roam the world until its end. Now the roving became a divine mission, with an edge that shone bright and hard, tempered in fire for a sure and direct thrust.

Reuben was, at once, both rootless and rooted. Rootless in the sense he stayed nowhere long nor, as he journeyed, thought longingly of a single distant place. Rooted in that he carried his home with him, a diamond carapace toughened beyond breakage in a blast furnace of searing heat.

Like any virtuoso, he seemed to tell his stories, share his thoughts and play his music as though each time was the first. Part of this was professional instinct, embedded over many years of service to the masters. But more was born of the fact that the truth never grows stale, as if the very act of its advocacy renews vitality and reoxygenates it to make its blood rich-red and ripe.

During long years of exile, Pablo Casals, estranged from his beloved Catalonia by Franco's fascism, ended every concert with a nostalgia-drenched folk tune, *'Cant des Ocells',* 'Song of the Birds'.

The sadness of severance imbued every phrase, the sliding of notes on the cello a heartbroken sigh for the distant homeland, out of reach.

Now Reuben emulated him. At the end of every telling of his tale he would take up the violin and play, first, *'An die Musik'* to note an unpayable debt, and then *'El Molei Rachamim'*. Each rendition spoke of people and events long passed and captured something for the future, so that the recital was never twice the same. It was a filter through which those who listened reflected upon what they believed – and what their lives had been.

So, just as those who heard Casals would allow their minds to drift to home and what it might mean to know the pain of exile, now audiences who heard Mendel were taken to the graveside and, craning for a view, peered in to see it overspill with the unnamed, innumerable dead. And on the starved, staring, sunken faces they perceived their own mothers and fathers, sons and daughters.

This was music that afforded no respite. Stripped of empty words which promised much but delivered nothing, played with a bitter, jagged edge, it existed for one purpose: to impregnate the mind with dark images, and so stir the intellect to ponder cause and import.

And everywhere that the Yellow Badge was active, those who had been dispossessed of their heritage fell upon the opportunity for cultural repatriation and kinship with a ravenous appetite, so that the final chords of the lamentation became more an anthem of belonging and a promise of a future than the solace at the end of mourning.

From the launch in 1960 for the best part of two decades, this was Reuben's life. Six months performing with the quartet, six months traversing the world on Fellowship business during which he played and lobbied, cajoled and advocated, and lost count of the number of letters he wrote, events he attended, causes for which he spoke. It was the very nature of the idea that in some ways counted against it. Reuben always made it clear that this was work which happened away from the public eye. All advocacy happened in private; no accounting was made of the benefits. Because of this discretion, some assumed that the Fellowship had failed. But he always used to say: 'Those who know, know. No-one else matters.'

At a personal level, it succeeded beyond his hopes. It gave him structure such as he had not known since Vienna. The calendar was fixed a year or more in advance. He knew where he would be, for how long, and was no longer susceptible to the unexpected.

During those near-on twenty years, inevitably he aged. Performances became more arduous, the process of remembering notes and of maintaining the level he demanded increasingly difficult. And as his quartet days waned, so he devoted more time to the cause.

Reuben was well versed in the art of appearing on the radio and television and being interviewed by the press. To cope with the inundation of invitations which followed the launch of the Fellowship, he tended to accept only those that were central to its purpose. So when he received a proposal for a special televised event to signify his eightieth birthday in December 1978, I felt sure he would decline.

Two things persuaded him otherwise.

One was the format proposed by an entrepreneurial Israeli broadcaster: a global audience, two clear hours for debate and performance, a number of friends and famous musicians flown in for the occasion. It flattered his ego beyond resistance, as he said himself: *So much interest, so much thinking on my account! It makes me rather uncomfortable but it does seem churlish to decline.*

The other influence was more profound, less tangible. Something had been weighing on his mind for a while. We never discussed it, but I could see he was wrestling with an enormous problem, a position that needed to be taken or a decision that had to be made but for which he had yet found neither conclusive argument nor concrete expression. I had learned over the years that he must be left alone to tackle it himself. But it was as if he felt that the imminence of a definitive date might concentrate the intellect sufficiently to resolve the issue, and so he perversely welcomed the pressure the event would exert.

During the build-up there were more than a few negative mutterings in the media. The religious authorities that he had lambasted in the now-famous speech in Los Angeles had long sought retribution. Since then Reuben had been essentially untouchable, his status as man and musician placing him beyond reproach. But now, for the first time, anonymous briefings hinted at a backlash, although I feel certain that it was never a question of *vox populi, vox dei*, but of *vox dei, vox rabbi*. Stories of a failure by the Fellowship to take off begun to circulate, with the implicit corollary that this was the real reason behind the broadcast. Other themes to corrode the newspapers, radio and television included the aged performer unable to accept the demise of his career and, of course, the inevitable, time-honoured 'charlatan prophet', another glorious member of the rich pageant of false messiahs to speckle his people's history now seeking the big show to propagate his insidious, dangerous drivel.

As the broadcast began the studio lights glinted off the golden six-pointed star which was by now his trademark and worn by Fellowship activists and other kindred spirits. Reuben immediately addressed the issues head on, partly to avoid their impinging on the whole event and partly to diffuse the uncomfortable atmosphere. The wry look which characterised his incredulity at the stupidity of his fellow man was dancing across his face, flicking from eyes to cheeks to mouth.

"I'd like to say something before we start, if I may. There's been a lot of talk about the Fellowship. Some people are simply unwilling or unable to understand it. I know that many are discomfited by the principles on which it's based. Well, that's their problem, not ours. We always intended to work away from the glare of publicity and self-congratulation. The essence of the Fellowship has been quiet success, to do good for its own sake with no expectation of reward or outward display of pride except, of course, in the Yellow Badge.

"With my *very* advanced years, I should know better, but even so I'm bemused that there is such distaste towards me. I'm not going to dignify the nonsense that's been written with a detailed rebuttal. These feeble attempts to undermine and discourage me pale into insignificance beside other events in my life.

"But I would like to dispense with one particularly absurd accusation: that I see myself as the new Messiah. It's ironic, isn't it, that I who, perhaps more than any Jew of recent times, has advocated atheism as the route to surviving and thriving should now be cast as an ambitious deity?"

He became more serious now, his eyes narrowing to extinguish the amused twinkle.

"You know, this whole messianic thing seems infantile to me. I quoted Shakespeare, *Julius Caesar* as it happens, when I launched the Fellowship. Well, in that play he also says: 'Men at some time are masters of their fates:/The fault, dear Brutus, is not in our stars,/But in ourselves, that we are underlings.'

"We have to stop this fantasy insurance that somehow someone will come along and sort everything out for us. We have to take control of our individual and our collective destiny. Praying for intercession, well, it's intellectually dishonest, self-centred and, of course, futile. Living our lives awaiting the Messiah, even more so. The notion that there are those who think that I think I'm the One, well, what can I say? Not merely baffling, but deeply insulting."

The fretful air that had coloured the start of proceedings receded into the background. Reuben fielded a number of not-too-taxing questions.

"Have you never thought of remarrying?"

"Would I like to have loved again? Ah, well, yes, I think that would have been nice. I remember so well the joy Sarah brought me. I do realise I've been fortunate to have known love like that. But the price for that happiness was so heavy. In 1918 I lost my first true friend; twenty-five years later my whole family. The thought of further loss, it would just be too much to bear. No, I don't think I could go through that again."

"Is there any music you wish you'd played?"

"Of the great classics I can't immediately think of any that I regret not having had the time to study apart, perhaps, from some of Haydn's amazing output. Eighty-three quartets – amazing! I follow recent music through the handful of students I occasionally guide but, at the risk of sounding decrepit, they are beyond my comprehension. I'd like to have played more Shostakovich. I met him, you know, in early fifty-four, just when things were beginning to go better for him after Stalin died. It was nerve-racking; he was intense, chain-smoking, anxious but, like the truly great, very generous and modest. I wanted to learn about his latest quartet, the fifth which he wrote in fifty-two but didn't actually publish for four years. His quartets, all fifteen of them, are amazing, like a secret, candid diary. He was wise, too; he refused to let me play the quartet, saying that after what I'd been through I may not yet be free from my history to see into its heart. It was as if he knew that I still required catharsis, so to speak, as if he sensed my reticence. If I were younger, if things had been different, who knows? Maybe I would have played these – and other new works – in public. But, you know, the works I played regularly are, for me, inexhaustible. If I may steal a famous verse: 'They do not grow old, as those who perform them grow old.' "

"Do you ever think what life might have been like had Hitler never been born?"

"Not for a single moment. I'm uncomfortable assuming that everyone's experience is the same, so all I can do is tell you mine. I view my life before all that happened *through* all that happened, if you see what I mean. It's as if I was forcibly infected with cataracts. Everything is viewed through an opaque film which colours all that I perceive. I hope that makes sense to you. There are no might-have-beens, no what-ifs. An ever-present is, has been, always will."

"I read recently that you will soon retire."

"Yes, it's certainly true that I am retiring from giving concerts and recording. I can't carry on performing with my powers waning. It would be a disservice to the composer and disrespectful to my audience and colleagues.

"Will I stop working and just relax? No, I can't ever see that happening. I'll certainly continue to contribute to the work of the Fellowship for as long as I can."

"Do you think you might live here?"

"Well, settling down's something I've been thinking about. You know, I've had no home since we left Vienna in thirty-four. I'm a real Wandering Jew. It's certainly true that I've felt as home here in Israel as I have anywhere. But I have to tell you. I cannot stay here."

He paused for a moment, as though to gather himself.

"The thing is, I don't feel that this country is being true to our ethical heritage. Where the Fellowship seeks to make sense of the Holocaust, it seems that much of Israel's behavior is designed to ignore it.

"Our self-image as Jews is one of pride in all that we've achieved, usually as outsiders. The greatest of us were strangers in their own land. Moses, Jesus, Spinoza, Marx, Freud, Einstein; they were all forced to go into opposition, and challenge authority and received wisdom. Mahler once called himself 'a Jew throughout the world; always a stranger, never welcome'.

"But here we now are, as insiders. And what are we discovering? That we're just as venal, dishonest, riven, hypocritical, manipulative and sanctimonious as the next race. Only we deflect criticism with accusations of anti-Semitism and hide behind a carefully constructed shield made from ash, hair, shoes and spectacles. We are faced with the awkward truth that when we are different, we are different, but when we are not, we're the same."

The atmosphere in the studio was becoming tense.

The master of ceremonies, who had hitherto merely invited

questions from the floor, intervened hotly.

"Are you saying that Israel was a bad idea?"

"Well, it's either a good idea, badly implemented, or an out-and-out bad idea. I'm not sure it actually matters. We are where we are. Does anyone think the current state of affairs can continue indefinitely? I mean, really, do they?

"I spent some time a few years ago with Pablo Casals. Many of you will know that he vowed never to set foot in Catalonia until Franco died. His was the only example to which I could turn to resolve a dilemma that has been gnawing away with increasing discomfort since the Six-Day War.

"We have to return all the land occupied since 1967. I know how difficult that position is for many, particularly with regard to Jerusalem. But I have belatedly, and much too slowly, come to realise that we have paid far too little regard to those who were on this land before we arrived en masse and were dispossessed. If Israel was established, even in part, as some kind of compensation for the evil perpetrated against us, we should be humble enough to recognise that those most affected by our arrival were nothing to do with the original sin.

"Maintaining possession of these territories is not only immoral and illegal, it is also bad politics, and will oppress us down the years. We have to apply the founding principles of the Fellowship to the Palestinian people. Sometimes we have to make the hard choices, the early sacrifice, in order to seize the high ground. It is clear to me that neither the present government nor any other party of influence will do this.

"Casals made it clear: there are times when you have to stand up and do what needs to be done, even if it causes discomfort. He is a man who voluntarily cut himself off from his beloved Catalonia, rather than pass even an hour there while Franco lived. That caused him abiding pain, but rather that than risk endorsing evil.

"Martin Luther was right when he said: 'Here I stand, I can do no other'. Only by taking such positions can we remain true to whatever moral code we each strike for ourselves. This is true for all of us, save children and those unfortunates unable to. It applies regardless of age, station or any of the categories into which we place ourselves. The fact that I am old and clearly have only a little time left urges on me the need for immediate, unambiguous action.

"I will leave Israel tomorrow and return neither to play nor stay until the pre-war borders are re-established and an equitable Palestinian settlement reflecting their legitimate historical rights is in place."

The hall went quiet as the force of his words sunk in. Then, uproar.

"Disgrace!"

"Shame! Shame on you!"

"Traitor!"

"Go then … we don't need you!"

Reuben eased himself to his feet and held up his hand. He gazed through sorrowful eyes, but said nothing. Gradually the tumult died, and he spoke again.

"Do you think this was an easy decision? This place gave me solace at a time when I thought all chance of it was gone. But the place I came for consolation in the Fifties is no more; 1967 and 1973 changed it, apparently forever. So what would you have me do? Everyone says I am a man of principle who has found reconciliation with a traumatic past. And yet now you would prefer me to be only part of that man. One is either moral or one is not, one cannot choose where one's conscience leads. It is a guiding star, to be followed with trust, or it is nothing.

"I shall immerse myself once more in the Diaspora. It was there where the flame was kept burning. I must go there and help it to re-exert its critical formative role in shaping Jewish history, a history that must now make sense of the existence of this nation. We each must ask ourselves only two questions: What is the right thing to do? And what can *I* do to make a difference?"

After a few moments of quiet that told him that he must move swiftly on if the programme was not to die on its feet, the MC sought a leavening question from his script and invited a schoolboy to ask it.

"You're not very funny, so I was wondering if *anything* makes you laugh?"

"Now, there's a question! Let me think now."

An uneasy pause ensued filled only with some nervous light laughter at Reuben's ruffled brow as he racked his brain for comedy.

"Well, you're absolutely right in that I don't tell jokes, but that doesn't mean I have no capacity to laugh. So I've been trying to remember what has amused me. I recall, for example, a time long long ago when I was a boy in London. My father, always very dapper, was wearing a fine new jacket when he took me to the zoo. We looked at all the animals, but my favourite was always the lions.

"On this occasion we were watching a lioness prowl in front of the bars, like she was eyeing up some prey. She stopped in front of us and seemed to hold my father's gaze. She then turned her back to him, as if to walk away. Then, in slow motion, her nether portions twitched and she peed all over him. He stood there, completely stunned. Well, after the initial shock, I collapsed, helpless with laughter and barely able to breathe. Oh, I can still recall the way the tears poured down my face. I've got to hand it to Papa, though. He was even more doubled up than I was. My, how he stunk; even now I occasionally get a mental whiff!

"The only other time I can recall really laughing was, believe it or not, in a graveyard. It was the Zentralfriedhof, Vienna's main cemetery, where, by the way, Beethoven, and Schubert are buried. I was wandering around there one day; it must have been in the 1920s, I guess. It was very peaceful, early spring, unseasonably warm as I remember. I was browsing the graves and came across one which made me stop and do a double-take. Why, I haven't thought of this for years, but I can picture the scene as though it was yesterday.

The headstone was a typically Viennese Secessionist design, in the style of Klimt or someone like that. In English it said very simply:

Sir Richard Fawcett-Davenport
Renowned entomologist and champion skier

He caught a bug and went downhill quickly.

"It was so moving and charming that this man who must have died far from home, was loved enough for what I imagine was a witty and dashing character to be immortalised for the amusement not merely of the mourners but generations of visitors. I walked back to the gate chuckling and with a very broad smile. I got some very strange looks, I can tell you!"

"How does it feel to be the destroyer of Judaism?"

Reuben looked up. He saw that this last question was spoken by a young Hasid, ultra-orthodox, bedecked in black from head to foot save only for the pallid skin of his face, emphasised by the sparse, straggly beard and an open-necked white shirt from which white fringes dangled.

"How does it feel to be the destroyer of Judaism?" The repeated question had none of the false gentleness of its first utterance. This time it was laced with venom.

"I've no idea what you mean."

"You seduce people away from the path of righteousness."

"I don't know what that means. I speak as I have found."

"You undermine the beliefs of millions so that you are not alone in your ungodliness."

"Words and music have the power to undermine nothing and no-one. They are like a flaming torch in a cave that's been cut off from the outside world by spiders' webs. When they're burned away, deep fissures in the walls, ceiling and floor are visible to all. But I – nobody – *caused* those cracks. They are there because the thing in itself is flawed, undermined in your term, lacking substance.

"And as for my ungodliness, well, there I am alone, as I am anywhere. Don't you think I would immerse myself in your world if I could? Don't you think I'd like to tear out my memory, overwrite all I have known? The price is my soul, the thing which makes me what I am. Hack off a portion, you damage the whole. If there's a God, he wanted me like I am, not as you would shape me. Far from attacking me, you should glory in your God that he should want me like this."

"The Talmud is what makes the Jew special; it is our covenant with Yahweh. By encouraging people away from its study you condemn Judaism – and so Jews – to death. You do the Jew-hater's job for him."

"What is the true way? What *you* believe? What about other strands of Judaism, or all the complexions of Christianity? How about Islam, Buddhism, other Oriental beliefs? What you are unable to grasp is that, for many, your 'true way' is unpassable. I see your contempt. You sneer because you perceive that anything less than rigid adherence is heresy, that all these factions are disabling Judaism. The converse is true. Splits don't cause weakness, weakness causes splits.

"Look," he continued, moderating his tone, "I think of the Holocaust like a deep, dark river, its waters washing on one bank or the other. To one side there are those who, like you, find solace and identity in the worship of Yahweh, according to the teachings of your chosen forefathers, even if reconciliation with that shattering event is beyond you. On the other side are those who believe that being a Jew is nothing to do with observance. How we use those fertile, ash-strewn waters will determine history's judgement of us. The future of all the communities which line those banks lies in our ability to bridge it. All that I have ever desired is to find a way for people to stay in contact with their heritage, no matter how far they may have strayed from the water's edge."

But the Hasid wasn't listening, couldn't listen, his ability to comprehend corrupted by a life of unflinching adherence and self-serving study.

"You turn people away from Yahweh, from the true way. Hitler is reborn in you. You shake the gas like the faceless ones. You murder the unborn babies by seducing their parents from the path of righteousness. You walk through the valley of the shadow of..."

It took a moment, then there was more fury.

"Too far, much too far!"

"Unacceptable!"

"Let Mendel speak, or we'll be here all night!"

Reuben's voice, which had even up to this point retained that softness which betrays the inner humility of those with nothing left to prove, now assumed an adamantine edge.

"I've seen that glassy glint in the eye before. In the camps I saw the inadequate raised to a level of authority way beyond their capability. Shorn of culture, they were damaged goods. What you are, what you have been made by your upbringing, is but half a man. You are a clone, an automaton, programmed to follow a path unquestioningly! *You* are the Nazi! Blind to opinion, deaf to criticism – unblinking in adhering to dogma, unflinching in believing the justice of your cause."

I had never seen him furious. His colour rose to a red glow. Sweat beaded his brow. He undid his shirt colour and loosened his tie.

"I want to pity you. I really do! You're a victim of some deep spiritual abuse. We are made to question, to challenge. You have been un-made to accept without question. And I believe you are beyond recovery. Return to your institution. Please!"

The young man stared at him, long and hard, eyes wide, with that look of mystification which comes with confronting an unknown language. For these words could never be understood by him. The sounds he recognised, the meaning passed him by. He knew his script, passed down by generations of similarly deformed men who learned by rote the line to tow, whose token curiosity was channelled into sterile discussion on arcane texts. He retreated, running, but not without a glance back, his face fixed in a rictus of fury and loathing.

To lighten the mood, Reuben took up his violin. But not the Guadagnini; since 1968, he had used it only for concerts. After every Fellowship event, he played the fiddle that had been returned to him in that package he received in Vienna. ("Well, it just seems so right," he told me when he first decided to air it in public.)

From that instrument which was so important to him he pulled a joyous medley of the old days: '*Sha! Stil!*', '*Rozhinkes mit mandlen*', '*Oyfn Pripitchek*': all tunes that evoked the long-dead spirit of life in *shtetls* like Skidel, a deceptive requiem for all the eradicated communities, all the disappeared.

A few more questions followed, most of the what-a-celebrity-likes-so-must-I variety. He answered them generously, explaining patiently what it was about their style that appealed, and which works particularly moved him. So that, despite the drama of the preceding events, the abiding image was his gentle passion as he enthused and informed about his favourite composers (Beethoven, Schubert, Bach), writers (Tolstoy, Levi, Shakespeare), poets (Whitman, Heine, Rilke, Rosenberg), artists (de La Tour, Rembrandt, Van Gogh) and films (none).

Although he was clearly fatigued and stressed by the evening, the programme still ended with his traditional closing. He played the two pieces with a breathtaking simplicity and quietness that, even by his standards, was a master class in control and momentum, the ending of each prolonged as in a reluctant but unavoidable farewell.

After the standard end-of-show hospitality, he declined my offer to accompany him to his hotel. Despite the fact that the burden of his decision had at last been lifted, Reuben seemed depressed, agitated by the audience's reaction to it and to the ferocity of both the personal attack he had suffered from the zealot and his own response.

His shoulders were hunched and his gaze was fixed firmly on the floor. As he raised his head he had about him a distant, absent stare that clearly was not focused on me or, indeed, anything in the foreground.

"I need some air, need to think. My head is swimming. This was a bad, bad idea. Why did I let myself get talked into it? What was I thinking of? Stupid, vain old man. Stupid, stupid, fucking stupid."

The night was cloudy. Reuben turned his collar up against the drizzle which had fallen long enough to mingle with the light brown dust and form an orangey paste which collected in the gutters. As he started the short walk to his hotel he looked back towards the few of us still left outside the hall and motioned towards the sky.

"It rained when I got my first violin. It rained in the trenches. When I met Sarah, it sleeted. It poured down en route to Lourdes and would have done in the camps had it not been snowing for much of the time. You see a pattern? Weather as a harbinger of something momentous."

As he set off along the road, the light changed. The feeble shower ceased and clouds cleared from the face of a full moon. Its white brilliance fused with a multicoloured neon and candle halo that oozed from the cafes and restaurants which lined his path.

I was still watching him as he entered a strange sphere of radiance, a kind of prism made of moon and smoke and rainbow lights. Reuben turned hesitantly to look back and made to wave.

At a tempo so slow even Beethoven would not have risked it, the right leg began to crumple. His shoulder subsided, the arm instantly useless. Neck twisting, the face of Reuben Mendel seemed to be of glass. One side of his mouth had already drooped, as his eyes, full of questions and bewilderment, fleetingly implored mine before emptying.

In the moments it took for me to set off toward him, he collapsed, and from my perspective one hundred or so yards away, resembled nothing more than a heap of clothes.

By the time I reached his side, little of him remained. But some part did. For his mouth was moving, though no sound emerged.

My mind may be deluding me, romance overcoming reality, but as I reflect back I become increasingly convinced that his feeble lips were striving, one more time, to form beloved names: Sa ..., Ma ..., Pa ..., Mi ..., El ....

Over and over again.

Postlude

Were I to live to a hundred, I do not believe I could endure any greater privilege than to sit by his bedside as a great man died.

It was early afternoon when, one interminable week after the stroke, Reuben Mendel's long war with Death finally reached its inevitable end. From a large tape recorder some of his own recordings had been playing, partly in the forlorn hope of calling him back, but mainly in the belief that the last sense to go is hearing and so he would not be alone in his passing.

The divine *adagio* of Schubert's string quintet filled the white room of the clinic. The tranquil beauty of the music masked his laboured, shallow breathing. Warm sunshine wafted in on citrus-scented wings. But while I could smell the melange of orange, lime and lemon that sweetened the air (without quite vanquishing the antiseptic smell), he no longer could. The noble head, framed as it had been for three decades by its statement cascade of snow-white hair, lay unmoving, half interred in the pillow, with only the strong Roman nose visible.

I stood up so that I could gaze down at that wonderful face, creased by the ravages of his life and with the faint scar running from the bridge across the cheek; the epitome of suffering not so much mastered as incorporated. It seemed to me that beneath the closed lids his eyes were stirring. When the music reached the return of the heavenly main theme, they opened, the left staring manically far out to some horizon that only he could see, the right barely unhooded.

His left hand began to move, driven by a cocktail of dissipating life force and the last potent dregs of that indomitable spirit which so endeared him to the world. At first hesitantly, then more purposefully, the palm turned skyward and the fingers, dormant but half a minute before, straightened before wrapping around an apparent violin. In perfect unison with the *adagio*'s dying embers, they shaped its final chord.

Until the music faded away to nothing, it held its position, the last vestige of an iron will. When silence finally reigned, it drifted limp and lifeless past the edge of the bed.

His expression, mad but a moment before, subsided and I saw for the first time what it looked like at complete peace. The ghost of a smile played on his mouth and eyes, as if he were greeting a long-lost friend.

In accordance with his wishes, I was the only journalist allowed on the special El Al flight carrying the ashes of Reuben Mendel. Nausea washed over me as the flight drew to a close, caused as much by nervous anticipation of what lay ahead as by the turbulence when the plane bucked and lurched during its descent through the bank of thick cloud separating the cold, sunlit stratosphere from a grey, wintery Kraków.

Despite the authoritarian regime of Soviet-controlled Poland customs formalities were speedily waived, and our cortège wove through the countryside west of Poland's ancient capital on the twenty-odd mile trip to the final staging post of Reuben Mendel's last journey.

It had been two days since the funeral took place in Tel Aviv, a modest ceremony without religious obsequies but widely covered by international media and attended by many political and cultural leaders. As executor of the estate I had agonised during his drawn-out departure over whether there should be any ceremony in Israel given his profound decision to leave the country for good. But the will had foreseen a pivotal role for the president, and I saw no way round it, hoping to correct any false impression of approval in a statement I prepared for the world's press.

During the trip from the airport, my car (and, I imagine, all the others) was silent. Were my fellow passengers pondering, as I was, our participation in the final clause of his brief will?

> Apart from my house in Toulouse, which I bequeath to
> Gaston Perrier and his heirs, I leave all my property to
> the Fellowship of the Yellow Badge.
> I desire a secular service the form and guests for which I
> leave to the wisdom of the president of the State of Israel.
> My only request is that Schubert's *'An die Musik'* be sung
> at the end, as people say their last farewell.
> My final request is this: that my ashes be scattered where
> the spirit and remains of my honoured parents, beloved
> wife and adored babies all await me. Let my long years
> of perpetual flight end at Birkenau so that, at last, I may
> know some rest among my family who, even as I write, I
> hear summoning me to their side.

Permission had been immediate, and now the plain terracotta urn containing what was left of him sat between my thighs as the infamous camp came into view. The railway spur that had brought so many to their doom nearly three dozen years ago was overgrown with weeds but its ineluctable progress through Hell's Gate could still clearly be seen.

The small party disembarked from the cars and we proceeded into the camp, following the railway line to its end.

As if to confirm his last words to me, the heavy cloud through which our plane had passed could no longer contain its load and the rain started, first slowly, hesitantly, then faster, harder, forming vast silver-grey sheets which began to obscure the bleak horizon, even the wire perimeter fence still topped with barbs. Although I had been before, never had it seemed so sombre, and never had I felt so powerfully the presence of the dead, as though their souls had gathered to welcome one of their own.

When we stepped from path to grass at the end of the track, the soggy ground gave way beneath our every tread, receding from grass to mud we churned the steps of our predecessors.

Even had it been planned, no music could have defeated the clamour of the beating rain as it drilled into the ground, hammered on umbrellas and ricocheted from the wooden roofs of the remaining buildings.

We reached the appointed spot, the ruins of Crematorium III where Reuben had played the Bach nearly a quarter of century before. A teenager from the tiny congregation which is all that remains of the once-thriving Jewish community of Kraków came forward and took the urn. She walked unsteadily through the clinging ground and began to clamber up the pile of rubble that he too had climbed.

Once she had confirmed her footing, the young woman turned her back to the wind which was blowing from the forest behind the camp. With the utmost care she removed the lid and began to tip out his ashes.

A ruddy-grey comet began to emerge, first dense and then increasingly fragmented, until it faded away to nothing. She stood stock-still as she turned the urn upside down to allow each fragment its freedom.

Apart from a few heavier particles that dropped quickly to the ground, the ashes eddied in the wind-whipped air, some catching thermals and, rising, separated into individual molecules. Others coalesced in the rain, falling into the sucking earth to mingle with the infinite atoms of those who had been lying in wait, trampled into the mud by broken, blistered feet.

As I watched the nebulous remains disintegrate, I pondered silently on those which, wind-borne, fled the dead camp. I imagined that some encircle the earth on capricious currents, rendezvousing with those of the long-departed, and, together for eternity, would surf the waves of time, forming clusters of dust to refract the starlight forever. But others are inspired by nightingales, reincarnated as song to charm all those who stop to hear. Some are heading out to sea, where they will await the gigantic maw of whales and inhabit their mystical apparatus to serenade the deep. Still more, trapped on an Arctic boreal, are whisked away to frozen wastes, there to slip through the steam-shrouded nostrils of white wolves when the pack, silhouetted against the unbroken moon in a clear black sky, rents the silent night with its prehistoric chorale.

And there are those, I fancy, which are drawn to towns and cities. Irresistibly they gravitate towards the places where music plays, to be interred in the dusty hollows of instruments, nestling silently among sheaves of yellowed scores, or finding refuge in the recycled air of auditoria, embedding in the acoustic for all time. There they will become subsumed in the mysterious propagation of music-making, forever to swoon with the ebb and flow, transmuting perpetually in that inexplicable alchemy of joy and sadness.

So, when the soprano's perfect note floats high and pure through the still opera house, or a plaintive oboe sings longingly of home, when the solo piano dissolves into silence, or a violin weeps for bitter histories and better futures, I, for one, will think of Reuben Mendel, and all that he was.

If Reuben were to know this, he would look at me in that way of his, puzzled, amused, and almost certainly with more than a hint of disapproval. But when the mood is right and I've heard a particular piece of music or read from one of his favourite authors, then, just occasionally, I indulge myself. Closing my eyes, I set my mind free to soar on a flight of fantasy that he was mistaken and there is an afterlife.

A vast celestial concert hall hung with crystal and stars is full beyond the scope of mortal vision. On the stage stand four spot-lit chairs. A quartet emerges from the wings. First comes Pablo

Casals, carrying his cello. He is followed by Lionel Tertis, violist, and thereafter Ignaz Schuppanzigh, whose eponymous ensemble premiered so much Beethoven. Reuben brings up the rear, holding a custom-made Stradivarius.

As they settle, a booming voice announces the first performance of Beethoven's one hundredth string quartet. The huge audience quietens to absolute silence, anticipation filling its every corner. Reuben gazes at the front row.

And there they all are.

Sarah with the composer on one side and Miriam on the other. Elias fidgeting between his sister and grandfather. Moses holding Leah's hand, even while she is turned away to reminisce with Isaac Rosenberg. Behind them, Fanny Hartmann advises Wilhelm Furtwängler and Szymon Laks.

Reuben smiles softly at them, nods, and raises the violin to his chin.

Author's Note

Apart from the unflinching support and love of my family, this novel arrived in its final form thanks to a great number of people, not every one of them aware of the fact.

In particular, Szymon Laks (1901–1983) who was conductor and arranger of the Men's Orchestra at Auschwitz, and whose memoir, *Music of Another World* (Northwestern University Press, now happily restored to print as a result of conversations with Susan Harris, then Editor-in-Chief) proved an invaluable source.

And Dr Jacques Stroumsa, whose own recollections of his time in the Orchestra and his personal interest were vital (*Violinist in Auschwitz* (Hartung-Gorre Verlag), and correspondence).

I'm also grateful to my friend the composer Michael Alec Rose for his honest criticism and valued insights, not all of which I agreed with!

Grosse Fugue was long in gestation and many were the times I thought it might reside for all time in the dark domain of my hard-drive. So I owe a special thanks to Janet Weitz and her team at Alliance Publishing Press for their confidence in my work, the many suggestions for making it better and their commitment in bringing it out of the shadows and into the light.

And, finally, to the people too numerous to mention who read early drafts and whose criticism and encouragement meant so much.

None of the above bears any responsibility for the content of this novel. For better or worse, that must be all mine.

If anyone's appetite to know more about the Holocaust has been whetted, one thought. It is a chapter in history so large, so three-dimensional that to study it is akin to learning a language. You must first familiarise yourself with the basics before moving more deeply into the subject. For those interested in making the journey, never forgot – it is not a voyage you can ever complete, because the enormity of the *fact* that it happened and its myriad implications defy comprehension.

If this book has kindled interest, then start with *The Kingdom of Auschwitz* by Otto Friedrich, with its own excellent bibliography. Martin Gilbert's *The Holocaust: The Jewish Tragedy* is a comprehensive and very accessible history of the events of 1933–1945. For a profound insider's insight, Primo Levi's triptych: *If This Is a Man, Moments of Reprieve* and *The Drowned and the Saved* is unavoidable, and repays repeated readings. The several anthologies of poetry that are available provide a unique artistic response both from survivors (like Levi and Paul Celan) and observers (see, for example, *Holocaust Poetry*, edited by Hilda Schiff). If you prefer a more visual approach then *The Pictorial History of the Holocaust* produced by Yad Vashem is definitive, while *Art of the Holocaust* (edited by Blatter and Milton) is outstanding (if you can find it).

A quick word about the novel's title. The correct phrase in German is 'Grosse Fuge' (or, to be strictly accurate, 'Große Fuge'). I've adopted 'Fugue' merely to simplify pronunciation for English-speaking audiences.

If anyone is interested in exploring the featured music, I have created a playlist on Spotify entitled 'Grosse Fuge: the music of the novel'.

Finally, for those who are curious, the quotation in German at the outset of Intermezzo #1 is a (deliberately stilted) translation of an English translation of Dante's famous inscription above the entrance to hell in *Divine Comedy: Inferno,* Canto 3:

Per me si va nella citta dolente,
Per me si va nell'etterno dolore,
Per me si va tra la perduta gente...
Lasciate ogni speranza voi ch'entrate!

This way for the sorrowful city,
This way for eternal suffering,
This way to join the forgotten people...
Abandon all hope, you who enter!

But I would prefer to sign off with a more elevating quote from the same work, this time Canto 26, recalled by Primo Levi in Auschwitz:

Considerate la vostra semenza;
Fatti non foste a viver come bruti,
Ma per seguir virtute e conoscenza.

Think of your breed;
You were not made to live as brutes,
But to pursue virtue and knowledge.

IP
London, Winter 2011/12

Lightning Source UK Ltd.
Milton Keynes UK
UKOW041557240412

191377UK00011B/20/P